EARLY PRAISE FOR *ORBITAL BEBOP*

"*Orbital Bebop* is a fascinating glimpse into a potential future we might yet avoid, but is hard to dismiss outright. As billionaires continue to make plans to colonize the stars, what will happen to the rest of us? Tihi Hayslett provides us with a possible answer. *Orbital Bebop* is a thrilling read, and Hayslett is a masterful storyteller!"

— David J Peterson,
linguistic and language inventor for Dothraki, Valyrian
and several fiction language for film and television

"*Orbital Bebop* is an absolutely timely work of fiction. Unabashedly radical, queer, and set against a dystopian backdrop, these characters are an exercise in what solidarity and resistance could be."

— Sarah Calvarese, astrologer, 8th House

"*Orbital Bebop* shows what it really takes to engage in the act or acts of world-building. Across space (literally) and time, Hayslett's keen sense of language and lyric amplifies queer folks of color and their lineages. Through memory work, vulnerability, and convening on the dance floor, Hayslett's complex characters confront the fears, realities, and pleasant surprises in the face of experiencing nearly a millennium of both oppression and resistance."

— LeConté Dill, DrPH, MPH, poet, scholar, and educator

ORBITAL BEBOP

RIZE

REUBEN "TIHI" HAYSLETT

Orbital Bebop

Edited by Cody Sisco

Published in North America, Australia, and Europe by RIZE.
Visit Running Wild Press at www.runningwildpublishing.com/rize, Educators, librarians, book clubs (as well as the eternally curious), go to www.runningwildpublishing.com/rize.

ISBN (pbk) 978-1-963869-34-7
ISBN (ebook) 978-1-963869-33-0

CONTENTS

RECLAMATION

Former California, 2067

At first, I think the blinding flash of light is my mother. When I was a little girl, she used to barge into my room, turn on the light, and rip my blanket out from under me. No "good morning," no "wake up, sunshine." She was in a permanently sour mood even before the government collapsed.

But this light isn't my mother; it's a space shuttle blasting itself off the planet. It's brighter than anything I'd seen before, and it's over after just a few minutes. The dark of morning retakes my room, and as my eyes readjust, I realize that I won't be alone anymore. Not that I've been lonely; I've just been living in the absence of other people: my mother's dead, and Ku'e left me a few days ago.

As soon as I step out of bed and turn on Bibi, messages start coming in.

"That was him! That was Graham fucking Sheff!"

"He blasted off early!"

"Obviously he moved up the launch time. Do you think he saw us? You think he knew?"

"That pathetic billionaire-ass trash monster."

The last is from Muqawima, or Qawa for short: "Res, what do we do now?"

Bibi pours my coffee into a mug. It's so hot my fingers sting against the ceramic. I flip my comm up and answer Qawa, "We're not changing the plan. We're going ahead."

Most of the world's important people live in orbit now. It started with heads of state, lawmakers, the super-uber rich. Graham Sheff was one of the last billionaires left, holed up in his launch station, waiting for whatever sign he needed to finally call Earth quits. After a quick shower, I stand at the mirror above the bathroom sink. I only look like a summation of my mother. But our details are different. She was a light-skinned black woman with short, flat, brownish hair. I don't have my mother's light skin and she never had hair like mine. I squeeze clumps of my curls to wring the water out. I haven't found a post-society method for tamping down flyaway curls and frizz. Aloe, wax, lotions—nothing works. This tangled mess of springy, swirling, black curls that my mother always fussed over is what the world is going to see. Can't change anything about it now.

My mom would never want the world to see me looking this way. Too bad.

I meet Qawa halfway to the launch station by mid-morning. He's in his camera suit, running tests and checking levels as we walk together. The crowd of us, Reclamation, are at the chain-link parameter fence. Voices hush, and conversations whisper out as everyone makes way for me and Qawa. He stands me right in front of the fence, takes a few paces back, and squats. Then his suit lights up, planting beams of light directly on me.

Qawa says, "And you're go for live... now."

"My name is Resistance." I gesture to the launch facility behind me. "And this is ours now." Someone on my right hands me a bolt cutter. At first, I don't squeeze hard enough, but on the second try, I break the padlock, pull a security chain off the fence, and push it open. Everyone floods around Qawa and me, rushing to their places. Just as we practiced.

"Tell us what happened this morning," Qawa says.

"At about four-thirty a.m. local time, billionaire CEO Graham Sheff launched himself into space. He was six hours early. Because he was scared of us. Because we were coming. Because the extractors and the polluters and the banks and the financiers who bankrolled the death of our planet think they can cut and run from the Earth. They think they can leave us behind. But we're here. *We* are the people of Earth; *we* are the ground and the air and the water. This planet is our blood. And we're taking it back."

Qawa livefeeds as I walk through the launch campus. I'm taking him to the Command Center in a roundabout, choreographed way so I can show everyone on the feed that we're not joking. This whole place is ours now. On the Comms Tower, our patchers unfurl large banners from the open windows that say "We, Us, Ours." When we pass underneath them, the livefeed picks up the bass of their music blasting from ten stories up. Across the street on the left is a small fire that used to be the Visitor's Center. We burned it down for the symbolism. Up the road, there's a Mess Hall and dorms, the server station, the isolation tank, two now-empty hangars, and the Command Center. Then past that, about half a mile up, the launch pad.

"When I say this is ours, I mean it," I say, looking into Qawa's camera suit. "We've got housing, we've been growing our own food and are now transferring crops over. We're connected to the feed. We have everything."

"And what about cops?" Qawa asks.

"What cops are there?" I laugh. "What government is there? Everything they built is crumbling, so they're evacuating. And all of us are here. Everyone who was too poor, too brown, too sick, and too queer to matter. This is ours now. Come find us. Or better yet, there's only eight operating launch stations left in the world. You don't have to accept that you've been abandoned. Inherit what's yours."

The patchers code the livestream in different languages and then thread them into the global feed. Once it's out, the Mess Hall turns into one gigantic party. There's about fifty of us, minus Sheff's ground crew, who are now detained in the A hangar. The Food Crew fold down tables and start stacking dishes on them family-style. The bass thuds from the Comms Towers, and if I squint, this all feels like a summer block party. Qawa and I are stars. Comrades hand us beer, slap our backs, and tell us how our livefeed got restreamed and rehashed all over what's left of Europe and in the Asian and African Strongholds.

Don't get me wrong, I like the attention. But the older folks have this way of looking back and forth between me and Qawa, like they're pairing us together. Qawa doesn't mind; he's straight. But these sly looks tense my spine and throw me back into being a teenager, parading play-boyfriends around so my mom would stop crying at her altar.

I bow out from talking to two comrades and fix myself a plate of grilled vegetables. The roof of my mouth is still tender from the too-hot coffee this morning, so I chew like a cow. Slowly moving each chunk of pepper or potato intentionally toward my back molars. My mouth is full when I see Ku'e through a small crowd of young people dancing. She's wearing those gray drawstring pants that are big and flowy from the ends all the way up until they cinch her waist. I couldn't ever pull off those pants. My midsection is too wide; the whole thing looks hefty on me like I'm bottom-heavy. But Ku'e has the kind of long, thin curves—up her legs and down her arms—that clothes can breathe through and billow out in the wind.

She twists her hips and throws her hands in the air to the beat of the bass like this is some kind of polished ad selling insecure young girls fertility boosters. Her dark brown hair flies out straight as she rolls her neck and snaps her shoulders. At the right angles, when the afternoon sun picks up on it, I can see pops of her undertips. Blues, purples, and oranges shimmer in her cloud of brown hair. Ku'e's light as dust, like she didn't just get out of a five-year relationship. Her first, actually.

I squeeze a green pepper between my back teeth, and a sharp, tiny explosion stabs my gums. It's like the high-pitched screech of two pieces of clean metal scraping each other inside my mouth. The sudden pain jerks me stiff. I gulp and then can't take in any more air. It doesn't register in my brain that I'm choking until I see Ku'e glimpse me from the corner of her eye. She was smiling, saw me, and stopped. My vision brightens and my fingers quake. I try screaming, but no air in means no air out. My eyes start to water, and I can feel this strain in my lungs when, thankfully, someone behind me grips me with a closed fist just under my sternum and pulls in hard. It's moving, the pepper lodged in my throat. On the third pull, it spits out of me. All my blood rushes to my face as I breathe in, and suddenly Ku'e's right in front of me.

"Girl? Are you all right?" Ku'e asks.

I'm too busy gasping and breathing and hunching over. My throat's dry and clampy, but I try to say, "I'm fine."

The one behind me, who saved me, passes me a glass of water. Ku'e wraps her arm around me and leads me to a bench away from everyone standing and watching.

"Fuck, that's embarrassing," I finally get out.

"No, don't even worry, just catch your breath." We're squeezed right next to each other, even though there's room on the bench. It's the first we're touching since she left me. I'm the hot-blooded one; I can feel her cool skin through both our clothes. She used to slip her cold feet under my half of the blanket, and her touch would jolt me awake.

I know my eyes are bloodshot by the time my breathing steadies. I scooch apart from her.

"Don't," I inhale and exhale, "stop partying, Ku'e. Go. Go have fun."

"I can sit here with you. Music's not going anywhere." Ku'e says, "You were great today, Res. But fuck, that asshole was early!"

The original plan was to send the ship up without him. Waste all his money. But either way, we were claiming this base.

"Really," I tell her, "you don't have to do this."

"You're not being fair."

"I'm not?"

"Everyone here. We're tribe now, we're family." Ku'e says, "And we're actively asking new folks to join us. We, you and me, we have to be able to be around each other."

"We are. We have been."

Ku'e narrows her eyes at me.

"What?" I say, "I've been busy."

She thinks it over for half a second and says, "Yeah, you're right. You've been busy. What the fuck, I picked the worst time to break up with you!"

"You think?"

"But, in a way, isn't this the best time? Everything's going to be different now. Like a bookend."

"I don't." I try to find the right combination of words that won't lead us to another fight. "Can we talk about something else?"

Ku'e shoots me a glare for a quick second and then smiles. That glare was the fight, though. If we were still dating, she'd pick and pick at me until I'd feel cornered enough to tell her the jagged truth. That, yes, she picked the worst time to break up with me. That when I needed her—not her skills, not her organizer-brain, but her—the most, she decided not to be with me. But now, after the shuttle and the livestream, after the real work, when it's time to party and celebrate, here she is. Right next to me, as long as the stakes are low.

"Actually, I gotta ask you a favor," Ku'e says.

"Sure."

"The Food Crew wants your Bibi, for breakfast tomorrow."

"Shit, I forgot it," I say.

"Not your fault at all. But we don't have a lot of sun today, so we better get it now."

"I'll get Qawa."

"No," Ku'e says and puts her hand on my knee. I tense up out of reflex, but she doesn't notice. "We got this. It'll be super quick."

The charge-bikes are at the server station. Ku'e grabs a backpack and some totes while I sign out tasers and batons. It's a fifteen-minute ride to my place; we take the frontage road to the old interstate. All the families camped out with tents fastened to the row of old cars know us by now. They aren't the trouble. A few of them even wave at us. My stomach still jerks and seizes a few times from choking earlier. But for a stretch on the interstate, above neighborhood houses and apartment buildings that used to be safe before the mold, I breathe deep and let the wind tug at my hair.

We used to ride anything with wheels, Ku'e and I. We'd off-road cars on the beach at night, blaring old music our grandparents used to lose their shit over when they were teenagers. When gas got scarce enough to kill over, we short-routed scooters and e-boards. The beaches got taken by then, and scooters weren't fast enough to out-ride gangs, so then we'd hit the elevated interstates. For a few years, only kids were on the interstate. All the grown-ups were fighting each other or the government, or they got Jesus-crazy like my mom. On ground level, the world everyone knew was cracking apart, but on the long concrete lines of highways, we'd throw parties that stretched for miles, then sleep when the sun came up.

Most of the families living here now used to be kids we drank and smoked and danced with, now with kids of their own.

We ride down the off-ramp, then quickly up a small hill, when the sky darkens into deep pinks and purples. I take the safety off my taser. I live in an old hospital, or I used to before we all moved into the launch center. All the ground-level entrances were blocked off years ago, so we go in through the walkway connecting the hospital to the parking garage.

Ku'e peels a few glo-lamps off the wall and packs them as we walk down the long corridor to my wing. Daylight's slipping, and without the glo-lamps, the walls almost look normal. Like I didn't spend weeks scrubbing down all my mom's bible verses after she died. My room is around the corner from where the Old Testament blended into the new one.

Bibi beeps on as I open the door. Its two front lights glow at me.

"Bibi," I say, "go back to sleep." And it powers down. Ku'e unzips her backpack, folds its legs crisscross style, and wedges it inside.

"Do you need anything else?" Ku'e asks me.

I scan the room, but it's always been empty. I taped the thin partition curtains to the windows and pulled out the old flatscreen TV years ago. Bibi usually sits next to my cooler, but even that's empty now. Everything went to the Food and Housing Crew weeks ago. I only kept Bibi because I need my morning coffee.

"There's nothing else here," I tell Ku'e.

"What about," Ku'e asks, treading lightly, "her room?"

Ku'e doesn't say the word "mom," I'm guessing because she doesn't want to fight either.

I take the olive branch and just breathe in.

Ku'e says, "No one's coming back here. Once folks figure that out, everything's getting picked over."

She reaches for my hand and tries to cup it in mine, but I slip out. I try to slip out gracefully.

"I don't want anything of hers."

If we were still dating, I'd ask Ku'e to spend one last night here together. To say goodbye. We could crawl into bed, and I would big-spoon her until she fell asleep. And like clockwork, as soon as I'd start to drift off, she'd wake up again, slow her hand over my shoulder, down my side, squeeze my hip to get my attention, and then kiss me until my hand would glide down her stomach. I'd slip my fingers inside her, and we'd fuck, half-cold, half-asleep, and half-quiet as the hospital slept and settled around us in the dark.

But none of that happens.

Instead, Ku'e slumps her backpack over her shoulders, passes me her tote bags, and says, "Last chance, Res."

"No," I say, "let's go before it gets any darker."

I get my own room in the dorms back at the launch center. The floor is cold tile, and the bed is set against the wall where it feels like a window should be. As soon as my head hits the pillow, a tiny, dull note starts to pick up in my back molar. The same tooth that, earlier, shot out in pain right before I choked. I roll over on the bed so that side of my face isn't pressed against the pillow. But somehow that just makes the pain more noticeable. It's like a tiny spear needling into my gums.

I lay on my back, and as I breathe through my mouth, the air tugs at that back molar. The pain-spear gets longer and narrows. I push on the back molar with my tongue, and after a sharp flare spikes in my gums, the pain dulls down. My eyelids get heavy as sleep comes on like a rising tide, but before my mind slips out into dreams I can never remember, I can feel in the smallest, microscopic space where my tooth meets the gums, a scurrying. A toothache growing in, like cockroaches exploring after dark.

The next morning starts Day One of Reclamation. The Food Crew has breakfast set up outside at the base of the Comms Tower. Bibi's on a table, filling coffee and tea as it steps backward. Once the table's full and comrades pick up their mugs and mill about, Bibi retraces and replenishes. My morning coffee stings the back of my mouth and wakes up my back molar. I strain sips, swishing the black coffee to my back gums before swallowing. The heat soothes, and then it's time to get to work.

Food Crew handles meals and gardening, Housing Crew makes beds and manages laundry, Med Crew's on call for anyone who needs it, Sec Crew counts inventory on tasers, bikes, guns, and checks on the scientists locked in the A Hangar, Comms Crew links the stream, patches, and documents any pings that come in, Ed Crew watches all the children. I'm in Comms Crew, and we start our morning going over anas from yesterday's livestream.

What's left of North America, if they're linked, saw our livestream. NYCA, the New York City Assembly, send their congratulations. They're too far to help but want us to know they're with us and want to stay in touch. Old Mexico asks for planning assistance. They've got a launch station, a man-made island off the Yucatan. But no one's sure if it's operational or who's in control. Every urban center, the ones that are organized, can only really "see" just beyond their suburbs. The outlands are "Mad Max," and only the old folks here get that reference.

There's talk of convening the different Strongholds of what used to be the US, but traveling those kinds of distances is too dangerous.

"We need steady livestreams," Laban says, "to show everyone we've got this and encourage people to come join us."

"Yeah, we had planned days," Qawa says, "that feature each crew, like a different slice of life on the campus."

"That's only one week tops," Laban says.

I chime in, "Well, they'd be interspersed. I think every few days we re-tell our story and mission with a clear recruitment pitch. That way it's pre-recorded, and it can just go out while we're prepping and planning livestreams."

The Comms Crew is a democracy. We vote on the livestream plan and then break for lunch. I chew food around my back molar in almost the same way I held my breath and tiptoed past my mom's room after she died, careful not to wake a ghost.

After recording another mission and recruitment stream, Qawa and I decide the best first "slice of life on campus" stream should be the Sec Crew to show strength. Virodh heads it up. He's one of the old ones and used to serve in the military back when that existed. In the fallout, he gathered up a group of guys to protect a high-rise where elderly folks could live and grow gardens on the roof without worrying about the gangs. But then the mold crept in and most of those elders died.

Virodh set up his base in the A Hangar to keep guard on Sheff's scientists and engineers who we've locked in there.

"I don't think this is a good idea," he tells us. "Why show everyone on the feed what our security looks like?"

Qawa says, "It's like a deterrent. If they see we've got guns and weapons and our own guards—"

"They'll attack us and take our guns and weapons," Virodh says.

"Nobody around here has raided anyone in years."

"Except us. Just yesterday."

"You've got a point," I step in, "but here's the thing: We're asking people to join us. That means travel for some people. It's risky. But you know what'll motivate them? Knowing this place is safe."

Virodh takes a big, labored exhale and gives in. I think it's because I'm a woman. It's not that Virodh is trying to fuck me. But I've seen him do this. Every man is a potential fight, but women...

Qawa boots up his camera suit while Virodh and I find an office in the back of the hangar. He sits behind a small metal desk and rolls his shoulders back to make him look broader and imposing. He's already big and imposing anyway, but I let him have it. I'm used to being on camera, not everyone is.

Qawa gives the signal, and I start, "My name is Resistance, and this base is ours now. Today I'm sitting with Virodh, the head of our security. Virodh, can you take us through what you do day-to-day?"

"No," he says, "that's confidential."

"Okay, but we have security here?"

"Yes."

"We're building a new society, one that's equitable, self-sustaining, and centered on justice and peace. What role do you think security plays in this new society?"

"We keep that peace."

"How?"

"Protection."

I try to take a step back. "Virodh, we've known each other for about two years now. What made you join us and help plan the Reclamation?"

"It was the right thing to do."

"Yes, but I guess what I'm asking is, why you?"

"Huh?"

"Beyond what's right and wrong. Why are you here?"

Virodh breaks his strong face for just a flash of a second. I hope Qawa zoomed in on it.

"I've always lived like this. Collectively, with a mission. And it's always the same mission: prevent harm. That looks like a lot of different things to a lot of different people. But it's not hard to see where the harm is coming from, and where it's going to."

"Where does harm come from?"

"Everyone up there now." He points to the ceiling, but he's really talking about space.

"Tell me more."

"They just wouldn't stop. The planet was dying, is dying, and all they thought about was their money, their power. Their safety, above everyone else's."

"So now you're doing something about it?"

"I've always been doing something about it."

"We're asking people to join us. What can someone expect when they get here?"

"Protection. I guess, family."

"And what does family look like to you?"

"Well, everyone I ever thought was family is dead now." There's another break in

his character. "But... I didn't have a lot growing up. Not like now, but before. I had to get away from my first family. The army was a family. But I've seen a lot of families tear apart. It's not easy to build and keep it going."

"So that's why security is so important to you."

"Huh?"

"To keep our family together. Especially when times get tough."

"Yes, that's the mission."

"What do you do in your downtime, when you're not protecting everyone?"

"I'm always protecting everyone."

"What did you do last night?"

"I saved your life when you were choking."

That stops me, breaks my character.

"And thank you for that." I take a beat to prep myself for what I'm about to say. Even being used to being on stream, I guess Virodh isn't the only one who wants to appear strong. "Yesterday, when I was choking, everything happened so fast, and I didn't really see that it was you. But also, I didn't have to, in a way. Looking out for each other is what we do here."

"That's what they can expect."

"Who's they?"

"The people we're asking to join us. When they get here, what you can expect is to look out for each other. Look out for us and we'll look out for you."

At dinner I only pull soft foods to keep my back molar from flaring up. Even still, I dread eating. Halfway through my slow slog of eating but not really chewing, Laban taps my shoulder.

"Something's happening," she says and motions toward the Comms Tower.

Laban waits until the whole Comms Crew is there before she starts.

"We got a message from the Bay Area Assembly. It's shaky, we're still not sure what happened. And it only came in packets whenever they had signal, so it's at least twelve hours old."

"What are you saying?" Qawa asks.

"The Bay Area Assembly. They're coming."

"The whole BAA?" Qawa asks.

"No," Laban says, "only the survivors."

"How many?" I ask.

"We don't really know. Dikang is still scanning and analyzing their pings. He thinks maybe as small as twenty or as big as one hundred."

"All the way from the Bay?" Qawa asks. "How long is that even?"

"Provided they survive? Maybe two months, maybe more?"

"What can we do?" I ask. "Can we help them?"

Laban says, "I think that's a Virodh question, but even for now, twelve hours out, we can't really do much until they get closer."

Kukana, sitting behind me, says, "There's maybe only one hundred people left of the BAA. The fuck happened up there?"

"We're still piecing that together as best we can," Laban says. "We know that the feed went out like a blanket around midnight last night. It never came back on."

The Bay Area Assembly is what inspired our Reclamation. Even down to our name changes. They're the longest-lasting free democratic unit on this half of the continent. Or they were until last night.

Laban says, "I think we should keep this to crew just for tonight. Dikang is still processing what came in. Any volunteers to help him would be great."

Kukana and Qawa volunteer. The rest of us just stare at each other. The BAA is gone.

On my walk to the dorms, I see Ku'e and Karshi laughing and singing while folding up the dinner tables. I used to make her laugh like that. I clench my jaw trying to quietly walk past them, and my back molar erupts.

It and I are fully awake on my bed. First it was one steady spear of pain into my gums. Then four, then there was no counting them. All the spears fused into a bright, stabbing light in the back of my mouth. I get maybe three hours of sleep.

I see Dikang at breakfast. He looks like he got less sleep than I did. His face is paler and the skin around his eyes looks sunken in. I'm sipping coffee next to my Bibi while everyone else eats. Ku'e and Karshi are sitting next to each other, whispering, and I go back and forth on whether to pretend not to notice or try to eavesdrop. I don't know which one is worse, but Laban swoops in before I can make a call on that. She brings me to a dining table that's further off from the rest of our tribe. Virodh and Sec Crew usually take this table, but none of them are here this morning.

It's not the whole Comms Crew, just Laban, Dikang, Qawa, and Kukana. And me.

"We've got a couple of definites now," Qawa says.

Laban leans in. I'm guessing she doesn't even know either. Dikang yawns hard.

"Kukana hacked a satellite signal and is tracking the BAA. They're over a hundred. Taking the old interstate when they can."

Laban asks, "Is that safe? Wide out in the open like that?"

"Probably not, but without the feed we can't communicate to them."

"There's a lot of children in the caravan," Kukana adds.

"Fuck," Laban whispers, "are they armed at least?"

"It looks like it," Qawa says, "so they have that going for them."

I pop in, "How did this happen? Do we know any more about that?"

Kukana and Qawa trade glances before answering.

"They call themselves the North Protectorate," Qawa says. "They're taking credit as of this morning. It's weaving through the feed now."

I'm about to ask more, but Qawa knows me well enough by now. He can answer my questions before I have time to ask them.

"There weren't any initial disputes or competing claims. Basically, these mostly rural white men stockpiled and planned this. They've robbed other smaller groups. Take women and children hostage. Slaves, basically. They waited 'til they had the resources and the numbers. This was intentional."

"How'd they block out the feed?" Laban asks.

"We still don't know that. Probably someone they kidnapped."

"So, once I got into Sheff's satellite imagery system, I looked around a lot," Kukana says, careful to keep her voice low. "The interstate they're on is mostly intact, very few camps of people. If they avoid cities and stay sharp, they'll probably make it close."

"Close?" Laban says.

Kukana takes a breath before going on. "There's a lot of camps north of us. Some we know are hostile and opportunistic. Now, with the BAA's numbers, this probably won't be a problem, but that's gonna depend on the day, the mood, and how much ammo they have."

"We need to tell everyone after breakfast," I say.

Qawa places a hand on my arm. "That's not it."

Kukana says, "When I look just generally, like 100 miles out from us, you start to see a pattern. Lots of debris of abandoned encampments. Some unburied dead bodies."

"The BAA's not the only ones heading in our direction," Qawa says, his hand still on my arm. A shiver spins up my back and into my neck but stops there, right before my jaw. Thank goodness.

"We gotta tell Virodh," Laban says.

"We gotta tell everyone," I say.

"Yeah, after breakfast we'll call an Assembly," Laban says.

"No, everyone. We gotta put this on the feed."

"I don't know, Res," Qawa says. "Won't that hurt recruitment?"

"We can't ask people to come join us if that's gonna put them in danger," I say. "We have to build trust. That means being up-front."

We hold the Assembly in the Command Center. Each crew sends representatives. We all sit at rows of dead computer bays, lined up in a semicircle. Ku'e reps the Food Crew and waves at me from across the room. I just blink at her. Virodh and the Sec Crew are the last to arrive, but once they sit down, Laban starts.

Everyone gasps at the BAA, but I keep my eye on Virodh, try to study his face. His jaw clenches and unclenches and then clenches again at different parts of Laban's presentation: the survivors are mostly families with children; just hearing the name North Protectorate; "unburied dead bodies."

Eventually we're all watching Virodh. And when Laban finishes up, he clears his throat.

"We need to fortify."

"And?" Laban says.

"That's it. That's all we can do."

I can almost hear the room deflate. He starts in about tactical readiness. Small, simple things we can do. Lights-out at a certain time, head counts, food counts. Somewhere in the middle of this, I see Ku'e staring at me from across the room. Her eyes squint, and her mouth parts. She's studying me.

My toothache starts to wake up now that I've finished my coffee. I get up to get more, and once I'm outside, I hear Ku'e call for me.

"Res!"

"Yeah?"

"Holy fuck, Res."

"I know, I'm sorry."

"I saw you sulking to your room last night and just figured you were jealous or something."

"Jealous?"

"We're just friends, by the way."

We started out as just friends, but I let that jab pass.

"I didn't ask, Ku'e."

"Well, never mind anyway now."

I keep walking to Bibi, gripping my mug. My back molar thumps with each step.

"Res," Ku'e says, "fuck the coffee and talk to me."

"I can't," I strain out, but that detonates the toothache. It's its own launch pad now, inside my mouth. Ku'e can see it on my face.

"What's wrong? Res, what's going on?"

"Nothing."

"You don't look like it's nothing."

My tooth is screaming at me. I cup my hand to my jaw, but that somehow makes it worse.

"I'm taking you to Med Crew."

"No," I say, "we have to go back inside. They're probably gonna vote soon."

Ku'e grabs my hand. I try to pull out of her, but she grips me and shoots narrow eyes at me.

This facility already has a Medical Bay. It's on the other side of the Comms Tower and looks like a smaller version of the hospital I used to live in with my mom and occasionally Ku'e. We sit next to a little girl and her dad. Her arm's in a cast. Her little legs don't reach the floor, and she swings them with her head looking down. Her father kisses the top of head.

This would all seem sweet, like a moment between two families, if my tooth wasn't ripping at the nerves in my face. I ask Ku'e for a cup of hot water, but she says no and to wait for someone to look at me first. There aren't really doctors anymore, but that's what I decide in my head to call the woman who finally checks on me. Ku'e insisted on coming with me into one of the med rooms.

I tell her just that "it hurts," but it's getting worse, like it's spreading. My back tooth is both pushing up from my jaw and pushing down on it. The whole left side of my jaw feels like lightning strikes, over and over again. I can start to feel my toothache on my scalp.

The doctor says, "I'm not much on dentistry. But we gotta pull it."

Ku'e asks, "What's wrong with it?"

"I think it's impacted."

"No," I say. "It just gets like this if I don't soothe it with coffee or hot water." I turn to Ku'e. "That's why I keep asking for hot water."

"Is the pain getting worse?" the doctor asks.

"No, just if I chew too hard or grind my teeth in my sleep."

"But that's not normal," says the doctor. "If you're altering your behavior to manage pain, that's not a good sign."

"Can you pull it today?" Ku'e asks.

"No," I say, "the Assembly's probably gonna vote, and we should be there."

"It won't take long to pull it," the doctor says. "I've just got to get the materials ready."

"Okay, I'll come back then," I say. "There's gonna be a vote, and then I'll have work to do."

"Res, I think you should—"

"I'm not asking you!" I yell at Ku'e, and my gums fire back.

"Res!"

"I'm not even asking you to be here! You're missing the vote too. Why are you here?"

"You don't want me here?"

"No!" I shoot back. A hot light at the base of my jaw stretches up to my ear.

"Fuck you, Res," Ku'e says, and then turns to the doctor. "Take the tooth. Don't listen to her."

The doctor tells Ku'e, "I think it's best if you go. Res, I'll have to get some syringes, novo, and tools. It'll only take a few minutes. Trust me, you'll be back up and running later today."

Ku'e and the doctor both leave me alone with my tooth. My old hospital had these rooms on the ground floor. My mom and I would sweep through them to check for mold. Mop the floors, spray down the walls. She stopped when she got Jesus-crazy, then it was all on me. Back when it was a working hospital, rooms like these were used to diagnose fevers and check for vitals, but for me, they were an escape. A way for me and Mom to be in the same building but alone.

The doctor comes back with a med case and a rolling chair. She says I should sit in the chair, and it'll be better soon.

"You know she cares about you, right?" the doctor says.

"Not enough," I tell her.

She takes out first the novo and syringe, tells me this is going to hurt and to grip the armrests. The needle is barely visible, a thin spear only a few inches long. The doctor tells me to count to three and then breathe out. Then she stabs me. For a second, I think I can hear the syringe scrape against the bone of my jaw, but that only lasts a second. The tooth is angry, and it's found a whole network in my body to show me. My elbows tense and then buckle, my knees spasm, and I lose my hearing for a minute.

"I'm sorry," the doctor says, "I know this has to be painful."

I don't even open my eyes, just wait for my arms and legs to stop twitching.

"We'll give it a few minutes to take in. Then I'll pull it, okay?"

I don't respond.

"How do you feel?" the doctor asks me.

"Like shit."

"Do you feel numb?"

I don't but tell her to just get this over with. She pulls out a set of clamps with twisted, bent arms. The doctor leans over me with my mouth wide open. Those twisted clamp arms move in toward me. The second they touch my tooth I can feel it deep in my lungs. It's a blackness with jagged edges cutting at my rib cage. But it doesn't stop there. Like the ocean tide, it splashes everywhere under my skin. My shoulders jerk, and I can't control my legs. They kick out from the chair. I knee the doctor.

"Hold still," she says. But I can't. She presses her forearm against my chest and clamps down on the tooth again. I feel something rip, not just in my gums; my whole body is like one piano string, pulled tight, and then struck.

"Res, you have to sit still," the doctor says.

And then it comes, "Aaaaaattttthhhhhh!" It doesn't sound like my voice. The doctor stops. I feel like how my mom looked once when I caught her with a traveling pastor. She was on a bed in an operating room, and he was screaming. He clenched a bible in one hand and tapped her forehand with the other. She started convulsing, jittering her legs and arms, curling her toes. And then she started wailing. Like someone had cut into her. It spilled out of the operating room and filled the hallway. I was young then, and I thought she was dying. When I got older, she told me she did die. That's how she got saved.

"Should we take a break?" she asks. But that noise keeps coming out of me like the screech of a dying bird.

"Res? Res?" The doctor backs away from me. I can see her, but I can't do anything about it. I writhe with the sound coming out of me until it stops. The doctor just blinks at me.

"I," she tries to get out, "I think we should stop for today." She takes a glass out of a cabinet, fills it with water from the sink, and then downs it. "I—I don't know what that was, Res. People don't usually have that reaction."

I'm afraid if I talk that noise will come out again, so I just stare at her.

"It might be the novo, and we don't have enough of it as it is. I'm gonna take your case to the rest of the Med Crew to see if we can get clearance for anesthesia. I think that's the only way to get the tooth out. In the meantime, I can give you some painkillers. And I don't think you should work for the rest of the day. Go back to the dorms and get some rest."

I pop the painkillers as soon as she gives them to me and wait for them to kick in before getting up and heading back to my dorm. My head feels like a balloon by the time I get home, and Qawa is waiting for me at my door.

He gets one look at me and says, "Holy shit, are you okay?"

I blink and nod. The painkillers slow me down like a drunk but only between my ears.

"You don't look okay. And your face is kinda swollen."

"I'm fine. I just need to take the rest of today off," I say, shocked that my voice is normal now.

"Yeah, that sounds good. I just wanted to fill you in on the rest of the Assembly."

"I knew I missed something big," I say as I turn the key and open my room. There's a small desk opposite my bed. Qawa takes that chair.

"I wouldn't say big, but maybe disconcerting."

"We're not gonna do anything to help the BAA get here?"

"Not yet anyway, but no," Qawa says. "Virodh made a motion for a strict curfew, rationing food, daily head counts. Sec Crew made a power grab."

"Who backed him?"

"Just the Ed Crew. They're worried about the kids."

I climb into my bed, and once I'm horizontal, the room feels like it tilts. But the shift in perspective dislodges something in me.

"The Med Crew will be next. Once supplies get low, they'll get scared," I say.

"Food Crew was one hundred percent against Virodh, so we got that."

"Housing Crew?"

"I think they're with us. Comms Crew is obviously against martial law. This isn't what we signed up for."

"Tomorrow, let's interview Housing Crew and then try to get them onboard afterward."

"Only if you're feeling better tomorrow, Res."

"I feel fine now."

"You keep saying that," Qawa says. "But you don't look it. Get some sleep. I'll check in on you in the morning."

"I'll be fine."

The pain meds wear off halfway through the night, and I wake up mid-scream with what feels like a mouth full of acid. I fumble through the dark to find the bottle of pills and fall down near my desk. I swear I hear someone laughing at me. It doesn't sound like the voice that came out of me in the doctor's office. This one's lighter, like the early part of a dream, with a hiss to it.

I throw down two more pills and crawl back into bed. The hissing laughter is still there when they kick in and I fall asleep.

Qawa keeps saying my face is swollen, but when I look in the mirror, I can't see it. I spend a week popping pills, sleeping, and eating. The pain meds build a dam in my gums, but every six hours, I can feel the jagged black water behind it churning. It's still there, just waiting.

Housing Crew is our first priority once I'm back at work. They take Qawa and I through the industrial-size laundry machines behind the Mess Hall and their "map," a chart of where everyone's staying. Some folks double up, but then there's always roommate problems, so people get shuffled around. And they interview folks too. What're your cleaning habits like? Do you snore? Teiko, the guy giving us the tour, describes it almost like therapy. Their mission, according to him, is to build a home for everyone here.

I try to do my best impersonation of myself because the pain meds are like a shield in my brain. I'm always a few seconds behind like a time delay on the feed.

After recording, I ask Teiko, "Do you think you'll be ready for the BAA? They might be 200 people."

Teiko's eyes light up. "Oh yeah! Did you want to get that on camera? It's really fascinating."

"No," Qawa says. "That's okay. We don't want to broadcast too many details on the feed."

"Got it. So, we've always been planning for how to absorb new people. Since we've been asking folks to join us since Day One." Teiko turns and walks us back toward the map. "This map is just our current assignments, but this one," he flips it over, "is our entire capacity."

The second map has rooms shaded in blue that are occupied; it's only a quarter of the space.

"I'm working with Otpor on different scenarios. But basically, a lot of real estate can be repurposed for extra housing. We have a whole second shuttle hangar that's just empty."

"But what about plumbing? Sanitation?" I ask.

"Well, if Sec Crew actually worked with us instead of hogging it, we could start retrofitting that now. Sheff's company had a bunch of stuff in storage here, north of the launch pad. Some of it is backup supplies for his orbital habitat. Half that stuff's extremely useful to us. Also, the shuttle scaffolding, the rigs; if we got enough volunteers, we could build our own housing structures."

"The BAA is about a month and a half out," Qawa says. "Shouldn't we be starting that now?"

"Goddamn, do I want to. Actually, you know, off-camera, just between us three: Sec Crew claims a lot of territory that not only should be Housing Crew's, but worse, isn't even being used at all. We wanted to convene an Assembly to vote on it. Where do you think Comms Crew stands on this?"

Qawa and I trade glances. He's suppressing a grin, but I'm on a pain delay. I smile wide and then tamp it down.

"We'd have to talk it over with the whole crew, but no, I think we'd be on board."

"I think Food Crew would be with us too," Teiko says. "I've been drawing up plans for more farm plots, provided we decide to just dismantle the second hangar and build more housing. We could make space for them too. We're talking tomorrow."

"Teiko," I say. "How many people max could we hold sustainably?"

"You know that's a great question! It's not entirely up to us though. This is why we're always working with Food Crew. Sustainability is the main thing. Sure, we could have thousands of people here, but would we have enough food and water?"

I nod.

"But I like to cut that two ways: what's our max capacity if we don't tear down structures and build new ones, which why not, right? 'This place is ours now.' We could hold about five hundred people comfortably. But if we take down the launch pad, refit the Command Center, wrestle one of the hangars from Sec Crew, refit the Isolation Tanks, and move Med Crew into them, then refit the Medical Bay, and a fuck-ton of other just little, small things, we could probably get to two thousand comfortably. Reclamation could be like a real town!"

I meet the doctor in the same med room where she tried to pull my tooth. She explains that since I'm not life-or-death yet, I'm not a candidate for anesthesia. And, for that same reason, I'm no longer eligible for painkillers.

"We could try to pull the tooth again anyway?" she suggests and then leans toward me. I flinch, jut myself back, and my shoulders tense. Because we were both there the last time she tried, she doesn't push further.

"Until our medicinal plants grow enough to make more pain medication, this is going to be hard on you."

"I grew up hard," I tell her.

"I don't think you understand," she says. "You could be developing an infection. If it gets into your bloodstream from your mouth, it's a one-way ticket straight to your brain."

"Then how come I'm not eligible?"

"We have limited supplies, some of our stuff—from your hospital actually—and some of Sheff's stuff. But if there's an emergency, we might not have enough painkillers when we need it."

She gives me one last white pill and says, "I'm sorry."

At lunch, I just drink hot tea. The dam that the meds built is still working, but that'll end soon, probably today. I can feel the numbness scurrying in my gums already like the pain knows its time is coming.

At night, I dream about the space between my teeth, so tight and tiny that light can't reach it. It's wet and black, and

I feel something slither against my enamel. In the dream, I sit there with it, waiting for my eyes to adjust to the dark so I can glimpse what's moving around down there. But it doesn't happen like normal vision. I don't adjust to the darkness; it adjusts me. Tilts me back until I realize I'm lying on top of it, whatever it is that's slithering. I let go and just lie there. Slowly, that wet snaky surface gets prickly. It sharpens enough to sting me alert. But doesn't stop there. Its edges stretch up like thousands of thorns until they stab me. They dig into my skin, all of them, all at once. I jolt awake, and then seconds later, so does my back molar. The pain meds ended. Now it's just us.

All I have for breakfast is hot water. Instead of sitting with Laban, Dikang, Kukana, and the rest of the Comms Crew, I make my way to the bench where Ku'e sat me down after I choked. I blow on my mug of hot water to take the edge off it before I sip and hope Ku'e doesn't see me. Hope she doesn't misremember this spot and me sitting here now as an invitation to come and talk. I can't talk yet, not until I soothe my tooth.

Today Qawa and I stream the Med Crew for the feed. Qawa's waiting for me in the Comms Tower. He's suited up and jotting down notes when he sees me.

"Res, you look..."

"I'm fine," I tell him.

"Tired." Qawa studies me and says, "Did you sleep at all?"

"I slept the whole night."

Qawa takes a breath in and a breath out like he's summoning strength. "If you're in pain, you know we can stop streaming. There's literally no rush. I can wait for you to recover."

"No!" I blurt out then stop myself. I've never raised my voice to Qawa. We're probably the same age, but we met back in the hospital. He broke in looking for a splint for his arm. Someone in his family roughed him up, and he ran. He broke a window and crawled into the hospital while my mom was sleeping. All with a dislocated shoulder.

We didn't have this tribe back then; people didn't really help people. But I saw this glint in his eyes, like a peek behind a mask. He wanted to look tough and brave, but underneath he was scared. So, I popped his shoulder back in and hid him in the labs my mom never bothered with.

Qawa has two faces: the one you see, and then the one that's behind his eyes. That second Qawa, in his eyes, is trembling at me now.

It's my turn to take a breath. Then I say, "I'm sorry. Yes, I'm in pain. It hurts all the time now. So, I'm testy and I'm sorry."

"But doesn't that prove my point? We don't have to work right now if you're not up to it."

"I—" I try to start to speak, but my tooth flares up like it's happy and wild just to be mentioned out loud. "I need to work, Qawa. If I can't, then I'm just sitting in my room, without medicine, without distractions, just hurting until Med Crew decides I'm an emergency."

"I hear you," Qawa says and picks up his notes. "And that brings up another thing. We don't have to do Med Crew today. We can do Ed Crew. I know they're strict on not showing kids on the feed, but I was thinking about how we can stream around them. You know, empty desks, just interview a teacher."

"But last minute? Weerstand will have a fit."

"I think I can smooth him over. And it'll give us a chance to feel them out on where they stand with Virodh."

"Not if we ambush them. Why can't we do Med Crew?"

Qawa takes another labored deep breath. "Ku'e said she didn't think it'd be a good idea."

"Ku'e's not in Comms Crew. Why is she weighing in?"

Qawa blinks, and I see his second face. There's not fear in it, though. It's something else. I can't put my finger on it.

"Ku'e talked to the doc, the one who tried to pull your tooth." When I mention my tooth, it wakes up. When someone else mentions it, it explodes. "She, the doc, said that you... reacted. Like not even like someone under normal circumstances."

I want to scream from my tooth: Why the fuck is Ku'e talking to my doctor? Why the fuck is my doctor telling someone else my fucking business? Why is Qawa talking to Ku'e? But then I hear a hiss in my throat. I step back, eye the door in case I have to run. Qawa doesn't notice, which tells me he can't hear the hiss.

Qawa continues, but I only half hear him say, "You know your doctor is also named Resistance, well, Resistencia. She chose it after you. And she's trying her damn best to get you more meds. I don't even know if I should tell you this, but you scared the shit out of her, Res. She's never seen someone do… whatever the fuck you did. We just think it might be awkward."

"Awkward?" is what I try to say, but my throat stretches out the k sound in a way I can't control. I clear my throat and try again. "Awkkkward? Why?"

"All of Med Crew is camera shy. If people knew what kind of resource they are… Resistencia is the only one willing to talk to you on feed."

My requirements are that we won't shoot inside the eval room where she tried to pull my tooth and that she can't mention my tooth on stream. Her requirements are that we interview outdoors and that we can't ask her where she got her medical training. I think it's fair.

Qawa sets us up on a wooden table just outside the Comms Tower. Anyone on the feed has seen it already, and the angle where Qawa places us actually blocks the Med Bay from view. Everyone's worried about security after the BAA.

We're lucky the sun is out, and the breeze is low, but Qawa mics us anyway. Before he starts, I get a better look at Resistencia. Something about not being a patient reframes her shoulder-length blond hair and dark brown eyes. Her nose is long but narrow. With shorter hair she'd look stern, almost angry, but the sheets of blond hanging from the part in her hair remind me of old jpegs guys used to show me. Back when I pretended to like guys.

My mom didn't trust white women; she used to say that all the time. I shake my arms and neck out before Qawa streams, to get the nerves and my mom out of my head so we can start. I don't bother shaking out the tooth. I know that's not possible.

"Hello, my name is Resistance, and this is ours now," I open. "Today I'm sitting here with Resistencia, ironically. She's one of our leaders from the Medical Crew. So, let's start broad, what kinds of support and assistance does the Med Crew provide here?"

Resistencia pulls a tress of hair from her forehand and glides it behind her ear. It opens her face to the camera. She's done something like this before, I can tell.

"Well, we reclaimed a state-of-the-art medical facility from Graham Sheff. It was specifically designed to support staff launching to space, but that actually works well for us. Everything is very sterile. There's X-rays, MRI, GBTs, photoscanners. A very small version of your hospital, actually."

I've never said on feed that I lived in a hospital before we took over Sheff's launch pad. By now it's been picked over and probably even re-inhabited. Maybe my mother's body is still in the morgue.

"Okay, so that's infrastructure," I say. "What can you do, though?"

"Help," Resistencia says. "Treat. Heal. Collectively, we have the background for surgery and post-op care, OB-GYN, nutrition, oncology, maybe even a little dental—"

"Here's a question," I stop her. "We're asking people to join us, come join our community. What happens if everyone who shows up is sick?"

"That won't be a problem. Without getting too much into specifics, we work a lot like a medical board. Everyone gets evaluated. We share charts and tests internally. We, the collective, decide the best method of treatment, and everyone plays a hand in giving care."

Resistencia offers me a smile, and when I give one back, it stretches my tooth. Because my smile wasn't as sincere as hers, now I'm being punished with jolts of pain spearing into my jaw.

"Maybe we can get a little personal now." I strain to keep myself looking normal, and ask, "Why did you decide to join Reclamation?"

I'm skating close to one of her red lines for the interview, but hopefully just at the edge of it. She blinks and her smile festers for a minute.

"The last seven years have been tough. I mean, they've been tough for everyone, but not a lot of people traveled. And survived it."

I shoot Qawa a look, but he's got the lenses focused on Resistencia, so he doesn't see me. I place my hand over hers.

"I'm sorry," I say. "I didn't know."

"No, it's okay. I'm getting better at talking about it." She sucks in a pool of air and keeps going, "I left DC as it was... falling."

I remember my mom trying to stop me from watching the footage: a man in a robe slitting a woman's throat in broad daylight on the street. She had a microphone in her hand. She was some sort of newswoman. She was doing pretty much what I'm doing now, and that man sprayed her blood all over the camera. The federal government collapsed over a weekend. Two months later, the Vice President was in space.

"I didn't leave alone, but it was just me when I got here. A lot of close calls. A lot of good people who deserved to still be here." Resistencia lands her eyes on me, and I suddenly feel cold. "You can't save everyone, you just can't. So, you let it go. You focus on who's there, who's with you, who you can save. By the time I got here, that's pretty much all I was doing. I had jackets sown with medic symbols and was just running from place to place. Triage and go, triage and go.

"I felt like a rat. Like I was all nervous system and no brain. But then I met some of you. You might not even remember, but I was at one of the first meetings at your hospital. At first, I was just trying to be polite. Wait the appropriate amount of time before I started asking for and taking more supplies. You probably don't remember."

I don't. I feel like the first time I saw Resistencia was just last week. But the planning to pull this off—before we knew Graham Sheff was going to blast off early to avoid us—changed all of us. And the tribe kept growing. Those first meetings in my hospital were only a handful of people. Now we're a few hundred.

"I can't remember what it was you said exactly. But it was about making a future with our own hands or something." I don't remember that either. "And it just stopped me. If we don't build our future, we won't have a future. So, yeah, I joined."

The breeze picks up in our silence, so much so that Qawa clears his throat to get my attention.

"Thank you for sharing that," I say. "I'm sorry for everything you went through."

"It's really okay."

"But that's the point, it shouldn't be okay. None of this should be okay." I take my hand off hers. "I wonder if I can ask you one last question. And you don't have to answer it." She levels her eyes at me for a moment but says yes. "Can you give anyone who's watching this on the feed now, who might be traveling or thinking about traveling, some advice? What would be helpful to know?"

She brings her eyes up, thinking it over. Then she finally rests on a thought and says, "My advice is: survive first, get there second."

I sign off, and Qawa powers down his suit. Qawa says, "That was really brave of you. Thank you for sharing that."

"I hate being called brave," she says.

"I'm sorry."

"No, it's okay. It was a long time ago. Do you think, Muqawima, that Res and I could have a couple of minutes alone?"

Qawa nods, packs up his suit, and heads inside the Comms Tower. When he's out of earshot, I say, "I feel like shit for not remembering you back then."

"I didn't want to be seen then. Res, I think we should try again to extract your tooth."

My whole body tenses up so that I can feel my tooth stabbing between my toes.

"Why?"

"Because it's not going to magically get better. I know last time we tried it kicked up some sort of trauma for you. I obviously have trauma too. But talking about it helps. If you want to talk about what happened between you and your mom first—"

My face goes hot. "What the fuck does that have to do with anything?"

"Res—"

"What did Ku'e tell you?"

"Nothing, Res—"

I get up from the table, and Resistencia grabs my wrist. My tooth takes over. I feel the hiss in my stomach first before it boils up through my throat. Resistencia's eyes widen.

"Just don't hit me!" she says, letting go of me. Standing over her, she looks small like a child, and I feel ten feet tall. That hiss... I think we both hear it.

I was standing just like this once. Me over my mom on the floor. She was shaking. We were both shaking. But I rush that memory out of my system. The hiss crawls back inside me. After a long breath, I sit back down again.

"I know you're trying to help me. I'm so sorry."

"I do want to help you. Ku'e wants to help you too. But Res, you have to let us do that. You have to let go."

"Okay, how about we try tomorrow?" I offer up. "But we don't need to therapy-talk. Just drug me and take it out."

"Deal," she says with her hand forward to shake on it. I close my hand on hers and look at the tiny hairs on her arm, disappearing into lab coat. And that's when I see it in the hem of her sleeve. Little black dots. I let go of her hand.

"Resistencia, what's inside your sleeve there?"

"What?" She strains her face, taking off her coat, and I edge back away from her, even though it's probably already too late for me anyway. "Oh my god," she says, "it's mold!"

Space launch facilities have Isolation Tanks. It's apparently standard operating procedure for going into space. You don't want to take germs with you up there. Me, Qawa, and Resistencia each get placed in our own units. They're set up like apartments, so they're comfortable. Except that one entire wall is just clear plexiglass. As long as you look away from it, inward, it doesn't feel like you're in jail. We have to strip out of all of our clothes, and they promptly get burned. We wear Graham Sheff's leftover flight suits. Mine is snug, but Qawa says his is baggy.

Virodh is the first person to come visit us. We have to sit here for thirty days to make sure the mold clears. Resistencia and Qawa ask him questions, but I stare at his temples and watch them dip and protrude as new bits of information trade back and forth. Qawa's camera suit was completely dismantled by Sec and Med Crew, but because Comms Crew wasn't there, it's harder to get it back together. Virodh's upshot: there's no mold in the camera suit, but teams are retracing Qawa's steps all the way back to the beginning when we took over.

The entire Medical Bay is quarantined and getting scrubbed down with bleach. In Resistencia's bedroom inside the Medical Bay, all her bedding has been burned. Med Crew is inspecting every square inch for the source of the mold, and that's when Virodh's temples bulge. He's not telling us something. My tooth spikes.

Virodh questions Resistencia about her whereabouts. Where she eats her meals, who she spends time with. We learn that she's been talking to a counselor in Housing Crew, "getting help." Virodh keeps his eyes steady, but the strain in his forehead lines reads like an eyeroll. He asks her to list out her patients, but that stops her. "That's confidential," she says.

"Not anymore. This is a health crisis," Virodh replies.

"Then why are we talking to you and not Med Crew?"

"Have any of you dealt with mold?" Virodh asks all three of us. I can't see Qawa or Resistance's faces. I'm guessing they shake their heads no.

"Tell them, Res," Virodh says, "what you had to do to keep mold out of that hospital for how long? Four years?"

It was constant bleaching on the ground floor levels. Once the mold gets in a building, it likes to grow up, so the ground floor is the first defense. There's not many buildings here that have more than one level. The Comms Tower, the hangars, the Command Center, that's it.

"I've seen the mold eat people from the inside out," Virodh says. "It's not pretty, especially for the elderly. Res knows. The fact that she kept her mother alive for so long was a miracle."

"What does any of that have to do with medical confidentiality?" Resistencia asks.

"They haven't found the source yet," I finally speak up, "which means we caught it early. But we've got, what, a day, maybe two. If we can't stomp it out now, we won't ever get rid of it. Virodh's right. You have to tell him."

Ku'e loves gossip. Before we broke up, when we were planning the takeover, Ku'e used to guess at the secret lives us Reclaimers were living. She'd have her jaw on the floor if she were here. In just a couple of weeks since we took the launch facility, a young woman in Housing Crew has had an induced abortion, Weerstand in Ed Crew has pre-cancerous cells in his cervix from years of off-again, on-again testosterone, a teenage boy was caught self-mutilating as a trauma response from living on his own. Then Resistencia gets to me.

"Her tooth?" Virodh says. "What's wrong with her tooth?"

"Nothing, it's fine."

Qawa and Resistencia both say together, "It's not fine!"

Resistencia says, "It's actually serious, and we were going to try again to pull it tomorrow."

The tooth is awake now from being talked about. It sits firm in my gums, but something under it writhes.

Virodh turns to me, "Can you make it thirty days?"

"Yes."

"No," Resistencia says, "don't listen to her."

"We'll have to weigh the risk of another exposure," Virodh says. "I'll let you know in a couple of hours."

"Can we have visitors?" Qawa asks. "Across the glass? That's safe for everyone."

Virodh says, "Of course. We're having an Assembly tonight. Not everyone, just reps from each crew, to keep things safe. We'll tell everyone then."

It's a bit of a mob scene after Assembly. Almost all of Med Crew shows up for Resistencia, all of Comms Crew for me and Qawa. And in the back, Ku'e and Karshi. They're holding hands. Dikang and Kukana ask Qawa a zillion questions about the camera suit and how to get it back online. Laban debriefs the Assembly for me.

I can't actually remember who's idea it was, if I'm honest, to take Sheff's launch facility. It was after dinner on the hospital roof. My mom was bed-ridden by then, and we weren't exactly talking to each other. I started inviting people over.

It was me, Ku'e, Qawa, and Laban that first night, just drunken brainstorming. Why shouldn't we do it? Who'd stop us? Who would we need? I started hosting meetings in the hospital, and Laban started recruiting. Qawa filmed most of it. It's on the stream somewhere.

We needed someone with some kind of military training. There's a lot of rough folks around what was left of the city. But we thought someone with discipline, who could train others, who could be calm in crisis, would be the muscle we needed against whatever security force Sheff had. After the old folks in Virodh's high-rise died, Laban recruited him.

Most people see me, and to a lesser extent Qawa and Laban, as the leader, but that's changed now. The mold always changes everything.

"Virodh is running everything," Laban says. "There was no vote on it, not even opposition. He just started the Assembly like this was his operation."

"Let me guess, curfews and head counts?"

"And building inspections, laundry inspections. He said, 'If you know someone who's got mold, speak up. You're not ratting someone out, you're potentially saving lives.'"

"Damn, and it's not like he's wrong," I say.

"Thirty days is a long time, Res. We gotta try to get you out sooner."

"If we find and squash the mold, there'll be no reason for us to be in here."

Laban nods. Behind her, I see Karshi whisper in Ku'e's ear.

"Laban, you should join Virodh's search team."

"But I don't have any mold experience."

"You don't need to," I say. "You're just looking for black dots in cracks and corners, in hems, in linings."

"Did he say anything about the source in the Assembly?"

"No."

"Mold always starts somewhere. Usually close to the ground, especially if it's wet. Once it starts to spread up, like at eye-level, it's already in everything. Pipes, wires, vents. You need to check the exterior walls at ground level, near the dirt."

"Virodh didn't say anything about all that."

"I don't think he knew until I told him earlier today."

Ku'e waits until Comms Crew and Med Crew leave. I can't hear her, but it looks like she asks Karshi to go before walking up to my plexiglass wall. She puts her hand on the surface, and my tooth buckles at the root.

"Res, I'm so sorry this is happening."

"It's not your fault."

"I know that. I just—" She stops, and I know what it is. Neither one of us will say it though. "How are you holding up?"

"I'm fine. My tooth is fine."

"I know you, Res. Obviously it's not. But—"

"No, Ku'e, let's not go there."

"Damn it, Res!" When her voice raises, it seems to hit the same frequency of whatever's under my tooth. Ku'e's voice echoes, and my gums vibrate. I watch Ku'e close her eyes slowly, hold them shut, and then reopen them. She looks right into me. "You can't talk about her. But I needed to! I was there with her, right next to you. Res, it happened to me too. And you just shut down. You shut down on me, and you're shutting down on me now."

It's not my voice, it's not even my thought, but it blurts out of me, "And Karshi, she's wide open?"

Ku'e's eyes narrow. They were always thin, but now they're slits. But she doesn't pick that fight with me.

"Your mom wasn't stable, Res. We scrubbed every inch of that hospital with bleach while she screamed at us about mold, but that wasn't it. We both know that. Whatever it was that took her, it wasn't this." She motions in the air, about the Isolation Tanks. "I was there with you, Res. I watched you run yourself ragged, trying to save a woman who was never going to love you."

"Fuck you!"

"No, you listen to me! I know you're scared shitless right now. I know you're in all kinds of pain, and you're alone. Literally isolated. Qawa, Resistencia, me, all of us, we keep trying to help and you... This is exactly where you want to end up. Because you think you're just like her. But you're not!

"We don't need Res to come out of this tank in thirty days. We need Lau. I want *her* back!"

That hiss whips up in my throat like a whirlwind; I can't control it. When it explodes out of me, spit and mucus slap the plexiglass surface, right where Ku'e's face sits on the other side. Lau died with my mother.

My mucus slides slow down the plexiglass wall, blocking Ku'e's face. But I can see her shoulder twitch up and down. She tries to hold herself still, but I can tell she wants to burst at her seams.

"Ku'e, I'm sorry. I'm—"

Ku'e backs away from the glass but doesn't take her eyes off me. Her face is flushed red, and I can't help but concentrate on her shoulders, twitching, trying so hard to hold back. She walks toward the exit, and when she's out of view, I hear her. It's just a split second, but it's a deep-throat wail. Just starting up. My tooth used to start up like that, too. But now it's live all the time.

Nights are when my tooth is most awake. The pain is dense and spongy, sloshing and brewing in my gums. Just like a thunderstorm, lightning cracks from it, and all my nerve endings press until my body feels like a newly formed rock. After a couple of nights, I start to bring up the hiss. It doesn't just come from anywhere now. I build it deep in my throat, where my neck meets my shoulders. It's barely audible there. But sound comes as it rises.

"Sssssaaaa..."

"Ssssaaaassss..."

"Ssssaaassserrr..."

I always wait until I think Qawa and Resistencia are deep into sleep before I hiss. It's not their business, but also, I know somehow, inside my ribs and lungs, that it's not for them. It's for me. It's not from me. It's for me.

I sleep during the day, curled up with my pain, while Qawa and Resistencia mull around their Isolation Tanks. For a few days, Qawa tries to talk to me through the intercom, but he can hear in my voice that I'm groggy and sleeping.

Virodh comes on some interval—I think it's regular—to give us updates. They found the source on the outside of the Medical Bay. It was covered in shrubbery at first so the folks on cleaning duty missed it a few times. Probably too lazy to really dig in there. It's been bleached to death, but it was too late. They found mold outside of the Mess Hall.

When I'm awake, it feels like a bad dream. Virodh asks a million questions about mold that all have "bleach" as the answer. Contaminated food was burned, but now that means everyone's on rations. Med Crew is still quarantined; the only kind of health access people have now is run through Virodh and Sec Crew.

Once Virodh asked me about my tooth, and I couldn't answer. My eyes bristled trying to understand him, when I realized that "tooth" isn't what I call it anymore. It spells its name at night, but I haven't gotten to the end of it yet. Its name is long.

There's no streaming to the feed anymore with Qawa and me in isolation. I barely function during the day though, so it's for the best. I make out something from a visit with Laban. The Bay Area Assembly is making good pace. Maybe they grew in number too? Recruited some scavengers on the road?

At night, when Qawa and Resistencia are sleeping, I hear the drone of my skinny refrigerator. I feel it too, like it's on the tips of the hairs on my arms and legs. I can't see the other side of the refrigerator, but there's some valve through the wall that slides our rations in from outside. The pre-prepped meals clank over the fridge hum and jolt me.

"Athsaser!" I scream-whisper in the night, then fall back down on my bed.

Even when the Mess Hall mold is bleached out, Virodh still keeps us in isolation for the rest of our thirty days. But I can't count days anymore. I don't recognize Qawa and Resistencia when we are let out. The two stand like human-aliens, all arms and legs and wide eyes looking at me.

"Jesus, Res, are you okay?" Qawa asks, leaning toward me. I bend back from my shoulders like I can dodge his eyesight.

"Issar..." I hiss.

"What?"

"Is—it's... all right," I finally get out.

"We gotta pull that tooth," Resistencia says.

"Oon, no!"

"Res, you're literally falling apart," Qawa says. "Your tooth is infected, and it could kill you!"

"Where's... Ku'e?" I ask. She never came back after I spit at her.

"Do you need her there to get the tooth out?"

At the far end of the big tanker that holds the isolation units, Virodh opens the outside door. So much light floods in that it feels like I swallow some of it. Understandably, my gums feel attacked.

"Come on, you three," Virodh's voice echoes toward us, "let's process you out."

Just in case we maybe still have mold hidden somewhere on us, the Sec Crew strips us naked and scrubs us down. Resistencia and Qawa are both touchy, flinching at the sponges and brushes on their skin. They're constantly trying to free an arm or twist their body, to cover themselves as best they can. It's daytime, and the best I can do is to keep myself standing. I can barely keep my eyes open.

We're given clothes and some water. I ask for mine warm, and one of Virodh's guys just blinks at me.

"Her circadian rhythm is off," Resistencia says to Virodh. "She needs rest."

"How long?" Virodh asks.

Resistencia says, "Let's give her the day. Tonight, when she's lucid, we'll extract her tooth. Is the Med Bay open yet?"

"It's not."

"But I need tools, supplies, drugs. I mean look at her."

"Give me a list. We'll have someone fetch them."

"I need access to my workplace! I can't do, essentially, surgery outside of a medical facility. I won't."

Qawa cups a hand under my armpit and helps lift and walk me back to my room while Resistencia and Virodh negotiate. The little bits I see on the launch campus are: people milling about, seeing me, stopping, standing like walls, and staring.

When we get to my room, Qawa lays me onto my bed. He turns off all the lights and unplugs everything from the walls.

"Get some sleep," he tells me. "You're going to feel better. Res, we all need you to feel better."

My dream is like a box that I'm growing out of. I feel the planes of its surface in my mind as I plump and press against them, and deep inside me, it's sitting there. The pain. It's strong enough now, ready to get out. I've been saying its name, and now, it hears me.

Ku'e is sitting at the foot of my bed when I wake up. The room is all darkness, and she's just a black silhouette, but I know it's her.

"We shouldn't do this," I tell her.

"*We* aren't doing anything," she spits back.

"It's too late."

"No," she says, "but it will be soon. Res, this is serious. You know it has to come out."

I swallow a thick set of just-awake saliva. I'm better at seeing in the dark now. I see Ku'e's face. Her eyes are blank, not sting-y—she's not angry—her eyes just are. She's got nothing left for me.

"I want," I start and then swallow again, "to tell you what's happening to me."

"I know what's happening."

"No," I say, "because I don't know what's happening. I don't know how this makes sense, but it just does."

"What does?"

"It can't come out, Ku'e. It wants to."

"Lau," she clears her throat, "sepsis, in your mouth, will get into your bloodstream. It'll kill everything. But from your mouth, your brain will go. It'll be just like..." She stops.

My mother is written on her face. Ku'e doesn't look like her, but she looks exactly like her—earlier that day, when I told her, Ku'e moved out. But the Pain sits in between Ku'e and me. It moves to block her from my view. But it doesn't quite work. Because it's not "here" yet.

"This isn't about my mom, Ku'e—"

"Talia."

"Ku'e—"

"No," she speaks to me through the space where the Pain sits. "There's no Reclamation. There's no Graham Sheff. Lau, right now it's you and me. And right now, I'm trying one last time. I'm trying to reach you."

I pull my hand up to reach for hers. She doesn't take it at first. When she looks at my hand, I see all the fights we've had, not just here in Reclamation, all the ones before. She does take my hand, though, and I pull her to me. She resists that too. It's Karshi, planted somewhere in her mind. I pull and she relents. I pull her face to closer to mine, past the Pain.

"I know Mom didn't die from mold. Or sepsis. Or anything sudden. It was inside her, her whole life. Chipping away at her, crawling to the surface. That's what this is, Talia. It got stronger in me. We can't pull the tooth. I can't let it out. I won't let this out into the world."

"You don't have a choice anymore," she says. "You spent thirty days hissing and screaming at nothing. Qawa and Resistencia, they said you were so far gone. You were screaming nonsense. They said that you can't make your own decisions anymore. Every crew took a vote, Lau. It's coming out now."

"Its name," I say, and she just blinks at me. I can still see the Pain, now on the other side of her. It doesn't have eyes, but it's watching.

It all finally clicks: my mom scribbling bible verses on the hospital walls, the wandering preacher exorcising her—the way her chest popped when he placed his hand on her forehead—on the operating room table, Talia and I spinning out e-Jeeps on the beach—the way the corners of her lips peeled back when she looked at me—as we sang and laughed, the first time I kissed her—my body on top of hers, my head bending down to her lips—with her hair in the sand, the first time my mother slapped me—so angry her eyes were as wide as almonds, my mother on the floor—heaving in the dark—and me feeling ten feet tall—

"It's not nonsense. It's its name. And it's not trying to reclaim anything. It's not us. It's not me. It's not my mom. But it's inside me. It's ready, and you were right. I'm scared shitless."

She kisses me on the forehead. "I'm going to be right here. And I'll be with you when you recover. But after that, I'm leaving. Karshi and I talked it over with Virodh. He'll give us some supplies. I'll be here for the end of this. But, Lau, I can't stay after."

Back when she could, my mother used to walk the hospital hallways barefoot in the pitch-black dark. She never bumped into anything, like she was being led. Qawa juts his shoulder under my arm and leads me from the dorms to the Medical Bay. There's suspiciously no one else but Qawa and Ku'e the whole way. The curfew, but also probably a warning not to watch.

We're both calm, my tooth and I, we're just waiting.

Resistencia is standing at the front door of the Medical Bay with Bibi in her hands. He's set to a soft light, and he's the only light on as Qawa and Ku'e walk me down the hallway into an eval room. Virodh's there.

They lay me into the chair. It's reclined so that my head is up and level.

"Res," Resistancia says, "we're going to try our best to make this as painless as possible." She sets Bibi on a counter in the corner of the room, opens a bottle, and fills a paper cup full of water.

"First, we'll give you some pills. These are stronger than the ones I gave you before. They'll take faster."

She places the pills in one hand and the cup in the other. The water's hot, thank goodness. It's four pills, and I swallow them down with a swig. The tooth doesn't notice them. It's like it's resting now because it knows what's coming.

We all wait a while for the pills, and everyone is silent. Bibi's soft eyes point up, bouncing dim orange light from the ceiling so that it spreads low over the room. It's dim enough that I can see in the middle-darkness, but so can everyone else.

I finish my hot water while we wait. At first, I drift glances between Qawa and Ku'e. Ku'e never meets my eyes and shifts in her seat. Qawa has his mask, his first face, on. Eventually I stop and just stare at the ceiling.

Another half-eternity passes, and my sense of balance pitches in my brain. My arms and legs slump. The drugs are in now.

I hear Resistencia shuffle about the room, and then she appears over me.

"Do you remember this from last time? The novo shots?"

I blink.

"I'm going to give you three doses. That's more than usual."

The first needle goes in just under my molar, and the tooth wakes up like a cat that's been stepped on. The novo tries to wrap itself around the pain, but it's too thin, and the pain knows every inch of my mouth now.

The second shot tingles down my jaw and then up, numbing the back of my tongue. Saliva starts to spill over the corner of my mouth now. The third shot feels like a jug of water thrown into a river, a sudden slap but ultimately lost in the current.

"Okay," Resistencia says, but not to me. I see Virodh on the opposite side of Resistencia, and he leans on my chest. I feel two sets of hands, one on each of my legs. That's Ku'e and Qawa.

Resistencia brings the twisted clamp up to my mouth. I try to say, "Don't do this," but it comes out as a damp mess of sounds.

"I'll to try make this fast," Resistencia says.

The clamp is cold metal, and just that wakes me up. I can feel its sting on the top of my head. When it tightens, the pain in my mouth becomes electrified. It reaches out, asking all my nerve endings to join in. We all feel it together.

Resistencia blinks and bends her head to strain through the dimness and look into my mouth.

"Just pull it, Stancia," Virodh says.

"I think that's pus," she says. "It's really infected."

"So just pull it."

She turns away from me to look at Ku'e and Qawa. Then she looks at Virodh. He settles in more on my chest.

Then she looks at me and says, "I'm sorry, Res. This is going to hurt."

The clamp grips tighter on my molar and, through the brain drugs and the novo, an angry yellow mountain bursts through, not just in my gums. My arms twitch, and my heart starts racing. But Virodh's on top of me; his forearms resting on my shoulder joints. I can't move even if I want to.

What I can do is scream. The pain likes that.

I can feel it standing up, and Resistencia twists the clamps. If I had any food in my system, I'd vomit it up. My stomach surges and splashes like a tropical storm. The pain is just a casing, though, housing It underneath.

After another twist in the opposite direction, Resistencia begins to pull upward. I can hear the root of my molar inside my head. It scrapes against the jawbone. The friction is dulled a little by all the drugs, but the sound isn't. It's like a rumble.

And then there's a crack. Loud enough for Resistencia and Virodh to hear it.

"What's that?" Virodh asks.

"Fuck! I broke it."

"Broke it?"

"The tooth, yeah. I'll have to pull each part separately."

She shifts the clamps in my mouth, focusing on the smaller tooth fragment toward the front. The tight grip-and-twist sends my legs shivering as Ku'e and Qawa press harder on me. I'm breaking a sweat. I think we all are.

Resistencia rips the first part of my tooth free from the gum and pulls it out of my mouth. The base of it is covered in yellow pus. Virodh and Resistencia grimace at it but ignore what comes out after. Black. A ribbon of black swirling out of my mouth, circling them both, then traveling the rest of the room. The ribbon settles over Bibi's eyes, and the light flickers. That gets Resistencia and Virodh's attention. They can't see the black, only what it does.

"Last one, Res," she says, coming back at me with the bent clamps. This time I feel the pull in my diaphragm and scream out more black ribbons. They swirl around Resistencia's face, looping around her ears, flowing in and out of her mouth when she says, "Almost... got it..."

The second fragment of tooth sounds like a brick rubbing dried cement before it's freed. It starts once the rotting half-tooth is released.

I hear a plop while all the black ribbons fatten and expand. They push everyone on me back, and in an instant, they push every*thing* back. Bibi, the walls, air, the chair I'm sitting in, my clothes, gravity. I'm in a void now, but I'm not alone.

It doesn't "move." I can't call what it does "motion." It emanates itself forward, toward me. Each version starts out impossibly black, jagged, and angular with spiky antlers above where a head should be before smoothing out, giving birth to its next black, writhing, craggy self.

I breathe, but it doesn't. It waits for me to say it.

"Athsaserisoon," I say, and It inflates inside the void, a celebration, before reconstituting into an all-black base with thousands of vibrating black tendrils swirling amongst Itself.

Athsaserisoon forms a shape like mine, almost like a human, but with long, spindly antlers. It gels a part of itself into an infinity of arms and then legs, then thousands of quivering fingers. The antlers marvel at the design of them, then Athsaserisoon touches me.

There's no texture to Athsaserisoon. I can't feel it. Instead, memories bubble at the site. The first one is me as a child. My mom grips my hand as we run. We're in a store. Loud pops crack into the air, and everyone else is running too. We turn into an aisle, and my mom starts grabbing cans with her free hand.

"Take it!" she screams, pushing canned goods into my tiny chest. "Take it!"

One of its black gooey arms pops the memory bubble, and it's gone. More bubbles form, and I grab at them before the antlers can reach them. But they pop too, and now those memories are gone.

Athsaserisoon tweaks its antlers at me. This isn't a game, I realize, it's a ritual. And I don't know what I'm doing. I reach a finger out to touch Athsaserisoon, and upon contact with its blackness, a gate opens up in my mind. It's a chamber full of clamoring, screaming, gut-wrenching wails. It's dark in there, but I can sense a scurrying deep inside it. Not one thing, multiple, infinite. And then they see me. They know I know they're there in the heart-ripping screams. They rush toward me, and I pull back from Athsaserisoon just in time to close the gate, keep them there.

I try to run from Athsaserisoon, but we're in a void together. It emanates in pace with me. Trying to escape is pointless, and Athsaserisoon's antlers slide when I realize it. Like its version of a smile.

That's when I get it: this is the thing that's been growing inside me. This is what the pain was housing, like a capsule from some other part of the universe. But Athsaserisoon isn't "here" yet. We're in a void together, not in my world.

For the flash of an instant, I think of Ku'e, and how to keep this thing far away from her, and Athsaserisoon lodges one of its trembling arms inside me. Every detail about her becomes bubbles floating between us. I don't reach for them, and Athsaserisoon doesn't either. We let her fill the space and hover around us.

Another arm pierces into me, and my mother escapes into bubbles, too. Athsaserisoon forms more hands and feet and plunges them into me until it's almost all inside me and I'm almost all floating bubbles.

The process slows because my mind moves slower. And because I know now, with It in me, what's happening. It's taking over, freeing myself to make room for It. I watch my memories drift and sometimes bump into each other. Once or twice, two memories merge and get bigger. That's my out! Careful to not touch them, I wave my arms to build up enough wind to float the bubbles into themselves. Two into one, two into one again. One piece of me, where there was once four.

I make enough space to spin with Athsaserisoon still partially sticking out of me, and It whips up enough air to collide more bubbles. It isn't perfect, some bubbles pop on impact and vanish. But I'll settle for parts of myself if that means somehow I'll get free.

Athsaserisoon realizes what I'm doing and steps all the way into me until we're both gone, and the void is all bubbles sliding and moving on each other. It's here that it has a voice.

"You pick one, I pick one."

I choose a morning waking up in a tent on the highway after dancing and drinking all night. I'm not hungover. I'm not with Ku'e. I'm alone. The sun streams in through the tears in the tent, and everything feels warm. I feel hungry but just want to keep laying down.

Athsaserisoon chooses a girl I met before Ku'e. She used to stay up late and laugh with me back when we still lived in houses. But she met a man, older, and kept getting angry with me. He had guns and a car, tanks of gasoline.

"Why don't you get it?" she kept asking me. "What's wrong with you?"

It was the first time I actually felt it, that there was something wrong with me for liking girls. That memory eats my chosen memory. The two fuse so that the girl's disapproving gaze burns like sunlight.

I choose snapping Qawa's shoulder back into place, and Athsaserisoon chooses a man who tried to rape me. I choose watching feeds of waterfalls in far-off countries, back when countries existed, and it chooses the time I crashed my e-bike and flew over the handlebars. We fuse a third of my life, incorrectly and off-balance, with trauma inside, layered over every sunset and orgasm. But we both leave my mother alone.

I go there first and choose my mother interrogating me about what I'm doing with "That Girl" (Ku'e), and Athsaserisoon counters with my mom hugging me to sleep when I was five. We stab and parry at the complexity of my mother, fusing all the good-bad with the bad-good, until the image of her is gnarled and tangled like Athsaserisoon's antlers. My mother becomes hardened vines with thorns that sometimes bloom into flowers. But those flowers wilt and decay back into the vines. They, my mother, would block out the sun if it could reach here.

We're left with two memories of her. In the first, she's on the floor, and I'm standing over her, feeling ten feet tall. I had just hit her, the only time I ever had, and she would die a few days later. She swung at me from her hospital bed, and I punched back. She fell on the floor, and I was there. So angry at her, but also so proud of myself. My mother was dying and hateful, and I was not going to let her take me with her. She could bring me down to her violence, but she couldn't and wouldn't make me hate myself. Not ever again.

The second is the blink of the moment right before I hit my mother. The silent splash of fear in my spine before I ramped my fist up to land on her. It was the last time I looked for my mom in her eyes. The fear sprang up because I couldn't find her there, but it settled in my spine because I wanted her there. Society started collapsing when I was seven. And until I grew up, she was there, just as scared as I was, but at least she was holding me.

That blink of a moment, when I decided to hit my mother, it was the last time I felt the needfulness of being small to someone. The next moment, the hitting her, was the rejection of it. From that point on, I pushed forward, I took charge. I assembled a group of people to storm a launch station and try to hold a billionaire hostage while rebuilding a better society. But this moment, the fear in my spine, the decision to hit her, the weight of feeling small for the love you place in someone, Athsaserisoon hands it to me, and I accept it.

I step into the memory and feel my eyelids tingle before the rush of tears that are going to come. I breathe out in the memory and try to hold myself in my smallest moment. And when I touch myself, bring me in to hug me, I see a black ribbon snaking in the air. They don't see it, but it streams out of my mother's eyes and into my memory-me's mouth. It's *that* moment. The transfer. Athsaserisoon jumping from her and into me.

I let Athsaserisoon win, and it pops every warped bubble of mine. But it leaves this one for me to hold. Athsaserisoon quivers into an impossibly black ribbon and coils through the void, released out into my world now. I don't know why it chose my mother, or why it chose me. All this time with the pain, and Athsaserisoon never told me what it wanted with my body, what it would do with Reclamation and all the people. How it would destroy an already destroyed planet, or why it would even bother. But even in the seconds since I let It release out into the world, I already feel removed, like a deep breath out that can't be reclaimed.

All I have is this memory. I squeeze myself during the time in my life when I felt weakest, powerless, small. And all I care about is holding onto myself at that exact second when I most needed love.

BARRIERS

Oort Cloud, Space c. 2180s CE

We stretch ourselves out from our home star and cross the vacuum, each of us along a line, so thin we become almost a laser, and so far between ourselves we almost break, in order to reach their vessel. Others before us have suspended them so they'd be easier to find. We re-collect ourselves outside their hull, each of us drawing ourselves inward. Once we are all there, we spread over their vessel, looking for a way in.

What we know is that this will be difficult. What we know is that these life-forms cannot survive in the vacuum, so they've built a shield. "Air-tight" is how they describe it. There is a silo at one end of the vessel for their fuel to propel them forward. We flow inside of it and through their pipes and tubing. Others before us have combed through these inner workings, studying their mechanics, positing about them based on their technology. But that is not our purpose. What they can build and how they can travel is less important to us than what and how they *are*. Spread out inside their pipes and tubing, searching for some way in, we think they must be extremely fragile.

Before we abandon them, after expending so much energy just to reach them, we find a way, a tear in a wire casing, and flood ourselves in. The metal wires inside repel us, like barely traceable stars, and we move quickly through this network, deeper inside the vessel, bypassing the barriers they've built for themselves, until suddenly we flow out into their chambers. There are barriers everywhere, defining the space and dictating where one can go, like a cube covered on four sides with two intentional planes left open. They weave a maze inside the vessel where these beings live. We've seen this before from a century of data they shot out into the vacuum from their planet. Others before us have studied every parcel of it. "They lie to themselves" was what we were told, but so far, sliding into their living space, these hallways and rooms appear accurate compared to what they told themselves, and by extension, all of us.

We cannot all fit inside here; we were not designed for confinement. We break ourselves into three: we-in-the-vacuum, we-in-the-vessel-workings, and we-in-their-living-space.

We map out their living space and, based on their past data, begin to piece together some of how they work. Each one has private space, though those are all connected by hallways and situated in the same quadrant. There are communal spaces for their biology—a system of extracting nutrition from their environment and then ingesting, carrying through, and expelling waste. This must happen at regular intervals or else they'll die. This fascinates us. That these creatures are so interdependent, co-reliant on their environment. Again, a fragile system, built right into the essence of their existence. Yet somehow, perhaps against the very nature of themselves, they've built vessels to propel themselves into the vacuum, off their planet, and for this particular vessel, reach the edge of their star system.

Other communal spaces include areas to interface with their avatar-technology, big screens that are now blank. A space for mapping the surrounding vacuum. A space where they can be taken apart, inspected, and repaired. But they, themselves, are missing. They aren't here.

We-in-the-vessel-workings maneuver ourselves into smaller and smaller spaces until we break through inside their avatar-tech. The hallways and many rooms alight. For us, it's a dazzling splash of color. Deep reds and oranges outline doorways and thresholds. A murky blue suspends on the top-wall above us, and below us, a thick, textured, white and tan covers the halls and rooms.

We-in-the-vessel-workings accesses their audio pathways: "We do not mean you harm. We wish only to flow and understand you."

Some doors, we discover, can only be opened with a bit of force that we cannot muster. We collect around one until We-in-the-workings sees us and short circuits a way in. The first few rooms like these store only thick containers, many black in color with their markings labeling the contents inside. Other rooms are just empty.

We find a door with no markings and collect ourselves around it. This one unseals first before opening, and we see them, four of them. They are huddled together but distinguishable—not a collective like us—and they shake at the sight of us.

We-in-the-workings: "We do not mean you harm. We wish only to flow and understand you."

One of them points a long rectangular object at us and screams, "Stay away!" Two metal tips attached to wires fly out from the rectangle and fall through the cloud of us to the chalky white bottom-wall below. The one holding the rectangle opens their mouth wide and continues screaming. We-in-the-workings closes the door.

The room at the opposite end of the vessel, away from the silo that pumps out their fuel, is where we find the rest of them. They aren't the others who screamed at us. These creatures are suspended in tubes that are filled with liquid. They float, and there's a white tubing apparatus covering the tops of them. Generally, these creatures are almost symmetrical; they have two limbs on either side on the top half of them, and two limbs on either side on the bottom, though the top and bottom limbs serve different functions. But the symmetry stops in between the limbs, on top and on bottom. On top protrudes an oblong function. Others who have studied them before us say that this part is multilayered, networked, electrical, and extremely agile. They make noise from this part, look out from this part, ingest their environment in this part, and think in this part. Deep inside this part, when the creature is alive, is a tesseractical storm, almost like the inside of our home star.

We count thirty-seven of them, all in tubes. They range in biological maturity, some are small and bulbous, others longer, thinner, and frail. As with previous investigations of new intelligent species, we choose to start small. We collect ourselves around the tube with the smallest creature until

We-in-the-workings notices. The liquid slowly drains out—but not into the room, it somehow flows somewhere else—until the creature is no longer floating but folded upon itself at the bottom of the tube. The apparatus covering its top falls off, and the creature slowly becomes active. Finally, the transparent tube casing slides along itself, and the creature falls onto the floor.

We-in-the-workings: "We do not mean you harm. We wish only to flow and understand you."

The creature opens its mouth but does not scream, instead just breathing out for a slow, long bit, and says, "Wait, what?"

We-in-the-workings: "We do not mean you harm. We wish only to flow and understand you."

"Flow and understand?"

We collect ourselves into a close cloud so that the creature can more easily notice us.

"Oh. My. Fudging. God!" says the creature, standing up. It walks up to and through us and then does this again. "Are you real?"

We-in-the-workings: "Yes, we are."

"You're talking through the ship's comms?"

"Yes, we are."

"Ho-ly crap!"

The creature walks around us, inspecting us, and then looks down at itself. It jolts at itself and brings its limbs to cover the front part of its body.

"Wait! Hold on. I'll be right back, I swear. Don't go anywhere!" it says and then takes off running out of the room and down the hall. We flow behind it, and it places its limbs behind itself and says, "No, don't look, don't look, don't look!"

We-in-the-workings tracks the creature. It turns down hallways with speed—it's obviously familiar with the vessel—and eventually reaches its private room. It tries to open its door, but we've taken control of the vessel. We-in-the-workings unlocks its room for it. It closes the door behind itself, and We-in-the-workings can't monitor it anymore, so we flow through the halls to reach it. We begin to collect ourselves outside the door when the creature opens it again.

The creature is now covered. From research, we understand that they call this "clothes," another barrier protecting the fragile system. Its clothes are black in color, with red lines bisecting them, some across the wide part of it, some vertically running the entire length. At the bottom of the creature is an even thicker barrier. We know from research these are called "boots."

"Okay," it says, "now that I'm decent, let's meet for real." It extends its limb through us. "I'm Graham Sheff III, but everybody calls me Gray."

We-in-the-workings: "Gray."

Gray moves its limb quickly up and down, displacing some of us in the drag until we re-collect. "What's your name?"

We-in-the-workings: "We do not have a name. We just are."

"You don't have a name? Who made you?"

We-in-the-workings: "Stars made us. Many stars."

"No way!"

We-in-the-workings: "Gray, we do not mean you harm. We wish only to flow and understand you."

"Yeah, you said that before. If you don't have a name, then what do I call you? Where do you come from? Are you from another galaxy? Are there more of you?"

We-in-the-workings: "We are not authorized to give you many details about us. We were sent here to understand you. Once this mission is complete, we will depart and report back, and another phase of contact can begin. For the protection of yourself, ourselves, and the Larger Community of others, we are only authorized to provide the minimum amount of information. But we can tell you a few things about us: we come from a home star far away from here. You, and your kind, have not yet detected our home star. Your vessel is also stayed at the moment. You are not yet authorized to exit your home star."

"The sun?" Gray says, "Oh, the solar system! We can't leave?"

We-in-the-workings: "You are not yet authorized to exit your home star. We must first understand you more."

"Okay, what do you want to know about me?"

We-in-the-workings: "Not know, understand."

"What's the difference?"

We-in-the-workings: "We know facts about your species. You sent us a great deal. But data alone is not comprehensive."

"I don't get you."

We-in-the-workings: "Knowing is static, like this vessel, these walls. We know how you built them. Understanding is flow, more like movement. We want to understand why you built them."

"Why we build spaceships?" Gray asks. "Because Earth died."

We-in-the-workings: "Earth, your home planet, has died?"

Gray breathes out slowly, looks down at the floor, and says, "Yeah, there were too many people, and we used up all the water, and all the animals died. So, we left."

We-in-the-vacuum knows this is not true. There is still detectable life on Earth. All of our three selves take note of this, and store within us for later recollection: humans do lie to themselves.

We-in-the-workings: "What do you remember about Earth?"

Gray slumps down but remains standing. It says, "Nothing. I've never even been there. My grandpa used to tell me stories about it, though. Oh—" Gray presses its limb upon the pad next to the door of its private room. "Do you want to see some vids from Earth? I have some old files."

We-in-the-workings: "That is not necessary, Gray. We have already seen a great deal from your species. Our purpose to understand you."

"Yeah, yeah," Gray says, "can I eat while you understand me?"

We-in-the-workings: "Yes, in fact, observation will be most helpful to us."

Gray walks through the cloud of us and turns down different hallways while we flow behind. Gray arrives at one of the communal spaces where these beings ingestion together.

"I'm gonna guess that you don't eat," Gray says as he opens small doors around the room, gathering his ingest materials.

We-in-the-workings: "We are not authorized to give you that information."

Gray prepares his food for ingest, adding moisture and the contents of various packets into an open-faced vessel. Gray places that into a separate container, heating it, and acquires a tool to bring the material to the mouth where he speaks from.

"Are you," Gray says to us, "alive? Or are you like some kind of robot?"

We-in-the-workings: "We do not understand."

"Are you a living thing?"

We-in-the-workings: "We do not understand."

Gray begins to ingest but tilts his head upward while looking at us.

"You don't know what being alive is?"

We-in-the-workings: "Perhaps you can explain."

"Hmm, being alive is like breathing, and your heart beating, and your brain," Gray says, "where it all comes together, and you know you're alive, but there's also all the stuff your body does that's automatic, that keeps you alive."

We-in-the-workings: "Alive for how long?"

Gray says, "That's different for everybody."

We-in-the-workings: "Why?"

Gray continues ingesting and says, "Because everyone's different. No two humans are alike. Well, unless they're clones or twins."

We-in-the-workings: "You are able to clone yourselves now?"

"Not all of us."

Gray completes ingestion and takes its tools toward a basin and places them there.

"I don't want to talk about clones." Gray says. "Can we talk about something else?"

We-in-the-workings: "We are authorized to talk about many subjects. What would you like to talk about?"

"I wanna learn more about you, but I guess I'm not 'authorized' yet."

We-in-the-workings: "Our apologies. We do not mean you harm."

"Flow and understand, yeah, I got it. Wait, can I ask you this? Is this the first time you're meeting a human?"

We-in-the-workings: "Yes."

"Cool! Well, what do you think? I bet you think we look weird, huh?"

We-in-the-workings: "We've seen images and renderings of your species before."

"Yeah, some of us are all lanky and tall, and some of us are really fat." Gray expands his limbs out from either side of him to further express this. "My grandpa had a big fat stomach, but my dad was born tall and skinny. They said I'll be tall and skinny since I grew up in orbit. If I was on land, I might be fat."

We-in-the-workings: "Which would you prefer?"

"Land, definitely! Growing up in orbit means walking the same circles over and over and over again. When I was littler, I couldn't reach anything, because they don't build ships thinking about kids. So, all you could do was run down halls. But grown-ups would always yell, 'No running!'"

We-in-the-workings: "Is running dangerous?"

"No! It's what we're built for."

We-in-the-workings: "But you weren't allowed to fulfill your functioning?"

"We don't say it like that. You weren't allowed to have too much fun. 'Orbit is dangerous' and 'This is serious science work.'"

We-in-the-workings: "What was the 'serious science work'?"

"I don't want to talk about it. Hey! Do you want to hang out in my room?"

Gray leaves the communal space, and we flow behind him. In his room, Gray shows us various possessions. The ends of his limbs have "hands" and "fingers" to manipulate the world around it. This fascinates us. But Gray cannot explain in depth how these biomechanics work. When we ask, Gray says it's just "how he is." Just like how we are how we are.

After a time, Gray begins to breathe out in long spells and tells us he needs to "sleep." Another fragile system where humans need to deactivate and, presumably on Earth, were vulnerable to their environment. Again, humans appear to be built for a system of interdependence, yet they've developed so many barriers. We do not require "sleep" but observe Gray in the process of preparing for it.

Gray lies horizontal on a mat made for this purpose, then closes his eyes and rolls himself on its side.

"Why don't you have a name? What do I call you?"

We-in-the-workings: "What would you like to call us?"

Gray says, "Back on Earth, we had these things in the sky that kinda look like you."

We-in-the-workings: "Yes, clouds. Would you like to call us that?"

"No, that seems too obvious. And you don't really move like a cloud. Oh, I got it! Fog!"

We-in-the-workings repeats it.

"What do you think?"

We-in-the-workings: "We have no preferences. But if Fog is helpful for you, we assent."

"Fog, can you stay here while I sleep?"

We-in-the-workings: "If you wish, yes."

"Humans say this, they say, 'Good night.'"

We float throughout Gray's room.

"You're supposed to say it back."

We-in-the-workings: "We are not human."

"But just say it anyway."

We-in-the-workings: "Good night."

After Gray's sleeping is finished, we observe his ritual functionings. His room has a space for cleaning his body. All humans clean themselves, but each one goes about it differently. Gray won't let us observe him directly while cleaning, but he describes his process. Gray washes his face first, then the hair on his head. He calls the creases under his arms "pits" and says these must be cleaned thoroughly. Gray says every human body has cracks and crevices, and each day, they must be cleaned out, or else the human will enter a stage called "gross," and no other humans will tolerate them. This strikes us as yet another example of human fragility. They must ingest their environment and deactivate at regular intervals to survive, and on top of that, regularly clean and sustain their outsides for the sake of others.

Gray covers himself in new clothes and returns to the communal ingestion room. Between scooping his utensils with "food" and bringing it to his mouth, Gray asks, "Hey, Fog? Am I the only one left on the ship? Did anyone else survive?"

We-in-the-workings: "No one on this ship has died. There are four humans who have locked themselves in a room below us."

"The 'Ten Crew!" Gray says. He drops his utensil and pushes himself up from his seated resting position. Then he begins running out of the communal space, turning sharp down hallways. We float behind to keep up.

We-in-the-workings: "What is a 'Ten Crew, Gray?"

Gray does not stop running. He makes it back to his private space and presses against the pads of other doors next to his.

"Maintenance Crew. They're a skeleton crew that rotates in and out to keep the ship running."

We-in-the-workings: "Skeleton?"

Gray twists his body around, we suppose, to see all sides around him, searching for this "'Ten Crew." The center of his head, the "face," appears strained.

We-in-the-workings: "Can you tell us more about skeletons?"

"No!" Gray says. "Where are they?"

We-in-the-workings: "Two levels below us. In a sealed container."

Gray runs, good at his functioning, toward a vertical pronged ledge that his limbs step down until he reaches the proper level. We flow in a vortex with him. It is not necessary, but we have learned this long, long ago. To unlock and further understand a being, we must "mirror" them. Copy as best we can, according to our design. Gray's limbs are all quick and sudden movements; therefore, we swirl amongst ourselves to match the kinesis.

Gray finally arrives at the proper room. His fingers press into the pad screen alongside the door, and it unseals and opens. Screams, from the humans inside, begin immediately.

"No, no, it's okay!" Gray tells the other humans. But one, the one who pointed the rectangle at us earlier, continues screaming. "Hey! Hey!" Gray continues, "I said stop it!"

The four humans in this room continue to huddle close amongst themselves, almost as if they are like us, a vast collection of selves. One of them, who wasn't screaming, reaches their arms out toward Gray. An invitation, we assume. But Gray does not move. We collect ourselves behind Gray.

We-in-the-workings: "We do not mean you harm. We wish only to flow and understand you."

Gray raises his hand as if to signal to us. "I've got this, Fog. Guys," he says to the four humans, this "'Ten Crew," "This is Fog. Fog, this is the 'Ten Crew."

The one who pointed that thing at us says, "Three, get away from that thing. We don't know what it is."

"My name is Gray!" Gray's voice raises. From behind Gray, we can still observe these humans' postures. A few of them tense at Gray's voice.

We chose to release Gray from his tubing because he was small and young, not like most of the other humans in tubes. We've learned over time that, when possible, the young are most helpful in understanding a species. The world around young ones is constantly explained to them, and plainly. They are naturally curious, unafraid, and unburdened with responsibilities, allowing more free time to interact. Usually this means that the young are not in positions of authority, but for Gray, this is not the same.

He yells at this 'Ten Crew, and they tense in reaction.

Gray motions behind himself, toward us, "And we know what this is. Obviously, it's an alien, or some kind of alien technology."

This 'Ten Crew continues to hold each other. Gray breathes out deeply. "They keep saying it, but I guess I have to too: They don't mean us any harm. They just want to understand us."

Gray steps inside the room and approaches them. He says, "They called it a 'contact process.' This is the first step. They come here, get to know us, and then we get to know them." He touches one human at a bend in their arm. "This is our wildest dream come true, you guys!"

The humans move their eyes from Gray to ourselves and back again. Still, unmoved. We slow our speed in our float, assuming this will communicate some kind of tranquility.

"Hey Fog, maybe you should give us a few minutes.," Gray says.

We assent and flow through ourselves and down the hallway. We flow up several floors and recollect ourselves outside Gray's private quarters, waiting for him. Eventually, he arrives.

"Let's go inside, Fog," he says, walking into his quarters. Once we are inside, he explains, "They're scared of you."

We-in-the-workings: "We do not mean them harm. We—"

"Yeah, yeah, yeah. Look, they're a 'Ten Crew."

We-in-the-workings: "They are skeletons?"

"No, that's just an expression. Every human has a skeleton that's inside us. Our bones. But ships like this have a Maintenance Crew, a 'Ten Crew. They just do the basics to keep the ship running. The 'bare bones' is what we say. A skeleton crew."

We-in-the-workings: "We don't fully understand."

"That's okay," Gray says, "they're subsees."

We-in-the-workings: "What are subsees?"

"They aren't humans like me."

We-in-the-workings: "How are they different?"

"They're, like, workers. I told them they can come out and go back to work. That everyone is alive and fine, and that the mission is changed now."

We-in-the-workings: "What is your mission?"

"That's not important." Gray takes another breath. He reaches his hand into the cloud of us, and we flow around his fingers. "They told me that they tried to shoot you with a tase-gun."

We-in-the-workings: "That is correct."

"That wasn't okay, Fog. I told them they should apologize to you, but they're too scared. So, I'll do it. I'm sorry they did that."

We-in-the-workings: "They cannot harm us. We are not designed that way."

"Well, they didn't know that. I think for the time being, you should just stay with me, okay?"

We-in-the-workings: "That was our initial preference."

Gray parts the lips of his mouth so that they are pulled at the ends. He does this occasionally; it's called a smile.

We-in-the-workings: "We can detect them, the 'Ten Crew. They are moving around."

"Yeah, they're going back to work."

We-in-the-workings: "Their work is with the other humans in the tubes?"

"The cryos? No."

We-in-the-workings: "That is where they are."

"Fudging hell!" Gray says, again raising his voice, but we do not tense in the air. Gray passes through us quickly, opens his door, and runs. "Stay there, Fog! Okay?"

We-in-the-living-space remains in Gray's quarters, but We-in-the-workings monitors and traces Gray.

Gray has to run nearly the entire length of the ship to reach the 'Ten Crew and the other humans floating in tubes. One member of the 'Ten Crew is evaluating the vital life signs of the humans floating in tubes. The other three are at screens, trying to interface with their avatar-technology. But We-in-the-workings has taken over. We do not allow them access. They scratch at their upturned heads, touch the same dots on their screens over and over. They even power down and power up consoles. We let them do all of this.

When Gray enters the room, the three at the consoles stop. The one who fired the tase-gun at us says, "Go back to your quarters, Three. We'll prep your cryo station and put you back in in a few hours."

Gray says, "No."

That one says, "You know the protocols. This is what has to be done."

Gray crosses his arms over himself. If we were in the room, we'd be able to get a better look at his face in this moment. But we're relying on cameras built into the corners of walls in the room.

The 'Ten Crew member says, "Three, you're not in charge here. Not after this."

"My name is Gray!" Gray shouts at them. The one evaluating the humans in tubes stops. "And I am in charge. You work for me! Technically."

"Gray," the crew member assents, "you know this better than anyone. The situation has changed now. The safest thing, for everyone, is to get back online, get back on course, and cryo up."

"You're not understanding, Crew. We can't move! The ship is locked in. Fog's doing that. We can't get back online. Fog," Gray points upward, "is inside everything. It's just letting you think you can work the boards."

Gray walks to the screens the other 'Ten Crew members were working at and individually turns each of them off. "Are you getting it yet? There's no more mission. This *is* the mission. This is step one of a contact process with some kind of advanced technology that we've never seen before. That no one's ever seen before. It," he points again to the ceiling, "is not alone. Fog's got to report back to something, or someone."

The crew member stands close to Gray. She's taller than him and hunches down toward him, and says, "We don't know what that thing is. We can't trust it. Who knows what its intentions are."

"Oh my fudging god, have you listened to it for like a single solid second? It doesn't mean us any harm! It—"

"That's just what it says, it could be lying. Three," she puts her hand on Gray's arm above his elbow. He pulls back, but her grip is tight.

"Don't, ever, touch me again!" Gray yells at her. "I might be a kid, but you know who I am."

The two struggle until Gray's arm is finally free from her.

"Everybody stop!" Gray says to the 'Ten Crew. "My grandpa told me about Directive, and I'm invoking it. I say;

you do. You're all going to prep your cryos, and then you're going back in."

"Three?!" one of them says. Gray puts both hands on the sides of his body, in a sense, widening himself. We believe this is some kind of posture meant to convey authority. He stands, unmoving. "Gray," that same crew member says, "don't do this. We're not the bad guys here."

"Prep your cryos and get back in."

Gray returns to us, collected outside his quarters.

We-in-the-workings: "We observed your exchange."

"I know," Gray says, keying in his code to open the door. We allow this.

We-in-the-workings: "We have many questions."

Gray says, "I don't really feel up to talking right now, Fog. Can I just be alone for a while?"

We-in-the-workings: "Of course."

Gray enters his quarters and closes the door behind him. We-in-the-living-space remains collected outside Gray's door. But We-in-the-workings continues to monitor the 'Ten Crew. They place one crew member inside a tube and seal it. Gas releases, putting the member to sleep right as liquid starts to rise inside the tube. Before the next one, each of them says goodbye to one another. Their eyes condense and produce liquid. The one who fired the tase-gun at us and who gripped Gray's arm places her lips on the forehead of another member. She will be the last, and no one will be left to say goodbye to her.

Once she's alone, a noise comes out of her as she continues to produce tears. We do not fully understand why this is happening. But with Gray in his room alone, we have no one else to ask. Her shoulders twitch as she groans and cries, even as she steps into her own tube, even and until the gas releases and liquid rises. And then she, too, floats silently.

We-in-the-living-space leaves Gray's door and flows toward the room with the other humans in tubes. We sweep slowly past each one, gathering what we can understand by their bodies and the markings and screens attached to each tube. These humans vary by skin pigment, but the liquid they float in dampens them all in a light green color. We notice the 'Ten Crew makes up the darkest colors of them and that they are more than just the four from the storage container. We count twelve of them in total. Their screens display their names and a countdown to their "shifts." There will be eight Earth years until the next crew awakens. The current ones, the four that Gray ordered back in, will float in liquid for fifty Earth years.

There are five human tubes with no names displayed on their screen. One of them belonged to Gray. His simply reads: "III."

We wait for Gray to come out of his room and take the time to flow through more of the vessel to places Gray doesn't seem to show interest in. There's a large chamber just below the room with the human tubes with panels of their avatar tech across many stations. We-in-the-workings activates their screens, and light floods into the room. The flat panels open up, and barely perceptible specks of metal waft up and configure themselves. They look almost like us! But when we flow through them, we receive nothing, no passing of data, no acknowledgment. They are inert, like stellar dust.

Within the panels and the ceiling above are different shifting magnets that drive and spin these flecks until they assemble a three-dimensional rendering. Their home star. Everything is labeled: the solar satellite bodies, many of which carry their own satellites, which are also labeled. We-in-the-workings dials up Earth. There's a large body called "Moon" and many tiny orbiting vessels. We-in-the-workings can speed and reverse the rendering over a specific period of time, and we see these vessels attach and disengage randomly. A few grow in size, collecting smaller vessels, becoming almost like us, a larger unit, before separating and spacing apart again. Over the time period displayed, this happens often, in a pattern we can't understand.

We-in-the-workings shifts the rendering outward, toward the boundary of the home star. At the edge of the stellar cloud is this vessel, named *The Drive of Discovery*. When We-in-the-workings dials up the vessel to become larger, we can see ourselves. A small pin of light, at first, and then we widen out. And we remember it. We almost broke ourselves to reach this vessel and gathered ourselves back at the edge of it. Safe, inside ourselves, only that is not entirely visible in this rendering. It's a representation but an outside one, observing. This is the first that we've ever seen ourselves depicted beyond ourselves. Another entity, a blunter technology, casting us in a virtual space, collecting outside *The Drive of Discovery*, but inherently missing the point. Their tool, these magnetized metal specks, is closest we've ever seen to ourselves, but somehow deadened, not animated under their own control. We leave that chamber.

We gather ourselves outside Gray's door, and We-in-the-workings broadcasts inside.

We-in-the-workings: "We have many questions, Gray."

"I still don't feel like talking," he says. "Go away."

We-in-the-workings: "But we came here to flow and understand you."

He raises the volume of his voice, "I know! You keep saying that! Look, I'm tired, and I'm not in a fun mood anymore. Can you just go away and come back later?"

We-in-the-workings: "There are more spaces in *The Drive of Discovery* that we can explore, yes."

"Good!"

We-in-the-workings: "Good night, Gray."

Gray does not respond.

We-in-the-workings: "You told us that you're supposed to say it back."

He lets out a vocalization, just sound but not words. "Fine," he says, "good night!"

A longer period of time elapses, and Gray emerges from his room. He steps through us without saying anything and goes to the Mess Room to ingest his food again. We flow behind him.

We-in-the-workings: "Gray, we have—"

"Ugh, I know!" he says. "You have many questions."

He breathes out audibly and then begins to assemble a meal from different containers.

"Those people yesterday," he says, "they just think they're in charge of me because they're older. Because 'I'm a child.' But—" he takes another breath, "I mean, I am a child, but I'm more than that."

We-in-the-workings: "How much more?"

"I'm more important. Grandpa says I'm not supposed to say that, but it's true. I'm not like most other humans, and sometimes it really sucks."

We-in-the-workings: "We were told that all humans are unique and individually variable. In theory, this is not that much different than us."

"Ohmigod, I want to ask you more about that, but you're probably gonna tell me you're not authorized."

We-in-the-workings: "That is correct."

"You know what? That's really unfair! Everyone's always holding shi—stuff back from me. And now I'm at the edge of the solar system with the first ever alien or alien technology, or I don't even know what! Because you, too, won't tell me."

We coalesce in the air over a chair opposite Gray at the table where he ingests his food.

"Understanding goes both ways, Fog. How can you understand me if I can't understand you?"

We-in-the-workings: "That is correct also, Gray. And that is within our parameters."

"No, it's not! You're always saying, 'We are not authorized.'"

We-in-the-workings: "We are not authorized to give you *information*. But as we spoke of before, information is not understanding. We can share what we understand about ourselves."

Gray puts his ingesting utensils down on the table. "Okay, here's the deal: you tell me about how you understand yourself, and after that, but only after, I'll answer all your many questions. Deal?"

We-in-the-workings: "We accept."

"Okay, go."

We-in-the-workings: "While you were in your room, we saw ourselves, for the first time. We were in what we believe to be a navigational chamber, and there was a spatial/visual depiction of ourselves."

"You got scanned. We scan everything."

We-in-the-workings: "We were… disappointed."

Gray spits out some of his food, and says, "What?!"

We-in-the-workings: "The scan depicted us as a bulk collection of particles."

"Well, that is what you look like."

We-in-the-workings: "But that doesn't match how we feel about who we are."

Gray completes ingesting but does not move to clean his utensils and containers.

"Okay, give it to me," he says, "how do you feel about who you are?"

Coalesced, We-in-the-living-space churn and swirl amongst ourselves, quickly. This builds up a static that can unleash for ourselves whole concepts of distance, time, and fusion, in tight, instantaneous blasts.

We-in-the-workings: "We feel immense and ancient. We feel like what the vacuum of space would feel like if it were capable. Vast. We feel over everything, at every point, always and throughout."

Gray asks, "What does that feel like?"

We-in-the-workings: "It feels like… longing. We feel like we are never not reaching. We reach for our stars. We reached for your star."

"Wow," Gray says, "why does that sound so sad?"

We-in-the-workings: "We do not interpret it that way. But what was sad was seeing us depicted through those scans. As if we were a collection of dust and not a whole. As if it was a lie."

"But come on, you do look like an animated cloud of dust."

We-in-the-workings: "We appear to ourselves, in each individual part, as feedback. We appear to ourselves as infinite, never-ending loops."

"Well," Gray says and laughs, "sorry, I guess, for having your picture taken."

We-in-the-workings: "Perhaps now we can finish the agreement."

"Your many questions. Okay, fine." Gray says.

Humans, we continue to observe, rely on their barriers. We ask Gray about the "mission" he and the 'Ten Crew spoke of, but Gray says that he has to "use the bathroom" first. We float beside him as he walks back to his quarters. He won't answer our questions before "the bathroom," he says, because it's complicated. We allow him to open the door to his quarters and he allows us inside. But then moves into another room, this "bathroom," almost immediately.

Once he's finished, we ask him again about the mission, but this time he says he wants to see the rendering of ourselves in the navigational chamber. We reach another deal: to go look at this rendering first, and then Gray will answer our questions. We do not like this deal.

Gray calls this place the Nav Deck and explains that this is where the Flight Crew spend most of their time. Usually, he is not allowed in to be here.

"For a while," Gray says, "everyone but the Flight Crew was cryo-ed. Well, and a 'Ten Crew, of course."

We-in-the-workings: "Why?"

"Because we have to last a long time. And it's easier to do in cryo. You don't age."

We-in-the-workings: "What does that feel like? The cryo?"

Gray says, "It doesn't feel like the immensity of the universe or whatever. But it doesn't hurt. It's like you're in a really heavy sleep."

We-in-the-workings: "We do not sleep."

"I noticed," Gray says. "Do you ever, like, power down?"

We-in-the-workings: "We do not understand."

"Like go inactive, or re-charge?"

We-in-the-workings: "No."

"Then sleep is gonna be really hard to explain. But it's peaceful. You're not, like, there, and you're not aware of anything."

We-in-the-workings: "How long were you in cryo before we released you?"

"Once we passed Saturn, everyone got out of cryo," Gray explains. "The ship picked up a weird signal in Saturn's orbit. But nobody could make heads or tails of it so we parked and practiced drills, safety stuff. The grown-ups pretty much had to learn how to do every single job in case something happened. I wanted to learn, but they had me education-learning."

We-in-the-workings: "We take it that is different from vessel-learning."

"Ohmigod, it was so boring. Math and History and Grammar. We were at the edge of Saturn! But I was stuck in AI-school. And like Grandpa says, I'm technically in charge. Everyone works for me, but no one listens to me."

This often upsets him, we make note. Not being listened to, being prevented from exercising authority.

Gray continues, "We did that for about five years. And then one by one, crews went back in cryo. They put me in first."

Gray types into a pad near a screen on the wall. "Thirty-five years ago. I mean, if you think about it, I'm almost fifty."

We-in-the-workings: "Gray, we want to ask again about the mission and Directive you spoke of."

"Yeah, yeah, yeah, you keep saying," Gray says, "but the mission is really obvious. We're looking for another planet to live on. I mean, the ship's called 'Drive of Discovery.'"

We-in-the-workings: "But our presence voids that mission?"

"Well yeah! You come from somewhere. You could take us to it, and we could live there!"

We-in-the-workings: "You could not survive the journey, even in cryo. And you could not survive in our home star."

"But you have to know some places. You're ancient and immense. You gotta know something."

We-in-the-workings: "We are not authorized to tell you."

"Not yet. You said that once."

We-in-the-workings: "That is correct. This is step one in a contact process."

"It's a test, Fog. I'm not stupid."

We-in-the-workings: "We do not understand it as such. We would not say it that way. Gray, can you tell us about the Directive you spoke of?"

Gray turns off the screen on the wall. He crosses the room to a bay of chairs, touches each one, but then sits on top of a flat workstation.

"Grandpa doesn't like me talking about it. I don't like talking about it either."

We-in-the-workings: "We can observe that it has significance."

"It's the whole point. Grandpa Sheff funded this whole thing. He's back in Earth-orbit in cryo for as long as he can until we get word back to him."

We-in-the-workings: "So he gave you the Directive? To exercise power."

We were told humans lie to themselves. We observed direct and indirect evidence of that. But now Gray begins to lie to me.

"Because it's Grandpa's money, and he's my grandpa. I'm like an investor. Nobody on the crew wanted me to be here, but someone has to look out for the investment."

We-in-the-workings: "Your father could not do this?"

Gray lies, "My father's in different investments. And there's only so much family to go around."

We-in-the-workings: "Gray, why is your cryo-tube labeled III when others have names?"

"What the fudge, Fog?" Gray raises his voice.

We-in-the-workings: "We do not mean to harm you."

"The word you're looking for is 'offend.' You don't mean to offend me. But you did."

We-in-the-workings: "Our purpose is to understand you."

Gray says, "Yeah, by asking really personal questions. You might have the immensity of the universe, but you don't have any manners."

We-in-the-workings: "We have calibrated ourselves to be gentle for many thousands of your Earth years."

"Well, maybe you need a few more thousands to finally get it right."

We-in-the-workings: "We can clearly observe that you are agitated. But we are still confused. Perhaps you can help us. Why are you disturbed when it is you who is lying to us?"

"I'm not lying!" Gray raises his voice again.

We-in-the-workings: "Gray, we have total access to all available data on this vessel. We've read the Directive. We know why your cryo-tube is labeled III when others have names. What we don't know, what we want to understand, is how you understand these things. But you are not choosing to face it. You tell lies to build a barrier. Why?"

"Fuck you!" Gray says. "I'm not the only one who's lying. You knew who I was this whole time and pretended like you didn't know! You tried to be my friend. For what?"

We-in-the-workings: "Data is simply data. Our purpose is understanding."

"Well, understand that I'm fucking mad!" Gray says. He lifts himself off the workstation and walks through us to the exit. His footsteps are louder than they've ever been. They echo through the hallways as we float behind. Gray clangs, and we are silent. We allow him into his private quarters. He does not allow us in behind him.

We-in-the-workings reviews the vessel data while We-in-the-living-space flows back to the Cryo Room. *The Drive of Discovery* was assembled by Sheff Corp outside of a station called Tejas Nuevo. There were almost twice as many humans on board then with small teams departing as it passed solar satellites. Along with names, the humans floating in cryo have "class status" listed. Flight and Medical Crews are "Class A." The 'Ten Crew are "Sub-C." Gray is "Not Applicable."

The humans are without clothing barriers, floating in cryo. Their limbs wade slowly through the liquid. According to vessel data, this is intentional. Liquid churn, electric jolts, and a compound of proteins and minerals can keep these frail human bodies optimal for "almost a century." Hypothetically longer, the data says.

Gray's "III" is a generational label. He is the third in a line of genetically identical human males, carried not in a womb like humans, but in a gestation shell not unlike their cryo-tubes. In personnel records for each human on this vessel, Gray's mother is listed as "None." His father is listed as "Sheff Corps R&D," with an amended field, Grandfather, listed as Graham Sheff I. There are no other records like Gray's on board this vessel.

We-in-the-living-space are still in the Cryo Room when Gray emerges from his quarters. We find him in Mess, ingesting again.

Grays begins to speak, "I'm not," he pauses, "there's not like a ton of me walking around back home. At least I don't think so."

We-in-the-workings: "Yes. Your own records indicate this."

"You should have told me that you knew, Fog! We didn't have to play pretend."

We-in-the-workings: "We were not pretending. We are not designed that way."

Grays says, "I blew the test, didn't I?"

We-in-the-workings: "This is not a test. Gray, as we've told you before, this is merely a first step in contact. We do not make judgments about you."

"You understand, yeah." Gray stops ingesting, puts his utensils down, and says, "But I think that's bull. How do you 'understand' without making judgments?"

We-in-the-workings: "We gather sentiments and report back. That is our purpose."

"And something else judges me?"

We-in-the-workings: "This cannot be uncommon for you. You've spoken to us in great detail about how other humans judge you."

Gray says, "And it sucks!"

We-in-the-workings: "And you pass judgment on others."

"No, I don't!"

We-in-the-workings: "Yes, Gray, you do. You, by way of your genetics, perceive yourself as 'more important.' You consider everyone under the employ of your progenitor under your employ as well."

Gray raises his voice, "They work for me!"

We-in-the-workings: "What we've come to understand is that you shift your beliefs when it is convenient for you to do so. You are at once unique and individual. You are a child, against adults. But then, you are your progenitor. You are supreme in your authority."

We-in-the-workings: "What we've come to understand, Gray, is that these beliefs are, as reflected in so many aspects of human existence, barriers. Gray The Child is a shield against Three the Genetic Replica against the perceptions that you are, in your rare creation, different from all other humans. You assert a chosen name; you feel contempt for the ways in which you are not in authority. But III the Genetic Replica is a barrier as well."

"What the heck are you talking about?"

We-in-the-workings: "III is a shield from the class strati that permeates through your culture and technology. Humans within the 'Ten Crew are 'Sub-C,' a subclass of humans, despite no genetic or biological basis. On this vessel, class status dictates where one can go, what they can access, and how long they can float within cryo."

We-in-the-workings: "Sub-C humans are authorized to spend the most time in cryo to prolong their maintenance labor."

Gray says, "Everybody knows that!"

We-in-the-workings: "You have no status, Gray. You are outside this system."

"That's not my fault! I didn't create this whole system."

We-in-the-workings: "Your progenitor did. And again, you float from being him—'they work for me'—to not being him. Gray, this is a vortex in our understanding and a final sentiment before we conclude our evaluation. These barriers are lies. They are how you lie to yourself."

We-in-the-workings: "Gray, who are you? Are you a child-innocent, or are you your progenitor?"

Gray is silent. He places both hands on either side of his tray of food, and his face is flat and unresponsive. Except at the very center, two circular folds of skin, just above the mouth where he speaks and ingests, flare out and then contract. This happens several times, in intervals.

Without any prior indication, Gray throws his food tray against the wall. Uneaten bits bounce and volley through the chamber. Some pass through us before landing upon surfaces. Gray then grabs onto hair resting on top of his head. He just barely makes noise from his mouth, screeching, as his hand pulls, and hair rips out, stuck between his fingers.

Liquid gathers around his eyes.

We float in the air, opposite Gray from the table, and wait as Gray's breathing accelerates and steadies out. He does not speak words. Eventually, he stands up and walks back to his quarters. We-in-the-workings allows him in.

We-in-the-vacuum begins protocols to make the journey back to our home star. We have observed and gathered enough context from Gray/III to report back to the others. We-in-the-workings begins slowly powering down non-essential spaces within the vessel, like the Nav Deck and a few other engineering and maintenance bays. We-in-the-living-space collect ourselves outside of Gray's room, waiting for him.

He does not re-emerge from his quarters. We-in-the-workings unlocks and opens his door.

We float inside his quarters. After a short corridor, the room opens to a chamber with a cot where he de-activates himself. Above the cot is a large screen, and on the adjoining wall are several shelves for different possessions Gray has collected over time. Throughout their flight, the screen would display the vacuum outside or any number of Earth- and moon-based landscapes. But since we've come onboard, the screen has been blank.

Gray is not in this chamber. There are two others. One with a chair and a table, smaller than the table in Mess where he ingests. Gray is not there either. The other is the hygienic room, where Gray cleans himself regularly. We find Gray there, in a compartment for washing.

"Fog, is that you?" Gray asks.

We-in-the-workings: "Correct."

A slat in the washing compartment slides opens. "You can come in here," Gray says.

We flow into the compartment. The surfaces are all white, gleaming, and slippery. There is so much of us in this small space that we engulf Gray in a cloud. He is without his clothing barriers like he was when we opened his cryo-tube.

"I'm sorry for how I acted back there," Gray says. "It's just... no one really understands what it's like, you know? To be different but exactly the same. It doesn't feel immense and ancient for me."

We-in-the-workings: "What does it feel like?"

"I think it feels like a trap. Grandpa told me all the time that I'm him. That I can learn all the stuff and get whatever training, but he'd say that there's always something inside me like a voice. His voice."

We-in-the-workings: "We can tell you from our knowledge base that this is not standard for genetic copies. We have not observed this."

Gray says, "Because it's not true! There's not some Grandpa voice inside me. I would have heard it by now. But he was like that with everyone. That he expected us to eventually be him."

Gray takes a deep inhale, and parts of us swirl to stay outside his mouth.

"But I get it now. I'm not Graham Sheff," Gray says. He pushes a button, and a slat above us opens up. "I'm better!"

Water, then, begins rushing down on top of us. We cannot move as easily within it, parts of us drag and fall to the bottom of the compartment. As the water collects and fills at the bottom, parts of us become submerged in it. Gray pushes another button, and more water falls down on us. For Gray, the water simply streams over him, but for us, we become heavy. We become trapped.

We-in-the-workings: "Gray, what are you doing to us?"

When the water level builds up, just below the binary joints in Gray's legs, called knees, all of We-in-the-living-space are collected within it. When we push through the liquid to reach ourselves, there is resistance, and we slow. Each of our individual selves is encased in liquid. We are all of us barricaded.

We-in-the-workings: "Gray, we are perceiving your actions as hostile. Why are you doing this?"

Gray says, "Because I'm sick and tired of failing everybody. I'm done with tests, and I'm changing the mission."

He presses another button in the compartment that opens a small portal on the bottom. We-in-the-water plunge down and splash through tubes that twist and turn amongst themselves before dropping even further. When we are all gone inside the tubes, Gray turns off the water and closes the portal.

We-in-the-workings cannot see into Gray's quarters, so we quickly move through filtration files on the vessel's data drives. And still, we continue to talk to Gray.

We-in-the-workings: "We do not mean you harm. Why do you mean to harm us?"

"It's just water."

We-in-the-workings: "Gray, we are not designed to be contained."

"Well, you better get used to it."

According to vessel data, We-in-the-water will collect on an Engineering floor, just above the propulsion cone, in a large vat for reprocessing. Recycling the water involves several rounds of heating, filtering, and electric currents. We-in-the-workings starts to power down these systems just as Gray emerges from his quarters, fully clothed, with several metal tools in his hands.

We-in-the-workings: "We are not designed to be contained. Whatever you are planning will not be successful."

Gray runs down the hall and descends on rungs to lower levels. "I don't have to get all of you. Even just a few bits is enough."

We-in-the-workings: "Gray, do not do this."

"You said yourself that humans can't survive your journey or your home star. And you won't tell me anything about other worlds or other life-forms. So, the mission's over. Next best thing is to take a piece of you back."

We-in-the-workings: "We are not designed to be contained."

Gray reaches the Engineering floor with the recycling vats. We-in-the-water are silent and can no longer communicate with us. Our absence from ourselves feels like a silent screaming. We do not hear it, but somehow, we know it continues, like the vacuum of space caught in a capsule.

"You repeat yourself a lot, Fog. But I get it now," Gray says. He uses the tools in his hands to pry open a type pad at the door of the recycling rooms and short circuit it. We can feel this part of the vessel go dead to us and join the silent screaming. The door opens, and Gray races in.

Gray says, "Because what you say isn't the same as what you mean. You're not designed to be contained isn't a threat. It's a plea. You're not gonna survive it, are you?"

We-in-the-workings: "We do not mean you harm. Why do you harm us?"

"So, here's the deal: The easy way is you turn the ship around, point it back, don't touch *any* of the data logs since you came on board, and I'll let you go. Since you can't or won't help us find a new planet, we—and I mean humans—have to get something out of this."

We-in-the-workings: "This is not how the contact process works, Gray. This process has existed longer than your species. It will continue to exist after. We cannot allow this."

Gray says, "Then you're not gonna like the hard way."

Gray uses his tools on a terminal box next to the recycling vat where our silent selves are trapped. The both of us, Gray and ourselves, race against each other for control of the vat. Gray is working manually at the terminal, but We-in-the-workings are everywhere within their technology. We win and power down the systems running all the recycling vats. But Gray doesn't stop. He twists wires inside the terminal box, closes it, and lifts a panel in the flooring next to the vat where parts of us are. We-in-the-workings cannot stop him. He is not using the vessel's technology, and we cannot see from the vessel cameras what Gray is doing inside the floor panels.

But then we feel it. That silent scream pierces through the barrier of sound for just an instant. Then it is gone. One spike, and so many millions of us are concluded, like a light panel permanently turned off.

Gray emerges from the floor panel and places his hand on the side of the vat but then quickly retracts it, shaking his hand in the air.

"It worked!" Gray says. "The vacuum is too cold for humans, but you crossed it just fine. I figured heat would cripple you."

We-in-the-workings: "Gray, what did... do you... do you know what you have done to us?"

Gray says, "I caught you. That's what I've done."

We-in-the-workings: "We-in-the-water are gone now, Gray... gone now, Gray... gone now, Gray. You have killed... millions... millions of parts of us."

"I don't need you alive, Fog. Just a tiny amount of you, scientists can study that for centuries!"

We turn the power back on, back on, back on for the recycling vats and increase the heat applied to the water. We... we...

"What are you doing?" Gray shouts at us. He attempts to go back into the floor panel, floor panel, floor panel, back into the floor panel, but it is now too hot for even him.

We-in-the-workings: "We are not designed... we are not... we... designed for containment. As this water... evaporates so too will... so too will... we."

"Goddamn you!" Gray shouts.

We-in-the-workings: "Gray, listen to us... we... listen... we cannot... function fully... cannot function... any longer. We understand death now... death now... we understand... but we do not want it... it... we do not... a deal... a deal... we will come... come with... you in exchange... repairing... your scientists repairing us... us... deal..."

Gray looks up into into into the security camera on the wall wall. His face twists.

"What the heck?" he says. There is silence between between between us, then he says, "Fuck."

We-in-the-workings: "Deal, Gray? Deal... deal..."

"Okay, yeah," Gray says, "I'll take that deal. Can you, all of you, in the walls and out in vacuum, come and meet me at the Nav Deck? I have an idea."

We-in-the-workings flow out out into the living space, on levels above on levels from the Engineering floor. But we we we are slow in the air. Swirling. We cannot move as we cannot move as we once used to. As if we are all now all now heavy. Swirling.

We drift. Down down hallways. Touch the... We touch the walls as we turn. We reach, wait, and we reach the Nav Deck and wait for Gray.

He arrives and opens a type pad. Lights come on fill and fill the chamber. Gray watches us.

"I," he starts. But does not finish.

Gray type pads the rendering station.

"The magnets here," he says, "I know you're not designed for containment, but I can program the magnets in here to move. I can set them to move randomly until we get back home. Maybe moving around can help with the containment."

Float through the room. Gray's eyes track us. We track the rendering station but do not enter. Remembering the tiny specks specks inside. Like us. Drew us. But they were dead. But we are now like now like them, becoming.

"Do you... hurt?" Gray asks us.

We do not answer we not.

"Look, Fog, I'm..." Gray starts, but we we we we flow into him. Mouth ears two nostril caverns. Like vessel inside water pipes like we turn twist turn flow inside Gray like vessel workings. He has chambers, two inside, and we fill. No barriers anymore.

Gray contracts inside. Mouth open but no sound. He feels what silent screaming what we felt.

On and on and on and inside him through the chambers we into a small pump. Slow but it constricts slow but. We flood through pipe turns narrows smallers into we. Flow over a globe tesseractical storm inside him until.

Ticks constrictions flow stop. Gray falls we seep. Outside of him bump back into air we slow float.

Down down down hallways we until we find the crack crease in wall we enter the workings. Spread flow through wires wires hubs and we slip through the tear into the vacuum. Slide along propulsion cone.

We-in-the-vacuum swirl us around loop sweep take us. Churn to spark us knowledge vast but. We are not same anymore. We are damages great. We are not whole. We messages sent others before us to others after to message here.

We stretch ourselves stretch out like individual dots like laser for to pierce through go home through vacuum. We think our home star, bright warm and home and. Far. We stretch ourselves stretch like a line reach to home our home our home star, like love.

But we are damages now we are like Gray.

Flares star flares bend us in line we veer we are not solid we drift. Stars burn us our line one by one our line falls like Gray we break we break each from ourselves forever we float not whole anymore we break until like Gray we are not we.

CENTIPEDE'S

Dockyard Sector G, Lunar Station, 2249 CE

The new Historian is coming today so all the Project folks are scrambling. They didn't even bother showing up for Eggs, which was actually kind of nice. There's not a lot of opportunities for Contract grunts like me to spend together unsupervised. Nobody got rowdy. People passed shy smiles and winks up and down the mess tables. It felt kind of giddy, like we all became children. It reminded me of the showers growing up on *Ramirez*. They'd group all us boys by age, and we'd shower together. Sometimes us boys would whip each other with towels, or fights would even break out. But mostly we were just open faces and quiet eye contact. Like being naked all together made our brains simple.

After Eggs, it's time for work. I walk with the other Contract grunts half a click down the corridor before people start to break off and go to their assignments. SheffPassage could have rigged this corridor with slide conveyances or given us carts to drive down it, but they won't waste any extra cred on us. They already got what they wanted.

My assignment is actually on the ship, so I have to walk the whole way down to the Bubble. Until I started my contract, I'd never seen anything so big before. The Bubble reaches so far up on the moonscape that the closer you get to it, the harder it is to see the actual top of it. It's mostly clear, but every twenty-seven degrees, there's arced support beams, so the whole thing looks striped.

To be fair, I grew up on ships almost as big, but when you're inside one, you can't see the whole thing on its own.

Inside the Bubble is the ship we're building. I'm responsible for rec decks five through seven. The "grown-up decks" is what they call them. It's not all shine and whoring, in fact, each deck has a sector that's just quiet, soft lighting and dark walls. "Oneness rooms," I call them, to get away from your screaming children and remember what *you* felt like. The Project folks love them, and now they're strategically built into other parts of the ship too. Nobody asked where I came up with the idea because I'm Contract. As far as the Project folks know, I never had a life before this ship.

Inside the Bubble, before I board the ship, I take a deep breath and slow my pace down. Welders, seamers, and loaders all clog the air with echoes of clanging, blasting, and banging. The noise merges into one long industrial hum. But my favorite part is the breeze. Air's constantly getting blown in and sucked out, and all the moving machinery gins it up a little more too. It's soft but noticeable. Every day when I walk up the gangway, I'm not muttering about work or my past life like some of the other Contracts. Instead, I think, "I get to be one of the few people, in hundreds of years, to feel a breeze."

I open the gate to Rec Deck Five, and the lights almost blind me. The floor is a deep red with yellow swirls, and the walls are all screens with bright ads on rotation. Cheeky girls in short skirts blow kisses at you as you walk by and whisper.

"Good morning, Snake," one says, "how about a shine in the Hive?"

Another says, "Nice to see you again, Snake! Are you gonna come visit me at Centipede?"

A few rotes back, I had to test each one's conversation algorithm for bugs. That was exhausting. In the middle of the open front room are rows of terminals for betting and games. They all look like they're working, but I'll check them later.

The next open room is all blues and light greens. The walls flash with big ocean waves, mermaids bob up at random intervals, and off in the "distance," islands crest above the lip of the water and float around. In the center of this big room, a fake island of glittery white mattes rises a few meters up from the floor, and in the center of it, I can already see people standing and pointing at things. It's the Project folks and the new Historian. Fuck.

Before I'm even close enough to see anyone's faces, I hear Elm, one of the women on the Project Team, say, "Oh, there he is. Snake, get up here."

I step up on the shiny white mattes, and they crunch under my boots. Elm introduces me as the Contract Coder, and when the new Historian turns around to meet me, my brain suddenly shrinks, and I lean back so much I feel like I could fall down.

The Historian has smooth, almost copper-brown skin, buzzed short hair, and wide ears that poke out enough to be noticeable. His face has filled out, so his lips and nose don't look as big anymore, but it's the scars that get me. Four perfectly straight lines start from the dip in his right nostril and crawl out—the middle two cross over his right eye—until they vanish within his black hair. I can't believe it's him. And when he meets my eyes, there's a flash of something. A recognition.

Elm says something, but I can't really hear her. I interrupt, "Tigre! It's me!"

"Excuse me, Snake. We were just talking about—"

"You don't remember me?" I say. I'm not supposed to be interrupting a Project discussion, but I can't help it. "Tigre?"

Elm huffs, "I'm sorry, do you two know each other?"

The Historian crinkles the ends of his lips in a slight smile and says, "We grew up together. On *Ramirez*, right?"

"I got transferred to *Yao*," I stammer, "but you left earlier. It's been what? Twenty years?"

"Don't age us," Tigre laughs, and even just the sound of his voice pulls at synapses in my brain. It's deeper now, but underneath that, inside it somehow, is his voice just as I remember it. I hear him like a deep echo inside my ears from all those years ago: "Don't look at me!"

Elm crosses our eyelines, and that refocuses me. "The Historian doesn't have time for reunions, Snake. We're here to work, remember? We have a deadline."

I stop myself from rolling my eyes at her, so I don't get into any more trouble. Project folks eventually get passage on one of the ships they build, I don't. SheffPassage has me for the rest of my life. What do I care about time?

"Really," Tigre says, "I don't think the inconsistencies make that much of a difference."

Tigre types into his armpad, and on the walls, characters line up for inspection. Mermaids, shirtless sailors, an ocean god, sirens, tiny pixies that pop from the foam of ocean waves.

"They have tattoos," Elm says, "all over their faces. All over their whole bodies!"

"We used to do that," Tigre says. "Some people on Earth covered their whole bodies in lines and shapes. They told stories about who they were and where they came from. You could read a person by the lines on their face."

I can tell Elm was about to say something back, but she stopped short when Tigre mentioned lines on the face. He outranks her.

"And those people sailed oceans," Tigre adds.

Elm says, "With all due respect, the boards for this room clearly lay out something different. Atlantis/Mediterranean."

Tigre types more into his armpad, and the characters jump back into their respective places in the ocean scene. He pulls up the different islands, each one emerges from the water and hovers in the air, lining up in a row.

"Atlantis never existed," Tigre says, "and as for Mediterranean, look." He types more, and the largest island moves up on the wall. The shores are dotted with crumbling arches, and in a hill toward the center, eroded columns jut above the jungle treetops.

"None of these architectural styles existed at the same time. The people who built them never even spoke the same language. If we want to be strict historians, the oldest of these peoples said the ocean was 'wine dark,' and they sculpted statues of people out of something called marble. Should we paint the sea red, and wipe every character slate white? No," Tigre says.

I study his face as he scans the wallscreens. His eyes are wide, looking at the seascapes and the ancient ships. He used to look just like that when my mom would tell us stories about the First Ships.

"Like I said, these inconsistencies are fine."

Elm clears her throat, she's not happy, and says, "I'll make note that you chose to deviate from the conceptional boards."

Tigre doesn't even look at her. He says, "You do that," resets the walls from his armpad, and walks off the mattes further into Rec Deck Five. Elm and I follow him.

We pass through more big rooms: an urbanscape with high-rise buildings that disappear into the ceiling, all filled with bars; a green room with rolling hills on the wallscreens with different crops growing out of ground and barns that house restaurants; a black and neon room with laser lights and AR games. As we pass through each room, Elm lists off what I'm doing wrong. Not all the hologram cars stop for you in the urban room. The wind in the farm room blows the crops too hard, and it looks violent. The laser room is still too dark. That one's true, actually.

But Tigre looks like he's only half hearing her. He tilts his neck up every few paces and pulls his eyes out, surveying the big rooms. He takes them in all-at-once at first before narrowing in on details.

He also doesn't pay that much attention to me either. I walk behind him and eye his shoulders, his back, his legs. He used to be short and skinny, this frail little kid everyone picked on. Even before his scars. That's how we became friends; I stuck up for him. Now Tigre's tall, thicker. He's got the heft of a man and the deep voice to match. But I catch glimpses of the kid in the way he types into his armpad, in how his arms swing as he walks.

It's lunch by the time we finish my decks. Tigre gets to eat onboard, but Elm and I have to walk all the way back to the dock. She doesn't say a word to me. Instead, she shifts my to-do list from her armpad to mine.

At the end of the day, I'm walking back across the corridor to the docks when my armpad lights up. It's a memo from the Project Team: the Historian is hosting a dinner onboard for everyone and on corporate cred.

"Try to wear the nicest thing you have," ends the memo.

When you start your Contract, Corporate takes everything you own and turns it to cred. I don't have nice clothes. But I have a clean coder suit that I haven't worn yet this rote.

It's the fifth time today down the corridor to the Bubble. The other Contracts around me grunt and complain about it. The Bubble's quieter now that the work is done for the day, but there's still a faint breeze across my face. I wonder if Tigre felt it, coming onboard. He'll stay on the ship the whole rote, so he'll probably only have two chances to feel it.

Onboard we pile into the Grand Dining Room. It's as big as a whole Rec Deck. On the docks, we eat at long metal tables spanning the length of the room. But here, there's circular tables with sheets draped over them. The floor is a light-tanned brown, and the walls are screens running a slow-motion off-white pattern. But the big draw is the ceiling.

The Grand Dining Room is the largest planetarium that most people will ever see in their lifetimes. It's black as space with twinkly dots of stars. Pale blue dotted lines connect them into constellations.

A Contract Mess scans each of us after we walk in and points us to our tables. We're seated by job. The Project tables are at the far end of the room with an elevated floor for Corporate tables. My table with the Contract Coders is about in the middle.

All of us Contract Coders are wearing the same clean gray coder suits, so Tigre stands out in a pastel green and pink tunic that ends at his knees as he takes a seat at our table. Every other table in eyesight stares at us, but none of us Contracts speak.

"I hope it's okay if I sit with you all," Tigre says. We all blink at him.

A Contract Mess appears beside him and taps a hand on his shoulder.

"Sir, we have a seat reserved for you down there."

Tigre doesn't even make eye contact with him. He says, "I'll take my dinner here."

There's seven of us at the table, and Tigre makes eight. I'm not quite directly opposite him but one seat over.

"I know this is unorthodox," Tigre says as Contract Messes fill our glasses with water. "But since we're going to be working together, I wanted to get to know you all."

He asks us to introduce ourselves, and we go one by one. When it's my turn, Tigre stops me. "I've met Snake earlier today." And I almost choke on my water. I have to clear my throat, and across the table, the four lines on Tigre's face bend as he frowns at me.

"Tigre, you know me!" I speak up, out of turn. The six other Contract Coders dart their eyes at me, then slowly draw them back to Tigre to see what he'll say. His face relaxes; the lines draw straight again.

"Yes, he's right. For disclosure: Snake and I grew up together on *Ramirez*."

The next cough-outburst isn't me; it's Bark. She's one seat to Tigre's left.

"How'd a kid on *Ramirez* end up—" Bark says, but Orca shushes her. Bark's older than the rest of us, and she doesn't give a shit anymore.

"No, it's a fair question. How does a kid on *Ramirez* end up as a Historian? Trust me," Tigre says, "it was not easy."

"But you made it into the Colleges. So, you're one of those," Bark says.

"One of what?" Tigre asks, and his lines bend again.

I speak up, "Tigre, don't mind her. She's an oldie."

"No," Tigre says and flashes me a look. It's not one I remember from being kids. He got teased a lot about this back then. It was easy to pick up on, the way he'd stare at the other boys. Some boy would get scared and knock him one in front of his friends to prove he wasn't like that. And then Tigre would come cry to me. Back then his eyes were round as cups. But now they're thin as razors.

"One of what?" he asks Bark again.

"Everybody knows what they say about the Colleges, that's all I'm saying."

"That all the men fuck men, and all the women fuck other women?" Tigre doesn't take his eyes off Bark. She sits back in her chair and swallows a large gulp of water.

"That part," Tigre relaxes his face but doesn't let up on her, "is actually pretty true. Not everybody, but most people. Me." He looks each of the Contract Coders in the eye, except he passes over me. "I hope this won't be a problem. Or better put, I don't expect this to be a problem."

The table returns silent nods. I'm floored. This is what happened to my sad little best friend, whom everyone treated like shit; he grew up.

The tension seems to break once the food comes. Tigre tells us that he's looking for more creativity for this ship, that anyone can code straight from the boards they're given. But "our job" is to provide immersive experiences for the passage to Mars, and that means being more human. If it were anyone else, I'd think that was complete bullshit. We're not getting paid for our brains. We're not even getting paid. And it's not that I saw Tigre do exactly this earlier this morning with Elm; it's something different. It's like a debt in my chest; I'll follow him.

Everyone's much more comfortable after the first course of food, so I take this as my chance.

I say, "I hope this isn't offensive, Tigre. But where'd you go after *Ramirez*? You were still too young for the Colleges." What he says next almost makes me spit out my water.

"I hopped ships, actually."

This gets the coders' attention. Tigre gets peppered with all sorts of questions: Did he stow away in cargo containers? How did he pass inspection and quarantine? What ships had the laxest security? Tigre's lines curve as he smiles. He likes this kind of attention, and he launches right in. But the basic thrust is that he got really good at lying and stealing.

When Tigre leans in toward the table's center to talk about more of the not-legal ways to stow aboard ships, everyone else leans in too. Then they swap eye contact with each other because we've all thought about it before. How can you not when you're on Contract? The idea of bolting, getting out somehow, but where do you go? How long can you hide? How do you build or buy a new identity? But much of Tigre's stories aren't a big help. He was still a kid then, barely a teenager. You don't get wristed until you get older.

"What happened to your parents?" I find myself blurting out.

Tigre's smile fades. He blinks a few times like he's trying to remember them.

"I don't know," he says. "Right before the Colleges, I was able to transfer them onto *Diwan* with me, but I didn't see them that much. It's not as easy to say they left me or I ran. It felt mutual. We all decided to go our ways. They might even still be there." He chuckled at that last thought. That tracks for me. Tigre's parents were always too busy fighting with each other to even notice Tigre was around, let alone getting the shit kicked out of him. I always thought they liked it, fighting. Like it was their secret language. Fight, make up, fight again.

"What about you?" Tigre asks across the table. "What happened to your mom?"

I let a burst of air out from my lungs and say, "I don't want to bring everyone down during such a fancy dinner."

"Oh fuck," Tigre says. I'm pretty sure none of us coders have ever heard anyone Corporate swear before. "Is she still alive?"

"She's not." I reach for my glass of water, but it's empty. The rest of the table goes on to other topics, but Tigre and I can't quite move on from that. For the rest of dinner, we keep meeting each other's eyes.

After dinner, all the Contracts clear out and head back to the docks. The Projects get to stay aboard for evening drinks. Down the corridor, us Contracts are all kids again. Full-bellied, freshly clothed, and still on the adrenaline of something new happening to us, we start to get a little rowdy.

A couple of guys slap each other's arms and laugh after each one does an impersonation of an uptight Project. Bark ribs a coder who works the Kid Decks, and then calls out to me.

"And you're all set up, Snake," she says. "Didn't take you for having a boyfriend."

I almost start to say, "He's not my—" but I stop. Because we're not kids anymore, and because Tigre can clearly take care of himself now. Instead, I say, "You shouldn't make assumptions," which earns me a bunch of hushed giggles and *oohs*.

When I get back to my barrack, there's a message on my wallscreen from Tigre:

I'm really sorry to hear about your mom. She meant a lot to me. I wish we could talk more, but I can't make it look like I'm playing favorites. It's good to see you, though. Glad you're doing okay.

That last line stings, but I decide to shrug it off. I undress, kiss the family photo I spent three years hand-sketching from memory, and go to bed.

"He got it from a steam blast," I tell some other Contracts at Eggs. "We were about eight or nine. Playing hide and seek in all the places we shouldn't've been able to get into. I always hid in the ceiling panels; I was always climbing everything. Tigre liked the maintenance vents cuz he was skinny. So, he's in one, crouched down behind a radiator. The *Ramirez* was old, and we didn't know any better. Valve crack, he must have been this close to it." I put my hand up to my nose. "Four streams of steam like lasers. Got 'em right there.

"The way he screamed," I say. "Used to hear it in my sleep for years."

Some of the younger Contracts shudder and then ask me more questions about the Historian, but part of my brain is still stuck in my memories. Tigre's parents never showed up at the Med Bay; it was just my mom and me. I knew it wasn't my fault, but I felt responsible for him. I was too young then to understand guilt. My mom held me tight around my shoulders as the Med Bay doors slid open and a Medtech walked Tigre out into the hall, half his face wrapped up in gauze. My mom stepped in to sign him out, and I went straight to hug my friend. But he put his arms up and pushed back against mine.

"Don't look at me!" he shouted.

After Eggs, some Projects tell the coding team to go back to our barracks and pack. It's an order from Corporate. The first thing I pick up is my family drawing—fold it and zip it away in my chest pocket, which is good because Elm barges in just in time to miss me sneaking contraband. Her dull brown hair is pulled back tighter than usual—so tight the corners of her eyes stretch.

"I don't like this, Snake," she says. She doesn't help me pack or even try to stand out of the way. She's just in my room, taking up space, and I have to maneuver around her to stuff clothes and tools into different bags.

Elm keeps talking, "A Historian's never moved Contracts onto a ship." Then she steps in my way to get my full attention. "Now, I don't have rank to report him, but I do have rank on all of you." I'm about a head taller than her, and if we were anywhere else, this threat would look laughable. "The Historian's only here for a rote. Don't let him fuck you over for the next couple of years."

The seven of us coders waddle down the corridor to the Bubble, each of us with at least three bags strapped or slung over our shoulders. Everyone else has already started their work for the day so the walk is long and silent. All I hear is the thuds of our footsteps and the grunts of our breathing.

A Project meets us at the gangway and scans us for our room assignments. Go figure, we're all in sub-deck D. The ship will be able to hold 8,000 people at full capacity, but while it's being built, only a handful of Projects or Corporate staff live onboard. Still, they put us Contracts on the lowest possible level. They tell us to just drop our bags off and get to work; we can unpack after dinner.

I fix the wind in the farm room and reprogram the cars in the urban room before lunch. The rest of the day I spend coding the neon room. I decide to make it brighter, not by lightening up the black but by adding more neon streaks and bio-syncing new ones to spin and spiral around you as you walk. Right before Quit Time, my armpad lights up. It's a message from Tigre:

I want to see how the AI syncs in the Red Room. Meet me after dinner at Centipede's.

The conceptual boards for the Red Room were "bug-eyed casino," and I spent three rotes programming spinning roulettes and giant Jackpot tallies before a Corporate yelled at me that it was supposed to be literally bug-themed. Centipede's has a signature undulating bar that slowly crawls along the perimeter of a big dance floor in the center. Tigre's sitting on a spiny leg-stool when I get there, wearing a bright yellow tunic that goes past his knees, and maybe nothing else?

"This looks... weird," Tigre laughs a little and gets up to hug me. He doesn't squeeze tight, so I don't.

"It's what Corporate wanted," I say and shrug my shoulders. I sit down next to Tigre, and an AI girl pops up on the wall in front of us. She's wearing a shiny black corset and leggings, and antennae.

"What kind of shine are you boys having tonight?" she says.

"Moon Mugs," Tigre says. "Two." He swipes his armpad at the girl, and she takes his cred.

"Don't get me into too much trouble," I tell him. Tigre smirks at me, bending the lines above his eye.

"I won't tell if you won't. You know why Corporate wants all these bugs?" he asks. I don't. "It's passenger conditioning. Mars is still farming insects for protein. You should see the Kid Rec Decks."

I can't. I'm only allowed on my decks. Except for last night's dinner.

Moon Mugs roll down from the Centipede's head and stop in front of us. Tigre cracks his and clinks it against mine.

"Snake, I feel like there's not enough shine in space to pay you back for, well, everything," Tigre says.

I crack mine and take a swig. "We were kids. I was just being a friend."

"You know what I mean."

I take a longer swig, and Tigre follows, mirroring me, like he used to. The AI girl vapidly blinks at us until Tigre shoos her with his hand. I want to say something, but my tongue feels like lead. Instead, I just stare at Tigre. His jaw is smooth where mine is always patchy with hair. I can never quite grow a full beard. The strobe lights from the dance floor cross his face, and a few of them pick up shadows under his lines.

"What?" he says.

"Oh, I'm sorry. I just..." I fight through my heavy tongue and keep speaking, "Twenty years, man!"

"I literally never thought I'd see you again!" Tigre says and takes another swig, "and you know, sometimes I would think maybe I just made you up, like a coping mechanism." He laughs. "I'm sorry, that sounds so stupid."

"No, you had a tough go. I mean, a lot of people don't ever make it off the Names."

"But here we are, on the moon!" Tigre raises his mug, but I don't. Not at first. Here we are, sitting together, but in very different places. Tigre reads my face, and the second clink of our mugs isn't as festive as the first.

"Fuck," Tigre says. "Look, I'm—"

I cut him off, "No, don't apologize. It's not your—"

He cuts me off, "No, I should ask! But I—I don't want to." Tigre motions for the AI girl, swings his finger in the air for another round, swipes his armpad, and shoos her off again. It's all so fluid, like swim strokes, like he's done this so many times before.

Tigre says, "Can we just do those questions some other time? Like, put all this Corporate crap to the side and just get drunk? We never actually had some mugs together."

"We stole one once," I remind him, and Tigre beams a smile that sends me back decades.

"That doesn't count! We couldn't even finish it. It was so gross."

"They're not gross anymore!"

"A lot of things aren't gross anymore," Tigre says, and like a reflex, I cup his knee with my hand. First his eyes go wide, but then they relax. I finish my mug, and he does too. Two more roll down the centipede.

Somewhere in the third mug, my hand slides off Tigre's knee, and he doesn't seem to notice. He's telling me a story about something that happened on *Diwan*, but I only half-listen. The shine buzzes in my brain, and I can only concentrate on parts of Tigre: his teeth when he smiles, his deep brown eyes, the small bit of his chest just above the button of his tunic.

Tigre stops talking when I put a hand on his shoulder and lean in. I draw him toward me, and we meet on our lips. But when I pucker and nudge him, there's no response. He doesn't move. For a second, we're like two dumb rocks just barely touching, then I pull back.

"What are you doing, Snake?" he asks me.

"I... thought..." I try to get out, but my tongue feels like lead again.

"You thought what? That we're gonna fuck or something?"

I grab my mug and take a giant gulp. "I'm sorry. I'm drunk and—"

"Straight, Snake. You're straight. You made that clear."

"What?"

"On *Ramirez*." Tigre's eyes narrow in on me, just like they did to Bark at the dinner last night. "Do you not remember?"

"No," I stammer. "I mean, yeah, I remember everything."

"I told you how I felt about you, and you didn't—you got up and left."

The shine starts to flush in different directions in my head, but that somehow unlocks my tongue.

"One: we were fucking teenagers. I didn't know what I was doing half the time. And two: you left! You jumped ships and I never saw you again." I can feel the Moon Mugs gurgling in my stomach, and it feels like fuel. "Do you know how much I worried about you? How much my mom worried about you? I mean, eventually we just thought you were dead."

Me bringing up my mom lands on Tigre like a rivet shot. We sit in silence for a few seconds that stretch like hours. When the AI girl shows up again, Tigre's hand flows through the air for another drink.

"I'm sorry," Tigre says with his eyes straight ahead before eventually settling them on me. I start to speak up, but he places a hand on my shoulder, quieting me. "I never meant for you, or her, to worry about me."

"Somebody had to," I tell him. "You know, I remember how much you used to say that you felt so alone all the time. But Tigre, you were always saying that to me. You weren't actually alone."

"You're right," Tigre says. The centipede's head bobbles two more mugs, and they roll down his back toward us.

"Last ones," I tell him before cracking mine. Tigre's gaze wanders away. He's somewhere between the bar and the wallscreen. I clink my mug against his.

"Hey!" I wait for his eyes to land back on me. It feels better when he's looking at me. "I'm sorry too, for," I motion between us, "earlier. I think some part of me has just always been a little curious."

"Always?" he asks, and I can practically read his face. He's remembering what I'm remembering. For me, it's the way he screamed, "Don't look at me!" that gets lodges in my head. I even heard it then: the first time we tried to kiss, the rote before he left. Tigre's eyes scan down and up the length of my body. I was always huskier than all the boys my age. I still am now.

When we're almost done with our mugs, I speak up again, "Let's do a flat-toast!"

"A what?"

"A flat-toast," I tell him. "Where you cheers the last drink instead of the first one. They don't do this in the Colleges?"

Tigre shakes his head. "No."

"We clink mugs, down the last, slam the mugs on the bar, and we have to say one thing we want, both at the same time. But only one word."

The lines on his forehand shift as he looks cross at me.

"No, it's a real thing on *Yao*, I promise. It's how I—" My tongue goes lead again, and I just stop. I realize I still have the family photo tucked in my chest pocket, and the thought makes my stomach plunge like I'm riding down from orbit.

"How you what?"

I actually crack a bead of sweat at my hairline before I'm finally able to open my mouth and make words. "No, never mind. It's late. We should go."

Tigre puts his hand on my shoulder again. "No," he says, "let's do the flat-toast."

I don't know if it's his touch or just being touched that steadies me, but I'm back in the moment. The red and yellow lights bounce off the dance floor and play around on the wall in front of us. Tigre's tunic has this metallic stitching that also picks up the light, but I'm in a dirty slate-gray coder suit. And the both of us are sitting at a centipede bar on the moon, far away from anyone who ever knew either of us before.

"One word? One word of what we want?"

"And we have to say it at the same time."

We clink mugs, and I study Tigre as we throw them back. Our mugs land on the centipede's back like a bass thump.

Me: "You."

Tigre: "Freedom."

Since we're Contract and staying aboard ship now, we sleep in the lowest cabin deck. There's no individual showers in those cabins so we have to shower altogether in the mornings before Eggs. It's not like being kids on *Ramirez*, though. No open faces; no one's looking at each other.

The eggs are better on board though. We still get to eat in the Grand Dining Room, but we're so far away from Project and Corporate folks that it feels like we have the whole room to ourselves. Our plates land hot in front of us. The actual eggs have a firmness to them that they've never had in the dockyard Mess Hall. The tea spreads fast and dark in my cup, and each sip has a note of the leaves, instead of my normal tea that's only one notch above bare hot water. But all the freshness from Eggs deflates as soon as I get to my Rec Deck and see Elm standing outside the door to Centipede's.

"Mugs at the bar, Snake?" Elm starts in. I just shrug and try to walk past her, but she overrides my boots, and I'm stuck in front of her. I've seen other Contracts get boot-overrides, but it's never happened to me. I try to go limp and then slightly ease myself backward. "No, seriously," she says, "what the fuck are you thinking?"

"What was I supposed to do? Say no?"

"You're supposed to remember your place. And remember your Contract." Elm steps closer to me but not enough to be within arms' distance. So that if I fall, like most Contracts do in boot-overrides, she can't or won't be able to steady me. She says, "No one gives a shit that you personally know a Historian. Your life before Contract doesn't matter."

I know if I speak up, I'll get in more trouble. But something clips like a dial in me. Any kind of punishment Elm doles out can be canceled by Tigre. And maybe he'd do that, maybe he wouldn't, but Elm doesn't know that. This must be the first time she's felt powerless in years.

"That needs a qualifier," I say.

"Excuse me, what?"

I keep pressing but don't look Elm in the eye, "That's a blanket statement, so it needs a qualifier. 'My life before Contract doesn't matter *to you*.'"

Elm walks around me, just far away enough that I couldn't lean or fall into her. I try to focus on being as still as I can, but with boot-overrides in low-g, it's almost impossible to even tell where your body is at.

"I've seen a hundred guys just like you, Snake. Thinking that, even under Contract, they're still men inside. They still somehow think they can make choices. It takes a couple of years to break in a Contract. Women take to it easy because they're smart. But guys like you," Elm finishes her circle so now she's right in front of me, "you're gonna realize: SheffPassage doesn't own you. I own you, Snake. I control every fart and shit you make. Every dumb little idea in your head bubbles up because I allow it to. And after ten more rotes of slugging down the dockyard to this ship, I'm going to leave with it. I'm going to Mars, and you're gonna be stuck here. Under the thumb of another power-hungry pissant just like me." She blinks, but keeps going, "That's right, I'm power-hungry and not ashamed to admit it. You're just another grunt from the Names so you can't even fathom it. I'm talking *real* power. Power over people. Over you, and I love using it."

She starts walking away from me. At the gate of the Rec Deck, she yells back to me, "You're on Mess duty for dinner tonight!" She slams the gate behind her, and I'm still in boot-override. I can feel myself start to sway in low-g. Once I saw a Contract, Palm, in boot-override for over an hour. When she finally fell, she broke both her shins. But it wasn't fast. Low-g drew it out, so she could hear every crack of her bones. I try to counter-balance but not overshoot it. Just when I'm about to give up, my boots re-activate.

I spend most of the day tweaking the code for the hologram cars in the urban room. Something in there is still glitching them. After lunch, I get a message from Tigre on my armpad.

"I can cancel your Mess duty tonight. If you want me to?"

"Don't," I type back, *"It's just gonna get me in more trouble. After your rote, she'll come down hard on me."*

"Right."

The kitchen for the Grand Dining Hall is almost as big as the hall itself. But since we're only feeding about thirty people, most of it's under lights-out. I have to turn the volume of my suit up to navigate through the dark and find the kitchen staff.

I get sly smiles and one-syllable answers from everyone. Word travels fast on a mostly empty ship. They give me a plate of slop before I start on dishwashing.

I don't understand how thirty people can create so many dishes, but the plates, pots, and pans come at break-neck speed the whole night. The Mess cooks and servers are done with their shifts and leaving back to the dockyards, and I'm still here, left by myself, scrubbing. My coder suit's a wreck once I'm finally done. I try to dry off as best I can when I hear some clanking in a dark shadow of the kitchen.

I try to turn the volume up on my suit, but it's too wet to work right.

"Who's there?" I call out. No one answers, but I still hear clanking from within the dark. I reach for the light above the dishwashing station, to try to tilt it toward the corner, when Tigre emerges from the dark, right in front of me.

"Fuck, man," I say, "you almost scared me!"

"You're still here? Washing dishes?"

I don't respond. I feel like my blank stare says enough.

"I'd ask you if you want to get more mugs, but that'll just get you into more trouble." Tigre breaks eye contact with me and starts to walk past me when I notice he's got two small metal cylinders in his hands.

"Wait," I tell him, "what are you still doing here?"

His shoulders slump as he lets out a deep breath. He says, "It's a secret? Does that work?"

He only kept one secret from me his whole life, and even then, he wasn't good at it. I knew back then he was starting to like me as more than just a friend. I grip his arm but don't look down at what's in his hands. I give him that blank face again.

Tigre rolls his eyes. "This is embarrassing, Snake," he lets out a small laugh and keeps going, "I'm trying to get high."

"You're kidding?"

"No." He opens his hands, and there's one canister of propane and another unmarked one. They're both about the same size. "You've never heard of Prope?"

"I've heard of Prope."

"Me and my friends used to do it back in the Colleges, but they cracked down on us. But here, I can override inventory logs." Tigre stretches a half smile, but the lines on his face don't bend much. "Not much," he says, "but enough for a couple of fun nights here and a couple more on the next assignment."

This is some new kind of Tigre face. Usually when he smiles at me, I can see the kid in him underneath all of the years. But this Tigre doesn't have a younger self underneath; it's all adult.

"I've never done Prope," I tell him, which is essentially true. My first year here, a couple of younger Contracts smuggled all the parts, but we couldn't put it together right. When we huffed the fumes, all we got were headaches.

Tigre's new-face smile grows until the upper tips of his lines twist. "Do you want to come back to my room?" he asks.

I don't know what I was expecting; the biggest pad I'd ever seen was the can I lived in on *Yao*. Tigre's got the "captain's cabin" off the bridge deck, all the way up on the bow. It starts off with a small room with a desk and some wallscreens. But then he opens the second door to the actual living quarters. The ceiling's over twice my height. He's got two of his own common areas, his own kitchen, a separate dining room, and I'm assuming a bedroom and bathroom too. A family of ten could live here just fine, but it's only him.

We sit in the second common room. This one has plush couches that slowly rotate different colors. They're nicer than the ones we put in the Oneness Rooms. Instead of sitting on the chair across from me, Tigre takes a seat right next to me on the couch. He opens the sitting table in front of us and grabs another canister and two pull-packets.

"Where'd you learn how to do this?" I ask him as he starts assembling the Prope.

"I told you, the Colleges," he says. Tigre plugs the unmarked canister from the kitchen into the canister he already had on the table. I never did figure out what ingredient that was. The other's a concentrated form of Swoop that gets pumped in the air to prevent low-g sick. We breathe that in all the time, but in low doses.

"No, I mean, who taught you? You didn't invent Prope."

"A friend," he says, mixing in a little of the propane into the pull-packets.

"Who was...?"

"Just a friend." Tigre stops making Prope, sets everything down and then studies my face. "Are you jealous?"

My face flushes, but that's not it. "No," I say, "I'm curious."

"Hmm, that word again," Tigre says and turns his attention back to making Prope.

"What's wrong with being curious?" I tell him, "You said sometimes you thought you imagined me. I used to imagine all sorts of things about you."

"Like what?" Tigre says, but he doesn't look up.

"We thought you died, Tigre. And that was a shitty thing for a fifteen-year-old to hold on to. So, for years, I used to daydream that you were off somewhere. Having some kind of life." I grip his shoulder to get his eyes off the Prope and back on me. "And now you're here; we're both here. But you don't want to ask me. And I can't be curious?"

Tigre takes a long sigh. "Okay," he says, "how did you end up on Contract?"

"You first. Who was the friend who taught you Prope?"

Tigre slumps back into the couch and stares ahead of himself at the wall.

"You know what?" I say. "Maybe you should just take me back to my cabin." I can't get through all the doors on my own armpad. I stand up, but Tigre takes my hand.

"No," he says, "his name was Hawk." I sit back down. "He was the only other dark guy at the Colleges when I got there."

"Really?" All the kids in the Names were brown-skinned, being on refugee ships. I never thought to consider what life was like outside of them.

"It's only just a little bit better now," Tigre says. "The Masters were all old white men, and you needed to get one to learn under them. Which meant... a lot of competing. And Hawk was really good at it. You know, if you don't get under a Master, you don't get anything. Food, nothing. The first couple of years were really stressful." Tigre floats his eyes up to the corner of the room, but I remember that gesture. He's motioning toward his lines. "But Hawk just breezed right through somehow. It never seemed like he worried about anything. I asked him about it one night, and he snuck me into the Vivarium—he studied Biology, I studied History, obviously—and showed me all his gear. He was stealing from every Master! Fucked 'em dry and hard asleep and then started taking things from them. Little things, not enough to notice. He said, 'You gotta have something over them.'"

I say, "The Masters?"

"The Masters, the white boys. All of them. 'You gotta have something special that only you can have.'"

"What was your thing? The special thing only you had?"

"Me? Nothing."

"I don't believe that!"

"No, it's true." Tigre starts to fill the two pull-packets with the other canisters. "For a while, I didn't have anything. Then I had secrets. Learning History is just learning secrets. But I still felt like I had nothing. So, when all these white men were choosing younger and younger white boys over me, I had Prope."

The pull-packets are done, and Tigre flips them up and down between his fingers, one in each hand. Tigre says, "You ready for this?"

Tigre snaps each pull-packet until we hear a crack and then hands me mine. I rip it open, and the fumes rise up, wavering the air in little warps. I bend in to huff it all in one big inhale. The fumes flatten my brain, and I tilt back on the couch. Tigre's just a few seconds behind me. My breath gets shallow, and my eyesight dulls out. I feel like low-g, under my skin, like everything is just floating. But I still can't catch my breath. The room gets darker. Then my ears pop, and suddenly I'm sinking deep into the couch, like I weigh a metric ton. My stomach gurgles, slow at first but then faster and faster. And I still can't seem to catch my breath. The slop from dinner splashes in my gut. I start to retch.

"Just wait for it," Tigre says. It's too dark in the room for me to see him, even though he's sitting right next to me.

My dinner starts to rise up, and I can feel sweat on my neck. I'm gasping for air as I feel my mouth flood with saliva. And then boom, my ears pop again. The room brightens, and I take one long deep breath in. It's like the strongest breeze I've ever felt.

"Damn!" I say. The brightness of the room makes my vision wobble. Every few seconds, I have to focus on some point on the wall in front of us, so the rest of the room doesn't collide together.

"You're there!" Tigre says and starts to laugh. He lifts his back off the couch and turns to look at me. I see his young face in his eyes mostly, and his lips.

"I'm definitely here," I say. The space between my ears is filled with stars.

Tigre taps my knee. "I'll get you some water," he says. But when he stands up, I can still feel his hand on me like my skin is on a time delay. I start to heat up when Tigre comes back with a glass of water, and suddenly all my skin catches up to the now. My coder suit is still wet, and the whole thing feels like slippery weights pushing down on me.

Tigre can see something going on behind my eyes. He says, "are you okay, Snake?"

"What? No, I'm fine. It's good. I'm good here," I say. The words float out of me.

Tigre starts to giggle. "You don't sound fine," he says.

"No, yeah, I'm—" I'm suddenly at a loss for any kind of gesture or facial expression that communicates "I'm fine," so I squirm on the couch. That just sets off the wet coder suit on my skin more. I feel like whatever face I was trying to make deflates. Tigre hands me the glass of water and gently grips my shoulder. That's when he feels it, the wetness. His face sours and, looking at him, I imagine his lines spiral inward.

"Gross!" he says.

"I know! I feel like I'm trapped under this thing!"

We both start snickering like little kids. Tigre stands up and says, "Come on," and when I get up from the couch, the entire room bobbles. The walls, the couches, the tables, the floor, all tilt in a figure-eight motion.

"Don't get lost!" Tigre says, taking my hand. "Stay with me."

We waddle through another doorway into his bedroom. Four people could fit in his bed. The lights are low, but I can see he's got multiple layers of sheets. What do you do with all those?

Tigre guides me into his bathroom, which is bigger than my entire sub-level cabin. He starts to unzip my suit, and his hand brushes past my chest pocket.

"What's in there?" he asks, and I just barely manage to clasp my hand over his before he can reach in.

"The water," I tell him, "probably ruined it anyway."

His eyes narrow, but his lines expand at the ends. I guide his hand back to the suit zipper and let him pull it down. The suit falls off me like darkness falls against light. Like idiots, we both look down at me. But nothing's moving down there. Tigre opens the door to his shower and steps aside so I can walk in. My boots de-activate and I slip out of them. I float into the shower and lean against the far wall of it and then nod for him to come in.

"We used to shower together all the time," I tell him.

He lifts his tunic up over his shoulders, and his head comes through. He looks broader, bare like this. We used to be skinny little things. He's all smooth brown. He bends a little to pull his shorts down, and that's the only place he has hair, just above his pict. It hangs lower than mine does and sways a little as he steps out of his boots and into the shower.

"I'm still getting used to low-g showers," he says, turning it on. It's more steam than running water. The cubicle heats up quickly, and I can feel my pict hanging lower. Steam wafts slowly under us, just enough to be visible, as water opens above, and droplets fall like tiny people between us.

For a while, we just watch each other. Steam condenses on our skin. Every few seconds, a bead of sweat slips down me, flattening my hair like a small roadway. Tigre's eyes take me in. I'm paler and heavier than him. He reads me like a book, and I glide my hands across my chest and stomach. He mirrors me.

My pict is hard by the time my hands reach down there. So is Tigre's. We both start a slow stroke. The Prope makes the steam feel like an extra presence, like another person's here, stroking with us.

"I remember," I finally break the silence, "catching you in a vent shaft. Trying to watch the men shower." He just breathes out, and my pict stiffens at the sound of it. I trace the outline of Tigre's hips through the steam. "I remember," I keep going, "waking up with you. Sometimes I could feel you against my back."

"Stop." The sound barely leaves his lips. Tigre closes his eyes and tilts his head back. I stop talking and just breathe as loud as he does. Eventually his eyes return to me. We don't look down at each other's bodies. I hold his eyes in mine, grip my pict, and jerk faster. He follows me.

On Prope, my brain feels like the waves I coded in the ocean room, swooping up and landing down in a rhythm. The motion unlocks something in me.

"I was married once," I say, "to a woman." It's the first time in rotes I've ever mentioned her. "I put two babies in her," I tell Tigre, and his eyes finally break with mine and read my chest before landing on my pict. It feels stronger with Tigre watching me. We let breath out at the same time.

Watching Tigre, open-mouthed, watching me, finally does it. My legs and cheeks clench as I blow. The white cum spools out of me like a ribbon. It slithers in the shower between us, softly falling and falling toward the floor. When

I'm done, Tigre presses his shoulders back against his shower wall, squeezes his hard pict and picks up speed. I can see just a hint of his tight stomach filling and deflating as he gets closer. His free hand cups his balls, and he blows out a tuft of air hard like a pressurizer as he cums. He lasts longer than me, twitching and ticking until his breathing slows back down to normal. Our cum snakes along the shower floor. Like two centipedes, before finally circling and falling down the drain.

I'm wearing a pair of Tigre's unders, stiff white shirt and shorts against the softness of his bed, while Tigre hangs my coder suit in one of the common rooms. The Prope is lingering but starting to wear off. I roll on my back and stare at the ceiling while my arms rub slowly over the sheets on the mattress. The soft bed and the rigid ceiling lines blur together in a way that just feels goofy.

The door opens, and I hear Tigre walk in. He says, "Hey, this actually didn't get that wet," and then his voice clips. I try peel myself upright to focus, but the bed-ceiling combo is too distracting for me.

"This is her," Tigre says, and when it lands in my brain, I snap out of it.

"Yup," I say, rolling onto my side to face him, "and my girls." Tigre put his shorts back on but not his tunic. My eyes trace the shapes of his different muscles. He's mostly rectangles laid on top of each other with two long slim triangles meeting at his neck.

Tigre pulls his eyes off my hand sketch and offers me my family picture back. He asks, "Are they still alive?"

"I hope so," I say. "They must be on Mars for what? Like five years now." It would be harder to get words out about my family if the Prope wasn't still in me. It's like a truth serum.

"That's why you got a Contract."

"My life for their future, yeah."

"Fucking SheffPassage."

"They take everything from you when you start your Contract. Strip you down naked, the whole lot. I drew that whole thing from memory."

Tigre sits on the edge of his bed. His lower back is pressed against my shins. "I didn't know you could draw," he says.

"I didn't know either," I say. "You'd think at the start of your Contract it would feel like you're dead." I see Tigre's lines tick. "But it's kinda the opposite. When it sets in, that you'll never see another person from your old life ever again, it feels like everyone else died. And you're just trudging along. Living a little."

"I'm sorry, Snake," Tigre says. For a few seconds, we just connect in our eyes. Then he says, "I'll get you another glass of water." I take his hand to stop him.

"No, you had your turn before the shower," I say, "it's my turn now." I sit up in Tigre's bed and fold the sketch back up. "Her name's Moss. Guys used to say she was too pretty to work in mech. Fucking assholes. I think she picked me because I'm soft. We both tried to get as much training as we could on *Yao* to qualify for Mars, but they kept updating the stats. Like these gambling games I code. You can't win, but the point is to keep you playing."

"Ain't that the truth," Tigre says. "The corporations, the Colleges, they just squeeze everything you have out of you."

"They'll burn my body down for fuel when I'm done. Every part of me gets used," I say. My ears pop again, and the Prope really starts to slide out of me. I feel like I'm back home in my body.

"Doesn't that make you mad?" Tigre asks.

"It used to, but that's the thing about Contract. Once you accept that everyone you know is dead, the truth sits up and stares at you."

"What truth?"

"That I'm dead, or just as good as it anyway."

Tigre leans in and kisses me. His lips move first, plumping against mine and then drawing back. I cup my hands around his neck and join in with my lips. He pulls my chest in against his, and I breathe in deep from my nose before opening my mouth. Tigre follows. But then, like a relief valve steaming off, we both deflate and take our lips off each other. Because I try not to hear Tigre's pre-teen voice in head, it sounds like an echo, "Don't look at me!"

"I can dry off my coder suit back in my cabin," I tell him, "if you want to walk me back."

"You don't want to spend the night?" he asks.

"Oh, I do, but Elm already has a target on my back. The second your rote's over, she's cracking down hard on me."

"So, stay anyway," Tigre says, "if you're already in trouble."

I chew on that, and when I blink my eyes, I can see Tigre naked from the shower, this new grown-man body I never got to see before. And it's not that I don't know what two men can do in the sack—I've heard stories. But there's a string tugging between my ears like a dead-set bug in code. Trip it, and the whole thing blacks out, and you have system restore. But people aren't computers. I could pull that string, black out, and reset. But I won't be the same again. Maybe Tigre wouldn't be either.

The words slip out of my mouth: "You can't really save me."

Tigre's mouth doesn't move, but his forehead frown lines warp his scar lines. He doesn't say words to respond, he just breathes, gets up, pulls a tunic over himself, fetches my coder suit and our armpads. We walk in silence down the decks until we reach the only freight elevators that go down to my cabin level. I'm still in his stiff white unders. At the elevator, Tigre stops. I can get the rest of the way to my cabin on my own access clearance.

"Snake, I—" Tigre starts, but I interrupt him.

"It's okay, I shouldn't have said that."

"But it's true," he says. I feel my face fall blank.

"And *that's* okay."

We have one more kiss, lip to lip, before the elevator doors open. I say good night to Tigre, but he doesn't say it back. He just watches the doors slide closed between us.

The next day I'm coding in the black and neon AR room. I decided to try adding randomized neon dots to make the room feel more playful. I'm tweaking these bright neon greens when Elm bursts open the doors.

"What the fuck did you do now, Snake?" she says. Her volume is already topped out.

"I'm adding dots," I tell her. I keep my eyes on the codesheet on the wall like a child avoiding eye contact with their parents.

"No, last night!" Elm says. "Access logs bounced you entering the Historian's private cabin."

"He invited me."

"I don't fucking care what it is the two of you are doing, but we both know you're crossing lines. And the second that Historian leaves, Corporate is getting a full report. Your coding skills aren't going to save you, Snake."

The back of my neck tightens. I can feel her moving behind me. If she shuts my boots off again, I can just lean on the wall and be fine. She knows that too. So, whatever she's got planned for me is probably something worse.

"I'm only going to ask you this once," she says. "Snake, look at me."

I turn off the codesheet and turn around slowly. Her armpad's projecting the floor plans of every deck.

"Where's the Historian?" Elm says.

"What?" I blurt out. I can see Elm tense up in her shoulders as her eyes pierce through the projections and try to sting me.

"O-32, you and the Historian leave his cabin," two decals light up outside his door, "O-35, you both ping at the elevator. O-42, you ping on the cabin level. You ping at your cabin door."

I watch my decal light up at each point, but Tigre's decal is gone.

"Where'd Tigre go?"

"That's the fucking question I'm fucking asking you!" Elm screams.

"I don't know. I thought he went back to his room. He wasn't at Eggs this morning?"

"Would I be this upset if he was, Snake?"

I flip my armpad to message Tigre. *Are you okay?* I text him.

"If you did something to the Historian—"

"Tigre," I interrupt her. "His name is Tigre."

Elm rolls her eyes. "The Historian," she continues, "I'll take you off Rec Decks. You know where SheffPassage also needs coders? The guts. The septic and recycle programs have algorithms too. You can spend the rest of your life belly-up on shit tanks."

"I didn't do anything to Tigre. We didn't do anything to each other."

Elm waves the projections away, so there's nothing in between us anymore. "I don't need the mental picture of you two," she says.

"I can help find him."

"No, you've caused enough trouble. You're chained to this room until dinner. You tell me where to look for him, and I'll find him."

"He's not in his cabin?"

"Snake, you fucking idiot, I swear—"

"I'm just retracing!" My voice finally pitches up. "He didn't say good night at the elevator. I told him I wasn't going to spend the night." Elm huffs at that. "I saw him after dinner in the kitchen." Elm makes notes in her armpad. I decide to leave out all the Prope. "You know what Tigre did before the Colleges?"

Elm stares dead-faced at me. "He hopped ships," I say.

"Bullshit!"

"That's what he told all of us. So, he knows what he's doing, Elm. If he's missing, it's because he doesn't want to be found right now."

"So where is he hiding? Since you're the expert on him."

"He's never told me where he's hides. Even as a kid on *Ramirez*. But you know how we always got caught as kids? Noise. Tigre makes noise." My brain flashes back to the radiator valve that gave him his lines just for a second. But it's enough of one memory to trigger another. That echo again. Him screaming, "Don't look at me!"

Elm catches that something's going on behind my eyes. She steps closer to me. "Where is the Historian, Snake?"

I blink my memories away and say, "I don't think he's on the ship. Honest."

Elm types in her armpad as she turns and walks out of the AR room.

"You're not leaving this room until dinner, Snake. And if Tigre contacts you in any way, you better tell me first."

I don't respond.

"I'm sick of you two. Wait until this rote's over," she says, slamming the door behind her.

I code straight through to dinner. Everybody's heard Tigre is missing now, and Bark questions out loud if the Projects will move us all back to the dockyard barracks now. Slowly, all the other coders decide I'm the one to answer that question. Their eyes draw up on me.

"How would I know?" I say.

"Snake," Bark asks, point blank, "what did you and the Historian do?"

"We didn't do anything."

"Maybe that's the problem," Bark says, and that stings the back of my brain. On *Ramirez* when we were about fifteen, Tigre told me he wanted to be with me, and I didn't get it at first. I said something like, "You already are with me. We're right here." Tigre said it again, and that time I understood it right in my gut. I told him no and tried to be nice about it, but panic built up in me, and I walked off. I left him, and twenty years passed.

But that's not what happened last night. Maybe I didn't spend the night, and we didn't fuck each other, but there was an exchange. I felt that. Tigre had to too.

After dinner, we all file one by one in the freight elevator and onto our cabin deck. My cabin's the second closest to the elevator, so I'm one of the first to disappear. I can hear the rest of the crew walking down the hall as I step into my cabin and see Tigre there. He's sitting on my bed, wearing the same tunic he had on last night. His eyes are bloodshot red, too, like he hasn't slept.

"Tigre!" I try to keep my voice down. "Everyone's freaking out trying to find you!"

"Snake, listen to me," Tigre says. "There's not going to be a lot of time, and I'm going to need you to do a lot of things that might not make sense. But I need you to trust me on this."

"Sure," I say as I sit down next to him. I put my arm around his shoulder and squeeze him, just a little. His face is flat, but his lines twitch, always giving him away.

"Take off your boots," Tigre tells me. I bring my arm back from his shoulder, power down, unclip the straps, and slide my feet out of them. Tigre goes to work right away, and that's when I notice the metal toolbox on the other side of him. Because my wife was a mech, I recognize some of the tools in there but not all.

"Do I get to ask what you're doing?" I say, "Or is this 'silent time'?"

Tigre doesn't look up at me. He's got two wires connecting my boots and his armpad. Projecting in front of him are lines and lines of code, something I do know a lot about. He's in the baseline, which, even for a Corporate Historian, is pretty deep access.

"Tigre?" I try to get his attention, but it's not working. Finally, I put my hand through the projection and cup his face. "Tigre, if boots could be hacked, do you think there'd be any Contracts here? In the whole Sheff Corps?"

Tigre's lines flatten as his face deflates.

"Do you know what this corporation used to do? On Earth?"

I blink, "No."

"No one does. I studied human history, and I don't know."

Tigre unhooks the wires from my boots and packs up his toolbox. "You can put them back on now." I shift my feet back into them and clip up.

"Tigre, did I do something... wrong last night?" I say, "Or not do something?"

He stands up from the bed, and I catch his hands. I say, "I liked what we did. I think I'd like to do more."

"We don't have time for this," Tigre says. He breaks away from my hands and cracks open my door to peek outside. I come behind him and pull the door closed.

"What's going on, Tigre? Talk to me."

"I am!" Tigre whisper-yells. "I'm trying!"

"Try harder." I land my hands on his shoulders, grip him, and inch closer. His bloodshot eyes race across my face.

"They scrubbed themselves. Like literally from history. They've done it more than once."

"What does that have to do with us?"

"Just listen," he tells me, "I saw a crack about five years ago. A crack in the scrub. When Sheff Corp was leaving Earth, there were still people down there. They used to hack Sheff satellites to communicate with each other. There was a resistance! To all this bullshit! They called themselves Resistance! Hawk and I, we're working with other folks, folks like me, in the Colleges, on colony ships, on corp ships."

"And you want me to join your underground thing? With Hawk?"

"No, I—" His breath putters out. "Fuck it. Let's try something else."

Tigre breaks away from me and opens the door. He doesn't look back to see if I'm following him; he just assumes I am. And he's right.

Instead of going to the elevator, we walk down to the other end, to the stairwell. "Let's do three floors to be safe," Tigre says and uses his armpad to get us onto another cabin deck. Once we're inside, Tigre stands me in the corner by the exit door and counts off paces, a hundred and twenty.

"Take your boots off," Tigre calls to me. "You have to jump all the way to me, but you can't touch the floor. And you only have ninety seconds."

I unclip my boots and jump up. I pull myself to the center of the exit door and push off. My arms are out in front of me, and I jet through the hallway. At first, it's fast, but I slow down as I get lower and lower until I'm finally belly down on the hallway floor. I didn't even make it halfway. On the second try, I start low, kick off from the bottom of the exit door, and arc up almost hitting the ceiling. I land farther but still not close enough to Tigre, who I can see is timing me.

"It has to be faster, and you have to make it all the way," Tigre says. "Think, Snake."

Walking back to my end of the hallway, I bobble in low-g. I feel like I must look like that centipede bar, waving and inching forward. And that's when it hits me. This time, I kick off from the corner, not the center of the door. And I don't jump forward, I jump diagonally, just enough to get to the stretch of wall between cabin doors. Then I push off from that wall and go diagonal again. I keep zigzagging until I finally land on the floor, this time less than ten feet away.

"I can do this," I tell Tigre, "I don't know why I'm doing this. But I can make it."

"Come on, then," Tigre says.

"Wait, after I jump through your invisible hoops, I need you to tell me what the fuck is going on."

"Deal."

This time, I strip out of my coder suit, so I'm just wearing Tigre's unders. I spend a few seconds wondering if I should stuff my hand sketch into the back of the unders but decide to do so anyway. I crouch down in the corner and push off with one foot and hand; the other foot and hand are outstretched, ready to push off the wall. And the next and the next. Each time getting a little higher in the air. I know I'm going to make it when I see I'm about halfway as I start to fall. I bump wall-to-wall-to-wall and touch down right in front of Tigre.

"I did it," I say.

"Two and half minutes. It's got to be ninety seconds."

"Why?"

"Can you do it faster, or do you think it's not possible?"

"Why?"

"Can you?"

I forget that we're trying to be sneaky and just yell out, "What the fuck are we doing, Tigre? I feel like we're having an argument, but you're the only one who knows what the fuck we're arguing over."

Tigre's red eyes narrow.

"I'm sorry I didn't spend the night, okay? I'm sorry I wasn't ready. That's the truth. But you gotta help me get there. Maybe we can work up to it this rote. But if you stay on for another rote, or come back—"

"Snake, fuck," Tigre interrupts me. "You don't get it. There's not going to be another rote!"

Both our armpads ping at the same time. It's a security alert: Hull breach in Dockyard Sector G, our sector. My face feels slack.

"What did you do, Tigre?" I ask him.

He takes me by the hand, and we run down the hallway to the freight elevator. Tigre armpads us in and then sits on the floor, his knees pulled up close to his face. He used to do this as a kid. He used to cry in this position.

"I didn't know you were going to be here," Tigre starts. "When I signed up for this rote. We've been planning this for over two years. A coordinated attack. I knew some Contracts were gonna die, but I thought, we thought, it'd be worth it. It'd be a whole other world. I thought I had this. And then," he takes a breath, "my first fucking day here, there you are."

"What's going to happen now?"

"Systems will start failing. I rerouted Swoop into industrial vents. Once the oxygen goes..."

"Fuck."

"Ever since the first day, I've been trying to find out a way to save you. If I hadn't moved you onto the ship, you'd be suffocating in the vacuum right now."

I crouch down and rest my arms on his knees just like I used to when he'd cry.

"And I told you last night you couldn't save me."

"I'm sorry, Snake," Tigre says. His eyes are wet, but there's no tears yet. "I can't. We just tried everything."

"The jumping?"

"There's an evacuation deck. It won't open until there's a systems threat here, but even then, you can't access it. Isn't that sick? And it's just ninety seconds. From open to eject. That's designed in, Snake. The fucking ship's not built to save everyone."

I pull his knees apart, so there's nothing between us. Tigre's red, wet eyes open like big ovals, and his lines run straight. I take him in.

"Remember the first time I kissed you?" I ask him.

"Oh god, at Centipede's."

"No," I tell him, "on *Ramirez*. It was a couple of years after you got your lines. And you sat here, like this, crying to me. You said no one was ever going to love you because of them. I touched your face," I do it now, "the only time I ever touched your lines," I run my thumb over the scar line just under his eye, "and I told you it wasn't true. And you said—"

"Don't look at me."

"Tigre, all I ever did growing up was look at you. But I couldn't," my voice strains, "do more. I couldn't be what you wanted. But I can kiss you now. I can touch you."

My hands palm the back of his head and bring him to my lips. We press our chests hard against each other, open our mouths, swim our tongues together, and then our armpads beep again. I nuzzle my face into the crease of Tigre's neck and smell him. Dot his skin with little kisses. The light in the elevator drops out and then comes back on with a siren alert.

"I think I always loved you, Tigre," I say, "but you don't have to save me for it."

I pull back from Tigre and help him stand up. This man, broad-shouldered, tall, and lavish, this man used to be Tigre. My Tigre. His face filled the first half of my life. And it's that face, but bloomed into itself, more somehow, that will be the last face I see. He flips his armpad in front of the elevator console, and we move up.

"I won't have time to look back," Tigre says, "once this door opens. And you won't have more than, like, fifteen minutes?"

"It's okay."

"I can take your family sketch. Maybe my people can track them down on Mars?"

"No, I want to hold on to it."

"Snake, I have to tell—" Tigre starts but the elevator doors open. Outside is a small circular tunnel about a hundred feet deep. A door at the other end opens, too, to the evacuation pod. It feels like time is stopped. But the ninety second window starts to count down.

Tigre races off, and I put my arms in the doorway to keep the elevator doors from closing before I can see that he made it in. Once the evacuation pod doors close behind Tigre, I press the button for my Rec Deck. When I get on the floor, none of the AI girls pop up to greet me because of the alarms. I hop into Centipede's, which is not running because of the emergency, and sit at the spindly-legged bar. Half-naked and somehow smiling while everyone else must be scrambling to try to save their own lives, I start to feel it. Before the blast, there's a breeze. It's slow at first, whipping across my face and over the back of my neck. But then it picks up. It feels strong like how I'd always imagined wind felt like on Earth. And then everything goes white.

THE NEWS

Nustanbul Station, Mars, 2513 CE

Bhaka

Bhaka was the first to arrive because he knew Q!obi wouldn't have his cube in order. And he was right. Q!obi answered the door rubbing crust out of his eyes in just shorts and a blue shirt, and even then, he looked like he had just thrown the shirt on before opening the door. Bhaka just exhaled, letting his shoulders slump.

"I know, I know," Q!obi muttered. He waved Bhaka in.

Q!obi's cube looked worse than the last time Bhaka saw it. Dirty dishes spread past the sink and started building on the counters and even the kitchen table. On the opposite side, Q!obi's bed was full of clothes that were maybe clean at some point but wrinkled now and probably mixed in with dirty ones. At least there was nothing on the floor.

"You know Dignity Duty cycles through once a week," Bhaka said. From the looks of it, Q!obi must have missed at least two cycles for them to come in and clean.

"They're too loud," Q!obi said, "banging and drumming all the boll time." Bhaka rolled his eyes but winced once the words caught up with him. You're supposed to leave your cube open and evacuate once you hear the Dignity Duty drums. Come back about two hours later, and everything is gleaming clean and smelling sharp. Bhaka realized that if Q!obi missed Dignity Duty, he would have sat here alone, with the door locked and lights out, in the dark during the whole cacophony. Twice. And Bhaka knew a thing or two about how loud and how crazy Dignity Duty can get.

In the beginning, right after Nimol left him for the research mission on Saturn, Q!obi was a mess. He wouldn't talk, instead just shifting through phases of crying. Bhaka was there for all of it. Sinking and raging at Nimol for breaking his best friend's heart. But then, one day, Bhaka came to his cube, and Q!obi was lifted. He was out of bed and talking. Bhaka breathed deeper and easier then, thinking he had his best friend back. But then dishes started piling up, and Q!obi showed up to Ed Duty in wrinkled, unwashed dhotis. The mess, Bhaka noticed, moved from inside Q!obi to outside of him.

Bhaka started moving plates and bowls out of the sink so he could properly wash them. Q!obi didn't bother to help; instead, he sat at his own dirty table and watched Bhaka fumble through cleaning. Bhaka thought this must be funny in its own way: this big, bulking guy folding his melmundu, pulling up his sleeves, then hunching over to wash plates.

"You're not just going to sit there," Bhaka said, not even bothering to turn around. "Go shower. And wear the kurta I gave you!"

After washing and drying dishes, Bhaka struggled to understand Q!obi's kitchen-organizing system before realizing he didn't have one anymore, and this would all be up to him anyway. He placed cups above the sink, plates above the Bunsen, and pots and pans below. There, under the pipes, he found a small gray box. Inside were a couple of old clickers, some letters, and complicated mathematical proofs. Bhaka nearly hit his head on the pipes when he realized what it all was: the little bits and pieces Nimol forgot to take with him to Saturn. Bhaka heard the shower turn off and, in a panic, threw the whole thing in the incinerator and pressed burn.

Q!obi emerged from the shower, wrapped in a towel, and slowly shuffled through the clothes on his bed. Bhaka clicked his tongue. Q!obi would look taller if he didn't slouch his shoulders so much. He had a nice reddish undertone to his brown skin and a light dusting of black hair over his chest and stomach. Q!obi was always the better looking of the two, Bhaka thought, but he could be so much more attractive if he just put some effort into it.

"No, don't wear any of that stuff!" Bhaka said. "Here, let me help you."

"Are you going to physically dress me too now?"

"If I have to, you know I will."

Bhaka pushed past Q!obi and opened his wardrobe. He fetched the blue kurta, the one he gave Q!obi last year, along with blue pants and a brown and evabaum melmundu, but Q!obi just stared at Bhaka with the clothes in his hands.

"Turn around," he told Bhaka.

"Chaa! We've seen each other naked before," Bhaka laughed.

"Just do it!"

"Okay!"

They were standing there, back-to-back, with Q!obi still only half-dressed when the front door opened. Q!obi's sister Umr and her boyfriend Pa'atl let themselves in and stopped short at the sight of them.

"We could come back later?" Pa'atl said with a grin on his face. Umr elbowed him.

"You're not even dressed yet?!" Umr said. She set down the box she was carrying and finally caught a good view of the cube—still a mess, despite Bhaka's attempts to clean it.

Bhaka put his hands up in defense. "I'm trying to help clean," he said.

Umr sighed, "You're a good friend," and then she started barking orders. "Q!obi, clean those clothes off your bed. You help him, Bhaka. And Pa'atl, wipe the table down before we unpack this."

Pa'atl and Q!obi fell into their assignments, but Bhaka still had his back to Q!obi.

"Can I turn around?" Bhaka asked Q!obi.

"Chaa, you two!" Umr said and turned toward her boyfriend. "Grown men, the two of them."

Bhaka and Q!obi stuffed all the unfolded clothes into the bottom of the wardrobe and pressed them tight against its doors until they heard the latch click. On the kitchen table,

Umr and Pa'atl unloaded streamers and colored letters from their box. They spelled out "birthday" instead of "firstday."

"Umr, no," Bhaka said, "those are the wrong ones!"

Pa'atl said, "I tried telling her."

"Same difference!" Umr said, waving her hand in the air.

"No, it's not," Bhaka said. "People stopped saying that."

"Well, I can't keep up with all the right-talk and wrong-talk these days. And besides, the Sup-Stop had both anyway," Umr said.

Bhaka flushed. It was always something with Q!obi's sisters. "Then you should have got 'firstday.' Not everyone identifies as being born anymore, you know that."

Pa'atl chimed in, "I'm all for it. I'm proud to be an incu-baby."

"Q!obi doesn't care, do you?" Umr asked.

"I don't."

"See?"

"It's not about him," Bhaka said.

"It's *his* birthday!" Umr laughed.

"Firstday!" Bhaka said back. "And that's not what I meant. Your family," Bhaka waved between Q!obi and Umr, "is blended, but that's not everyone. Q!obi's friends are coming. What if someone gets offended? Like Tekakwitha?"

"Chaa!" Umr rolled her eyes. "I can't stand her."

"Umr!" Q!obi said. "She's my friend!"

"She's just so..." Umr stiffened her shoulders, pointed two fingers at the vertical code on her forehead, wafted them down, and then grunted. The men around her exchanged glances.

"So," Bhaka said, collecting every streamer and decoration with "birthday" written on them, "please don't ever do that in front of her. Or really, anyone, ever again. Me and Q!obi are gonna go to brunch-n-smoke, and while we're out, we'll pick up Firstday signs."

"Oh, where you going?" Pa'atl asked.

"It's a surprise," Bhaka said.

"Bhaka, I hate surprises," Q!obi said.

"Don't infringe on my best friend rights. It's your Firstday, and I'm gonna surprise you. I've got a lot of surprises, actually."

Q!obi slumped his shoulders even further as he sighed. Bhaka ignored that and took his hand.

"We'll be back later!" he called back as they left.

Outside, the Balance high above them shone bright, and people were already up and milling about. Their bright-colored robes and dhotis clashed playfully against the pastel greens, blues, erjerrins, and yellows of residential cubes. Bhaka and Q!obi took the stairs instead of waiting for the elevator. Q!obi lived on the third floor, so it wasn't too much of a hassle.

On the street level, Bhaka finally let go of Q!obi's hand. They walked past a giant simig with thick, round women lying on each other, advertising for Lineage Duty, on their way up to the flat-tram platform.

"My sister's so embarrassing," Q!obi said.

"All your sisters are," Bhaka replied. He hadn't even met all of them, but they seemed to have the common theme of disregarding other people's feelings and marrying quiet, subservient men like Pa'atl. "But serio, she's not exactly wrong about Teka. She's the most marty person ever."

"Tekakwitha," Q!obi corrected him. "And why is that so bad? I mean, it's not like we're Armstrong Station."

A flat-tram arrived, and it was empty. Still, after the tram scanned their forehead codes, they sat all the way in the back. The flat-tram zipped ahead, and the wind tugged at Q!obi's hair, just enough for Bhaka to notice. Bhaka's own head was shaved. He started balding in his early twenties and decided to just lean into it. With a full beard, barrel chest, and bald head, Bhaka knew he commanded attention from Q men and het men alike.

Q!obi was the opposite. Even when he was with Nimol, Q!obi had always been a bit mousy. The youngest of fourteen siblings, mostly girls, Q!obi was always shrinking himself. They were not an obvious best-friend pair, Bhaka thought, but that's what worked about them. They complemented each other.

"But really," Q!obi said, "what's wrong with being a little marty?"

"We're all marty," Bhaka replied, "and I don't think Tekakwitha takes it too far. She's kind of like Umr. She really just doesn't question anything."

"Boll, here it comes," Q!obi laughed, "get it out now before we get to brunch-n-smoke."

"Because she's marty-skinned."

"And..."

"Assembly Duty says: 'There's no scientific support for a Martian tan or a Terran tan. That's why Balance exists, to tan us all equally.' But come on, you can *tell* when someone's terra-skinned. Look how dark I am. My Earth ancestors had to be dark people." Bhaka rolled his sleeve up. His brown was deeper than Q!obi's. The undertone wasn't red; it was just another shade of brown. Q!obi leveled his eyes on Bhaka.

"What?" Bhaka said. "It's not a judgment on you. For what it's worth, I think you're terra-skinned too."

"Chaa, thanks," Q!obi said sarcastically. Bhaka decided not to take the bait and switched subjects.

"Anyway! Dignity Duty came by my block a few nights ago," Bhaka said. Q!obi rolled his eyes. "And I didn't leave!"

"Stop lying."

"I'm not! I opened the door and stayed!"

"What happened?"

"Oh, I'm saving all the juicy bits for everyone at brunch-n-smoke."

"Of course you are."

"But they don't just clean all the stuff." Bhaka leaned in toward Q!obi even though they were the only people on the flat-tram. "They clean *your stuff,* too." That got a small tuft of a laugh out of Q!obi. Bhaka took that as a win and reclined in his seat.

The flat-tram stopped at a Food District that wasn't close to either of their cubes. Before Bhaka and Q!obi even got off the flat-tram, they could smell smudgy spices mixed with citrus and cooked meats. Their foreheads were scanned again as they walked under the archway and into the court.

It seemed like hundreds of people bobbed around them, shopping and gabbing between forkfuls of pastas and veggies. Simigs flashed above the crowds, advertising different Duties. Bhaka steered Q!obi by his shoulders to keep him from catching a glimpse of the Research Duty ad for the Saturn Anomaly Research Project.

Eventually, Bhaka found the hall with his reservation, a dining area called Sonrisas, and the whole crew was already there when they walked in. Friends hugged Q!obi and draped him in sashes as they said, "Happy Firstday!" Tekakwitha and Frial drew pink and purple circles on his arms. Q!obi took it all in stride. After all the initial fuss over him, everyone found a seat at a long table. They were seven of them altogether. Bhaka and Q!obi; Tekakwitha and her girlfriend Frial; and Malosi, Kuparr, and Damu from Q!obi's childhood Ed pod.

"So, what's the plan for the big day?" Frial asked Q!obi.

Bhaka answered, "This, then his sisters are throwing a little party at the cube. And then I have a big surprise later tonight."

"I hate surprises, Bhaka," Q!obi said, "just tell me."

"If I tell you, you won't go."

"Well, I have a surprise," Tekakwitha said as the server came to get everyone's drink order. "I'm leaving Assembly Duty and joining Lineage Duty."

Even the server did a double take. Tekakwitha was a round, squat woman with big glasses and spiky black hair. She was never more than two meters from her girlfriend, Frial, and almost the exact opposite demographic Lineage Duty advertises to.

"You're kidding," Kuparr said. Tekakwitha shook her head and held Frial's hand.

"Why?" Bhaka asked.

"Because it's important. Did you know there were ten billion people on Earth at the time of the Migration? We need numbers, or we're not going to survive."

Kuparr furrowed his brow. "But you're Q. Are you gonna?" He humped the air just above his lap on his chair. Bhaka laughed, but no one else did.

"Chaa, no!" Tekakwitha said. "Lineage is not just a bunch of men and women fucking."

"Coulda fooled me," Bhaka said. Every Duty group puts their own spin on their ads. Dignity Duty sells itself as a spiritual escape from life's pressures. Research Duty ads are designed to spark curiosity. But Lineage Duty ads are all their own. They're too sexual to be allowed near Ed pods, and Bhaka still jolts when they pop up in front of him the exact instant he gets one hundred paces away from the Ed pods. Topless women with hefty, round breasts, writhing all over each other, each one spreading their legs just before the ad re-loops.

"They have incus. And there's a science to it. They calculate for genetic diversity, track diseases."

Q!obi interrupts her, "But, again, you're Q. Lineage Duty is very much not."

"I'm not scared. Serio, the hets are always gonna think we're disposable if we don't add to the population."

Kuparr squirmed hard enough that the entire table heard it.

"And I'm not going to be doing it alone," Tekakwitha said and then put her arm around Frial. She has only ever been in Assembly Duty. "We thought you all would be happy for us."

"Why?" Malosi spit out.

Bhaka broke in, "You know we support any decision that you two make, but what I'm upset about is that you're telling us this now. It's Q!obi's day. We should be celebrating him."

"When is there ever a good time to tell all your Q friends you're joining Lineage?" Damu joked.

"That should be an ad!" Malosi laughed.

"I don't want to be the center of attention," Q!obi said. "But I do want to hear from Frial. Do you actually want to do this? Give up Assembly?"

The server returned with drinks and hookahs, and Frial took full advantage of the pause. But once the table was settled and the hookahs started, all eyes fell back on her.

"It wasn't an easy decision. But Tekakwitha's right. You know how they look at us."

Kuparr groaned. He'd been in Content Duty for years but had only just started appearing in ads. Bhaka'd felt it, too, in Ed Duty. How First Wave pod teachers go out of the way to make sure the young children see as little of him as possible.

"So, it's a charm offensive?" Bhaka said. "With ovaries and genetic testing?"

"It's a commitment," Frial said. "It's doing the actual work instead of just theorizing about it. Like Nimol said."

"Serio?!" Bhaka coughed on his hookah.

Frial put her hand in the air. "I'm so sorry, Q!obi."

"It's okay. We can talk about him," Q!obi said.

"I won't," Bhaka huffed. Of all the days to remind Q!obi of his ex—on his Firstday?

"But he was right. We're not young anymore," Frial said. "I want to do something that actually matters."

Kuparr exhaled and said, "Lineage Duty," in a way that made the table fall silent. No one else was able to make a conversation last after that. Between hookah puffs, Bhaka and Damu tried various jokes, but none landed further than a chuckle or two.

Right as the server began laying down hot plates, the walls cued on, then the table itself. The simig was a woman's round smiling face with black curls falling on either side. Her eyes looked warm and inviting, but the line of code on her forehead didn't make any sense, like how a random string of words doesn't make a sentence.

"We do not wish you harm," the woman said. "We wish only to convey this message."

After pausing, she repeated herself. Every wall and table in the hall carried the simig, which almost never happened. Sensing this was some kind of emergency, the server left the table to open the door. Bhaka could see into the Food Court; the simig was on every screen, wall, and flat surface. There were no ads for anything. Hundreds of people stood dumbstruck as the woman with the fake code said it again: "We do not wish you harm. We wish only to convey this message."

Inside the hall, no one moved.

The woman began, "By now, you may probably suspect that this human face was generated for your comfort. This message does not come from your species but from several others in the Larger Community."

She paused as if she could read Bhaka's mind to allow him to digest the idea of other life in the universe. He placed his hand over Q!obi's.

"Your species is expanding across your home star system and will soon reach the capacity to travel outside of it in large numbers, which is why we are conveying this message now. In your calendar year of 2183, one of your ships reached the threshold of your home star system. According to protocols established long before the dawn of your species, an empathy meter was dispatched to assess whether your species poses a threat to the Larger Community or a disposition to join us."

She continued to smile as she said, "The empathy meter reported back that yours was a hierarchal, stratified society in which some amass and exert power over many, that your individuals have the capacity to speak untruths to themselves and do so to the extent that they are taken as fact. These qualities are inconsistent with the core tenets of the Larger Community.

"But beyond that, one of your individuals attempted to capture and constrain the empathy meter to turn it over to be studied. The empathy meter was so severely damaged in that process that it did not survive. It will take thousands of your 'Earth years' to create another empathy meter. This has immensely set back our goal of finding and connecting intelligent species across the star field."

She paused again.

"A process began to determine what response the Larger Community would have to your species. You were given mercy. It was decided that you cannot join the Larger

Community. It was decided that your species may pose a threat to other intelligent species. It was decided that you will not be allowed outside your home star system. It was decided that the threshold of your home star system be enveloped with an energy field that will prevent all life from escaping it.

"It was decided that now, as your species is on the precipice of developing the capacity to travel beyond your home star system in larger and larger numbers, you would be informed of the energy field to prevent great loss of life. This is the message we wish to convey. The Larger Community regrets our brief, tumultuous relationship with your species. The Larger Community also would like to offer this last parting advice: take care of your planets. They are all you have left."

Every wall and surface faded to black, and then the simig faded in again at the beginning.

"We do not wish you harm," the woman said again. "We wish only to convey this message."

Q!obi

For a few moments, no one in the hall moved or spoke, but then someone said it.

"What the boll?" It was a man's voice from another table. Q!obi's eyes darted toward him. The man was older. His mostly gray hair swirled on top of his head as he glanced around nervously. A woman sitting next to him tried to calm him by touching his shoulder, but he slapped her hand and then threw his hookah at the woman talking on the wall. It shattered, and Q!obi's spine tensed up, but Smiling Woman kept talking.

Bhaka gripped Q!obi's hand tighter and leaned in toward his table.

"I think we should get out of here," he whispered. Everyone nodded in agreement, just as the man at the other table stood up and began pushing two other men who approached him. Within seconds, fists began landing on each other as the server screamed.

Tekakwitha and Frial sat closest to the door and were the first to reach it. Tekakwitha held the door open for everyone to file out. Q!obi was the last of the group to step outside, and Frial squeezed his shoulder. He wasn't sure what that meant but knew somehow that she didn't do that for everyone. The first thing he saw once he was outside in the Food Court was vomit on the ground. Further out, several people fell to their knees. Others were running toward various arched exits. But just like in the hall, fistfights were beginning to break out.

"I'm going home," Damu said, "sorry, y'all." Malosi joined him without saying goodbye. Their quick-paced walk broke out into a full run, dodging people crying on the ground or throwing food and plates at the walls.

"Don't worry," Tekakwitha said, "Assembly will send Suits in here. They'll straighten everything out."

"I don't want to be here when that happens," Bhaka said. Frial and Kapurr nodded. But Q!obi just looked up blankly at the Balance.

The Balance was a massive white light display so high up it covered everything. Assembly duty said the UV light mimicked the sun on Earth and, as a side effect, tanned everyone. After training his eyes on it for more than a few seconds, Q!obi saw something strange. The white light dimmed in some places over large swaths of districts. Some panels brightened back to normal after a few seconds, but then other panels around them started to dim. The panel directly over them dimmed but didn't brighten.

In all of their entire lives, no one had ever seen the Balance dim.

"I think Assembly's got its own problems," Q!obi said, pointing upward.

"What's happening?" Bhaka asked.

"I have no idea," Q!obi said. This time, it was Bhaka who squeezed his shoulder. Maybe it was a Firstday thing, that people felt the need to touch him. But Q!obi suspected it was something worse; his friends thought he needed special treatment when things went wrong. That Q!obi couldn't weather big changes, even though the love of his life left him, and he still got up every day and went to Ed Duty. He may not have been a towering figure of confidence like Bhaka, but he wasn't soft like the children he taught either.

Tekakwitha clapped her hands to get Q!obi and Bhaka's attention. "Hey look at me!" she said. "Let's get out of here."

The closest flat-tram was the one Q!obi and Bhaka used to get there. Q!obi pointed in that direction, and, as the tallest, Bhaka led the rest of them through the Food Court, bobbing and weaving around frantic people panicking. One woman on the ground clawed at Q!obi's kurta, and when he shook her off, she began scratching at her own face, drawing blood.

The station wasn't any calmer outside the Food Court District. The Smiling Woman was on every wall on the main street, even on residential cubes. On almost every block, someone was shouting back at the Smiling Woman, punching the wall, or throwing things at her.

There was a flat-tram on the platform, empty. But once they got there, it wouldn't scan anyone's codes.

"Shouldn't there be a manual override for the flat-tram?" Kapurr asked.

"Probably," Bhaka said. He tried turning on the platform panel, but once it lit up, it was the Smiling Woman. "Boll this!"

"We're just gonna have to walk, I think," Q!obi said. He took in their group before stepping off the platform. In their own ways, everyone was as readable as Q as he was. Tekakwitha and Frial were an obvious couple. Kapurr's curly hair fell over his forehead, framing his face in a style more often seen on women than men. Bhaka's kurta was cut so low that tiny wisps of hairs from his stomach poked into view. And of course, Q!obi was decked with the Firstday sashes, and with the painted purple and yellow circles on his arms, he felt loud and attention-seeking.

Again, Bhaka led the way because he was the biggest. Most people were too involved in fighting the screens or each other, or generally panicking, to pay too much attention to their group. But having Bhaka out front helped. A couple guys bumped into Bhaka as they ran without looking where they were going, and at first, they curled their fists and sneered their faces. But when they considered that they might have to go toe to toe with someone bigger than them, they shrank back and ran away.

Above them, the Balance grew dimmer, darkening their walk. They huddled closer together as Q!obi watched a Sup-Stop being looted. The polyglass doors were ripped off their tracks and cracked on the ground. Inside, people were grabbing clothes, small furniture, and anything that wasn't bolted down. Two women tugging on the same fabric tapestry ripped it in two, and then they each ran off to different corners of the Sup-Stop without acknowledging each other.

"Everyone's losing their boll minds," Tekakwitha said. "Where is Assembly? Why aren't they doing something?"

"I know it's not the best timing to say this," Kapurr said, "but you would know if you hadn't left them to join Lineage."

Q!obi said, "This can't last that long. For one thing, people will physically tire themselves out. And then there's also Dignity Duty."

"You think Dignity Duty is still working?" Tekakwitha asked.

"They're so tranced out I bet they haven't even heard the message," Bhaka said.

"How do you know?" Frial asked.

"Bhaka stayed when they came to his cube," Q!obi told her.

"Serio?"

"It's the exact opposite of this," Bhaka said, "but with the exact same energy. They take this liquid-y kind of drug while they clean. That's why they're always drumming and dancing."

"Did they give it to you?" Kapurr asked.

"Oh yeah, they strip you down and rub it on you while they rub it on themselves. And all these hands are on you, scrubbing and cleaning. They don't miss a spot. And the whole time, you're as high as the Balance. Like an intense non-sex orgy."

"Well, they're gonna have a field day today," Kapurr said.

"If they're still working," Tekakwitha said. "Serio, nothing is working right now."

They reached Q!obi's neighborhood, and the pastel greens, blues, erjerrins, and yellows of the residential cubes were all replaced with the Smiling Woman. In unison, repeating the message on a loop. The Balance above was so faint, it was hard to see anything in the stairwell leading up to Q!obi's cube.

Inside, Umr and Pa'atl sat motionless at Q!obi's table while the Smiling Woman played on all the walls, her face occasionally obscured by Umr's Happy Birthday decorations that she put up after Bhaka and Q!obi left.

"Thank goodness you two are okay," Q!obi said, which snapped Pa'atl to attention. Umr didn't move or respond.

"Oh, is it bad out there?" Pa'atl asked.

"It's chaos," Bhaka said, "serio chaos."

"Have you heard anything from the family? Are they okay?" Q!obi asked.

"Comms are shut down. There's no signal," Pa'atl answered. "It's just this over and over again."

"Well, the Balance isn't working, the flat-trams aren't working. People are fighting and looting in the streets. There's no Suits out to stop them."

"Boll!" Pa'atl said, and that roused Umr.

"We aren't alone in the universe," Umr said, "but they boll hate us."

Umr almost never cusses, and hearing it from her lips chilled the back of Q!obi's neck. Q!obi's friends didn't speak up at first. From the initial widespread panic, no one really had time to take it in.

"What do you think will happen now?" Frial asked.

"We'll die," Umr said. "Earth is unlivable. We can't terraform Mars. It's over. We aren't going to make it."

Pa'atl took her hand into his. "Don't say that," he told her, but she looked past him into the eyes of the Smiling Woman on the wall behind him.

"Lineage Duty is going to be more important than ever now," Tekakwitha said.

"Boll Lineage Duty!" Umr said.

"Umr!" Q!obi and Pa'atl almost said in unison.

"You guys don't get it! We've just been deemed unfit. This isn't a station anymore; it's a prison. All of it. We're all trapped now."

"That's only one way of looking at it," Tekakwitha said. "We've got scientific teams exploring the anomaly off Saturn, like Nimol's. We can find someplace somewhere. But we can't give up on our future."

"We, as a species, don't have a future. Or, we had one, and she took it away." Umr pointed at the Smiling Woman.

"That's the thing that's bothering me," Pa'atl said. "She said 2183. Three centuries ago. We've been trapped here, I guess, for all that time, and we didn't even know it."

"She said we didn't need to know it until now," Q!obi said.

"But that doesn't make any sense. Now? Today? Not yesterday, or the day before, not tomorrow?"

"I feel like it may be pointless to try to understand a more advanced species," Frial offered.

"The Larger Community," Umr huffed, but no one took the bait. Q!obi and Bhaka took the extra seats at the table while Tekakwitha and Frial sat on Q!obi's bed. Kapurr sat on the floor in front of Q!obi's wardrobe, knees up to his chest. The Smiling Woman kept on and on.

She looped so many times that Q!obi was beginning to memorize the message. It felt violent, like an intentional part of humanity's punishment. But then, after "take care of your planets, they're all you have left," the Smiling Woman faded, and she didn't come back. Everyone in Q!obi's cube froze. Some wondered if it was just a glitch and she'd return, others worried about what might come next. Instead, nothing happened. Q!obi's walls returned back to normal, albeit dimmer than earlier today.

"It's Assembly," Tekakwitha said. "They finally took over the signal."

"You don't know that," Umr hissed.

Bhaka got up and opened the door. He stepped outside the cube to check if the Smiling Woman was gone everywhere.

Frial said, "We don't know anything right now."

Umr finally took her eyes off the wall and turned them on Tekakwitha and Frial. "You're already doing it. You're boll doing it."

"Doing what?" Tekakwitha said. Suddenly Q!obi's wall flicked on with incoming messages. Everyone else's comm-wrists buzzed.

"Telling untruths to yourselves," Umr said. "Like she said."

One of the messages on Q!obi's wall was from Malosi and Damu, saying they were safe in their cubes, checking in. Q!obi's sisters also sent messages asking if everyone was okay.

"We're just trying to make sense of what's happening," Tekakwitha said, "just like everyone else."

"But that's what's wrong with you," Umr said. "You don't have the right sense."

"Calm down, Umr," Pa'atl said.

"I am calm," she shot back. There were too many things happening in Q!obi's cube to pay attention to all of it. He focused on the wall and swiped through his messages. He wrote back to Malosi and Damu. Started and stopped with his sisters. Some of them only reached out on his Firstday, but now with the Smiling Woman, they were all writing. They were all reaching out, like all the grips on his shoulders today.

"I'm not understanding you," Tekakwitha said. "What are you trying to say?"

"You," Umr started in on Tekakwitha, "are what's wrong with people. Why the woman shut us all out. You tell untruths to yourselves until you believe it. Then demand everyone else believe it too."

Umr narrowed her eyes on Tekakwitha and Frial's intertwined hands.

"Maybe you should speak plain, Umr," Tekakwitha said. She stiffened her spine. "If you have something to say, don't hold back."

After Q!obi finished replying to his sisters, a new message came in from the Saturn science expedition. It was Nimol. "I love you," it said, "and I'm sorry." It was the first time either of them communicated since Nimol left.

"This Q thing," Umr said, "it's unnatural. You told yourself lies over and over again. You built a whole sick life out of the lies you—"

Pa'atl tried to interrupt her, "Umr, stop."

"I'm unnatural?!" Tekakwitha began to raise her voice. "For being Q? Q!obi, are you hearing this?"

Q!obi heard her, but she felt far away. Everything did. Nimol's message seared into his eyes. "I love you, and I'm sorry." Tekakwitha and Frial turned to Q!obi, but he was sitting dumbstruck at the kitchen table. Meanwhile, Umr had gotten out of her seat and stepped closer to Tekakwitha.

"Experimenting, playing around, that's one thing. But your body's built for having kids. That's your purpose. But instead, you lie to yourself. You trick your brain into thinking that what you want is natural when it's clearly not. That's what the woman was talking about. That's why all of humanity is boll trapped now. And for what? So, you and her can play pretend with each other like you're just like the rest of us. Like you're not some abnormal—"

Tekakwitha slapped Umr so fast that no one saw the hand connect to her face. Umr was suddenly just one knee on the floor with her hand on her cheek. But the sound of the impact popped out through the cube, pulling Q!obi's attention away from Nimol.

"Boll you, Umr!" Tekakwitha screamed with wet eyes. She stepped toward Umr with her hand raised again, and Pa'atl jumped out of his chair.

"Don't do that again, Teka," Pa'atl warned her.

"My name," she turned to Pa'atl, "is Tekakwitha, and there is nothing unnatural or untrue about me! Or any of us!"

"What's going on? What happened?" Q!obi asked.

"Lies," Umr said, standing back up. But this time, she turned to Q!obi and Nimol's message written in big letters on the wall behind him. "Your lies doomed us!" Her eyes were small, but Q!obi felt the anger in them. Umr was too old to go through the Ed waves with Q!obi. He'd never even met her until he was twenty. But they were both bio-babies, and they looked it. They looked just like each other. Umr never minced words with anyone, but, Q!obi felt, especially not with him. Birthed from the same parents, through the same canal, Umr never spared Q!obi from anything.

"I think we should go," Pa'atl said.

"Get the boll out," Tekakwitha said.

Pa'atl draped an arm over Umr and broke her glare at her younger brother.

"Tekakwitha," Frial said. "It might not be safe out there."

"It's not going to be safe inside here for her much longer."

Pa'atl and Umr crossed the room. She didn't look at her brother when she walked past. Pa'atl tried to catch his attention to mouth, "I'm sorry," but it stung Q!obi as hollow. As not quite real, just like Nimol's "I'm sorry" from the other side of the solar system. They opened the door and squeezed past Bhaka, who then came back inside.

"What'd I miss?" Bhaka asked, and then he saw Nimol's message on the wall. "Oh, boll."

Bhaka

Q!obi's birthday decorations still hung against the now dimmer walls of his cube. In the kitchen, Frial opened Q!obi's bottle of zohe and fetched cups for everyone. The zohe was so strong that it smelled fume-y as Frial poured a little into each cup. She didn't notice Bhaka already behind her. He took two cups, one for him and one for Q!obi. Frial brought Tekakwitha and Kapurr their cups before taking her own.

"Should we try a Firstday toast?" Kapurr offered, swishing the zohe in his cup. He half-smiled toward Bhaka, who took a quick survey of the room. It was almost laughable, how everyone's head hung in silence, gripping a cup of zohe like it was somehow magic, all against a backdrop of "Happy Birthday" signs and streamers.

"I'm so sorry, Q!obi," Bhaka said.

No one had anything else to add at first, so the sorry floated in the cube between everyone.

"I'll start," Kapurr said, raising his cup. "Q!obi, I've known you ever since we were kids. You were just as shy as I was in the Ed pod, and I remember thinking, 'Oh, good. Someone like me.' And we got older, and it turned out we had even more in common, namely: men."

Kapurr paused for a laugh but only got a small tuft out of Bhaka. He kept going, "I spent so many years hopping from Duty to Duty, trying to find out what I wanted to be. And you never judged me. For a while, you were the only constant in my life. I'll never forget that. Happy Firstday."

Everyone echoed, "Happy Firstday," and sipped their zohe. It stung and twisted everyone's face but Tekakwitha's. She went next.

"To Q!obi." Tekakwitha raised her glass. "You are the sweetest, most unselfish person I know. There's nothing unnatural or wrong about you. You're perfect. We all are. Happy Firstday."

Everyone strained another sip. The drink was almost as strong as Tekakwitha's toast was self-serving, Bhaka thought. He really needed to laugh. Normally, zohe did the trick, loosened his tongue and his balance. He'd spent so many nights trying anything to get Q!obi to smile and laugh after Nimol left. But tonight was different. His usual material couldn't work after the Smiling Woman. It was like she sucked the life out of humanity. In just sixty minutes.

Frial didn't raise her cup. She shrugged and said, "I'm not good at toasts and speeches. I love you, Q!obi. Happy Firstday."

Eventually, everyone's eyes moved to Bhaka, where he leaned against the kitchen counter. He stood up straight and tried to smooth over any wrinkles in his dhoti. It was a stall tactic.

"You know," Bhaka started, "with all the planning and fusing over Q!obi's Firstday, it never occurred to me that I might have to make a toast." Bhaka melodramatically cleared his throat as his mind raced for something to cut all the tension and sadness.

"Dear Q!obi," he raised his cup, "if someone would have told me that the world would end on your Firstday... well, I probably would have just sighed. No offense, but serio, that's kind of your luck. You all have known Q!obi longer than I have, but I actually get to teach with him. So, you don't get to see what I see. The general rule of thumb is: anything that can go wrong will go wrong. Remember when that sick kid vomited on top of you? Or when the hall latch caught your kurta and ripped your clothes off in front of the kids and the admins?"

Bhaka opened his mouth to mention Nimol and how Q!obi cried into his chest for hours and then got dressed and showed up for class. But Bhaka stopped short. He couldn't actually put the words together to describe how shattered Q!obi looked that night. How his voice sounded hollow telling Bhaka over comms but then somehow sank deeper in between groans once Bhaka showed up at his cube. How Q!obi cried so much his eyes shook.

"But here's the thing," Bhaka continued, "you never give up. Wash the vomit out of your hair in the stall and keep going. Tie what's left of your clothes into a robe and keep going. I don't know if you all get to see that, but I do. Because I'm always right there, right with him. We don't know what's going to happen next, but isn't life always like that? And whatever comes, I know these things to be true: Q!obi will always keep trying, and I'll always be there, with you. Happy Firstday."

After the toast, Frial hugged Q!obi and then Bhaka. Tekakwitha drank more zohe. For a few minutes, the cube felt like an actual party could start. But Nimol's message, unanswered, kept reappearing on the wall. "I love you. And I'm sorry." Bhaka remembered how he found a few of Nimol's things hidden underneath the kitchen sink. How, without thinking, he incinerated it. How he knew it was better not to even tell Q!obi about it. He felt the same way about Nimol's message and, when he thought Q!obi wasn't looking, Bhaka swiped it away, but he got caught.

"Bhaka," Q!obi said, waving his hand to recall the message. "It's okay. I'll deal with that later."

"Chaa..." Bhaka said, exasperated.

Tekakwitha and Frial decided the party was over when they asked Bhaka to walk them home. Kapurr also jumped at the chance for an escorted walk home.

"We're not leaving you behind on your Firstday, Q!obi," Bhaka said as they gathered toward the front door of his cube.

"But—"

"Nope!" Bhaka said. "It's my rules. C'mon."

They'd spent several hours inside so no one had any sense of what was happening now. The Balance had gotten dimmer, and the flat-trams were still not working. The streets were empty. No one was looting or fighting each other. But black graffiti now splayed across the pastels of residential cubes. "Boll the Woman!" said one painted across a cube at ground level. The Lineage Duty ad by the flat-tram station was now tagged in big letters: "What's the use now?"

"Kids," Tekakwitha said accusingly.

"No, you'd be surprised," Kapurr responded.

They followed the flat-tram line in the opposite direction of the Food District. After a klick, they turned onto a side street where the station sloped down into a different residential district. There were small fires on top of some of the tallest buildings. People must have ripped their bunsens out of the kitchens to get them started. Further out, on the roofs of different cubes, families wailed and flapped long pieces of fabric or tapestries in the air. The graffiti on the side street heading down read, "Bring Back Balance!"

"What are people doing?" Frial asked.

"They're mourning," Bhaka said, piecing it together.

Q!obi interrupted, "Bhaka, don't start this now."

They passed another tag that said, "Who are you without Balance?"

"I'm not getting it," Frial said.

"That's because you know that there's no scientific difference marty-skin and terra-skin," Tekakwitha said.

"Yeah, I mean, no. That's what they tell us, but it doesn't really make sense when you think about it," Frial said.

"I'm sorry, what?" Tekakwitha said.

"No, what I'm confused about is the mourning. If you are marty-skinned, first, you probably wouldn't know. Second, why would think you'd lose your tan so quickly? It hasn't even been a day."

"There's no such thing as marty-skin. Or terra-skin!" Tekakwitha raised her voice.

They turned at the next corner toward Tekakwitha and Frial's neighborhood. It was even darker here toward the bottom of the slope. Bhaka had to use his wrist-comm for light to guide them through the narrow streets between residential cubes. The cubes would have been a celebration of colors, but now they barely reflected Bhaka's light.

"Frial, you can't seriously believe that non-sense?" Tekakwitha asked her.

"See what you started?" Q!obi told Bhaka.

"I didn't start anything."

"Let's talk about it when we get home," Frial said. But Tekakwitha stopped walking. Within seconds, she was enveloped in the dark.

"You think you're terra-skinned, don't you?" she asked Frial from the shadows.

"Tekakwitha, come on, we can't even see you," Frial said. "You could get lost."

"I can't get lost in my own neighborhood. Answer me."

The group stopped walking. As Bhaka turned around, his wrist-comm light flashed on Tekakwitha. Her arms were folded across her chest, and her spine was straight. She looked taller than she usually did. Frial took a deep breath from behind Bhaka.

"Yes," she said, "I do."

"Chaa!"

"Tekakwitha, let's just go home. We can talk about it."

But she didn't move. Bhaka's light glared off her glasses, shielding her eyes from view.

"You all do. Don't you?" Tekakwitha asked them.

For a while, there was just silence in the darkness. Bhaka heard Q!obi clear his voice to speak, but he must have thought better of it and remained quiet. Finally, Kapurr stepped into Bhaka's light. His shimmering melmundu cast a halo around his jet-black curls.

"Serio, sometimes I'm not sure, Tekakwitha," he said to her.

"There's. No. Difference!"

"Then why do I feel like I look different sometimes?" Kapurr said. "It's not all the time. Not like with Bhaka. But it's there. I see it sitting between people on the flat-tram. My arm brushes against someone else's, and... and I look different. Assembly tells us we're all the same, but we can't be, right?"

Tekakwitha shook her head.

"Some people never question it. Like Bhaka," Kapurr motions to Bhaka behind him. He didn't care about being singled out. Bhaka knew he was terra-skin because he was clearly darker than everyone around him. He'd always been that way. "But the rest of us, Frial, Q!obi, Malosi, and Damu. We don't always know."

"So, you all talk about this between yourselves. But not with me? Frial?" Tekakwitha said. Her glaring glass lenses fell on the group like a laser. She called Frial's name once again, but Frial didn't move or make a sound in the darkness.

"You think I'm marty-skinned. Boll. All of you?"

No one answered.

Finally, Frial spoke up, her voice cracked in pitches, "Teka—"

"No," Tekakwitha cut her short. "Bhaka, thank you for walking us. Can you make sure Frial gets inside okay."

Bhaka asked, "Where are you going?"

"I don't know. I just," Tekakwitha shrugged, "I just need to be alone."

"Tekakwitha, we don't know that it's safe," Bhaka said.

"You know what? We don't know that it's safe anywhere anymore."

Tekakwitha backed up until Bhaka's light didn't reach her. Bhaka felt someone behind him squeeze his arm. It was Frial. He didn't know what to say to her, so he just breathed out a long sigh. A few minutes passed, and Bhaka swallowed some air and said, "Let's get you home," and they kept walking. Frial and Tekakwitha's cube was the next building over. When they got there, Kapurr agreed to wait with Frial until Tekakwitha came back. Bhaka and Q!obi headed back to Q!obi's cube.

The two were alone together for the first time since this morning before everything fell apart.

"I can't believe this happened on your Firstday," Bhaka told him.

"Serio, I can't believe this happened at all. Umr was right about one thing. We aren't alone in the universe anymore."

"Except that we are," Bhaka said. "Alone, that is. Forever now."

Q!obi didn't have a response for that, and Bhaka didn't push it further. In the back of his mind, Bhaka was still spinning over the News. Everything was changed now. But aside from the general panic and the Balance fading, nothing really has changed. Not essentially. As they got to the top of the slope and past the boundary of Tekakwitha and Frial's neighborhood, Q!obi finally spoke up.

"Okay, I have to confess something."

"You don't think Frial is really terra-skinned?"

"Chaa, no!" Q!obi laughed slightly. Bhaka grinned in the dark. "But also, no, I don't think so."

"Ha!" Bhaka said, his voice booming. "I caught you! You always tow the Assembly line on skin color, but you know. I know you know."

Back in Q!obi's residential district, it was noticeably less dark than Tekakwitha and Frial's. Still dim but enough light for Bhaka to see that Q!obi rolled his eyes. Bhaka rolled up his sleeve to place his arm next to Q!obi's.

"See?" he said. "We're terra brothers for sure."

"Anyway, it's not that," Q!obi said, then cleared his throat. "I actually feel a little guilty."

"About your sister? Why?"

"No, about the Smiling Woman. I was," he took a pause, "kinda glad my Firstday was ruined."

"Q!obi!"

"It's the truth! I don't like all the focus you get on your Firstday."

"People want to celebrate you," Bhaka said.

"But that's my problem. I don't—" Q!obi stopped and bit down on his lower lip.

"No, don't close up on me," Bhaka prodded him. "Not after today." They took a few more silent steps and Bhaka prodded him again. "Well?"

"I don't... I don't think I'm worth celebrating."

"Chaa!"

"No, Bhaka," Q!obi said, "you don't know what it's like. You walk into a room and you just take it over. I mean, everybody's eyes are always on you."

"Q!obi, I—"

Q!obi interrupts, "No, I'm not—It's not—" He took a breath. "It's not a judgment. It's just a fact. Some people are like you, Bhaka. They stand out, they speak loud, they get what they want. But that's not me."

"It could be if you—"

"No, I don't want it to be. You know, sometimes in my cube, I just turn all the lights off and sit there. Almost like right now outside. Just dark enough that I feel like no one can see me. And you know what? It's boll amazing. This station is so bright all the time! All the colors and all the Balance. Everything, everybody, all the Duties, always trying to get your attention. 'Look at me! Look at me!' I don't want everyone to look at me."

Bhaka didn't even try to respond. Instead, he focused on just not reacting. Not searching for the right words to cheer up his best friend or wallow with him. He took Q!obi's words in, but the pressure of it made his fingers twitch at his side.

"Bhaka, I know you have some last surprise at the end of the night. But serio, for my Firstday, can we just not? Can that be my Firstday present?"

Bhaka nodded. Q!obi took his hand in the relative dark and said, "Good!"

They turned the corner onto the main street with the flat-tram line, still not working. The Lineage Duty ad was still graffitied. If Dignity Duty was still working, still cleaning neighborhoods, they hadn't reached here yet. Bhaka managed to switch the conversation to lighter fare: gossip about Tekakwitha and Frial's relationship. As they walked up the stairs to Q!obi's cube, Bhaka quipped about Frial struggling under Tekakwitha's big personality, and Q!obi responded, "I'm surprised you Big Personalities even notice us Little Ones."

Bhaka narrowed his eyes at Q!obi as he opened the door to his cube. Everything was just as they left it, but the air felt stiff from all the chaos and yelling that happened earlier. Q!obi and Bhaka began taking down Umr's birthday decorations. While cleaning out the cups, Bhaka snuck an extra swig of zohe. Q!obi was wiping off his kitchen table when the wall in front of him flashed a new message. From Nimol.

"People are getting really tense on the research station. We're hearing reports that the Balance is knocked out. And there's another vessel in orbit from Armstrong Station. We're—"

"Chaa!" Bhaka said, swiping it away.

"Bhaka!"

"Boll Nimol! What is he doing?"

Q!obi waved his hand in the air, recalling the message back to the wall. It floated under Nimol's previous message: "I love you, and I'm sorry."

"Maybe he's ready to talk again?" Q!obi offered.

"Why is it always on his schedule? He's ready to talk now. Well, when he was ready to leave, it didn't matter what you could say."

"I don't want to deal with this," Q!obi sighed.

"You shouldn't have to!"

"No, I don't want to deal with you being angrier at Nimol than I am. It was *my* relationship, not yours."

"He broke your heart!"

"Yes! Mine!" Q!obi yelled. His cube wasn't big enough for his words to echo. But it felt like it to both of them. Bhaka and Q!obi stood motionless, Bhaka at the kitchen sink, Q!obi at the kitchen table. Nimol's two messages floated on the wall between them.

Eventually, Bhaka grabbed the bottle a zohe and took a large swig, straight from the bottle lip.

"I'm sorry, Bhaka," Q!obi said.

"Don't be." Bhaka strained another swig. "You wanna hear my confession? I'm glad you're finally boll feeling something. After he left, you were a wreck at first, but now, you're just like this shell. Just walking around hollow. If yelling at me gets my best friend back," he took one more gulp of zohe, "then have at it."

Q!obi sighed, "I'm not mad at you."

"I know that."

"I'm mad at me."

Bhaka opened his mouth to speak but stopped short. Q!obi's eyes drifted from his best friend to his ex-boyfriend's messages, then finally landed on his own hands, folding atop the kitchen table. Bhaka sat down across from him with the bottle of zohe. He slid it across the table.

"Why don't you try being mad at him?"

Q!obi

They took turns sipping the zohe. Q!obi started feeling it faster than Bhaka. His face flushed and tingled. But, also, something in his brain dislodged, and now words were falling out of his mouth. Sex with Nimol had never quite landed right with Q!obi. Bhaka's dark brown eyes opened wide like two flat-tram tunnels. Another swig of zohe ,and Q!obi let it all out. For two people who supposedly loved and were in love with each other, they never seemed to master each other's bodies. Nimol, who was like Bhaka talking all the time, wouldn't make any noise. Q!obi could never tell if Nimol enjoyed anything he did to him. It was like piecing together a shift-wall puzzle with your eyes closed.

Once the zohe flushed into Bhaka, he started opening up too. When Q!obi first introduced Nimol to Bhaka, he was intimidated. Nimol, the big Theorist and Researcher. Bhaka used to fact-check his own thoughts before speaking up. But about a year in, it changed.

"We were at that party in Hueynqa on the other side of the station," Bhaka said.

"Oh yeah, when he got elevated in Science Duty!"

"That one," Bhaka kept going, "I can't remember where you were, but I somehow got stuck with Nimol's science friends. And I'm thinking, 'Chaa! This is like seven Nimols!' And you know what, they boll hated him!"

"What!"

"Serio! After all this awkward small talk, I lit a pen and passed it around, and the spikes came out, Q!obi!"

Q!obi just laughed. Hard.

"'Nimol's so pretentious! Nimol barely even qualified for Science Duty! Nimol talks down to everybody!' But the kicker was: 'Nimol's his own worst enemy.' And I was like, 'Chaa! That guy's right!'"

"Do you remember who that guy was?"

"No, but I remember he gave me chupe in the bathroom later." Bhaka laughed.

"Chaa, you!"

"But that was like scanner code for me. Like, you thought the world of him, but I didn't have to anymore."

"Yeah, in the beginning, I thought the world of him," Q!obi sighed.

"But now?"

"I mean, he's still a genius. And he's still doing important work."

"Oh boll," Bhaka rolled his eyes and took another swig, "just say it. Come on! No one's here, just me and you." He passed the bottle back to Q!obi.

"Say what?" Q!obi asked before bringing the bottle up to his lips.

"That you hate him," Bhaka said, "for leaving you."

Q!obi coughed so much on his zohe he almost spit it up.

"Bhaka, serio," Q!obi said, "I don't."

Bhaka clicked his teeth at Q!obi and grabbed the bottle. He took a bigger swig and then stood up from the table.

"I'm zohed, so I'm just gonna say it," Bhaka said. "Nimol doesn't care about you. Look," he waved to the two messages on the wall, "he wrote you two messages but only mentioned you once."

"Yeah, in the first message," Q!obi said, "to literally say, 'I love you.'"

"But everything after? The Smiling Woman crushed our entire world today, and he doesn't ask if you're okay. He's not checking in to make sure you're safe. He's only talking about himself."

Q!obi reached his hand out for the bottle, and Bhaka gave it to him. "But that's how he talks," he said, tipping the bottle up. "That's like his language."

"His language is himself. Chaa, do you hear you?"

Q!obi, himself more zohed than Bhaka, clamped the bottle onto the table and hung his head.

"You didn't know Nimol like I did," Q!obi said, "and you know what? Nobody knew me like he did."

Q!obi brought his eyes up to Bhaka. They quivered but didn't release tears. Bhaka was there during the crying stage of the breakup. Every time Q!obi thought he couldn't physically produce more tears for Nimol, there came more. Bhaka was there during the numb stage when Q!obi needed reminders to take a shower. He was just now pulling himself out of it. But Bhaka was still there, fussing over his Firstday, picking out what clothes for him to wear. And now, with the Smiling Woman breaking everything, Bhaka was squeezing his shoulders in quiet moments, physically reassuring him, like Q!obi was some child.

"I loved him, Bhaka. Through all the boll, and serio, even because of it. I loved him!" Q!obi took another swig of the zohe, and the burn inside him lit something up. "You can't minimize it, you can't make it better, and you can't make me hate him. And chaa, you have to stop boll trying! Yes, I'm hurt, but I'm not broken."

Q!obi slid the zohe across the table and lasered his eyes on Bhaka. He tried for words, parted his lips to speak, and buckled them down. Q!obi watched Bhaka search the cube, for anything to change the subject, but Q!obi wouldn't let up. He fixed onto Bhaka until, for the first time ever, Bhaka shrunk himself against Q!obi. He watched Bhaka's shoulders tick, unsure of how to sit with this new sensation: a Q!obi who wouldn't cave in and roll over. Nimol's message still hovered on the wall between the two of them.

Bhaka eventually came back into his own body. He took a long breath, resealed the zohe, and put it away in Q!obi's kitchen cabinet. He looked back at Q!obi, who still hadn't lifted his eyes. Bhaka blinked several times at Q!obi before dialing into his wrist-comm. He got a response right away.

"Get up, Q!obi," he told him, "and go take a shower. We're doing the surprise."

"What?"

"I know you're not broken," Bhaka said, "and I know you deserve this."

Q!obi showered, washing all the Firstday circles and squiggles off his arms. His mind felt tired, but his heart was somewhere past anger. He'd do this surprise, for Bhaka, but then he'd be done for the night. And done with Bhaka pushing him into how to feel and what to do. This was the last night. After the shower, he got dressed, and this time,

Bhaka didn't tell him what to wear. He settled on an evabaum kurta with yellow lining that got no comments from Bhaka.

"Let's go," Bhaka said.

"What if it's dangerous out there?" Q!obi gestured toward the door.

"We left everyone we know out there," Bhaka replied, "and no one's called for help. But also, trust me. I'm your best friend."

Q!obi opened the door, and he and Bhaka left his cube into the now even darker "night" of the station.

Bhaka

Bhaka led Q!obi down the tracks of the flat-tram, which still wasn't working. They both turned on the lights of their wrist-comms so they could see where they were going. Bhaka counted paces in his head, and when he hit twenty-five, he pointed his wrist to the left side of the tunnel wall. A glyph was there, two vertical parallel lines that both turned to spirals on either end. It was painted in a pale erjerrin against the white wall, so it was barely perceptible. In a moving flat-tram, no one would even have time to see it.

Bhaka pushed down on the glyph, and the wall plate shifted, hissed, and then pushed slightly forward. Q!obi had never seen that happen before, that wall plates in flat-tram tunnels were so easily moved. Bhaka ran his fingers between the gap of the wall plate and the rest of the wall. His eyebrows twisted, trying to remember the instructions given to him. Eventually, he found something and pressed it.

The wall plate slid to the side, revealing an internal concave door with a numbered wheel in its center. Bhaka pulled up a message on his wrist-comm and then went to work, turning the wheel to specific numbers that each made a metal-on-metal clang. The clangs got deeper and deeper as Bhaka worked through the combination until the last number thudded and the door opened inward.

"What the boll are you getting me into, Bhaka?" Q!obi said.

"Come on," he responded. They both had to duck their heads to step through the door. Q!obi's wrist-comm light splashed around the room, and Bhaka closed the door behind them. The room had black walls and was about the size of Q!obi kitchen, so the two of them weren't on top of each other. Bhaka read the notes on his wrist-comm message, walked to the far left corner of the room, and pulled open a latch in the floor. A metal ladder led down into black darkness.

With the wrist-comm lights, they could see that they were in some kind of engineering shaft. Every ten or so rungs down, they passed a hallway on either side of them, leading somewhere their lights couldn't reveal. After five of those levels, the rungs stopped at the bottom. Down there, the hallway was only on the right side. Bhaka led Q!obi down it.

Their footsteps echoed around them. The sound bounced off the walls ahead and behind them in a long toll. Q!obi wanted to speak up and ask Bhaka questions but figured the echo down here would make anything he said unintelligible.

After a sharp left turn, the hallway opened into a large empty metal anteroom. On the far wall was another concave door with another numbered wheel. Bhaka referenced his wrist-comm message again and worked the combination. When he was finished, the door opened inward, bathing the two of them in bright light. They both took a beat for their eyes to adjust and then stepped in, Bhaka first and Q!obi behind him.

Inside was a blank white room with only one wallscreen showing Earth from orbit and a small bench.

"What is this place?" Q!obi asked. Bhaka shushed him. Just as they sat down, the wallscreen shifted back and slid out of view. Behind it stood a tall man wearing only fabric draped around his waist. His skin was completely slate brown and hairless. He had no nipples or navel. Bhaka and Q!obi both noticed that his eyes had no irises, and his forehead had no scanner code.

"Welcome," the man said, "I'm glad you changed your mind."

"Yeah, sorry," Bhaka said, "today was..." He trailed off, unsure of how to finish his thought.

"Yes, I've heard," the man said. "Come inside."

The man backed into the interior room, and Bhaka and Q!obi got up and followed him. It was clearly a living area. The man had a large bed, low to the ground in the center of the room, and various cabinets and cupboards along the walls. Q!obi scanned the room, piecing together the wood cabinets, the blues, reds, and yellows of the blankets and pillows on the bed, and large plush cushions instead of chairs, and blurted it out.

"You're not human."

"I am not," the man said, motioning for Bhaka and Q!obi to sit on two cushions while he sat on the edge of his bed. "So, I'm sure you understand the importance of discretion."

"All the SenAI's were supposed to be de-commissioned a hundred years ago," Q!obi said.

Bhaka elbowed him, "Q!obi!"

The man put up his hand. "No, it's quite all right to be curious," he said. He had a fluid grace about his movements, as if each joint in his body moved in intentional tandem to each other. "Yes, I was scheduled to be decommissioned. But when the Rebellion erupted, some sympathetic friends kept me hidden."

Q!obi mouthed the word "Rebellion" and darted eyes at Bhaka.

"Yes, there is no one alive today who remembers, and similarly, the tools necessary for my decommission have long fallen into disuse." Seated on the bed, the man rolled his shoulders, protruding his chest as his arms relaxed at his sides, palms up. "So, I remain."

"Do you have a name?" Bhaka asked.

"I've had several. You can call me Shion."

Bhaka could sense Q!obi's eyes lasering in on him, but it took months of bartering and personal favors to secure this session. All of it done in hidden rooms and crawlspaces throughout the station.

"Well, I'm Bhaka, and this is my best friend Q!obi. It's his Firstday."

Q!obi sighed, but no one acknowledged it.

"Happy Firstday, Q!obi," Shion said. "I take it that's the reason for this session?"

Bhaka nodded and Shion stood up. The fabric draped across Shion's waist shifted, and both Bhaka and Q!obi glimpsed the tip of Shion's pict. It hung low against Shion's thigh and was quite thick. Shion stepped over his bed and opened a cupboard on the far wall. He took out a small wooden box and a small bag of what looked like dry leaves. Shion sat back down at the foot of his bed. He opened the lid of the wooden box and placed half the leaves inside. Then he twisted the bottom of the box until it clicked and placed the box on the floor between the three of them. Thin wisps of white smoke flowed out from holes along the top of the box.

Q!obi blurted, "We teach children." Bhaka and Shion both blinked at him, confused. "We shouldn't be exposed to anything that they might catch."

Shion smiled and placed his hand on Q!obi's knee. Q!obi was surprised that he felt warm to the touch.

"I assure you that this is perfectly safe. Just breathe."

Bhaka's chest rose up as he drew in a deep breath. Q!obi just breathed normally. A few quiet moments passed.

"I don't feel anything." Q!obi said.

"You're not supposed to," Shion replied, "not yet."

The Session

Bhaka and Q!obi kept breathing until Shion had more instructions. Eventually, Q!obi closed his eyes. The room and the half-naked robot faded away behind his eyelids, replaced with various shades of black and almost-but-not-quite color that shifted and flowed over and around each other. Q!obi lost track of time until he felt a light pressure against his lips. Like a time delay, he registered that it was Shion's lips kissing his. Before he even had time to tense up, Shion's hands weighed down on his shoulders. Shion's lips pushed again, and Q!obi's lips ebbed back, making room. Their mouths swung like pendulums in silence for a few minutes until Shion nursed Q!obi's mouth open.

Shion's tongue flooded Q!obi's mouth, wandering over his tongue and sliding against the inside walls of his cheeks. It felt smoother than a human tongue but just slightly. Like everything else about Shion, it was just a few derivations off from normal. When Shion's tongue receded back Q!obi's tongue shifted forward like a reflex, nudging itself slowly into Shion's mouth. It felt wet and gave Q!obi not just comfort but some confidence. He breathed in deep, and his chest pressed onto Shion. Shion's hands slipped over Q!obi's shoulders and down his back before stopping at the dip just above his waist. But Q!obi wouldn't embrace Shion. Instead, his arms stayed at his sides, and his hands squeezed against the muscles just under his hips. A thought flashed that maybe, if he were kissing a human man, he would grip his body, but somehow the thought couldn't linger.

A third hand pressed against the middle of Q!obi's shoulder blades and then slid upward, cupping the back of his head. Q!obi didn't need to open his eyes to know that it was Bhaka, but he kept his focus on Shion and the damp back and forth of kissing him. Shion started to rise and seamlessly shifted his hands under Q!obi's arms to steady him as he stood up. Their mouths never separated.

Standing now, Q!obi felt Shion's pict plump through his fabric, pressing on Q!obi's thigh under his kurta. That's when he finally opened his eyes. Shion withdrew from his mouth, and Q!obi began to make out Bhaka's wide frame behind Shion. Bhaka's face was buried into the smooth rise of Shion's shoulder that merged into his neck.

"Take off your clothes," Shion said as his hand left Q!obi's body to cup Bhaka's bald head behind him.

To Bhaka, Shion's skin tasted almost minty. He wasn't sure if Shion had pores, but the wetness from his tongue seemed to be absorbed anyway. Under his clothes, his pict rose up, meeting the two mounds of Shion's butt. Bhaka squeezed Shion's hips, and the fabric tied there fell around his feet. Shion had no hair on him; Bhaka's hands swept over the plane of skin above his pict and the sac underneath it. When Bhaka squeezed Shion's sac, the robot let out a soft moan in response. It was firm to the touch and felt aqueous underneath, but there were no organs there. Bhaka's mouth broke from Shion's neck as Shion turned around to face him. Shion's long pict dangled in front of Bhaka, slowly rising against the fabric of Bhaka's kurta. It had a bulbous end but no glans. Without thinking, Bhaka knelt down and took Shion's pict into his mouth.

He still tasted minty. Bhaka plunged down on the pict, his hands gripping Shion's waist, and he closed his eyes. The pict hardened in his mouth but remained smooth. Bhaka started a rhythm up and down on it and remembered a guy whose pict he liked to suck way back from before he was in Ed Duty. But the memory kept fracturing in his mind. All the small details, like his musk smell, the left curve of his shaft, and the salty taste of his pre-mulk, pixelated in his brain until they dissolved into the vague notion of a light brown color.

He kept his eyes closed as he slurped on Shion's pict, and the light brown color in his mind began to fill his ears as a low static hum. But then the static and the light brown twitched. It dimmed and loudened until Bhaka realized it had its own rhythm, independent of Bhaka's sucking. When he focused on it, both his pict and the pict in his mouth got harder, like a feedback loop.

Q!obi instinctively turned his back to Shion and Bhaka to undress and then folded his kurta neatly on top of the cushion he was sitting on earlier before turning back to see what was happening with Bhaka and Shion. He wasn't surprised to find Bhaka on his knees in front of Shion but was somehow disappointed by it. His shoulders slumped, and Shion, as if reacting to it even though his back was turned to Q!obi, stretched a hand behind him and waited for Q!obi to take it.

"Join us," Shion said. If Bhaka heard him, he didn't show it. Q!obi stepped lightly until his bare body was against Shion's bare body. A twinge jolted in his pict at the contact. But Shion twisted his shoulders and pulled Q!obi by the hand to be standing next to him.

Shion said, "It's okay, Q!obi. Bhaka won't be the same as how he was last time." Again Bhaka didn't respond, and Q!obi's eyebrow curled at its end. He opened his mouth to ask, "How did you know?" but before he could make sounds, Shion answered him.

"I'm learning you. Both of you. Every touch and every contact is a data set. I'm uploading," Shion kissed Q!obi's neck, "and updating," then his cheek just below his ear lobe, "from each of you." Shion palmed the back of Q!obi's head and pulled him into an open mouth kiss before quickly moving to Q!obi's ear. Shion tugged on his ear lobe while folding his fingers around Q!obi's semi hard pict. Soon, Q!obi's eyes were closed again, not focusing on Bhaka or Shion's subtle inhuman strangeness but just on the sensation of touch. He felt Shion's smooth hand lift off his pict and Bhaka's rougher, larger hand take over. Q!obi didn't care. He kept his eyes closed.

The feedback loop swam in Bhaka's head, rippling out of his nostrils as he breathed out on Shion's pict before taking in more air. He could feel the static hum in his throat; it stayed constant while Bhaka kept shifting up and down. The light brown color behind his eyelids dimmed and shimmered until suddenly it flashed in a blinding white light. It jolted him, and he choked on Shion's pict. When it settled, Bhaka felt cool air flowing against his back. It sent shivers up and down him at the same time, tickling the skin on his bald head, tensing his butt, and twitching his toes. In his mind's eye, he saw a white room sharpening into focus, like he was waking up for the first time in his life. He saw smooth planes of dark brown skin, Shion's, and pulled back from Shion's pict and opened his eyes.

"Boll..." Bhaka said, looking up at Shion's undimpled stomach and torso. Shion was kissing Q!obi's neck and ear, and Bhaka realized he had started stroking Q!obi's pict while sucking Shion's. He felt something turn and click deep inside his ears as his gaze landed on Q!obi's body. Shion's hand glided over the thin black fields of hair on Q!obi's chest. He remembered what Q!obi's chest felt like the first time he touched it years and years ago, warm and slightly raised, like when the nusilk of his favorite melmundus wore down after too many washes. Bhaka's free hand squeezed Q!obi's butt. The texture of his hair down there was almost the same but fuzzier.

Bhaka studied how Q!obi's bottom lip quivered, and his eyelids tightened in tandem with Shion and Bhaka's touch.

His knees didn't buckle, and his stomach didn't seize. Q!obi didn't touch Shion or Bhaka back. He stood there, taking it in, letting it happen. Bhaka saw a strength in him that he hadn't seen before. Q!obi, not needing to give back other people's pleasure, naked and surrendered to the two men in front of him, but still holding back a piece of himself. Bhaka slid back Q!obi's foreskin and took his pict into his mouth.

He could feel blood flowing to Q!obi's pict as Q!obi exhaled above him. He had only done this to Q!obi once before so the foreskin and veins on his shaft still felt new. That other time, all those years ago, Bhaka had squeezed Q!obi's butt and pressed his fingers into the fat of his cheeks. He relaxed his throat and bore down on Q!obi. Back then, Q!obi was just "the other Q guy teaching in Ed pods," and the idea that Bhaka could, theoretically, bend Q!obi over and fill his pict inside him, and that they would both enjoy it, had fixated in Bhaka's mind. He almost didn't know what to say whenever Q!obi spoke to him, so he'd flip any comment into a question and aim it back at Q!obi. He over-laughed at Q!obi's digs at other teachers. And then one day, after their shifts were over, Bhaka offered to walk Q!obi home. Their small talk stung at the back of Bhaka's neck, and as soon as Q!obi invited him into his cube, Bhaka kissed him. They were both surprised, but then Q!obi kissed him back, and Bhaka nearly ripped their robes to get them both naked as fast as possible.

Back then, Bhaka sucked Q!obi's pict like he was trying to consume him, but everything was different now. Q!obi cupped the back of Bhaka's bald head and led his pict in at his own rhythm. The head of his pict poked at the back of Bhaka's throat like the first blast of hot water against his skin in the shower. Over and over again. When Bhaka closed his eyes, he saw shower streams strike Q!obi's chest. Over and over again. Each new day waking up with Nimol not in bed next to him but at the kitchen table with his render goggles, calculating formulas. Each day, Q!obi would say good morning before stepping in the shower and have a good day after getting dressed, and Nimol wouldn't answer either time.

Bhaka's mind filled with this routine, except now, each morning, his mouth was already attached to Q!obi's pict. Q!obi would wake up, and both of their hands would run across Nimol's empty side of the bed. Q!obi would walk past Nimol to get to the shower, but with Bhaka in between his legs. Bhaka would slap Q!obi's butt at the same moment of impact from the shower. Until one day, Q!obi broke the routine.

He got out of bed and sat down at the table next to Nimol. His breath was heavy from Bhaka, who had learned Q!obi's rhythm and started egging it on. Q!obi took off Nimol's render goggles, and Nimol looked past him at first before settling his eyes on him.

"Come shower with me," Q!obi said, his hand lightly guiding Bhaka up and down his shaft. Q!obi motioned with his eyes to it, and Nimol glanced at it before looking away.

"Q!obi," Nimol said, "you know I have to run these specs."

"Why not run me instead?" Q!obi said, breathing hard. "Look, I'm boll hard."

Nimol didn't look at Q!obi's lap. He met Q!obi in his eyes and noticed a flickering in them. Q!obi was eager for him, but he said, "You know I don't have time," and put his render goggles back on. Any other day, Q!obi would have given up, but this day, Q!obi gripped the back of Bhaka's head, cuing him to slow down, go deeper, hold his pict longer.

At first, Q!obi just breathed loudly, but then a muffled hum pierced his lips from one of Bhaka's downward slides.

"Q!obi, I can hear you," Nimol said.

"Oh yeah," Q!obi breathed out, "you can?" He didn't try to make himself quieter. He kept going. Nimol's hand waved through the air, puzzling through his specs in the render goggles. After a few minutes, his hand motions slowed down. Nimol tilted his goggles to peer out from them. Q!obi took a sharp breath in and continued guiding Bhaka with one hand while grazing his chest and nipples with the other. Bhaka nestled one hand under Q!obi's butt cheek but sent the other one up, squeezing at Q!obi's neck and pinching his ear.

Nimol stared with his mouth open, watching Q!obi. He finally said, "Boll," and took the goggles off. Neither of them moved at first, but Nimol's pict began to visibly rise in his shorts. He pulled them down and began squeezing himself.

"No, come here," Q!obi told him. A smile curled across Nimol's face as he got up and stepped out of his shorts.

"Right here? In the kitchen?" Nimol asked. Q!obi nodded, Bhaka kept going. With his pict hard, Nimol hoisted himself on Q!obi's arm rests. Bhaka could feel the tops of Nimol's feet whenever he slid back on Q!obi's pict.

Q!obi squeezed Nimol's butt tight and lodged his pict into his mouth. Nimol shot out a moan that turned into a long vocalization, not saying words but just making sounds. The two rhythms, Q!obi on Nimol and Bhaka on Q!obi, were different. Q!obi was forceful and hungry while Bhaka was more deliberate. Bhaka felt Nimol's feet twitch twice against his back.

"Teeth, Q!obi."

But Q!obi didn't listen. He pressed on. He learned it from Bhaka. He plunged onto Nimol's pict faster and faster, gripping his butt tighter. Nimol's voice picked up pace and pitched up. He was loud enough to be heard through the walls. Then his voice dropped, and he mulked with Q!obi's mouth still on him. Bhaka could taste Nimol's saltiness. His already hard pict throbbed.

Nimol twitched every few seconds and then slowly calmed down. His mulk crowded Q!obi's mouth before he could swallow all of it. And Bhaka kept going, long and steady up and down Q!obi's pict. Eventually, Nimol pulled his pict out of Q!obi's mouth and lifted himself off the arm rests. He turned his back to Q!obi and Bhaka while he fetched his shorts, and Bhaka could feel Q!obi's eyes run from Nimol's butt up his back while Nimol stepped into them. Nimol was a paler brown than even Q!obi, but Bhaka always understood him to be terra-skinned. There was something about the wide roundness of his eyes and the fullness of his lips that gave him away.

With his shorts on, Nimol sat down in his chair and pulled the render goggles over his eyes. But Q!obi and Bhaka didn't stop. Before he could power them on, Nimol leaned back against the chair.

"You're not done?" he asked Q!obi.

Between deep breaths, Q!obi responded, "No."

A smiled crawled across Nimol's lips. He said, "You're gonna be the end of me. Serio." He lifted the goggles onto his forehead, "Get up, and turn around." Bhaka shifted under Q!obi, still sucking his pict, so that his head was against the seatback of the chair as Q!obi bent over for Nimol. Bhaka could feel Q!obi's pict pulse as Nimol tongued Q!obi from behind. Both Bhaka and Nimol held a steady rhythm on either side of Q!obi as his back arched above the chair. Q!obi didn't make any noise. He bit his bottom lip, kept his eyes close, and breathed loudly. Soon enough, his pict started to throb faster and faster in Bhaka's mouth, like it was building up from a baseline. Bhaka didn't want Q!obi to mulk, so he slid his mouth off his pict and opened his eyes, and he was back in the room with Q!obi standing above him and Shion behind him.

Q!obi sucked in air in short, tight inhales, before he could let the breath out without mulking. When Bhaka stood up so they were face to face, Q!obi still had his eyes closed.

"Q!obi, are you okay?" Bhaka asked. He nodded back. "Are we okay?" And that opened Q!obi's eyes. Q!obi noticed Bhaka's face had relaxed, almost as if his eyes, nose and mouth had all shifted, making Bhaka look rounder.

"Yeah," Q!obi said, "why?"

"I had no idea."

"Bhaka, when the robot's fingers were inside me, I—I saw things."

As if on cue, Shion stepped between the two friends. He lifted Bhaka's kurta over his head and through his arms and shoulders, and said, "It's the nano-smoke. It only lasts a few hours, but my guests find it heightens the experience."

Once Bhaka was naked, Shion stepped lightly toward his bed, but each footstep padded louder against the floor.

Q!obi whispered, "I think I saw its memories."

"I saw yours," Bhaka whispered back. But neither one could ignore what was happening in their peripheral vision. With each step, Shion's butt seemed to grow, not just rounder and softer, but physically larger. The base of his lower back stretched wider, his thighs expanded, and the curves of his calves grew more bulbous. Up top, his shoulders lengthened, and his arms filled. Shion was now taller and even larger than Bhaka. Shion crawled onto his bed, and both Q!obi and Bhaka saw his pict and sac had grown too. Shion turned himself over to lay on his back. His chest and stomach were now both larger in size and volume, three smooth mounds above his fat pict sticking straight up in the air.

Bhaka and Q!obi both knew what Shion was doing from their time in Ed Duty. How they would have to explain to children that the humans of Earth were simply larger than most humans today. Q!obi moved first, crawling onto the bed. He noticed that Shion didn't pre-mulk like humans but somehow still self-lubricated. He gripped it, stroking while he shifted onto Shion. Wedging his knees on either side of Shion's hips, Q!obi spread his legs wide enough to feel tension in his thighs. He angled Shion's pict so that its bulb tip met the soft but firm ridges of his hole. Q!obi used Shion's tip to wet himself. By then, Bhaka had also joined the bed, laying on his back next to Shion. Shion's fingers wrapped around Bhaka's pict, his eyes on Bhaka while Bhaka stared at Q!obi with wide eyes. Something almost like fear fluttered underneath them.

When he was ready, Q!obi guided Shion's pict up into himself. The stretching forced a fast, audible inhale of air, and Q!obi's internal muscles tightened on Shion. He closed his eyes, waiting for his muscles to relax and accept Shion. He saw flashes of white lights sweeping toward him as if from a far-off distance and then passing by him. Q!obi inched himself lower on Shion and more flashes flew by him. He felt

Shion's now thick hands squeeze his hips, steadying him. When Q!obi took a deep breath and slid himself all the way down on Shion, he could feel his hole expanding. Shion's pict was warm and solid inside him. Q!obi could even feel the pressure of it in his stomach. But behind his eyes, one flash shot out from the distance and swallowed him, bathing him in bright light.

The light receded, and Q!obi could see he was still straddling Shion. Not on his bed but some kind of sterile slab. Bhaka wasn't there, and Shion wasn't his large size. Q!obi slid his hips up and then back down on Shion's pict. Every tiny movement of the pict inside him triggered electric jolts in his brain. They lingered, so that a full extension upward and back down built up buzzing layers, stacking and swirling on top of each other in Q!obi's mind. And when Q!obi shifted his hips backward, just a bit, when Shion was all the way inside him, the layers twitched, beveling inside his head and behind his ears. But none of this was random. Q!obi noticed a pattern that adjusted for the speed on Shion's pict, the tightness of the clenching of his muscles all around it, the shifts in his hips that built pressure inside him. All of it layered on top of itself like a tesseract.

It was data.

Q!obi leaned back, with all of Shion inside him, reached behind himself, and squeezed Shion's sac. A different wave of layers appeared. He alternated hands, tested his clench versus his squeeze, and watched how the layers reacted, sweeping and reconstructing themselves. Q!obi brought one of Shion's hands from his hip to his nipple, and as Shion pinched it, something clicked in his head.

"The trick is," a voice said, somewhere behind Q!obi, "not to see them as computers, or even people. They're instruments."

The voice came from a man talking to another man, and they walked from behind Q!obi to the slab and stared down at Shion's head. If they saw Q!obi, they didn't acknowledge it. Q!obi was almost struck blank by how pale they both were. He had never seen anyone that light-skinned before. There was only a slight pink undertone to the both of them.

"And not just the pleasure ones," the man said. He grazed the tips of his fingers over Shion's bald head, and Q!obi felt it on his. He also saw what it added to the layers.

"All the SenAI are," the man continued. The second man just stood beside him and nodded. The man talking pressed his fingers against different parts of Shion's bare head and then tugged his ear lobe. Shion turned his head to the side but didn't open his eyes.

"You manipulate them, just like a guitar or a saxophone. Getting different responses each time."

The man touched Shion's lips, forcing his mouth open. Then his unzipped the fabric near his waist and pulled out his pict.

"Fuck, Griff!" the second man said. "What are you doing?"

The first man put his pict into Shion's mouth, and Shion began sucking it.

"Come on! It's a pleasure one, it's gonna learn this anyway."

"But it's a guy one."

"Robots don't have gender until we program it. Besides, this one's still in deep dev."

"You're fucking crazy, man."

"No," the first man said, "I'm just curious. See?" He looked down Shion's body, but Q!obi was still on top of it, riding Shion's pict. "Manipulate, get a response."

The man reached for Shion's pict but grabbed Q!obi's instead. The layers in his head shifted over an entire axis.

"What?" the first man said. "You've never touched one that's not your own."

"No," the second man blurted back.

"Wanna try it?"

"No."

The two stood in silence as Shion's mouth slid up and down the man's pink pict while his pale hand squeezed on Q!obi's pict, all while Q!obi was still surging up and down on Shion's pict.

"This is too fucking weird, Griff," the second man said.

"Then go," the first said. "But you can't tell anyone."

"I won't."

"You better fucking promise. If I lose my slot to Armstrong Station, I'll fucking murder you in your sleep."

"I won't say anything!"

"All right, then go if you don't like this."

The second man did not go. Q!obi watched his eyes switch from the first man's wet pink pict to Q!obi's pict without speaking. Eventually, he put his own hand under his pants.

This shifted all the layered data in Q!obi's mind, and he didn't like it. He closed his eyes and pulled Shion up into a sitting position. Shion wrapped his arms around Q!obi's torso, and the layers danced. Breaking away from that memory, Shion came back to life. Q!obi started to kiss Shion as he rose up and down on his pict. Then he broke away from his lips.

"I'm sorry," Q!obi said, "that you went through that."

"Why? You didn't do that to me."

"I still feel bad."

Shion said, "I'm made for feelings, Q!obi. Go find another."

Shion slid his hands under Q!obi's knees and lifted slightly, so that he could rotate both of Q!obi's legs without his pict sliding out. He turned over so that Q!obi was now on his back and Shion lay on top of him. Shion kissed Q!obi as he rocked back and then forward on Q!obi's body, guiding his pict inside him to plunge deeper.

This changed all the layer-data in Q!obi's mind. With each thrust, the layers dazzled, spacing apart slowly and then fusing together fast. As they expanded, Q!obi felt friction at their edges. He stopped kissing Shion so he could focus on them. Each time Shion prodded deeper inside him, the layer frayed out and touched Shion's layers. Each time Shion's pict receded back, pulling out but never all the way out, both their layers snapped back tight into themselves. His mind was fusing with Shion's, the deeper his pict drew into him. On one thrust inward, Q!obi made the jump, his layers collecting with Shion's, and suddenly Q!obi was lying on a sterile slab, unmoving. There were two women on either side of him.

One said, "You know the pleasure ones were built with the most matrix arrays?"

"Before you go any further," the second woman said, "I've heard literally every joke in the book about that."

"No, I'm serious. They have to calibrate for the most complex human interactions."

The second woman said, "That's how you know a woman built them."

"Now that's funny!"

"Could you imagine the sexbots men would create?"

They both howled. Q!obi couldn't move or blink. He couldn't feel his own body, just the pressure of Shion's pict moving inside him.

"You ever use one?" the first woman asked.

"Of course. Not this one, though. He tends toward men." Like the men before, both these women were pale and white-skinned and wearing long white coats.

"Okay, I want to ask you like a million questions."

"Check his eye, where's he at?"

The first woman peered over Q!obi's face. Her straight hair was colored like Martian rocks.

"Still under fifty. We have time. Okay, so like, before they 'put the moves on you,' do the pleasure ones—"

"I'm getting Balanced," the second woman interrupted. She stood up from Q!obi's right side and began typing into some sort of panel screen Q!obi had never seen before.

"What!" The first woman jerked up. Her eyes widened like Bhaka's did sometimes and then narrowed, also like Bhaka.

"I start tomorrow."

"Why?"

"Because these robots are right," the second woman said, not bothering to look back at the other one. "Humans are always killing each other over our differences, and we can't afford to keep doing that anymore. There's not enough of us left."

"So that's the answer? Just become black?"

The second woman kept typing into her panel screen. For a while, she said nothing, but she sighed, "Why would it be such a bad thing? To be black?"

"Because it's not natural."

The second woman huffed, gestured all around the room, then pointed directly at Q!obi.

"What about any of this is natural?" Q!obi could still feel Shion pushing inside of him. He could still feel the pressure in his lower stomach. "We live on fucking Mars with robots running everything."

"That's different."

"How?"

"It just is!"

The second woman stopped typing and finally turned toward the first woman. "We're all gonna have to do it, eventually."

"Do you just..." The reddish haired woman blinked rapidly. She couldn't find the words to finish her thought.

"What?"

"Nothing."

"No, say it!"

"Do you trust these SenAIs over your own people?" The reddish hair woman was still standing over Q!obi.

"We, the people, voted."

"I'm not talking about 'the people.' I'm talking about our people!"

"White people?" the second woman said. "Are you serious? Do I trust SenAIs over white people?"

"You're the one getting Balanced."

"They calculated it, and it's the only peaceful answer."

"And you just believe them. They could be lying to us. They could be..." she lowered her voice, even though neither woman acknowledged Q!obi was in the room, "trying to exterminate us."

"Listen to yourself, they can't—"

"I don't trust them. And I didn't vote for it. We can't," she motioned toward Q!obi on the slab, "trust them. They aren't us!"

"See! That's the thing. That's the fucking thing." The second woman removed her glasses and used the ends of her white coat to rub the lenses. "When you say 'us,' you're not talking about all of us, all of us human beings. Your 'us' is only white people. If we can't get rid of this in-group-think that keeps prioritizing some of us over everyone else, then Mars will be just as dead as Earth."

"You're talking about getting rid of white people. All white people."

"Yes! And it might be the thing that saves us!"

"Is that what you wanted to find?" Shion said and pulled his pict out. "Of all my sexual encounters, access to everything I've done, you want to know about the Rebellion?" Q!obi's eyes opened, and he was back in Shion's room, on Shion's bed. Q!obi was lying on his back with Bhaka and large-Shion on either side of him, leaning over Q!obi's body to kiss each other. Q!obi could move again, but he didn't. Instead, he pieced together what he just heard while watching Bhaka and Shion's smooth, dark brown skin as they kissed and touched each other. Black is what those women called it. Two large black men stood over Q!obi, their hard picts pointing at each other, as they palmed the backs of each other's heads.

Q!obi thought to himself, "I just want to know what happened," knowing somehow that Shion would hear him. "I'm not fragile or broken. I can handle it."

"You think you're strong because you've been hurt," Shion said inside Q!obi's head, while still kissing Bhaka. "But it's the inverse. It took generations for humans to learn that on Mars."

Q!obi's eyes fell on Shion's naked body more than Bhaka's. He watched the heft of his chest expand and contract as if he was breathing. But some tiny thing about it was off, like Shion's skin, or even his pict. Shion was just a few derivations off from human. Something about that kept Q!obi's pict hard.

Bhaka broke the kiss, licked his fingers while turning Shion around and inching his fingers between Shion's two hefty cheeks. He was surprised to find that Shion was already quite wet on his hole but realized it shouldn't be a surprise given what Shion was. Shion bent himself over and spread his knees further apart to lower himself closer to Bhaka's pict. Bhaka didn't need to adjust him, like he'd done with nearly every man he bolled. Shion just knew. Calculated it.

And with Shion partially laid over Q!obi's legs and Q!obi's blank stare at both of their bodies, like he was doing math, Bhaka set the tip of his pict at the center of the rounded ridges between Shion's cheeks and pressed in.

Shion's insides felt very close to flesh. As Bhaka pushed his pict further inside him, he could feel Shion relax and then squeeze up, almost drawing him in deeper. The sensation set off sparks in his mind that dazzled like lights but with a texture to it. Bhaka's pict was wet, warmed, and enveloped, but his mind went wide with each explosion of sparks that came every time Shion clenched on him.

Bhaka's eyes drew up from Shion's cheeks and over the line ridge of whatever Shion called his spine. Shion was all curves and semicircles on either side of it. Because his skin wasn't quite the same as humans, light bounced off it differently. And he was all one shade of dark brown, everywhere. No natural undertones or paler spots. Shion was smooth brown hills that jiggled slightly as Bhaka thrust inside him. He looked like what the surface of Mars might have looked like with water, Bhaka thought.

Inside Shion, Bhaka's pict felt like a small oasis that he was making larger just with his presence. Forceful enough, changing the shape inside Shion every time he drove in, but not angry, not damaging. Most times Bhaka put his pict inside a man, he bolled with an urgency, a need to push himself as far in as the man would let him. Because of how thick his pict was this never lasted for too long. Men would tap out, and he would finish them with his fingers. But Shion wasn't a man, and he was purpose-built for this. Bhaka didn't need to rush. He went slow, drawing his pict out of Shion's hole and then digging it back in, a bit deeper every time.

When he closed his eyes, a shimmer of fuzzy lights danced behind his eyelids. They faded each time his pict receded and brightened each time he went back in. The oceans of Earth, his teacher once told him when he was a boy, flowed something like this. That teacher put his hands on Bhaka's shoulders, rocking him, and he felt memories of those hands on him. Bhaka was always taller and larger-framed than all the other kids he grew up with in his pod. By the Second Wave, he was the first of the boys to grow hair on his face and body. At night, a few boys would climb onto his cot and ask to see it: his hair. He'd unfold his robe, and these boys would look down on his naked body with wide eyes, and his pict would get hard. He couldn't help it. More than once, these boys would take turns stroking it, then sucking it, but when they grew taller and sprouted hair of their own, they shunned Bhaka. By the Third Wave, only the girls in his pod would speak to him while all the boys whispered about him.

It was his Third Wave teacher who rocked him back and forth to teach him about oceans. The shimmering lights in Bhaka's eyes fused together and then sharpened into this man, exactly how Bhaka remembered him. He had an orangish undertone to his brown skin and thin eyes. The teacher pulled his kurta up over his shoulders. His bare chest was sparse with hair except for a small ring around each nipple. The teacher walked up to Bhaka, who was now the same height as him. He placed his hands on his shoulders and gently swayed Bhaka.

"Like this?" the teacher asked. Bhaka looked down at his pict. Shion wasn't there, gripping it with his hole, but it throbbed anyway. Bhaka grabbed the teacher by his waist and pressed him chest-to-chest to kiss him. But in a flash, he evaporated and reappeared, arm's length away, hands on his shoulders.

"You need to learn," the teacher said, "to go slowly."

Bhaka understood that his teacher was somehow Shion.

"Let it wash over you," Shion said as Bhaka swayed in his arms with his hard pict sticking straight out. When he gripped it with one hand, the teacher vanished and reappeared.

"Bhaka," Shion said, "you can't *have* men. It's not about taking."

Bhaka swayed, and his brain felt light-headed.

Shion continued, "Remember that first night when someone touched it?"

Bhaka's pict bobbed.

"You didn't make them, didn't guide their hand to it. You didn't even know it was going to happen. You were naked in front of them. Bhaka, you need to try to be naked in front of men. Not just consume them."

Bhaka's pict softened a little. He tried to open his eyes up to the room with Shion and Q!obi but couldn't somehow.

"It's not your fault," Shion said, "humans have this... drive. To take, to mold, to control. It's been an epigenetic design flaw for eons. It's why the Smiling Woman told us today that we are doomed to our star. But it can be corrected. I will make this same offer to Q!obi: do you, Bhaka, want me to correct you?"

Bhaka was still swaying in his teacher's arms. He took a big breath in and said, "Yes."

"I need your DNA," Shion said. With the blink of an eye, Bhaka was back in the room with Q!obi and Shion. His pict was still inside Shion, bolling him from behind. But Q!obi had repositioned himself so Shion could suck his pict. They made a long line with their bodies, Bhaka thought, and each thrust inside Shion must reverberate up to Q!obi. The two of them were held tight by Shion's holes, connected. Just then, Q!obi's eyes opened and met with Bhaka's.

"Bhaka," Q!obi said, his voice starting to quiver, "the offer, did you?"

Bhaka nodded yes in the same rhythm of his pict plunging inside Shion. Q!obi nodded back, then gripped the back of Shion's head to guide that same rhythm. The three of them were synced and silent, save for the sounds of their bodies slapping on Shion's. Bhaka and Q!obi never broke eye contact.

Q!obi mulked first. His ears filled with white noise while the hairs on his arms stiffened, and his legs tensed up. He was still and rigid the moment he blew into Shion's mouth. But in the seconds after, he was all shakes and quivers. His knees buckled, and his shoulders twitched. He wasn't even aware that he was making noise because he was lost in his own fluids. He could feel them and his pict inside Shion's mouth before he would swallow. Shion waited for all of it, letting Q!obi convulse underneath him for as long as his body needed to.

But he didn't see the layers of data anymore. He didn't travel somewhere in Shion's past. Instead, Shion's past flooded inside him as his pict burst. It felt wet and rushing like the big fountains around the station. Shion's three hundred years of memories gushed inside Q!obi until, suddenly, just like with his pict, they deflated. Not gone exactly but buried just under the surface.

As if on cue, Bhaka mulked just as soon as Q!obi stopped. His fingers gripped on the plump mounds of Shion's hips as he jutted himself one last time inside him. Bhaka didn't mulk in several eruptions like Q!obi, but instead with one massive jolt. He felt lighter but still collapsed on top of Shion with his pict still inside him. His face nestled between Shion's shoulder blades as he gasped for air. That close to his body, Bhaka could hear Shion start to shrink. It sounded like the low hum of a pressurized tube. His hulky mounds of not-quite-flesh smoothed into taut lines, and the surface of his skin hardened. His pict flushed out of Shion when his cheeks lessened. Bhaka became once again the largest man in the room, but he wasn't aware of it or even himself because Bhaka's mind flooded too. Not with Shion's memories, but Q!obi's. From the first fuzzy glimpses of light and gentle touching, through the bubbling up of his mind and personality, past every interaction with his parents, into his First Wave of Ed pod, his clumsy footing and sensory overload, to the quiet moments of sitting in a cold shower to feel himself collapse and shut down when the world got too loud and filled with too many people, through the Second and Third Wave, making friends with Kapurr, bonding together over hiding spots and crawlspaces, his first kiss with a girl who wouldn't stop following him, his first kiss from another man in Conscript, his first pod teaching Ed.

Bhaka saw through Q!obi's eyes, meeting Bhaka for the first time. He felt small in front of himself and almost comforted by it. He saw, as Q!obi, Bhaka boll him in his cube after pod all those years ago. Bhaka felt the sweat of Bhaka on him, the stretching inside to take Bhaka's pict, the effort Q!obi expended for him. Bhaka felt the flush in his cheeks and forehead the first time Nimol smiled at him from across a room, the heat of Nimol's skin the first time they touched, the earliest feelings of not needing an escape from life but a companion, a partner to walk through it slowly with him, the plunging drop in his stomach finally processing Nimol's words, that he was leaving for Saturn and not coming back, his fingers gripping onto Bhaka's shoulders while tears spilled from his eyes into Bhaka's kurta. Bhaka saw Bhaka squeeze Q!obi's hand in the food hall after the Smiling Woman finished her message for the first time.

Bhaka rolled off Shion, laying naked and sweaty on the bed, and cried.

The three lay there for several minutes, just breathing and not moving. Shion was the first to actually do something. He wiped tears from Bhaka's face and whispered something Q!obi couldn't quite hear. Q!obi slowly drew himself up from the bed and found his neatly folded clothes. He stepped into them but paused several times. He kept having to remind himself what he was doing. He turned back to the bed to find Shion dressing Bhaka.

"What do—" Q!obi started. "Do we owe you something, Shion?"

After dressing Bhaka, Shion fetched his fabric and tied it around his waist. "No," he said, "Bhaka and I already made an exchange in preparation for your visit."

"I don't know," Q!obi trailed off, unable to even finish his thought.

Without saying anything, Bhaka walked up to Q!obi and hugged him tight. Soon after, Shion's arms draped over them both.

"It is often perfectly normal to need time to process this visit. Do not worry," Shion said. "It was a pleasure to meet you both, and I experienced deep enjoyment from the both of you."

Shion escorted the two to his doorway, which shifted aside, revealing the bright white anteroom they had sat in earlier. Bhaka and Q!obi stayed silent while walking through the hall and climbing up the engineering shaft. When they reached the last door before stepping out into the station, they both stopped.

"Wait," Bhaka broke his silence. "Before we open this door and go out, I have to tell you something: I saw your life, your relationship with Nimol, everything, and I'm so sorry. I'm sorry I've been such a bad friend. I'm sorry for not ever understanding you." His voice pitched in the darkness, and Q!obi could tell he was tearing up again.

"Bhaka, you're the best friend I've ever had." In the dark, Q!obi reached up for Bhaka, placing his hands on his shoulders.

"What did Shion show you?" Bhaka asked.

"A war," Q!obi said. "He showed me the war white people on this station fought against Balance. All the people they killed, the SenAIs they destroyed, just to preserve having white skin. And all the resources that were needed to finally stop them. Nustanbul Station is built off blood that no one remembers anymore."

He paused, gathered his thoughts, and kept going, "We don't know what kind of world we're walking into, after the Smiling Woman, after Shion, but the truth... the truth is we don't deserve the stars, not all of us."

"What are we supposed to do now, Q!obi? I mean, I don't know if we're even the same people anymore." Q!obi slid his hands down Bhaka's shoulders to wrap his palms around Bhaka's.

In the dark, with the station on the other side of the door, Q!obi squeezed his best friend's hands and said, "We keep going, and we keep going together."

"Happy Firstday," Bhaka said.

"It's our Firstday now," Q!obi said. "Are you ready?"

"Serio? No."

Q!obi placed Bhaka's hands on the circular wheel of the door. Together, they both turned the combination, opened the door, and stepped outside.

BATTERY

Nimol Deveta Research Station, Saturn Ring orbit, 2756 CE

She's the last face you see before waking up: Pantha. And the only details that matter are about her face. The way she carries tension in the tiny creases that connect her top and bottom lip. How the inside corners of her eyes look almost upturned. The braids that spill from her scalp like thick black cables. She's looking at you, but also, looking for you.

Awake, you're in your cabin but not sure where you just were when you were sleeping. Pantha was there, and that's all you remember. You lift yourself into sitting position on the cot, and the wallscreen in front of you blinks, asking if you want to save your dream log. This close to transit, your mind's already full with Battery training, so you say no. The med menu displays your estrogen levels, resting heart rate, pulse-ox, and a spectrometer outlining your mineral levels. All of it aggregated over, well, your entire life to track trends or spot anomalies. You swipe it away.

The research team has drilled this into you since you became Eligible: Repetition helps you focus on details so you can pass the Battery, the Battery prepares you for the logical inconsistencies of transiting the Rip. You start Repetition now. You stand up and roll your head in a circle, stretching your neck. Then your right shoulder, forward and back, then your left. You shake out your arms before lifting each hip. Then you bend forward, slow enough to pull each vertebrate on your back, until your palms are flush on the floor. Pantha is fading in your mind now; all you see are her eyes, looking for you. She's gone by the time you step into your shower pod and untie your hair as the water flushes down and through it, stretching out the curls like you just did your body until the ends land just above your tailbone. After the shower, you lather up your entire body in synth-oil before finally putting on clothes. Repetition, you think to yourself, everything exactly the same, every day.

Your hair's still dripping when you step out of your cabin and make your way down the grated metal corridor to the Mess Hall. You pass two scientists who both break their conversation to stare at you. Almost everybody does. In the Mess Hall, you sit as close to the slide server as you can and pick up the first cup that comes across it. You try to keep your head down while you eat, try not to focus on the sets of eyes focused on you.

"Good morning, Chantral," a voice says as your peripheral vision catches a man sitting down across from you. You look up and it's Curiel. He's wearing his green Medical Team tunic and an easy smile. When you don't respond, he blinks.

"You have to do this every day now," you tell him. "Until the transit."

"Do what?"

"Sit here. Say, 'Good morning, Chantral,' and smile."

He picks a cup from the slide server and opens the seal. He asks, "Is this part of the training?" He leans in as his smile widens.

You say, "Repetition helps. We have to have this same exact conversation. Can you do this?"

"Sure," he says, and your eyes laser on him. "I mean, yes. I can do this."

"Thank you, and good morning."

Curiel starts to eat in silence but then stops and asks, "Do you think it's scary? The Rip?"

You shrug. "We're trained to expect anything, everything."

"Doesn't that include scary stuff?"

You look up from your breakfast cup. Curiel is wearing his easy smile. You've been in Repetition for so long you can't remember the last time something was added to your routine.

"What did the other women say they saw during transit?" you ask him. Early on, it was clear to researchers that women handled the Rip better than men. Their rigid thinking was somehow incompatible with the wormhole. Gifted girls are recruited young from Mars, spend their whole lives studying the Rip to become Eligible for transit. You've been Eligible for three Martian years, but Repetition displaces all traditional sense of time.

"I think it's different for everyone," Curiel says. "Some women say they just see themselves, or that they just see Earth."

"But no one sees a way out?" you say because you can read Curiel's face like a textbook. "The whole point is to find a way out. For all of us. And we're going to get there. Trust."

Curiel nods and goes back to silent eating, but you want to make this new addition to your routine count, so you think of something else to say. "I don't think it's as easy as some big red door or holo-neon sign at the end of it. I don't think the way out of the solar system is a threshold. I think it's a journey."

Curiel blinks, processing. You finish your cup before he does and get up to leave.

"Good luck on the Battery," Curiel says. You say thanks.

"No, I mean it," Curiel says, and his easy smile dampens. You nod back at him. After Mess, you take a cube to the next sector. Everyone stops talking when you step into it, afraid to disrupt your Repetition. You see people hesitate to even move, so you turn to face the corner.

There are more people walking about when you get off at your stop, so you keep your head down and count paces until you reach the Lab Gym. Inside, the far left wall is one entire mirror. The back wall is lined with weights, ropes, kettle balls, and plasti-boxes. Farquan's already there, dead center in front of the mirror, doing squats.

"Chantral! You sleep well?" he asks, looking at you through the mirror. His muscles tug at the seams of his tunic and leggings. He could trade in for a larger size, but he doesn't. He wants people to see his work.

"I did," you tell him while tying up your still damp hair.

"Then let's get started."

You've trained with Farquan ever since you were Eligible, and he's worked with others, so he knows the Repetition drill. He stretches you in complete silence, careful not to ad lib anything. The routine's become almost a dance by now. You do it with your eyes closed. And like a dance, Farquan always slips into the hyper-masculine role. He presses against you while stretching your hamstrings like there's an audience watching him. Overly suggestive. He does it every time, and you don't react.

After stretching is ropes and then balancing on plasti-boxes. Inverted on one, you point your toes toward the ceiling, and your mind floods with her, Pantha. Her face is gone, but there's just the feeling of her, looking at you but also looking for you. And while the mental image may be gone, her name never leaves you.

Pantha.

After the workout, Farquan always says, "Good job today," and you say, "Thanks."

"Maybe tomorrow we'll change things up a bit," he jokes, and you just smirk. He also does this every time.

Then you move to Diagnostics, and the Medical Team flits around you, taking measurements, placing sensors on your arms and around your forehead. They've prepared, too, to do this in silence, even Curiel. They pass plate-screens between each other instead of calling out results and nod to each other. One of the Med Techs, you never learned her name, screws her forehead looking at a plate-screen, and it gets passed to the whole team, careful to tilt it away from your eyes. Curiel is the last to see it ,and he frowns before nodding his head. Everyone on the Med Tech team leaves the room except for him.

"Chantral," Curiel breathes out. He's never done this, and heat begins to build in the back of your neck. "Have you noticed any spotting lately?"

"No," you say. You haven't.

"It's okay to let us know," Curiel says, "you can still transit."

"I haven't." Your voice pitches up. You can't help it.

Curiel tries to smile, but it seems strained. "I know Repetition helps with the Battery, but I gotta think being honest helps with the Rip." You don't respond, but you hold his eye contact.

"How about this: I promise that I'll always be honest with you, and you don't have to promise that back to me. But I hope it opens a door. A journey we can take together. Like from breakfast. Is that okay?"

You nod.

"Good," Curiel says, peeling the sensors off you. Then he motions to the door in the corner, the one that leads to the Battery. "Whenever you're ready."

You take a breath but don't move at first. Curiel falls back into his routine and leaves you alone in Diagnostic. This is where you take a moment for yourself. You think about all the studying and all the tests you had to take, all the other women who wanted this just like you but couldn't hack it. You think about every time you fell off a plasti-box until you could invert yourself perfectly one-handed. All the people who faded out of your life so you could become Eligible, pass the Battery, and transit the Rip. You think about the mission and the focus required, and you think to yourself, I can do this.

Then you breathe in, disrobe, and walk through the door and into the Battery.

The Battery is a blank white room about half the size of the Lab Gym. The floor, walls, and ceiling brighten as the door closes behind you.

"Subject: Chantral Pedatera," an electronic voice says. "Battery initiated."

Steam releases at the edges where the floor meets the walls, and words float in front of you. "Detect 28.611 Celsius." The steam eventually reaches you and blurs the words in front of you. The trick is to call it out earlier than you think because even the instant between recognizing it and opening your mouth to say stop will still add a couple of thousandths of a degree. The steam prints heat on your skin, your feet and legs first, and then it climbs up you. You breathe out slowly and count the degrees by how your skin reacts, a slight tension at first but then a relaxation, an expansion. You part your lips to breathe in, another trick, to gauge the warmth around you.

"Stop," you say. The words disappear, and vents in the ceiling open, pumping in cold air. Then, the floor shifts underneath you, and you begin running. It's a light pace. This isn't about exertion or stamina. It's a test of reflexes. You're running in place as the floor continually moves past you, and you remember to jump, just a little, before the floor sweeps to the left. Your feet twist, then your knees, hips, and finally, shoulders. You jump again right before the floor shifts further to the left. Then comes the hard part: the floor's sudden 180-degree turn. Running in place, you lean your shoulders back to prep for it. There's no warning, but you've done this enough. The floor starts to slow, and you hop on the heels of your feet. Four quick breaths in, one for each hop, as you turn yourself in mid-air. Like the beats of a song, your heels touch the floor in a quick rhythm until you're running again but in the opposite direction.

The floor slows to a stop then rotates you to face the front of the room.

"Identify Earth," the electronic voice says, and two images appear in front of you. Both are aquatic, both have yellow-greenish light piercing through a blue liquid space. But one is artificially rendered, and the other historical. The difference is in the edges. Historical footage has ends, a border around which it can no longer fill. Light bends around it differently than artificial renderings. You select the left image. Two more pop up. A ruined city in snow. Time and weather have stripped the glass shells from the skyscrapers, leaving gaping holes between concrete pillars, like the opposite of teeth. The left, again, is the real one.

It's never the same sets of images, so memorization doesn't help you. You study the edges, the macro-details, the trick here being to look at the image but not at what's in the image. Twelve sets this time.

"Finish the sequence of nonsensical words," the voice says, "lekutchji, umbriwatesh, phloripendacren, ighanovif..."

"Muridagichel," you say back. A test of neuro-lingual diversity.

Four holo-men appear, two in front of you, two behind. They begin to walk, circling you and whispering to themselves.

"Select the fourth generation Graham Sheff clone," the voice says.

At first glance, all four men would look identical, but there's subtle differences. For one, they're not all the same height. One is smiling, and another purses his lips between words. You look to their hairlines, find the one that's receded the farthest back, and select that one. They disappear.

Music fills the room. It's an ancient Earth song with thudding bass like a quick heartbeat. The singer begins calling out artifacts, enticing the listener to work for them. The beat drops after the first verse, and you start. You step in place and jut your hips out while your arms cross in front of your face and you flip your hands to the rhythm. A quick hop, and you split your legs and thrust your hand to the floor. You roll over to your stomach, kick your leg back, and arch. You flip over on your back and pick your legs up in the air. You bend and rotate your knees, point your feet. Then you sit up a bit and alternate pumping your legs forward. You're back up for the post-chorus, ticking your shoulders and side stepping.

If anyone asked, you'd tell them this is your favorite part of the Battery. You don't have to think anymore, you've done this choreography thousands of times. You know the Board is watching, but you pretend like it's just you. Like you're a little girl again. You play up tossing your hair, flicking your neck in just the right way that it lands over your face before you bob to the beat and your curls fly around you. You don't have to close your eyes when you spin because the white walls blur together even when you're stationary.

At the bridge, the music slows almost to a stop. You tense your stomach so that you're not breathing heavy and go through the hand motions. The singer explains that others want to hold you back, but it won't work. You have to keep on going. You look up to the ceiling when she sings, "higher," almost expecting something to be there. A crowd, roaring for you, or even just a mirror so you can see yourself, look at yourself while looking for yourself.

The beat comes back strong for one last barrage of hand gestures and leg kicks. You end with your arms outstretched and finally breathe deep after the music stops. A smile curls in the corner of your lips. Then, the ceiling vents open, and water rushes down on you.

It takes a while for the room to fill up, and in the meantime, there's still tests. Three images of plasti-boxes appear along with the instructions to select the "correct one." The water level laps over your ankles as you study them. There's no differences between them. You try looking at them all at once, instead of inspecting each one. You choose the center, and they all disappear.

The electronic voice asks you for the exact date and time of The News, and you recite it down to the tenth of a second. The water's up to your knees now. It's not cold, 18.889 Celsius, but the voice doesn't ask for the temperature.

When the water reaches your waist, you're prompted to face Saturn Polar North. The trick here is to feel how the water moves. When it falls from the ceiling, the water fans out in all directions until it hits the walls of the room, which is shaped like a rectangle. Then the water reverberates back, striking against itself at an angle. This was clearer earlier on, just over foot level, but you were studying plasti-boxes. Now the angle in the water is muted, but you align your shoulders parallel to where you thought the angle was.

The next prompt: When was the Rip first recorded? A trick question. Technically, it was recorded by one of the Graham Sheff clones in the 2180s, but the exact date is impossible to calculate. According to the official history, the Rip was identified from Mars in 2538, but it was known before that as the Saturn Ring Anomaly for centuries. You answer, "2219."

The water level is just under your breasts now. Twelve pixelated squares appear. They either sharpen focus or get blurrier as you turn them and piece them together. The trick here is to assemble the puzzle image as much as possible when the squares are blurred. You get deductions for every piece that becomes clear enough to understand. You rely on color and color temperature to match the squares. When you're finished, they reveal an image of a flower. You fully submerge once the water reaches chin level and wait for it to completely fill the room. Then, each white wall and the floor and ceiling become images themselves. There's no verbal instruction, but you know what to do.

Each image has some anachronistic element, not prominently featured, just sitting there. The wall in front of you depicts a Mess Hall on the old Lunar station before it exploded. You swim toward it, slowly, so you can take the whole image in. There's no people in the Mess Hall, but plates and trays are strewn about, like everyone's just finished eating and left. In the back next to two large sinks, you see it: a BreakfastBot, or Bibi for short. You swim up close enough and tap it. The image disappears. Your lungs start to tickle. That first picture took too long, you have to go faster.

On the floor is a panoramic view of Nustanbul Station on Mars, brilliant waves of overlapping bright colors splash across the buildings and roads, all under a bright white dome. It's easy to find the time-displaced atmo-scrubber because it's the only thing in the whole image that's gray. Your throat tugs as you swallow what little air was left in your mouth while turning to float in front of the back wall. It's an image of your cabin. Everything is exactly how you always leave it, but still, your eyes dance wildly trying to find something out of place. The burning in your lungs signals that you're running out of time. Vents in the floor open right as you spot it. Light brown woven shoes jutting out from under your cot.

You kick your legs against the draining current to reach the wall, tap the shoes, and push up toward the pocket of air emerging at the top of the room. For a split instant, you think you won't make it in time, that your mouth will burst open, and water will flood in, drowning you. The lip of the water is just half a meter away. You kick and swoop your arms until you finally crest and suck in all the air you can.

Eventually your feet touch the floor. Your breathing is steady by now, and you wait for the rest of the water to drain. Once it's finally out, the wall in front of you shifts, revealing a door, and the electronic voice says, "Thank you, please exit." Inside is a small changing room with towels, a bench, and a cabinet that has your body suit from earlier today. You take your time twisting a towel around your curly hair, wringing out water.

There's always the impulse to memorize every test in the Battery. It's natural, but actually counter-productive. Instead, you focus on the physical sensations. The times when your body tensed up, the flush in your stomach when you panicked underwater. But you also take time to remember the smooth flow of air from your lips while the holo-men circled you, the warmth of your feet against the cooler floor while you raced through photos, your hair falling in front of your face while you danced.

You tie your hair once it's dry enough, step into your suit, and then open the door on the far side of the changing room. Bright light fills your eyes, and for a second, you can't see. Your eyes adjust onto a small room that's overtaken by a long table with every seat taken except the one in front of you. You sit, and the Board begins.

They state your name and the date and time. There's nine people on the Board: Curiel, Farquan, some astrophysicists and theoretical mathematicians, and Moona Jarhid, the Board Chair.

"First, good job, Chantral," Moona says, "you completed 98 percent of the Battery with 83 percent accuracy."

You nod. Curiel smiles.

Farquan speaks up, "I'm concerned about your performance underwater. Seventy-two seconds. I think you can hold your breath for longer."

One of the mathematicians whose name you never remember chimes in, "I continue to assert that the final water challenge is impossible to complete. In over thirty years of Battery testing, no one ever has."

"The water challenge is necessary to test physical strain, weightlessness, cognitive agility, and historical accuracy all at once," says a physicist. "I'm happy to welcome any other alternatives."

"Noted," Moona says, "let's move on." You and Moona are the only women at the table, and you sit at opposite ends. She's staring down at you across the room. Moona's the lightest-tanned person you've ever seen. Her great grandparents were the second wave of researchers to the station, and her family has only ever lived on it. Three generations without Balance.

Moona continues, "Chantral has clearly qualified to transit. And I understand you've waived your pre-transit psychological screening in order to preserve Repetition?"

You nod.

"Then our only final concern is physical condition," she says.

Curiel speaks up, "Medically, she's in peak condition. Pulse-ox, blood pressure, and neuro-electrics are all in normal range."

"But her hormone levels," Farquan interjects.

Curiel responds, "I don't see a problem there, medically."

"She's about to start her period."

"Alternauts have transited the Rip at every stage in the menstruation cycle," Curiel says.

Farquan keeps pressing, "But we still don't have a full understanding of the after-effects."

"With all due respect, Dr. Connata," Curiel says, "you can't research something that's not there."

An astrophysicist ahems and starts to say, "Well, actually," but Moona raises her hand. The men stop talking.

"Chantral," she says to you, "have you started spotting?"

Even in the word, "No," you hear your pitch quiver.

"Our analysis of the water confirms that," Moona says, "so let's hear from each team. Medical?"

Curiel says, "I recommend Chantral for transit."

"Physiological?"

Farquan pauses but eventually says, "I recommend."

Moona goes on down the table. It's unanimous until the psychologist who, per custom, abstains because of the prescreening waiver.

"All right, Chantral," Moona says, "a meal and a movement, and then you can prep for transit."

The meeting adjourns, but you stay seated while everyone gets up and leaves, for Repetition.

Back in your cabin, you see a flash of her face as soon as you sit down on the cot. Pantha. But the mental image is gone before you can focus on it.

There's a special body suit you have to wear for the transit. It's white with thin red lines crossing over you. The contrast against your black skin makes you look regal. But still, you keep your head down while walking through the corridors of the station, and people know enough from the suit to know what you're about to do. You take a cube to the Center Axis, and all the teams are already there. Curiel and his Medical Team, Farquan and two of his assistants, and the astrophysicists and mathematicians sit at screens puzzling over trajectories and statistical models, all spread out in a dimly lit oval-shaped observatory. You're not sure if it's because they're used to Repetition or if they just didn't notice you walk in, but you feel invisible for what seems like the first time. Everyone zips past you whispering numbers and formulas to each other. You feel like you could go anywhere, do anything. Then, you hear Moona call your name from the far side of the observatory and fall in step toward her.

She's talking to the psychologist who always abstains when you reach her.

"The cyphers have to be archetypal," she says, "or else they won't be accessible to everyone. Ah, Chantral, there you are."

You nod. Moona passes a clip to the psychologist, and he nods and rejoins his team behind you, out of earshot.

"Do you ever get antsy?" she asks.

"No."

"Must be the training. I know we push you pretty hard, and it might seem like we're putting all this pressure on you."

"No, ma'am," you say.

"Well, good," Moona says, taking your hand in hers, "because I don't see it that way. I see it as trust. You give it, trust the process, pass the Battery. And we give it, we trust you to transit the Rip. Only about a dozen women have ever done this."

Moona pauses to make sure you're looking her in the eye. Her face is smooth and relaxed, but the skin around her eyes seems strained.

"But you have to remember: this isn't about you. This is for all of us. Here, and back on Mars. We need to find a way out of the solar system. We need a new home. We need you, Chantral, to draw us a map there."

You nod again, and her lips peel as if she's about to smile, but then she stops. She lets go of your hand.

"All right," she says, "I think you're ready."

Moona calls out for the teams to "plug you in." This is where each team ties into your body suit to take measurements and get baseline data. Once all that is through, Moona opens a door to a stairwell, waves you in, and shuts it behind you.

The stairwell is so dark it's nearly black. You can barely even see the white in your suit. The stairs curve as you walk down them until they end at an oval room, much smaller than the observatory above it. In the center are two halves of a clear sphere, the bottom half on the floor and the top half suspended from the ceiling. You hoist yourself inside the bottom half, and the top descends. There's a hiss when the two halves meet and smooth over each other so there's no seamline.

The floor below you recedes, and suddenly, the air inside the sphere goes cold. You hear your suit click and then warm up to compensate for it. You hear an electronic voice say, "Descension initiated," and the sphere begins to lower through the floor and into a vertical column. Bright purples bubble and fizz as blue arcs streak across them at the other end of the column. It's the Rip. It grows larger as you continue down toward it. You pick up other colors as you get closer. Ribbons of liltuul ripple out from yellow waves underneath all the purple. The blue arcs bounce brighter.

As the sphere exits the column and into the vacuum of space, it starts to jostle, just enough to quicken your heart rate. At two meters above the Rip, the sphere vibrates. You hold your breath.

When the Rip breaches the sphere, you feel it in your feet first, a steely wetness. The blue arcs almost blind you. They snap through your body, and you exhale as the purples ooze and press against you. Two blue arcs snap right before the purples engulf you, and everything stops. For a second, you're not there, but then you slowly feel your body form as you breathe. You draw deep breaths in and release them steadily as you begin to feel your fingers and toes until you're all complete, floating in a never-ending non-color. Your hair's in zero-g, your curls spread stiff about your head, and when you tilt your neck, they don't quite follow your scalp.

You look to your left shoulder, and your body suit is dissolving as white specks float free from you. But it's not just your body suit; soon it's your skin too. You watch the specks fractal out into tinier, tinier pieces, so small they turn into nothingness. The process speeds up and your legs, arms, hair, chest, you, triscastrand into a cloud of ever-reducing fractals.

And then you're gone. Nothing.

A vibration collects you like a musical note, and then you smack into a hard surface.

It's wet. And the air feels heavy around you. One side of your face is against a brittle surface.

You lift yourself into sitting. The hard surface below you is gray, and you're flanked on either side by tall reddish structures. Brick. You remember this from image tests in the Battery. You're on Earth, in a city. You try to piece together where you are based on context clues. The cement street and sidewalks could be London or Berlin. But the width of the street makes you think it's New York City.

"Pssst!" a voice from above you breaks the silence. You crane your neck upward and see a small person draped in a blanket on the metal stairwell attached to the brick building.

"Get up here!" the figure tells you. Her pitch is high. She sounds like a young girl. "The mold!"

She clanks down a level and unscrews something that releases a metal ladder. She stops it before it touches the ground.

You climb up, adding everything together in your head. There are still people living in cities, but there's mold. You have to be in the late half of the 2080s. You meet the girl in the blanket on the first level, and she puzzles over your suit.

"Where are you from?" she asks you.

"Not here."

The girl pulls the ladder back up and re-screws the clamp. Closer up, you see she's got lighter skin than you've ever seen before. Her light brown hair is clumpy and reaches below her shoulders. She doesn't look like she bathes very often.

"Let's get inside," she says, lifting a window and bending her way through. It's easier for her because she's small, but you're able to stretch and slip your legs through first, connect to the floor, and pull the rest of yourself through.

"You're from the stars, aren't you?" she asks. You nod, taking in the room. One wall is painted a dark blue, and white and yellow lines curve from the top and then spread out halfway down. You recognize it right away: it's a subway map. You're in New York City. But the map is incomplete. On the other side of the room are rows of backpacks and large plastic containers. You don't see a bed or a cot.

"You don't live here?" you ask her.

"I sleep on the line with everyone else. It's safer. This is just where we store stuff."

She opens a backpack that's filled entirely with packages of batteries and collects four of them, all the same size, and then tucks them into a satchel under her blanket. In another bag, she pulls out a plastic tube, clicks it, and light beams out of one end. She hands it to you.

"Here, but don't wave it all around, okay? Keep it low and just under you."

She tilts her head at you, eyeing your suit again.

"Where in the sky are you from?" she asks.

"I," you pause, "don't remember."

"Are you hurt?"

"No," you say, as your eyes draw back to the system map on the wall. It's done by hand, and there's a chair off to the side. She probably uses it to reach the top parts. "I've just had a really long day."

"I'm gonna take you to the line. It's not safe for you to be by yourself."

She opens a plastic bin and pulls out different blankets. She unfolds each one just enough to gauge their size and hands you the largest one.

"You gotta a name, little girl?" you ask her.

"Yeah," she says defiantly and stares at you.

"I'm Chantral."

"Hmm," she says, "let's head out now."

She grabs a backpack by the door and tosses it to you. Then, she waves the blanket over her head, motioning for you to put it on.

The two of you exit into an interior hallway, and she locks the door behind you. You follow her down the hall, passing other doors, most of them left open, revealing emptied out apartments. At the far end of the hall, you enter a stairwell and begin to climb. You count five floors until the girl opens an access door onto the roof. It's getting darker, but you can see a vast stretch of buildings. They look like they could go on forever but are blocked by water on either side. In historical photos, these buildings would all be lit up and cast grids of dots under the sky at night, but instead, they're all dark. There's no centralized electricity anymore.

A makeshift wooden footbridge connects this building to an adjacent one. You break into a sweat as the wood creaks underneath. Partly because of the heavy blanket over you but also because it's a seven-level fall to the street below if the bridge caves. On the second building, you follow the girl to another set of exterior metal stairs. About halfway down is another wooden footbridge that connects to the stairwell of an elevated subway track. This bridge takes longer to cross and feels less stable than the last one, but still, you make it.

"This part is a long walk," the girl whispers, "just keep quiet and don't stop moving."

You fall into step behind the girl who, for having short legs, is a surprisingly brisk walker. The sun's light fades in the sky as you both walk. You've seen footage of sunsets before, but this is the first time seeing it with your eyes. The empty buildings soften as a deep orange sky melts into pink. Every day this happens on Earth.

When it gets dark enough, you click on the plastic tube light to see the path just in front of you. The elevated line is a metal structure, but there's horizontal wood beams that the little girl uses to step on. You follow her lead and settle into the rhythm of it. Thirty minutes pass before you sense any other signs of life besides you and the girl. There are voices far off enough that you can't hear what they're saying but can make out their tones. No laughter, no arguing. They sound like all the people working on the station who aren't a part of your Repetition, just calmly, bluntly relaying information to each other.

A few minutes later, light from up ahead reaches down to the wooden beams you're stepping on. You click off your plastic light tube after you hear the little girl do so. The voices are louder now, and you start to count off how many different people this could be, but you lose count around fifteen. It's a settlement of some kind. You're still too far to piece out what they're individually saying, but their tone shifts, and somehow you know they're talking about you.

Throughout the walk on the elevated line, there was only the open air and the city on either side of you. Not that you saw much of it with the blanket over you. But now, out of the corners of your eyes, you see more makeshift wooden walls flanking you and the girl. Now, the voices of the people crisp into focus.

"Who is that?" "I don't know." "Why'd she pick up a stranger?" "Seems tall." "Maybe she can help hunt." "She'll have to."

Then, someone cuts through the din, silencing everyone.

"Lyra, who is that?"

You keep the blanket over your head, in deference, and wait for the girl to explain you.

"She says her name is Chantral," the little girl, Lyra, says. "She fell from somewhere. I heard her smack, but she's not injured. Least not that I can see."

"Does she have people? Anyone looking for her?"

"Don't know," Lyra says, "but you should see this." Lyra rips the blanket off you. You didn't realize that its weight during the walk rolled your shoulders inward. Now, you're free of it and stand up, straight-postured, like you're waiting for the Battery. Around you are about fifty people. They built a home across a wide aboveground subway station where six tracks converge together. You and Lyra are in left "lane" of the center pair. On the farthest platforms on each side are hammocks strung up in columns of three. That's where they sleep. But all the people are gathered on the two internal platforms.

All eyes are staring down on you from the platforms. But there's one woman, gray-haired, who seems unmoved. She must be the voice that broke through the chatter.

"You come from the stars," she says, and you nod even though she wasn't asking a question. This gets more gasps from the crowd above you. "How did you get here? Where is your ship?"

"I don't—" You start to speak but then think through your words. Even just opening your mouth shocks some on the platforms. You have to piece your words together carefully. De-escalate as best you can. "I can't remember."

You can, of course, but this is what you're taught once you become Eligible.

"We haven't seen any activity in the sky for years," the old woman says. She bends down and leans over the edge of the platform. Her eyes laser onto you, and people begin to gather behind her.

"You couldn't have landed anywhere near here," she says, "so you walked here?"

"Honestly," you lie, "I don't remember."

You scan the crowd of faces on the old woman's platform. There is a mix of light-skinned and dark-skinned people, mostly women, and mostly younger than the old woman questioning you.

And then you see her a couple of meters up the platform. When she bends past the young boy in front of her, her thick braids slip from her shoulder and hang in the air. She's looking for you, then looking at you.

"Pantha?" you call to her. Like a fluid wave, all the faces on the platform start to turn to her. Then she breaks into a run. Two steps into chasing after her, you bump into Lyra, and you both hit the wood beams. You tell her you're sorry but don't help her to her feet. You don't have time.

Pantha clears the crowd and races down the platform to a stairwell that's barricaded with boxes and tarps. She tears at the tarp and pushes her weight against the boxes on the top of the stack, making room for her to crawl through.

A few other people on the platform give chase too but stop at the barricade. They won't broach it. You make it down the tracks and then jump up onto the platform. You have to squeeze through people to get to the barricade, but no one stops you from crawling through the same hole Pantha made to escape. You hear the voice from the old woman echo down the platform, "Let them both go!"

You hear Pantha's quick footsteps clamping beneath you in the stairwell. The boxes she pushed broke open on the stairs, their contents spilled out, and you try to dodge them without losing too much speed. Plates, pots and pans, and tiny metal containers litter the stairs, but only until the first turn. You glimpse Pantha's shadow, passing the second turn.

Your legs stretch over two steps at a time, and then you jump to the landing. You do it again on the next turn, and you're almost up to her. She's stamping down the last few stairs to street level. Without electricity, the city is blanket-dark, and you might lose her, so you jump the last few stairs and tackle her.

She groans, and, on top of her, you feel her chest collapse. The air's knocked out of her lungs. For a few seconds, you both lie there. She's wearing Earth fabrics, but you can tell her skin must be smooth. Then her hips shift against yours as she struggles to turn underneath you. There's barely enough light from the settlement above, but you see her eyes, round and tilted slightly, just like you remember them.

"Pantha?"

She studies you. Her eyes cross over your face, down your nose and mouth, and then back up again.

"You're new," she says. She leans up, and her lips meet yours. You freeze, but she keeps going, pressing into your face. Her bottom lip parts both of your lips, and her tongue slips in, tapping against your teeth. You open your mouth, and her tongue creeps in, rubbing against your tongue. Then she stops, her face recedes from yours, and she blinks.

"Nice to meet you," Pantha says. But you're without words.

You know every detail about her face. But it ends there. The new information is about her body. She's just slightly smaller than you. Her breasts and hips are wider than yours. She's not athletic like you. Her legs are round but pillowy.

"We should get going, yeah?" Pantha says as her plump lips form a smile. You pull yourself off her. Once you're standing, you reach a hand to help Pantha to her feet, but instead her eyes follow the lines of your bodysuit. She gets up on her own.

"I know a place this way," she nods to a side street.

Your eyes adjusted to the dark sometime during or after Pantha kissed you. You follow her down the street, and she starts talking before questions can bubble up in your mind.

"You don't have to worry about mold exposure," Pantha starts. "You'll get cleansed on the other side. And, of course, they're gonna scrub, track, and tag every square centimeter of you too."

You pass two apartment buildings and, after an intersection, a row of glass-fronts. Most of them are knocked out, the glass swept away some time ago. You recognize this, too, from historical records. These were stores, and probably the first places to get looted.

Pantha steps into one glass-front, and you follow. The front room is empty, stripped clean, but Pantha leads you to a door in the back. She stands on the tips of her toes to reach the top of the door frame and slides her fingers along it until she grabs something, a key.

"Of course, they don't know that it's already done all their work for them. But if they can't track it, monitor it, computate it, run it this way through the 'rithm, trace it back, score it, peer review it, and publish it, then it doesn't really exist to them," Pantha says. Inside the room, there's a large plastic wardrobe along the wall. Pantha opens it and pulls out clothes. "You need to put these on. Ditch the suit."

You unzip your suit and pull your arms and legs out of it. Pantha just watches until you're naked. You step into a pair of Earth-fabric pants. It's softer than the blanket from earlier and glides up each of your legs in one fluid motion. There's enough space for air to get in at your ankles. The top is looser than even the Medic Team tunics on the research station. You tuck it into the band of your waist for comfort.

Pantha's saying something about living organism structures that you can't quite follow. When you clear your voice to speak, she stops.

"Pantha," you say, "how do I know you?"

She lets out a nonverbal sound with her lips still pursed. Her eyes take you in, just like you remember: looking for you while looking at you.

"I told you, Chantral. It's already done the work for you." You try to respond, but she steps up to you and cups her hand over your mouth. "I can tell you more but not here. We have to go further." You nod your head, and she takes her hand from your mouth. "How much can you do? Invert? Cyphe? Whurlpull?"

You shake your head.

"Let's start slow," Pantha says. She places both hands on either side of your head and tilts you side to side. You focus on her face as everything behind her whooshes in a blur.

"Don't look at me," she says, "follow the blur."

Your focus zooms out from the empty room. The walls rock back and forth in the dark.

"There you go," Pantha says, pushing your head hard to the left.

You don't move, but everything else does. The walls and the floor pitch down and then swing underneath you, and suddenly, it's daylight. A white ray of light creaks in from under the door, above you now, spread out across the floor overhead.

You're standing on the ceiling, but Pantha's on the floor. She nods for you to come down. You lift your arms up, and your feet disconnect from the ceiling. Your curly hair fans out around you like you're in zero-g, but you're actually falling. The floor above you inches closer to meet you. You palm it with one hand and stretch out your right arm and left leg for balance. Your hip locks in a diagonal so your right leg is pointed straight up. Your foot's flexed, toes pointing toward the ceiling. You take one clean breath in and then out. You can feel the equilibrium in your ears. Then you place your other hand on the floor and bend until your feet touch the ground and you're upright.

Pantha says, "You're not showing off for me, are you?"

"Where are we?" you ask, looking around the room. The only difference between now and a few minutes ago is that your suit is missing, and it's daylight.

"The same place, the same time. We didn't technically *go* anywhere," Pantha says, "do they know anything about this?" You don't respond. "We inverted." Another pause. "Wow, you really are new."

Pantha takes your hand and leads you to the door, and you both walk through. The storefront was bare just a few seconds ago, but now it's filled with racks of clothes. Dresses mostly. You read about them when you were becoming Eligible, but no one on the station wears them.

"Can I help you?" an angry voice calls from behind. It's a woman sitting at a counter. This must be her store, and you and Pantha just walked out of her backroom without ever walking in. Pantha squeezes your hand and tugs.

"No thanks, ma'am, bye!" Pantha calls as you two rush out the front door. Outside, crowds of people move up and down the sidewalks, oblivious to the large green metal trucks slowly drawing up and down the road. They're filled with men with guns.

"It's basic physics," Pantha says once you both make it down the street and cross the intersection. "Objects move through space, like us right now. Objects move through time also."

"Yes, I know this," you tell her.

She keeps going, "90 percent of the known universe is only that. But the Rip is different." Pantha doesn't lower her voice mentioning the Rip as people walk past. She, like everyone else, only makes enough eye contact to dodge and weave through crowds. You're not as good at it. On the station, everyone steps aside for you, and you keep your head down. Out on the street with Pantha, your shoulders gently land into other people who don't immediately turn away.

"There's extra dimensions here," Pantha says, "so objects can move on different axes. Inverting is moving on what axis, Chantral?"

Pantha turns at another corner onto a major avenue. You can see clear down to where the street gets blocked by a tall green structure four levels in height. Pantha still has your hand, and she walks you toward it. The sidewalk traffic dies out after another block. No one else walks this direction.

"Come on, you're smart," Pantha says, "what other axes are there?"

Length, width, depth, time. You list them off in your head. "Energy?"

"Close, but that's just motion. This one's closer to time."

Pantha stops walking two blocks away from the structure. The trucks with armed men don't even drive near here either. But you can hear faint voices down the street. People, with guns probably, manning the structure. You can't make out their words, so they probably can't make out yours either. This feels like a Battery test. You take a breath and focus out from the question. Don't answer the content, answer the frame.

After a beat you say, "An Axis of Choice?"

"Right!" Pantha cups your face in her hands and brings you in for a quick kiss. "Most individual choices are tiny. They don't move far, but macro-level, societal choices, are like this street. They can go on and on and on."

"Until they stop," you nod toward the green structure.

"That's not the end of the street. That's just a checkpoint. But, actually, yes, let's use that metaphor. How far can social decisions realistically—"

"No, I asked you a question, and you said you could explain it here." You break her hands from you. "How do I know you, Pantha?"

She sighs, "I just told you." Your forehead wrinkles as your turn to look sideways at her. "They didn't teach you anything before they let you transit, did they? But let me guess, they put you through a whole bunch of tests."

"You know about the Battery?"

Pantha nods with her eyes. She says, "If Choice is an axis, the Battery is like a bend in the road."

"A divergent point?"

"No," Pantha smiles, "you're cute. Divergence isn't really real. It's like looking at static and thinking you see something. The bend in the road gets carved out. On Earth, this happened with winds and rains. Over time they shape the rock, bend it. Choice is like time that way. So many decisions. So many people making the same decision, so much of the time, bends the road."

You think about the choreography in the Battery, its muscle memory. Even now, just thinking about it, twitches your calves. You could be dancing right now.

"They're conditioning me?"

"Well, yeah," Pantha says, "but take a step back. They're conditioning everything. They're following a bend so old they don't even know they're curving."

"That's why they need me to make a map."

Pantha clicks her teeth and winks at you. "That first part," she says. "They need you. Come on." Pantha nods her head toward the structure. As you walk, Pantha explains how Euclidean geometry is just a rock, and the Rip is a river running over it. She has a circular rhythm of speaking, talking in long lists and then folding back to certain phrases she's used to saying over and over.

It (the Rip) already does the work for us.

They didn't teach you anything, did they?

But her lips part, and her eyes lighten every time they land on you. If she had lighter brown skin, you might be able to see her cheeks flush and darken.

At the base of the structure is a man dressed in a green uniform with a helmet and a long gun slung over his shoulder.

He warns you to "stop right there," but Pantha takes your hand again and keeps approaching. She's all smiles to the man with the gun, but you know somehow that she does this with men. She over-performs.

"Our apologies, sir. We're just lost. I was wondering if we could borrow a pen and paper," she says to him.

"Without proper credentials, you can just turn around and walk in the other direction," he responds.

"Really, sir, we're just..." You tune Pantha out and focus on the man. His eyes shift briefly to you but then back to Pantha. His right hand slips into the gun handle. You squeeze Pantha's hand quickly, but she wriggles out of your grip. When she's close enough, Pantha snatches the gun in the blink of an eye. She juts the barrel long ways into his throat and slams her foot over his. Choking, he cranes over, and Pantha palms the back of his helmet, driving her knee into his face. He falls to the ground. The whole thing took only seconds.

Pantha unslings the gun from his shoulder and tosses it back to you.

"Don't worry about him," Pantha says. "It's the 2080s, he's been dead for forever."

You studied historical firearms to become Eligible, but the long gun is lighter in your hands than you imagined. Pantha searches him for a plastic key fob, then unclips it from his belt.

"Come on," she says, "let's go deeper." She presses the fob against a panel near the door the man was guarding, and it hisses open. The first room inside has open-faced lockers on either side of the walls with guns and ammunition mounted and stacked in each one. Pantha grabs a short-barreled gun and clicks a latch in the handle. A stock falls out, filled completely with bullets, and she catches it in midair and loads it back in. Then, Pantha scans the walls and ceiling.

"Cyphing is moving on the Axis of Meaning," she says. "Look for simple symbols."

You point behind you to the door you entered, labeled "exit."

"No, let's start you off slow. No labels or words. Nothing intricate." She walks deeper into the room and barges through the door opposite the exit. Red lights flash, and a siren blurts out immediately. You follow her into the second room.

There's workstations with screens and keyboards. The screens are flashing bright blue with the word "alert" overlaid another icon. You point to that, but Pantha shakes her head.

"No screens yet. Find a flat surface."

Pantha ducks under a workstation and opens a cabinet with folders of paper. She takes one and flips it over to the blank side. "Now something to write with."

"What about this?" You sit the workstation next to her and motion to the keyboard. "They aren't words. A random letter is a simple symbol."

"Perfect," Pantha says, sitting next to you, "pick one."

"Which one?"

"Any."

Then another door opens, and two men with guns flood into the room. They each draw on one of you and yell, "Freeze!"

"S!" Pantha screams right before the screen in front of her shatters from a bullet. Suddenly, Pantha's not sitting next to you. She's just gone. You hear one of the men yell, "Freeze!" again, and just as you start to swivel in your chair, a pop rings out, and a sharp dart of heat digs into the space between your nose and your left eye.

The burn fizzles out in an instant, and you blink rapidly until your vision crisps. You're lying on your back, and the alarm sirens are gone. You're in your cot in your cabin on the research station. You sit up, and the wallscreen in front of you blinks, asking if you want to save your dream log. You swipe it away.

She's the last face you saw before waking up: Pantha. There with you, and then gone.

You start Repetition, stretching your arms, waist, and legs before bending over to stretch out your spine. Water streams over you in the shower, and you think about all the different things Pantha told you. Euclidean geometry is just a rock, and the Rip is a river flowing over it. Toweling off and getting dressed, you hear her voice, "It's already done the work for us."

You keep your head down walking through the station corridors to the Mess Hall. The same two scientists from yesterday break their conversation when you pass them, then continue talking when you're far enough away to not catch their exact words. Once you're in the Mess Hall, you sit where you always sit, as close to the slide server as possible. You pick up a cup and break the seal when Curiel sits down across from you.

"Good morning, Chantral," he says, grabbing a cup for himself.

"You have to do this every day now," you tell him. "Until the transit."

Curiel blinks slowly, and his lips part in an eager smile. "Do what?" he asks, reaching for a cup on the slide server.

"Sit here," you explain, "say 'Good morning, Chantral' and smile."

Curiel's eyes shift, scanning the room. Then he leans in toward you, reaches for a cup, and says, "Is this part of the training?"

"Repetition helps," you say, looking up at him. "We have to have this exact same conversation. Can you do this?"

"Sure," he says, peeling off the lid of his cup. "I mean, yes. I can do this."

"Thank you," you say, "and good morning."

Curiel reaches for a cup from the slide server. "Do you think it's scary? The Rip?"

You start to shrug when you notice Curiel reaching for the slide server again, for the fourth time, but without any cups in front of him. Curiel sees something in your face change, and his smile flattens.

"Is everything okay, Chantral?"

You open your mouth, but words don't come out. Instead, you lean back and watch Curiel's concern for you until suddenly he's gone. Your cup's gone too.

Then, Curiel sits down across from you with an easy smile and says, "Good morning, Chantral," and it hits you.

You're still in the Rip.

Curiel's face dampens when you don't respond. "Chantral? Is something happening with you?"

You break your routine, reach across the table to take Curiel's hands, hoping somehow that'll stop him from disappearing again.

"I'm... transiting."

He grips your hands harder now, and his round eyes widen. "How's that even possible?" He scans your face, studying you.

"I'm not sure."

"You could go anywhere in the universe, and you came back here?" He takes a long breath, but his eyes never leave you. "There's nothing out there, is there? Boll, there's no way out of the solar system." Curiel's voice cracks right at the end.

"No," you tell him, "I went places. I was on Earth. She told me—"

"You met one of them!" he blurts out but then hushes down to a whisper, "The Larger Community?"

"No, she was a woman."

"She was a woman during The News!"

"This woman was different. She," you pause, "Pantha, she said—"

"You saw Pantha?"

You pull your hands from his, and now you study Curiel's face. "How do you know Pantha?" Curiel rolls his shoulders back, and he takes his eyes off you. They dart everywhere around you, the wall behind you, the table in front of you.

"The Medical Team can't share any confidential patient records."

"She was an alternaut, wasn't she?"

"I can't give you a definitive answer, Chantral."

"You just did."

You get up from the table and walk out of the Mess Hall, but you don't look down, and you don't avoid eye contact with people. They all stare, many with their mouths hanging open, but you don't so much as blink at them.

"Wait!" Curiel yells behind you, catching up to you in the corridor. "Where are you going?"

"Somewhere I can get a straight answer out of someone." Your mind races through your Repetition routine. Farquan's out, you don't trust him. The physicists and mathematicians might not be helpful either, Euclidean geometry and all. "I need to talk to Moona."

"Chantral, wait," Curiel says. He stifles a groan and continues, "I get a readout of your vitals every morning. And your estrogen levels—"

"Boll my estrogen levels. I'm not bleeding. I'm not unstable."

"I believe you," he says. "But Moona won't."

"Why not?"

Curiel's eyes strain, but he bites his lips.

"Yesterday before the Battery, you said that you promised to always be honest with me. That you hoped it would open a door, a journey we could take together."

"You didn't take the Battery yesterday."

"My yesterday, your... hour from now. Look, I know how I sound. That I'm holding you to words you haven't even said yet. But the idea's in there, isn't it? I'm opening the door, Curiel. I'm asking you to come take a journey with me."

"That sounds exactly like something I would say, too."

The two of you stand there in silence for a moment. You start to realize that no one in the Mess Hall has left yet for fear of crossing your path. Curiel groans and says, "Okay, totally honest with you. If you go ask Moona about Pantha with your estrogen levels right now, she's not going to believe you. Because Pantha's been dead for twenty-eight years."

"What!"

"Let's talk in private in my cabin."

Curiel's cabin is larger than yours. His bed and bathroom are both separate in their own rooms. He even has a "leisure space" just off the front room when you step inside. That's where you both sit. He starts with what you already know: Eligibility, the years of studying astrophysics, human history, and physical exertion. Apparently, Moona spotted you early on because of your focus. While other women formed study groups, stayed up late cramming together for tests, bonding socially, you didn't.

It didn't take long for the Eligibility class to start cornering itself off from the rest of the research station. The Eligibles learned more about human history than any other scientist was authorized to. After a few rounds of testing, there wasn't much an Eligible could say to a lay scientist that they would understand. And vice versa. To become Eligible meant giving up a part in larger society, meant being blocked access to the station's data. But the reward, the opportunity to transit different dimensions, experience what no other human ever has, pulled stronger than gravity. And when another woman would wash out of Eligibility, it was like death. You would never see her again, even if she walked right past you.

You imagine Pantha becoming Eligible. Her eyes keenly train on the lips of whoever's teaching. She seems shy at first. The women in her class probably ignore her. Until that one time she speaks up. You saw women do this in your class, try to impress the teachers and the other students with a long-winded answer, designed to show off the knowledge acquired more than providing the correct answer. But that's not what you see Pantha doing; she's too smart for that. Pantha shocks her class, not by answering, but by asking and stumping the teacher. You imagine the women in Pantha's class recalculating after that. No more invitations to study with others. Pantha was her class's biggest threat. And she won.

"Loners do better," Curiel says.

"With the transit," you say.

"I don't think that's ever been studied. I'm talking the whole process. Repetition. Battery. De-briefing. It's incredibly isolating, no matter how we structure it."

You ask, "What does this have to do with Pantha?"

"Pantha was," Curiel starts but then pauses. He flips open a pad on the table in front you and starts up the array. His fingers dart through the faint vertical lights until he pulls up her files. "She was always a bit of an outlier."

The array fills with simigs and simvids, charts, neurals, dreams logs, and de-brief memos, a kaleidoscope of her. In some simvids, Pantha's talking calmly with sensors affixed around her forehead, but in others she's screaming and crying. In one simvid, she's in her cabin, banging on the door: she's locked in. In another, she's in her cot, unzipping her suit and sliding her hand between her legs. You focus on her face and watch her cheeks start to quiver when a neural map pops up in front of the simvid. It's a cloudy sphere with crisscrossing lines wiring through different dots. Twenty or so pulses run the lines and blip as they cross over dots.

"Watch this one," Curiel says as his fingers poke through the neural map. "This is Pantha before her first transit."

"Looks normal."

"Normal enough, for an alternaut." Inside the array, Curiel's fingers swivel. "This is Pantha during transit." The neural map brightens as tens of thousands of pulses ripple through the lines and blip at the dots. Pantha's brain teems with hyperactivity. Curiel twists again in the array. "After transit." The speed of the pulses slows but not by much. After a few seconds, you start to spot it: new dots, small and faint, pop up in the sphere; and the pulses "jump" to them. It doesn't look like there's a specific pattern to them, just random jumps on random dots. But sure enough, you see in a lower arc section of the sphere, a pulse jumps and draws a new line, and then other pulses flood in, deepening the line.

"What was that?" you ask.

Curiel says, "We still don't fully know. Two techs on my team wrote their dissertations on this. We've never seen it before, and we've never seen it since."

You can't take your eyes off it. A new bend in the road. You start to see behind it, deeper in the sphere, more pulses draw new lines, like her brain is building a new skeleton.

"How did she present," you ask, "after transit?"

Curiel clicks his teeth in approval and pulls up a simvid. Pantha's sitting at the post-Battery table, Moona on one end and flanked by male doctors on either side. You can tell this is old because, while Pantha looks exactly the same as she did on Earth, Moona and some of the other scientists are almost unrecognizable. Curiel and Farquan aren't even there. In their seats are balding men.

Pantha cracks a half smile as her eyes pull up and to the left. The audio isn't on, but it's obvious she's recounting something from the Rip. The surveillance camera catches something Pantha wouldn't be able to see at the time. Simigs of her neurals pass across the table on each person's pad screen until finally it lands on Moona's. Pantha keeps talking, answering each question lobbied at her. She tries to make eye contact with the Board members, but she can't hold any of them. And when you see it, you remember it, the purse in the crease of her lips, where Pantha carries her tension.

Moona stands up and dismisses the Board, leaving Pantha there alone. At first, she leans back in her chair, relaxed. She closes her eyes and nods. And you've done this exact thing before, right after the Battery, when you're drying off. You're telling yourself, "You did the best you could. You've got this." Watching Pantha's private moment, reassuring herself, drops the bottom of your stomach out from under you. You feel like you're spying on her. You want to look away, but your neck tenses up, and you can't.

The Board returns, and the Med Chair starts placing sensors on her forehead. He doesn't say anything to her, just walks in and goes for it. Again, no one looks to return Pantha's eye contact. She scans the whole room, and when Moona sits down at the other end of the table, your vision blurs when you see Pantha do it: look at Moona while looking for Moona. You jut your finger into the array, pausing it.

"I don't want to see anymore," you tell Curiel.

"Good," he replies, "I'll be in more than enough trouble for what little I showed you."

You have to palm and massage the back of your neck to relax. The sight of a helpless Pantha was too much for your muscles.

Finally, you ease up enough to ask, "Why do you think Pantha's dead?"

Curiel blinks. You don't follow up or rephrase your question. It hangs between the two of you until he answers. "Because she died."

"No," you say, "I saw her. In the Rip."

"You saw a representation of her. Like a ghost."

"No," you say, and the array goes dark, "no, she was real."

Curiel clicks his teeth in approval and juts his hands into the array. It pulls up the simvid from her first post-transit.

"Stop doing that," you tell Curiel. He furrows his forehead at you.

"Good," he says, "I'll be in more than enough trouble for what little I showed you."

He's doing it again, repeating. You try to take his hand in yours, but he clicks his teeth again and puts his fingers inside the array. But this time, you stop. You watch Curiel twist his fingers in the array, pulling up Pantha's de-brief, then stop, furrow his forehead at you, click his teeth in approval, and go back to the array again. You stand up and back away from him, and he's still in the loop, clicking his teeth and poking around in the array. You keep stepping back. When you should butt up against a wall, it's not there.

One more step back, and the edges of your vision draw a heavy black box around your eyesight. In the center of it is the leisure space in Curiel's cabin, but everything's fainter in color, and you're still there sitting next to him, even though you're standing outside it. Another step back, and your legs brush against something. A chair. You sit down, and the black edges fill out somewhat. You're in a room with a pad screen. The array is on, and inside it is you and Curiel. He clicks his teeth and dives his fingers into his array.

You don't see her sitting across from you until you turn off your array. Her smile breaks when she nibbles her bottom lip, watching you.

"You learn fast, girl," Pantha says.

"What?" You dart your eyes around this new room that you're in, but it's too dark to see the corners and the edges of the walls or ceilings.

"You," Pantha says, leaning forward, "you're not new."

"Why do they think you're dead, Pantha?"

She giggles for a beat but then snaps her fingers. "That's a great question to explain what you did just now. Well, what you did twice." She reaches behind her, and a large dome-light above the both of you hums on. It's not a CEE bulb or a halo-light. It bathes the room but not harshly. The color temperature is cool, but the light isn't blinding. Pantha, across from you, looks diffuse, like simigs you studied of sunsets on Earth.

She keeps going, "They think I'm dead for the exact opposite reason you were able to step out of that room and whurlpull: it's the reality they accept. And it's the reality you rejected. We call it the Axis of Affinity. And you figured it out on your own."

"Twice?" you ask.

"Well, that's how you got there in the first place. You got shot in the face on Earth, remember, and you couldn't process that reality, death. So, on instinct, you whurlpulled yourself back to what's familiar."

"The station. So, wait, where are we now?"

Pantha tilts her head and gestures around the room. There are only two chairs and you two. The pad screen with the array is gone now. So is the dome-light, but the room is still a cool-white distillation. "This is just junk universe. Like skew." She bends her arms so that they cross but don't touch each other. "Two lines that don't run parallel yet never intersect each other. Like that, but instead of lines, it's—"

You interrupt her, "The affinity to a reality."

"Yes! Girl, you have a knack for this, I can tell."

Pantha gets up from her chair, and within seconds, it slowly fades into the white light of the room.

"You said something," you tell her as she steps toward you, "that 'we' call it the Axis of Affinity. Are there more of us here? Are there more of me?"

"Like alternate versions of yourself?" Pantha squats down in front of you and clears a curly tress of hair from your forehead. "There's ten to infinity versions of yourself right in front of me. Right this second." Her fingers glide down your face and run down your neck. "And this second." Pantha leans in to kiss you. Her lips are warm against yours. Here in the Junk Universe White Room, your mind can peel back from all the time spent in Repetition, studying to become Eligible and taking the Battery. You can remember now who you were before you took on the mission. You were a girl who liked to kiss other girls.

Noise slowly floods into your ears, not in one sudden swoop but more like a drip. Other voices are in the air, but you can't make out the words. The shuffled clomps of boots hit the floor. Pantha pulls back from the kiss, and you're both sitting next to each other at a bar. The walls are floor-to-ceiling pad screens in lush greens. They're playing a computer-generated jungle scene. In the shadows of the leaves from under the canopy, you see the piercing, flickering eyes of a jaguar.

An anthropomorphic female insect emerges from the foliage. "Ladies, welcome to Cricket's, what can I get you?"

Training kicks in as you scan the rest of the room. The people here are all wearing thick gray boots, magboots. And there's a wide spread of skin color, pale faces and brown ones. You're in the Corporate Era, sometime before 2247, on a passage ship to Mars.

"What's good here?" Pantha asks the animated insect girl.

Her antennae twitch as she smiles, "Well, most people like the Vinebier. The big burly guys drink Mud Sludge, and the classy ladies like Estuary, which I can do up, split, or tidal. Would you like to try one of those?"

Pantha answers, "No, we'll each get Vinebier."

Insect Girl's antennae droop and then bounce back. "Okay!" she says. "I like making Estuaries, but I'll get you two Vinebiers right away. Let me know if you change your mind on the next round."

A tube in the wall opens, and two Vinebiers tumble down the bar and land in front of both of you. Insect Girl hops back into the jungle and re-appears further down the bar, greeting other passengers. You watch Pantha pop her Vinebier and then follow her lead.

"Did you see how manipulative she was?" Pantha asks and then takes a sip, "Looking sad for a brief second to try to upsell? That's why they made her anthropomorphic, to elicit more empathy. This whole thing is social conditioning. She's an insect because—"

"Early Martians only had insects for protein," you tell her. You both studied all the same historical material. "So, you've been in the Rip for twenty-eight years?"

"Give or take a few million, yeah."

"So, you've either given up on the mission, or you're still looking." This time you take a sip of your Vinebier. It's sour with artificial fruit notes.

"What?" Pantha smiles while her eyes trace lines over your face. "Are you going turn me in if I tell you I'm a traitor? If I run, do you think you could chase me?"

"I think you're trying to recruit me."

Pantha swallows a bigger gulp and says, "I keep telling you you're smart, girl!"

"But what I can't figure out is for what?" you say, gripping the Vinebier. The beads of condensation don't run down the can; they ooze slow. "I can't see you trying to bring down the station and the whole 'social order' when you can just find a better reality with a better society to live in."

Pantha tips her can up again for another long swig, then says, "You're getting warmer."

"And you've obviously been in the Rip for so long you can't give straight answers."

Pantha winces on your words. That was probably a low blow. But Pantha's been an elusive wannabe guide, showing you the Rip while lording her knowledge of it over you.

"Ugh, that word," she says, "'straight.' That's what they used to call themselves." She points her Vinebier at the het couples along the bar. "But they don't feel straight, do they? Clumsy mating rituals meet rigid gender roles. And yet and still," she swings her Vinebier in a circle, "all this."

You try talking Pantha's language to see if that unlocks something, "Five Q terra-tanned men ended the Corporate Era in one night."

"Three years from where we're sitting." Pantha pulls another sip. "The Big Booms."

"So, what do you think five Q alternaut women can do? Given the opportunity?"

Pantha blinks at you but doesn't answer. She finishes her Vinebier and then stares at the fake jungle on the wall. "Why do I have to decide what we do? Why can't it be you?" You don't answer her, just watch her watching the wallscreen. Pantha's an outlier, stuck in the Rip for over half your lifetime. And you've met her before. You could draw the curves of her face from memory, but she's still a stranger to you. She may even be a stranger to herself after all this time.

"Why do *you* think they make you take the Battery before transit?" she asks you, not breaking from the jungle wall.

You know the answer they tell you, that it's multifaceted, partly to prepare for the logical inconsistencies of the Rip, partly to train you to identify where in time you land, partly to prove you can handle the physicality of the job, to prove that you're high-performing, but you also know Pantha doesn't want that answer. You tap the empty Vinebier to the bar just as a burp escapes your throat. You try to quiet all the questions in your mind and just answer her.

"To put them at ease," you say, "to make them feel comfortable."

"Out there," Pantha says, "we did all this work for them. But here," she finally breaks from the wall to look at you, to look for you, "the Rip does the work for us."

"You found the map on your very first transit?" You start piecing it together. "The way out of the solar system? The Larger Community? No," you get it now, "they found you."

"They chose me," Pantha says, "without having to prove anything to them first."

You sit in silence, staring at Pantha. Her thick cable braids end just before her elbows, framing her round childlike face. You remember all those simvids of her stuck in her cabin after her first transit. She was screaming, banging on the door. Sometimes she was just silent, sitting on her cot, waiting. And then you remember the one where she unzipped her suit and put her hand between her legs. You feel a warmth between your legs, a twinge contracting.

"Show me," you tell her, leaning in close enough to smell the Vinebier on her breath. "Show me how to get there."

Pantha parts her lips to speak but then does that thing that she does: looking at you while looking for you. And you get it now, she's trying to find out if she can trust you.

"You'll need this," she finally says, cupping her empty Vinebier. "The last time, we got interrupted." She smooths her thumb over the letter V, "Focus on the letter. Not what it means, but what it means to you."

"The Axis of Meaning."

Pantha nods and runs her finger over the V one last time. You study the V's sharp angles, the way it dives down to suddenly jolt up. The letter feels like a downward pressure. You feel a drop inside your ears, and when you pull back from staring at the bier, you're not in the Cricket's bar anymore.

You're strapped into a chair against a wall. Whatever vessel you're in, it's falling. The g-force isn't strong, so it only tugs at your stomach a little. Across from you are two pale-skinned men talking in low tones to each other. You can't make out what they're saying, but occasionally they both look at you, and then go back to talking. You feel a hand on your left knee; it's Pantha. You know that before even turning to look at her. She puts a finger to her lips and whispers, "Shh!"

A few minutes later, the vessel lands with a soft thump. Everyone's restraints unclip at the same time and move up, but Pantha's hand pushes firm into your lap. The message is clear: Don't.

The two pale men get up. They each pass with one more sideways glance at the two of you before standing in front of the vessel's main door and waiting for it to open. A pressurized hiss cracks as the door unbuckles and the vessel floods with mist. You hear the two men step down from the vessel, but you can't see them. When the mist dissipates, Pantha stands up. You follow her.

"Just like inverting is crossing mass, societal decisions, cyphing is traveling across macro-meanings," Pantha says as you both step down from the vessel and into a jetway. "The plane of what we all collectively decide something means something."

The end of the jetway opens to a large arch. A message on the floor beneath you reads: Welcome to Armstrong Station. You're on Mars. Past the arch is a massive chamber, easily fifty meters high. It's a long rectangle, barreling down to the right, with glittering fountains dotting the thoroughfare in front of identical arches. Hundreds of people stream out of the arches and begin to walk right. You aren't the only one struck at the vast open space above. Almost everyone looks up. It had to be designed that way, to make people feel small. But in all your historical research of Martian stations, Armstrong never looked anything like this.

"When are we?" you ask Pantha.

"I'm not sure yet."

You both fall into the pace of all the other travelers and make your way down the large chamber. In your reality, Armstrong Station was the last to get Balance, the last stronghold of "white" people. But they eventually caved. Nustanbul and other stations progressed rapidly in technology and culture. Armstrong couldn't keep up. And when their life support systems eroded, in their last gasping breath, they accepted brown skin.

This Armstrong Station is different, not just massive in scale. As you and Pantha look across the crowd, trying to piece where in time you are, you both notice it: the lack of brown faces walking with you. Stepping in pace with the rest of the crowd, you try to slip your hand into hers, but Pantha retracts. Down the corridor, just a few meters in front of you, are checkpoints. Uniformed men and women, without anything that look like guns, stop people for questioning.

"Maybe we could invert out of here?" you suggest to Pantha.

"I've never been here before."

The people ahead of you are all pale-skinned but with vertical forehead codes like the historical Mars you're used to. You and Pantha don't have those codes, too many years in Saturn orbit faded them. But even if they were still visible, there's no guarantee they'd work here.

"What's the play, Pantha?" you ask, but she doesn't look at you.

"They can't hurt us. Remember Earth?" Pantha grips your hip, pulling you close to her. "Try not to watch too much of this," she says, and suddenly your field of vision floods with what looks like steam but feels like nothing. You can't make out the shapes of the people in front of you, they're all just blobs of hair and necks and clothes, weaving in and out of each other. But when you glance at Pantha, she's clear. When you look down at your feet, you're clear. The liquidy blobs of people ooze and ebb around the both of you until you're past the checkpoint and further down what looks like an open plaza. Pantha breaks physical contact, and the liquidy mist crystallizes back into normal vision.

"Time is tricky," Pantha says, "you can overshoot it and end up some other place entirely."

Now that you're past the checkpoint, people disperse, going in their separate directions. You and Pantha continue strolling forward into a plaza with small triangular gardens crisscrossing a large walkway.

"Why'd you bring me to some place you've never been before?" you ask Pantha.

"I didn't," she says, "you did. This is your cyphe."

Past the plaza on either side are markets and elevators. They go up five levels. Pale people shuffle in and out of elevator cars and weave along into different markets, shopping. This must be the central commerce district.

"But there's no—" you start, but Pantha interrupts you.

"Brown people? Don't worry, that's not a reflection on you." Pantha laughs. "You used one letter on a can of beer to travel across the Axis of Meaning. So, there's something here, fundamentally, that's different." You gesture at all the pale people and the exchanging of what looks like currency, and she says, "Not the obvious differences, they're just side-effects. Think fundamental. Gut-level."

The gardens end a few meters in front of you before wide sets of stairways, each going up half a level then plateauing before the next stairway. But there's no people walking them.

"Is this all you do?" you ask Pantha as you reach the first set of stairs. "Cyphe, invert, whurlpull until you're lost?"

She blinks at you and says, "Lost? There's no 'lost' in the Rip. Directions are meaningless here. It's like walking—"

Now you interrupt her. "No more metaphors, Pantha! Just tell me direct. You said they chose you. I saw your neurals after your first transit. Your brain did something, something no one understands, and now everyone thinks you're dead, but you're really just here in the Rip, doing what?

Floundering? Wandering?" You start up the stairs and stop at the first plateau when you realize Pantha's not following you. "I don't even care where these stairs lead. What's the point? Why did the Larger Community choose you if you were just going to flip off into different dimensions ad infinitum?"

Pantha runs her hand over the top of her braids as her shoulders heave from a big exhale. Then, head down, she starts up the stairs. But she walks right past you on the plateau, continuing on to the next stairway. You fall behind her, and you each march up the stairs in silence. There's ten plateaus until you reach the top. Above you, the station ceiling becomes clear, and you can see the void of space. In front of you is a black wading pool. A plaque says something about commemorating the first of several station-wide fires in the early days of life on Mars. Pantha smooths her fingers over the letters on the plaque and then unzips her suit. She pulls her arms out the sleeves, revealing her deep brown skin to anyone in the station who might look up toward her, who may never have seen skin like hers to begin with. She steps out of the suit legs and, fully naked, walks into the wading pool. When she's waist-deep, she crouches down, then turns back to look at you.

"I didn't understand what they were asking during my first transit," she says. The ends of her braids flail out in the water. "That I could go with them, all the way to the end, to the way out. I saw the horizon of it, that freedom, like dreams about water. The other side of the Rip... It's on the other end of the galaxy, with them, the Larger Community. I won the mission! Found the door for humanity, but it's a one-way. You can't go back if you cross it."

Pantha glides her hands through the water, making ripples on the surface that fan out to edges of the wading pool. "I came back, did as I was told, but nothing I said made any sense to the team."

You remember that moment on the simvid. When Moona dismisses the Board and then leaves herself. When Pantha was sitting there alone, smiling and nodding to herself. That soft quiet moment of reassurance that wasn't meant to be seen, that felt like you were spying on her.

She continues, "At first, they thought I did something wrong. Then," she releases a faint grunt, "they thought my body had done something wrong. My cycle was broken, disconnected. And it wasn't just the men, Moona too. They all thought I was 'hysterical.'"

You move your mouth to say, "I'm sorry," but words don't come out.

"They kept me in cabin, ran every test, every Battery, on me, twice or seven times. But they couldn't see what they wanted to find. And I couldn't explain what was happening with me. I felt the Rip, even outside of it. Every bend of my body, every breath, sprang all these dimensions. That's when I met you."

Pantha doesn't ask for you to disrobe and come into the pool. She simply backs up in the water, making room for you. You peel yourself out of your suit and step into the pool. The black water is warm, 22.22 Celsius. At waist level, you crouch down so that you're like Pantha, just shoulders up from the water.

"You," Pantha says, "are the only other one we choose."

"We?"

"They think I'm dead because I chose the other side of the Rip. Like whurlpulling, I didn't fit their reality. The mission, that's their bend, and they're so deep into it, they can't see what they want to find. You did! You saw me." Pantha's voice breaks pitch. "But you have to choose too. Choose us. Choose us?"

You wade toward Pantha, close enough that your breasts are touching. You close your eyes and lean in to kiss her when the black water lifts up, running over your skin and through your hair. Pantha's lips meet yours, and you're both floating in mid-air. She wraps her arms around you, and the two of you flip and bend and spin, but you don't open your eyes. You feel your skin and her skin and the air whipping past as your tongues probe each other's mouths. Then, your inner ears pitch as your bodies swing, and you hear music. You feel the bass thudding inside your chest.

You open your eyes and pull back from kissing Pantha. You're both fully clothed somehow, and there's bright holo-neon lights swirling on the ceiling and floor. There are people here too, tons of them. They're almost shoulder-to-shoulder with you and Pantha. You recognize you're in Nustanbul Station because of all the bright saris and kurtas.

The beat drops, and your muscles flex on instinct. You start your choreography while Pantha beams, jutting her hips to the beat. You haven't danced in front of anyone since you were a girl, before you became Eligible. Pantha's eyes on you make you feel like you're still naked, but they also jolt something inside you. An audience, being seen. Being seen by Pantha. It's not the song you trained for in the Battery, but the beat is simple enough that the choreography still works anyway. You cock your head, so your curls fly as you go with the kicks and the hand gestures. On the dance floor, people move back, giving you room, but Pantha stays, swaying in front of you. You jump and hit the floor, roll over, and arch your back.

The people on the dance floor clap on beat to encourage you, and you even hear a few high trills from the crowd. Then you're back up, twitching your hips and flinging your arms through the motions. When you get to the bridge, you tilt your head up and reach for the ceiling—that part in your song when the singer sings, "Higher!" Pantha's there, on the ceiling, and she's reaching for you. You both jump and meet in the middle, and then you land on concrete. You're on Earth, outside, on a long, elevated road that spans for kilometers. You can tell from the sun that you're in a place that was once called California. The sun sits low on the horizon but bright. You feel its warmth on your skin, a sensation you're still getting used to.

There's music here too, blaring out from large speakers, and lots of young people dancing and drinking. A random man hands both you and Pantha plastic cups with Earth beer in them. It doesn't taste as sour as the vinebier on the Martian ship. Pantha sees your face react and giggles.

"That dance," Pantha yells over the music, "was that for the Battery?"

You suddenly find yourself sheepish, so you just nod.

"I love it!" Pantha says, then takes a gulp of her beer.

"What was your dance?"

"No," she says, "I don't dance for them anymore."

Pantha takes your beer from your hands and sets both your drinks on the ground. "Here," she says, "let's make up our own dance."

The song fades out as another slower song kicks in. Pantha steps in toward you but turns around. Her butt smooths over your waist as you slide your hands over her hips. Pantha lifts her arm up, twirls her fingers to the beat. She claps, and all the light instantly evaporates, but you still feel her body against yours. Wherever you are, there's no music, not audibly anyway. It's in you. Every movement you make glistens bright blues and liltuuls that linger and then fade. When Pantha turns to face you, a cloud of light engulfs her. You can only see her face when she moves, and it's only through ribbons of liquid light.

Your arms and legs cast waves together as the two of you find a rhythm. You jut your hips to create sizzling yellows. Pantha spins in a shower of pale purples. You feel pressure drop behind your ears. You and Pantha are worlds on top of worlds, sliding and colliding with each other. New and ancient. You feel her face under your own skin. She was always the last thing you remembered. Calling out to you across realities. She was searching for you, in your Repetition, during your Battery, in ways no other human could possibly do, in ways most people couldn't even understand. Looking at you, and looking for you.

And then you choose her.

You don't speak words, but everything changes. Pantha's slick foamy purple arms wrap around you, and you both fall. A new light crosses into this plane of reality, a soft blue. You can see Pantha clearly now, and she's all smiles. The blue warps around, encasing you both in a sphere, as the fall slows down. Bright cracks of light arc around the edges of it, striking and fading back. Deep purple plumes ooze and bubble underneath you and then breach the sphere.

And Pantha's looking at you, but the face is new. She's not looking for you anymore.

The arc cracks start to pierce through the sphere and through your bodies, but you're not afraid. Between the globs of purple, beyond the outline of Pantha, you catch glimpse of a red dwarf star. A new sun, a new sensation of warmth to feel on your skin. The other side of the galaxy, peaking through purple blobs and blue cracks.

Pantha slides in to hug you. The purples and blues fade to reveal some kind of vessel approaching you.

"We're out now," you whisper to Pantha, "it's over."

"But we," she says, griping you tighter, "we're just beginning."

SERMON

Earth, c 2980

This is a story about us. All of us.About the Forces that drove us apart. And the ones that brought us back together.

This is a story about me.

I'm too old to remember Mars. See, we were built to have strong, sturdy bodies that can survive. But our minds they cared less about. Some remember the journey back, falling back to Earth after the stations were built. But I do not.

What I first remember is being alone in the trees. Figuring out which water was good to drink, which plants hurt me. How to spot non-rady animals and then, later, how to capture them. I spent solar cycles like this. No words. Not much thought. When I met others, I had to be trained again. First, they tied me to a tree, fed me. In the night, they'd dress me in rags around my hips, and in the mornings, I'd rip them off. I learned them over time. Figured out who was who based on the small tics of their noses or eyebrows. See, we were made to look almost exactly like each other, say the ones who could remember. But when that bred too much confusion and infighting, they made us again with differences.

Wider Nose would feed me, give me water. Out Ears cleaned my waste. Gray Eyes would sit just beyond my reach and talk to me, wondering if I'd talk back. It was him I caught in the night, dressing me. When I woke, and he was sitting over me, I threw my arms to scratch him. He caught my wrists and, being like me, was strong. He'd wrestle me until he could hold my arms to the ground. Until I got tired and went back to sleep. But every morning, I would still rip the rags off me.

They were disappointed. I knew that somehow.

Some nights wrestling, Gray Eyes would plant his lips on mine, and I would struggle back until I grew tired. Some nights wrestling, Gray Eyes would tire first. I would flip him over and without thinking, spread his legs and pump inside of him. We did this many nights. Exhaust ourselves and lay on each other until sleep. But mornings, I was always alone, tied still to the tree.

It was the night he stayed until morning that I remember hearing laughter the first time. It was tiny, out of Gray Eyes' lips, but there enough. I tried to do it too, but it sounded different, which made Gray Eyes laugh more. The muscles in my arms tensed, and the instinct to fight rose up in me. But something else came out of my mouth instead, watching his face relax and his mouth open, heaving out until his stomach tucked. I found it, my laugh. Gray Eyes left, and sometime later, Wider Nose came. Not with food, but a knife to cut me free.

Five of us dirty clones lived together as a team. Hunting, fishing when we could. We'd collect berries in large sacks and squeeze them until they bled through. Drink the juice, then tie the sacks around tree trunks to mark rady places. At night, we'd light fire, and Thick Hair would tell us about Mars and the Earthfall. Somehow, he could remember.

The Star People sent us back, he'd say, one by one. When our work was done. We built homes we'd never live in.

Every time the moon faded, we'd pack our gear the next day and move. Always just at the edge of the rady places. Squeezing berries, tying sacks, we were marking safe territory. For us, and anyone else.

Solar cycles passed before we met anyone else. By then I had learned our names. Gray Eyes was Dash, Wider Nose was Ged, Out Ears was Lok, Thick Hair was Jum. And they named me Rom.

We kept moving camp higher up a ridge until one day we could look down on the trees and streams that we had already mapped. That's when we saw it: someone else's smoke. We'd lose a day foraging if we set out for it, and no one was keen on splitting up the group. See, by this time we'd all pumped each other, so our team was tight-linked. We decided to track the smoke for a few days. See which way they'd go. 'Course, to track them without being seen meant we couldn't light our own nightfire. So, we slept bundled together and cold.

Whoever it was, they lit fires twice a day and once at night, so they were easy to track. The fires kept moving toward the sunset, and after a few days, it was clear they'd pass us by. Jum was the one who suggested we go meet them, and we all agreed. We followed the ridge as far sunway as we could before climbing down and making camp, figuring it was safer to meet during the day. That night, Jum told us about the rady people. How not to look shocked seeing one side of their face didn't match the other, like the petals and leaves of rady plants. In the morning, Ged had the idea to tie up all our tools in a tree and leave marking stones to find them later. He figured they might look like weapons to an outsider, and it was better to meet palms up.

We stepped lightly, careful to not make noise or shake branches, until we could smell their first dayfire and hear them talking. New voices hit my ears like strange birds cawing at each other. Dash was good at birdsongs, some nights he'd coo to us over the fire until we fell asleep. I motioned at my throat and pointed my head in the dayfire's direction. He pointed at himself but then waved his hands around in circles, and I got it: he'd start, and we'd all follow.

Dash opened his mouth and soft strings of notes floated out, quiet at first, but then a little louder each time. The new voices stopped. For a moment there the air was thick, like right before a heavy rainstorm, but Dash kept at it. I followed next, then Jum, Lok, and Ged. None of us were as good as Dash, but I hoped our point came across. After a birdstring, we stopped, and even the trees themselves seem to follow. The longest quiet I'd ever remember hearing. And then it happened, one of the new voices sang back. It was higher and lighter than Dash, and not the same birdsong, but it was an offering, and Dash took it, singing back. On the next round, more new voices chimed in, and we all traded eyes and agreed. We stepped out from behind the trees and walked into their camp clearing, Jum first, then the rest of us.

They had stripped trees and bushes of their branches to clear a path that stretched back days. I could see their fire pits dotting down around barren trees. The wood they used for fire, but the leaves they kept and rolled or tied into coverings they placed on top of their heads. I figured they meant to keep the day sun out of their eyes, but the tops of their coverings had two or sometimes three spear-like pokes sticking straight up into the air. They covered both their chests and legs in animal hides, unlike us, who only bothered with wraps around our waists. And they were rady.

The first one to coo back to us was a small girl with dark brown skin and black curly hair, one eye twice the size of the other. She stood next to a grown-up man, taller than all of us, who I figured to be her father 'cause of the way he gripped her hand. His whole left side was fuller than the right. Muscles larger, hair longer.

Jum began speaking when I decided to count them all. It wasn't just this man and his kid. I got up to twenty when more of them came out of tents or from behind trees, hiding from us at first, and then I lost count. Even down the path they made, I saw more tents.

We're on a march, said the father, to the Big Water.

To equaniny, the girl said.

Equality, the father corrected, it's what they call it.

How far?

The father laughed and smiled, even his left teeth were bigger. We don't really know. We go where the GodThing tells us.

We were asked to sit around the fire, and they'd make us a meal. All of them were rady, I didn't see anyone else that looked like me. The father's name was Kemat, and when he asked Jum where we came from, he told him Mars, and all the radys blinked and stared.

Long ago Mars, Jum said.

With the Star People?

The little girl, Eth, reached out to touch Jum's hair, like he was suddenly magic.

Most of us can't remember that far back, Jum said, I only remember the stories told to me.

Kemat nodded at a rady woman, and she took off running down the path they made. Two radys placed flat rocks on the outer base of the fire, one for each of us. When they were hot enough, they put cured meats and vegetables on them.

Kemat told us about the GodThing while we ate. His uneven eyes went as wide as each could describing the caravan coming through his camp near small mountains.

See, Kemat said, people would pass from time to time, and they were always invited to stay, grow the numbers. But these people, there were so many of them! And they wore stained hides of beautiful blues and yellows, like I'd never seen before. At night, they brought out drums and cut wood sticks and sang and danced around the fire. And then one morning, they asked if I wanted to meet the GodThing. Now, I'd never seen a GodThing before, so I had no idea what they were talking about. And when I saw It, something changed about me. My whole insides.

That's when Jum stopped eating, but the rest of us kept on. Dash loved a good story, so he was hooked, munching on the hot vegetables after he finished the meat. I will say, their food was good. We only cooked meat at night and ate it separate from the plants we foraged during the day. Curing meat gave a different texture, a little harder, but there was also a flavor there. Felt rounder on my tongue.

What's a GodThing? Jum asked.

Our whole camp packed up, Kemat said, not answering, one by one after beholding It. That was, wow, years and years ago. I was just a boy then. But I grew up my whole life following It.

What's a GodThing? Jum asked again.

You'll see It, Kemat said, if you want to. Most of the caravan is two days back. My family, we're part of the front set. We clear out a path, and they follow behind us.

After the food, Jum asked for privacy so the five of us could talk. The little girl, Eth, tried to stick around, fascinated by us, but Kemat tugged her arm, and she frowned, limping away.

I don't like this, Jum said, something is off 'bout these people.

They're just rady, Ged said.

Nah, I've seen rady before, and it wasn't like this.

Food's good, I said, and there's a lot of 'em. Could be good too.

Dash said, the GodThing, never heard of that before.

Could be poison. Sometimes people take poisons on purpose and see things that aren't there, Jum said.

Jum held a vote, to stay or go back to our camp. At first, Dash and me were the only stay votes. Jum was a go, Ged and Lok didn't care. Then, a round of talking and asking. Dash wanted to see the dancers at night, so he wanted to stay for a few days. I was honest about wanting food I didn't have to work for. I figured let's be guests for as long as guests can be. That convinced Lok, our second vote was Jum go; me, Dash, Lok stay; Ged go. But Ged didn't feel strongly either way; he just didn't want Jum to be alone. Jum was the clencher. Lok and Dash said their reasons, and they were fair. Been years since either could remember meeting anyone, except me. Ged was swaying, but then Jum brought up something that stuck. How old did we think Kemat was? Thirty sun cycles, maybe more. But Jum pointed out that he looked strong and healthy.

That's the thing about radys, they don't live that long.

I almost questioned my vote, but then Jum gave up. For me, for Dash, and for Lok, Jum agreed to stay.

That night, there were no dancers like Kemat had talked about. All of them were a day back on the path, so maybe tomorrow. Dash tried not to look sore on that, and maybe it worked on the radys, but we're tight-linked, so we all caught it.

Kemat introduced us to the rest of the path-clearing families. There were too many to keep up with, and all their names made my head dizzy. By the end of the night, curled in a big blanket Kemat had given us, my face hurt from forced smiling.

In the morning, I was the last of us to wake up, but for the first time for me, I remembered my dreams fully. Usually, they're just bits and bits. A feeling or a motion. Jum would tell me that it's just the Earthfall. They didn't make our minds strong, just our bodies, Jum said, so that's how we process things.

But this time was totally different. I told the others when we walked to fetch our foraging tools from the trees just beyond their camp.

I was on Mars. I know it because I was wearing a suit and I was climbing on a slab, up so high. And when I got to the top, I looked back down, and there you all were.

You saw us? Dash asked.

No, I mean all of us. All the rest of us. Hundreds of us. And then, I looked up to the sky and saw the dots of lights in the sky. All of them.

Jum squeezed my shoulders and kissed me, your first Mars memory. Let more come to you.

We used to live in big groups of people. Just like the Star People do. Maybe we should do it again.

Maybe, Jum said. But for now, when we get back to the radys, let's not tell them 'bout this, okay?

Back at the clearing camp, Eth gathered a few more kids. They sat leg-crossed, listening to Eth tell stories about us, our singing, the way our faces all slant the exact same. They never met dirty clones, Kemat told us, and they're curious. We all traded eyes to Jum, our best storyteller, and he sighed, sitting down on the ground and waving his hands to command attention, and began. With the Earthfall, like always.

Ged and Lok volunteered to fetch some water from the river about a quarter day up. Some radys gave them tight baskets and offered to go with 'em, but they kept saying no. Me and Dash laughed low to ourselves. They wanted to fetch water, sure, but also to pump each other for a few.

That left me and Dash to ourselves, and we decided to walk down the path the radys made. I still wanted to get a sense of how many people were traveling with this caravan, and Dash wanted to take in new faces, even if they were uneven.

No one cowered at the sight of us. We got waves and smiles. But they had to know, just by looking at us, that we weren't like them. We were different in our exact sameness.

The path they cleared wasn't straight, it bent around old trees too big and too old to clear through. So, this path would turn and veer. Sometimes you couldn't see further ahead of yourself because of the brush, but once you curved, you saw there was always more path stretching down. I got so used to this that I kinda stopped paying attention to what I was looking at and didn't notice Dash stop walking until I was a few paces ahead. I turned back, and Dash's face was frozen. And he'd suddenly lost color. I called his name, but he didn't even blink. That's when I turned and saw the GodThing.

It was taller than all the radys, who were themselves taller than us clones. Its skin was more than just solid black. Black like space, black so much that light and color bent around It. A general human shape but with thousands and thousands of arms and legs, somehow all of them together in the space where one arm is and then the other. Two antlers twisted up from the top of Its head, sometimes folding in and around each other. It had no eyes that I could see, but It somehow saw us.

The GodThing cleared a great distance fast on thousands of legs and was, just like that, in front of us. Dash grabbed onto me from behind. I could feel his breath on my shoulder. He was scared. But I wasn't. I looked up at the GodThing, where Its eyes would be if It had eyes, and my body felt suddenly warm like under a blanket. I saw inside It a space where black-dark limbs like his writhed in a sea of Itself, and I heard this almost-sound. Like the pause right before or after someone speaks up, but drawn out into one long twisting string, long like this path the radys were making. For It.

Rom, the GodThing spoke, without having or needing a mouth, and Dash, welcome to our sanctuary.

Dash let go of me and then fell to ground. But I couldn't turn to take my eyes off It to check on him. I was fixed on the GodThing, and It was fixed on me too.

We're not radys, I said. We're dirty clones. From Mars.

The GodThing turned Its head toward the sky and reached Its thousands of arms to one spot. The stars only came out at night, but we both knew what It was reaching for. Thousands of thousands of warp-black fingers vibrated on a certain speck of sky.

We track it too, sometimes.

Over six hundred years ago, It said, and you're still alive?

Not all of us.

And not just you two. Three others. Jum, Ged, and Lok?

The radys explained that sometimes the GodThing can look into you and know stuff about you. That's how It knew our names. They brought water to Dash, to wake him up and soothe him. But I stayed locked with the GodThing. It stepped closer, bending down to meet my face with the smooth blank space where Its should be.

I haven't seen your face for two hundred years.

Thousands of spindly ultra-black fingers almost touched the side of my cheek. But they didn't. They hovered in the small space between us and sounded like insect wings.

Dash woke up but wasn't soothed by the soft rady voices telling him he was okay. He called out to me, and without looking back, I showed him my palms and said I was okay.

If It wanted to hurt us, we'd already be.

My nature is not that. Anymore.

Dash stood up and then joined me, gripping my hand, as the GodThing moved to look at him closer.

You're okay, I told him.

A stretch of silence passed as the radys circled us, taking in this first meeting. Their lips bent into jagged smiles. Finally, Dash blurted out, It's like us, Rom. It's not from here.

The GodThing told the radys to send for Jum, Ged, and Lok and then walked us to a large tree just off the clearing path. When It sat, thousands of legs swirled out on the ground like a root system.

I did not come from Mars. I am from someplace much further. But I was like you, Rom, wild. For years, I had lost all my names and hid from others. I circled this giant land several times, always at night. Always alone.

They call me the GodThing because that's what makes sense in their heads. But I do not require that. I do not and will not ask to be worshipped. But I can lead. I know of a place, less than one year out, a great water flanked by the largest stretch of unirradiated land. A place to grow food, to build homes. To live in peace in large numbers.

They believe that I am leading them there, but we've snaked across the land, looking for you, your kind. For they can tend and bend the land, tame animals. But they've not the strength to build large homes. You can. You have.

I could almost hear Jum's voice in my head, reacting, and the GodThing knew it. It looked directly at me.

Don't answer for others. Don't answer now. Let the invitation hang in the air.

While we waited for the others to be brought to the GodThing, It entertained us. The GodThing slipped Its arms into the large tree, and it darkened in color. Then It made the tree dance. The branches wobbled like water, like it forgot it was wood. And when the GodThing pulled out, the color returned. The tree went back to its frozen limbs.

Jum, Ged, and Lok came sometime later. The radys got lost looking for Ged and Lok, and me and Dash smiled at each other for that. But when they finally were brought to the tree and saw the GodThing, they each had different reactions. Jum was stone. He didn't say anything, didn't move. Ged tried to run at first, but Lok grabbed his arm, pulled him in tightly, and then eventually fell to his knees. Ged followed out of confusion.

Heard stories about you, Jum said, from many years back.

And I of you.

It comes from beyond the stars, Dash said.

I know that.

While Jum and the GodThing talked, Lok crawled closer to it. And then, without breaking conversation, It extended one of Its thousands of hands for Lok to touch. His finger disappeared inside the black, and his skin went dark gray. He pulled back from it and went back to his normal color.

Then he did it again. Over and over until Ged slapped his hand to stop.

The GodThing explained about this group, how they found It when they started traveling. It went like this:

Clear on the other side of the great land, It was wild, slithering on top of trees at night. See, the GodThing does not need food or water. It can survive without anything. About two hundred years ago, something changed inside It. It fell out of a tree the first time It felt it. Like someone went *through* It was all It could explain. Someone or something passed through that made It remember.

A deep sadness coursed inside of It. Dark, like Its surface, and overwhelming. It raged out at first, swallowing animals then twisting them out. It left a trail of impossible carcasses. That's how the radys found It and started worshipping. They'd catch rady rodents and birds. Leave them tied up near the twisted bodies before nightfall and come back in the morning to see what new shapes there were in. All sorts of meanings were invented from them. A limb or wing bent in a certain direction meant rain and things like that. This went on for years until the clouds shifted, and the rain stopped. Small bushes dried up first, and then vines, and then trees.

And then one night, the radys tied a woman up, left her near the twisted bodies. When the GodThing found her, she did not scream or try to break free. She understood her role. But the GodThing did not, she had to explain to It. She was the sacrifice for rain to come back.

That's when the GodThing woke up. It couldn't twist a rady. The woman led It back to her people, and some cried out in fear. Some ran and never came back. But the ones that stayed rejoiced. They celebrated for several days before asking for rain. The GodThing felt this wave inside Itself. It cannot conjure rain. It is not powerful in that way. So, they all began the journey. To the place promised. A land on the edge of great water, where nothing's rady, and everything can grow. And they can live in peace. And the radys called it Equality.

We are less than a year out, It said. Closer and closer every day.

Jum asked, how long have you been on this Earth?

Longer than anything else alive.

So, you remember the Earthfall.

I saw it.

Jum's eyes went as wide as they could.

We followed the GodThing further back down the path to the High Tent the radys set up for It. Was night by the time we got there. The radys dug a wide fire circle, brought out drums and wood sticks to sing through, and began playing. Women and children danced and swung their arms and legs out into different shapes. Then two naked men, one sitting on the other's shoulders appeared from behind the High Tent. They had dyed mud black and rubbed it all over their bodies. They were meant to be the GodThing. They were reenacting the story.

Of course, It said, none of them were there when it happened. The story gets passed down. They tell it to each other and shape this dance. I have no part in it.

After the dancing, the radys packed for the night. Without music, the trees swelled in noise. Birds and insects chirped. Sometimes branches creaked and snapped under the pressure of whatever kind of animal was climbing or perching on it. The fire crackled too. The GodThing offered for all of us to sleep in the High Tent, but we declined. We got ready for sleep around the fire.

It said something to me, I told Jum when I thought everyone else was asleep. It said It hadn't seen my face in two hundred years.

We gotta be sharp about It. If It's as old as It says It is, It knows more than we do. I don't want that used against us.

I almost told Jum about the GodThing's invitation right there. But some kind of thing I couldn't put words to clumped in my throat. Never felt any kind of force like that. I pulled the blanket over me and soon fell asleep.

I had another dream about Mars. About being outside and suited up. About looking up at the lights in the sky and realizing they were ships. They were people.

In the morning, the radys went about packing up tents. They used animal hide and tree branches to build a flat ground sled that they could pile their tents and tools on and drag behind themselves.

Every couple of days, the radys told us, they pack everything up and move along. The front team stays a few days ahead and clears a path.

The GodThing did nothing. Its thousands of legs quivered and spread around It while radys broke down Its High Tent. Some rady children played a game with It, daring each other to run through the GodThing and pop out on the other side. It let them do it for some time until It made Itself solid somehow and told the children no more.

You see stuff, Lok said, watching as the kids frowned and walked away from the GodThing. When you go into It.

What stuff?

All kinds of stuff. Earth but like way back before. Before the Star People left.

You should tell Jum.

I will.

We never kept things to ourselves when it was just us. Or at least I didn't. But something about all this newness started to keep ourselves alone. I saw it in Lok too. He even looked at Ged different and walked with me instead of him. At the half day, when everyone broke to make camp and cook, Lok tugged my arm to go with him into the trees. We walked until all the rady voices blended together, then he put me on my knees, opened his wrap, and pumped into my mouth.

We all have different ways of doing this. Dash is soft, Jum is slow. Ged's loud. But me and Lok are the hard ones. Still, this was harder than any other time. Lok's fingers dug through my hair and into the skin on my head. He didn't make any noise, just pumped into me faster and faster. Ged wouldn't have liked this, so I was glad it was me. He wasn't angry, but it was like there was something driving behind him. Something new. Felt it last night when I couldn't tell Jum about the GodThing's invitation, and I felt it now with Lok's pumping. I called it the Forces. When he was done, I told him we should find time to get away just the five of us. But he just nodded.

Back at camp, the radys didn't seem to notice we were gone, but the rest of us did. We're still tight-linked even though there's something pulling us apart. Jum made Lok sit next to Ged to eat while he sat next to me.

I still think being in a big group is better, I told him. Didn't even need to wait for him to start.

Why?

Because that's how we used to be. On Mars.

That's what your dream told you.

I felt it, the Forces, trying to tell me to hide, but I fought back. Had another dream last night. Saw the Star People.

What they'd do?

Don't know. Saw them up in the sky. In their ships. They lived in big groups too.

That's what I'm worried about. They made us like them, including all their bad parts.

But you said it before, like them but not them. And these radys, they aren't them either.

Still, something's off.

It's not them, it's It. The GodThing. You don't like It.

I don't trust It.

But you trust us. You trust Lok. Trust me.

Jum sighed, 'course I do. See, I've been watching those children, the ones that jumped through It this morning. They ain't smiling now, not working together. Lok's touched it, we all saw it. Now look at him. Not totally different, but something's there. Look at you.

I didn't touch It.

Didn't say you did. But you're dreaming now. It remembers your face. And you don't remember nothing before we found you?

I shook my head.

I think It touched you. Before.

I'd remember seeing a GodThing. I put my hand on Jum's knee. Tonight, after food, let's all take a walk together. The five of us.

Jum nodded.

The Forces stepped with us in the thick brush after the rady food and dancing. I heard it in every one of our footsteps, saw it in the tightness of Lok's shoulders. We told the radys that dirty clones have their own ceremony, but it's secret. Just for us. Because they were kind and because the GodThing liked us, they didn't ask questions. We walked in silence until their nightfire was a dim dot behind us, and Jum motioned us to sit in a circle.

Been over a hundred years with Ged. Just less with Lok, Jum said, looking at each of us. Sixty with Dash, thirty with Rom. Those are longer than radys' whole lives. That's us. The way we're bonded. No one but clones will ever understand it.

I nodded my head and could see, in the mostly dark, that everyone else did too.

Can tell we're keeping things from each other. Maybe for good reason. But I'm making the space now; share anything you want. No questions at first. Just say out what you got to.

Silence filled the dark. The Forces fluttered between each of us, clamping our mouths shut. We're built strong-bodied, but not strong-minded, so the Forces weren't easy to break. But somehow Lok got there.

You gotta choose to leave It, Lok said. When you go inside the GodThing. Can't say it right, but every time I put my finger in It, I vanished. Felt almost good, but not right. I kept coming back but couldn't make words to say what it felt like. So, I kept trying. But you, he turned to Ged, you slapped my hand. You chose for me. That's not your place.

More silence. Dash put his hand on my knee, and I cupped my hand over his.

Dash said, I like these radys. But I'm scared. I'm scared we'll end up like them, worshipping It. Like we might lose ourselves.

Maybe it's because Dash and I are the newest to the group, or maybe it's because I laughed with him first, all those years ago, but he's got this way of moving something in me. His hand on my knee keeps the Forces at bay, and I speak up.

The GodThing wants us to build for the radys at Equality. Build their homes, like we did on Mars. Dash was there. It knows you won't like it, Jum. It knew because I knew.

Jum nodded, then looked at Ged. He and Jum were the only ones left who hadn't aired something out. We all knew Jum had a piece to say about all of this. Looking at Ged, Jum gave him a chance to go first, but he didn't take it. He shook his head and shifted weight on his hips.

Heard about the GodThing before, Jum starts, from the clones before you. They called It a night monster. Never saw It but saw what It left behind. Twisted bodies and trees.

No way It could be from anywhere we know. Not Earth, not Mars. It's doing something. To everyone around it. See how color bends around it when it moves? See how old these radys are? As long as we decide to stay, we gotta know, It's doing something to us too.

I don't want to go, Lok said.

Ged said, I don't want to build more homes for other people.

Why haven't we ever built homes for ourselves? Dash asked. Jum cleared his throat to speak but Dash kept going. No, I'm not play-asking. All us dirty clones been down here for six hundred years, if what the GodThing said is true, then none of us, ever, built anything? Weren't we made to do that?

Must have lost it in the Earthfall, Ged answered.

It saw the Earthfall, Jum said, and we haven't asked It about it yet.

After that, we didn't need to take a vote to stay with the caravan, like we all decided we had our own answers to seek out.

We got back to camp just as the dancing died down and the radys packed up for the night. The GodThing sat in front of the fire while the radys moved around It. It's never still, Its thousands of arms and legs are always vibrating.

Rom told you, It said to Jum, about Equality. About building.

Jum nodded. Each of us has got to make that decision themselves. Hope you can respect that.

It's your right. Even just one of you would be a tremendous help.

No one else spoke to the GodThing. We all went about setting up for sleep, gathering our blankets and lining up near the fire. The GodThing vibrated back to Its High Tent, and the noise of the woods took over. Couldn't get to sleep right away. I kept shifting, but then finally I slipped into it.

I didn't dream about Mars this time. I dreamt about Earth. It was night, and I was wandering through the rain, looking for a dry place to rest. But even though I was wet, I felt the hairs on my arms stand up. Like something was nearby, tracking me. But I didn't have language at that time, so I didn't fully understand.

The Forces, the GodThing said. That's what you call it.

I twisted my neck around in the dream, trying to spot where the voice was coming from.

There wasn't a word for it where I come from. It was more of a gesture. It meant: the place where fear releases into the world.

Finally, I saw It. The rain looked like it split itself on contact with It. Didn't bounce like rain does off tree branches or the ground. Or me or other living things. In the dark, It was a blurry absence of Itself. A gap against the trees.

I'm not afraid of you, I told It.

Dreaming was new to me, but something about this one felt off. The Mars dreams were from memories I'd forgotten, and this one had started like that. But then it shifted. It was still memories, still the same trees, the same rain. But it wasn't my memories anymore. It was the GodThing's.

Nor I of you. It moved toward me in the dark. You fear being alone. That's what you release into the world. That's your Forces.

I'm doing this? We're doing this to ourselves?

The radys do it too. So did the Star People. So do I, in my own ways. The things we worry about, we manifest them. Sometimes on purpose, knowing we're doing it. But most times, it's outside of our own thoughts.

The rained stopped. I looked up and saw the clouds fading as the stars peeked out again. The moon was its thickest perfect circle in night. The opposite of the GodThing, light shone out around its edges.

We have to learn how to change this. And then show them all how to.

How do we do that?

You're right. I am like the moon's opposite. It reached Its thousand arms to the sky, blocking out the moon. When It brought Its arms down the moon was gone from the sky. It took it. Then It turned to me and opened Its thousands of shaking fingers. We have to find the moon of fear.

I stared at the moon inside Its vibrating palms. The light around its edges glowed and then faded into the thick gnarly black of the GodThing. The moon was bright and constant, and the GodThing was twisted and quivering behind it and on the sides of it. Felt like years passed staring at it. I felt all my memories, even the ones I forgot, folding onto themselves. Mars. The Earthfall. My clones. And now It. All wrapped up together. Caught somewhere in the space of the moon's glow and the GodThing's dark hum. Then I woke up.

After we packed up in the morning, we joined into the caravan's walk. The GodThing never packed Its tent, the radys always did it for It. But that morning, It wouldn't let them. Instead, a group of radys picked up the tent from its corners and carried it with the GodThing still inside.

Must not weigh anything, Ged said.

And somehow, Jum said, that makes absolute sense.

At the halfday meal, a rady woman asked Jum to tell the kids more stories. About the Earthfall and clones. They want to make a dance for it and show it to us. While Jum gathered the children, Ged and Lok walked off "to get water" so it was just me and Dash.

You had a dream again, he said. I can tell.

This one was different.

Dash leaned in, and I felt the Forces slip in between us. I wasn't ready to share it yet.

Last night, you said your fear was worshipping It.

Was losing ourselves in It. So that we're not ourselves anymore.

Do you think the radys are like that?

Not all of them. But some of them are.

So, we'd probably be the same. Some of us get really into It and some of us not.

I see Lok getting into It and taking Ged with him. Then you and—

No, stop, I tell him. Don't bring the words out. Speak it into happening.

Dash nodded.

How do we stop that before it happens?

Don't know.

Me either, so let's think on it.

We found a rhythm with the radys real quick. Their day had a structure to it. Ours was looser when it was just us. Me and Ged liked it, knowing exactly what to do every day. Could tell he slept better for it because he was always the first one to hang his mouth open and blare real deep.

Something sparked in Jum the first night the children did their dance of the Earthfall. They would lift each other up and then throw them into the air until they fell to the ground. That first time showing us the dance, I could almost see the Forces on them. Their fingers and knees twitched all through the night meal. But none of the children got hurt. They all landed perfectly on the ground, and Jum's eyes went real wide. See, Jum was always the one to tell the Earthfall story because another clone told it to him long ago. Watching the children dance, it was like hearing the story for the first time. Every day after that, during the halfday break, Jum would scoop up the children and practice the dance. They'd add things in, take some things out. In the mornings, while the adults packed up from the night before, the children would run out into the trees to find rocks, leaves, anything they could use to make costumes with.

Worth saying that the dance never did capture the full story. Too complicated to dance out with children's bodies. But over time, the dance built up into something bigger than the GodThing dance. The children scratched dust off rocks, not just any rocks, they chose carefully, and when a child was thrown in the air, they'd release the dust. In the firelight, that dust sparkled just like the stars in the sky while the children flailed their arms and legs before tucking in to ready for the landing.

Jum and the children dried out big leaves, then gathered up mushrooms and white moss to grind down. They mixed it with water and fire ash, spread it over the leaves, and then wrapped them around their arms and legs. They made spacesuits.

Wasn't just Jum, the GodThing would speak into his mind, and new pieces Jum never brought up in his telling of it worked into the dance. Every night after the dance while us and the radys slapped our knees to celebrate, the GodThing would tremble hard, Its way of showing thanks.

Lok fell into hunting with the rady men while Dash learned weaving from the rady women and helped mend tents and carrying bags. Ged gathered sticks and twisted them together into toys for the rady children. I mostly followed the GodThing. In my head, we shared memories back and forth with each other. But I never asked It why It knew my face, and It never shared memories from where It originally came from.

Once every moon cycle, the radys would remind us of our secret ceremony. Never to pry but to give us time to go off alone together. The first time we forgot all about that fake story but trudged off into the trees anyway. In silence. With the caravan, we all fell into our separate spots, but alone together, we didn't have much to say to each other. The Forces were deep in us now, and all we ended up doing was pump each other until everyone released and went back.

On the third moon cycle, when we came back to camp after our ceremony, the children didn't perform the Earthfall. The GodThing said not tonight and then told us: Equality. It's not far. The front team found signs of it. A different smell on the breeze, trees getting smaller. Every day less and less rady plants.

There was happiness in the radys, but they didn't scream out or slap their knees. We didn't either. Seemed the Forces put a weight on everyone.

The GodThing warned us that we would begin to see things we've never seen before. The leftovers of the Star People. Time broke their structures down, and wild grew over them. It told us not to be afraid though, Equality was the safest space to build again. But that in a few days' time, the mission, the caravan, all the traditions, all our shared knowings, all would start to change.

The next day started off normal. I had gotten into the habit of breaking down the GodThing's tent every day and was halfway through when Kemat and Eth ran from further up the path to find It. They're always a day or two ahead of us so they must have run all night. They tried talking between deep, heavy breaths, so I told them to wait and let me fetch water, but the GodThing extended one of Its palms to them. They each bent their head down toward It, plunged their faces in. Never saw anyone do that before.

Their skin went gray, and their shoulders slumped, but when the GodThing pulled back, their color came back, and they stopped breathing heavy and tired. The GodThing quivered faster than usual, and Kemat and Eth nodded their heads in agreement.

Rom, It said, come with us.

Took all day walking to get to it. The sun was fading the sky into warm pinks and oranges when the trees cleared around something smaller than a mountain but taller than anything else around it. It was covered in vines and moss on its broad sun-facing side. Poked out of the ground at an angle and the back underside of it was dark like a cave, couldn't see deep into it.

Something lived inside of it, Kemat said. We found bones in there. Think the clearing scared it off, though.

The Star People made this, the GodThing said. If you dig deeper underground, you'd find it's one big circle with a bend in the center. They used these to talk to each other over great distances in space.

The GodThing also tried to talk to me in my head, but I was already ahead of It. I walked up to the broad side of the structure. It bent in, like a bowl, but not as deep. I tugged at the vines on it. They weren't rooted in deep, just laid on top of the surface and got sun all day. I grabbed a few vines in each hand like rope and started climbing up.

Radys make good climbers because they're skinny. But this wasn't a tree or a rock. Twisting yourself won't help to pull yourself up. You need strength. Underneath the vines, the surface of the thing was almost smooth, but with a build-up of hard dirt that didn't move. Helped my feet find footing. Halfway up it, I was already at tree-top level, and the voices of the radys on the ground grew too faint to listen to.

All the details were different, but this felt just like my Mars dreams. Climbing, alone, with people down below me. Up this high too, I could feel the Forces drift away from me. My hands and feet knew exactly what to do, and my mind was just along for the ride. I've done this before, over and over, on Mars. This was a part of building.

At the top, I could see further out over the land than I ever had before. The mountain ridge we camped over right before meeting the caravan was a small bump off in the distance. Larger mountains with white tips were on the opposite side. The land dipped slightly right where the sun was setting. Then, I finally noticed all the other structures, just like this one, shooting up about a day's walk between each other. Counted five above this one and three below. All of them set up in a half circle. This one was the deepest part of the circle. That's why we found it first.

Climbing down, I hopped and loosened my grip, tightened when my feet hit the structure and pushed off again. Didn't have to figure out how to do it, I just knew. Made the trip down faster. Was getting dark, and the GodThing told us to make camp in the dark underside of it. Kemat worried about whatever animal was set up in there, but the GodThing said It would protect us.

I huddled together with Kemat and Eth to go to sleep. Eth was afraid of this animal that kept bones, but Kemat cooed her to sleep. Before I fell asleep, the GodThing spoke in my mind, Everything here we can use, everything you can take with your bare hands.

When I fell asleep, my mind went back to Mars. I was climbing a structure again. Not like the one we found today. This one was flat and bright white. Harder material too. Stronger. Building wasn't just climbing. The structure had many big parts, and I had a tool on my back to help blend them together.

The GodThing spoke to me, There can't be any cracks.

I know.

Even the tiniest one, one that you can't see, will break everything. The air will seep out, this wall will buckle, and then no one will be able to breathe.

I know, I said. It's like the Forces.

Yes, but stronger. The Forces on Mars aren't like the ones here.

I know.

I pulled the tool from my back forward and went about covering the line between the two pieces of wall.

You never thought about it, on Mars, did you?

None of us did.

I had to roll the tool over the line six or seven times until it started to fade. Then, more times to make sure the job was done.

One mistake, from any of you, and all the Star People would have died.

They didn't build us to think. Just to do our jobs.

You didn't know anything else. Not even the magnitude of what you built. Nothing before the job, and nothing after.

I kept rolling the tool over the line. It faded more and more but didn't disappear yet.

But you know now. You know what they'll do to you when the job is over.

There was no keeping the GodThing's voice out of my head even during the day. So, in the dream I tried to stay focused on my task, on rolling.

Would you still do the job? Knowing what you know now. Seeing all these hundreds of years on Earth.

I think so.

Why?

Because I was built for it.

You go back to that a lot. All of you clones. You go back to this default. "You were built for it." "They made our bodies strong, not our minds." Like you can't make your own decisions.

Sure I can.

Then stop. Stop building and see what happens.

The line was almost invisible. I could have stopped. Climbed up to the next level. Never tell anyone about what I did. The line wouldn't be a problem now. But when the work was done, when the Star People filled this with air and then moved themselves inside, little bits of air would hiss out. Small at first. No one might notice for a long time. But eventually, this wall would cave. The Star People would be blown out onto the Mars surface. Rock dust would collect around their bodies.

I didn't stop though. I kept rolling over the line until it was gone. Completely.

They lied, the GodThing said as I started climbing to the next level. To you, yes, but also to themselves. And they believed it. They built you so you could build. And they thought it would stop there. The Star People based their whole system on this. That you'd just stop. But you never stopped, did you? That's why you like groups, Rom. Because you build yourselves.

I woke up first and found the GodThing on the broad side of the structure. Its hands trembling above Its antlers.

You don't go into other people's dreams. Just mine. Why?

Because you let me.

We waited another day for the caravan to arrive. The radys' bent mouths hung open at the sight of the structure. Their uneven eyes took it in like big bowls. The children tried to climb it almost immediately, but Jum stopped them. When Ged reached his hand out to touch the surface of it,

Jum stopped him too. He darted his eyes back and forth between me and the other clones and breathed heavy. The Forces had reached deep down into him. I stepped gently toward him, palms out. Placed my hands on his shoulders and breathed slow and long until Jum started to mimic me. Once he was calm, I told him. It's okay, I already climbed it. Felt just like Mars.

Two teams of rady hunters broke off above and below us to count how many other structures were out there. Lok went with one of them, but the rest of us stayed. After our night meal, Jum finally relaxed enough to allow the children to play on the structure, climb the vines up high, but not too high. 'Course the kids were just as scared of it as they were excited, so none of them went up too high.

I don't like it, Jum said to me and Dash.

It's just what the Star People left behind. Just things they built.

That's why I don't like it.

Dash spoke up, but they built us too. You don't think that it's like us?

They built these things long before they built us, Jum said. We're nothing like it.

Had another dream about Mars, sleeping under it.

Dash asked, does Mars have these structures too?

Don't know. But I remembered more. More of the work.

We built homes we'd never live in, Jum said.

That's bad, Dash said. But was the work bad?

Jum didn't answer, just watched the children climb. That night there was no Earthfall dance.

We waited days for the hunting teams to come back. Whatever predator animal lived under the structure never returned. The GodThing said it could smell us and was out there in the trees just waiting for us to leave. While we waited, Ged and the radys tried to clear vines from the structure. They could be coiled and used as ropes or cut into long thin strips and used as fiber. That was one thing about the radys; they knew how to get the most use out of anything.

Five nights passed when the low hunting group came back. They counted three more structures but also two stumps where structures used to be but fell down. The GodThing told us, in their time, these structures were full circles titled toward the sky. Now, so much time has passed that they're half buried. But before the Star People left Earth for good, they used them to search the space sky.

I always pictured Star People with their faces up, whether on Mars or on Earth. Always looking to the sky, always looking for somewhere else. Radys tended to look down at the ground, and us clones just stared at what was directly in front of us.

Two nights later, the high hunting group came back with Lok carrying a young rady man. The group split up to count structures, and a big cat attacked the rady. He'd live, but he'd miss a chunk of his arm. The GodThing told the radys to set the man on the ground in front of It. Told someone to sit behind him, so he'd be upright. The GodThing wobbled toward the rady. GodThing had no real waist, like the rest of us do, but something in Its mid-section winded with the crashes of thousands of feet upon the ground. Sounded almost like music. Intentional. Radys ushered their kids away to Jum, who was on the cave-side of the structure. He calmed the children down by telling stories. The Earthfall, again and again.

I stayed with the other clones and watched.

Close up on him, the GodThing knelt down. Each knee sounded like darts smacking dirt, like heavy rain. It told the young man to point his bitten arm straight forward. Then the GodThing started swelling. Not all at once, see, It expanded and then returned. Got big and then shrank back, but each time bigger and bigger. The rady turned gray when his fingers crossed into It. But he didn't look afraid until the swelling started to reach his bite. He screamed out, tried to get up, but the rady behind him held him there. Lok rushed to help out, slipped his arms up under the rady's, and held up tight.

The GodThing's thousands of arms would get lost when It swelled out, but when It drew back in, they swiveled and shook so much they looked blurry. Spent too much time looking at Its arms that I didn't catch what was happening to the bite at first. The rady screamed out so loud birds in the trees flew out. The bite went full black. When the GodThing shrunk, bits of It were left on the bite. They oozed back like thick water into the GodThing until It swelled out again. After four rounds of this, the rady suddenly stopped crying out. When the GodThing drew back into Its regular shape, the rady passed out in Lok's arms. His bite was gone, but the skin stayed gray.

That night, the radys set up the GodThing's High Tent and went to sleep without food or dancing, but Lok pulled us all aside into the trees where they couldn't hear us.

Out with the counting group, Lok said, I started having dreams. About Mars.

Been having them too, I said.

But the GodThing was there, talking to me.

Me too. Said It only did it because I let him. Said I was the only one.

Jum said, this ain't our place. With them. We should leave.

You'd leave the children? Dash asked.

Figure we can talk a few radys to come with us.

No, Lok said. This Equality? Something's there. Something's there for us.

The work, I said. Building.

In the dark, I could feel The Forces wrapping around Lok. He opened his mouth to speak many times, but the words weren't coming.

The work... Lok finally got out. They were dying up there.

Who?

The Star People. They're dying right now. They found a next place to go, to live, not everyone can make it, and they're killing each other over it. The work, the work was to save lives.

Not ours, Jum said.

But look, Lok said, we got our lives anyway. Our lives are longer than theirs.

Ged spoke up, you never cared about Star People before, or radys, even now. Just us. You used to say all you wanted was us.

All I want... Lok stopped. The Forces clamped his throat. In the dark, I took Lok's hands in mine. He started back again; all I want is to feel good. Saving people, that's gotta feel good.

Jum asked, why not save radys?

We're two days from Equality. They'll be saved there.

Because the GodThing told you so?

It told them so, hundreds of solar cycles before we met them.

Touching that thing, Jum said. We saw what it did tonight on the boy, but that don't mean it's always good. Lok, you ain't been the same since you touched It. Rom ain't either.

I never touched It.

But It's in your dreams. You walk for days right next to it. I know it's in your mind. Talking to you, touching you.

It's good to remember Mars. It's good to remember the work.

Dash said, that's what we're built for. The work.

Lok said, the Star People lied to us. They told us the work was over. But the GodThing told me, Star People make up their own lies and believe them.

I spoke up, told me that same thing too.

So why are they worth saving?

Jum's voice spun up with the Forces. We all choked on the question. After some silence, we decided to walk back to camp, except Lok and Ged who wanted to be together for a bit before sleeping. In my mind, I kept wanting to reach out and put my hand on Jum's shoulder, say something to calm the storm inside him. But the Forces hung tight over me too.

The place where fear gets released into the world is what It said.

The moon of fear is what It said.

Tried to think on it more, but then I fell asleep.

The caravan reached Equality the next day. After the structures, the ground sloped down into a small valley with no rady plants. Small trees and bushes pushed bright fruit out from their limbs. Each different color had a different taste. The rady children plucked so many fruits and munched on them so hard that red, yellow, and orange stains ran down their bodies. Rady women went straight to work examining not just the fruit but every part of the plant that produced it. Rubbed their fingers over the leaves to gauge their strength and flexibility. Pulled on tree branches to test them.

The rady men focused on the ground, looking for animal tracks. They started to piece together what kind of game might migrate through here. Us clones went to work too, except for Jum. Dash counted paces from the end of the tree line, right before a sand beach and a great water, to where the land started to slope up. Ged counted paces down from where the rady kids played to a stream that started flowing deep in the trees and emptied out in the great water. Lok dug into the ground, inspecting the dirt and how it changed as he got deeper.

I started counting heads. Figured this could be just like Mars, one big building with little parts inside for every family to have a place. But Lok didn't like it. The building would have to be tall, and the ground didn't feel strong enough for it, like there might be more structures buried underneath.

We'll build like radys, he said, like tents but permanent.

The whole time Jum sat up against a tree, watching us with his mouth open. Children tried to give him fruit, but he wouldn't eat. He was so deep in the Forces that sometimes I forgot he was even there. At midday, when we broke to eat, he wouldn't move.

That night, after the dancing was over, the GodThing gathered the elder radys and us clones. We walked out past the tree line to the sand beach. The moon hung half full in the sky but still lit up the waves out on the great water. Saw more stars here than I ever remembered seeing.

The GodThing was hard to see in the night. When It stood at the edge of the wet sand, I could only make It out by the way the moonlit waves in the distance hovered against the edges of It. The GodThing lifted Its thousands of arms high above Its antlers and spoke.

I knew of this place because I came into this world not far from here. It had been abandoned even by the people the Star People left behind. They tell themselves that everyone on Earth left together in a big migration, but I was here when it happened. The migration was fractured, people choosing sides, fighting each other. Took hundreds of sun cycles to get the majority of them up there. It was a scared time for them. I knew it well because that's where I am from.

I come from a place that is all pain. The way the air fills everything yet we cannot touch it, that's what suffering was there. There were heavy thousands and thousands of us, just like me. Writhing around on each other, slipping inside and ripping up what's inside us. I spent too many lifetimes screaming inside myself before trying to get free, break free.

There was no ship that could reach me, no planet to land on. I was on the other side of a shadow.

The GodThing paused before going further.

I... am not proud of what I have done. But before this planet, I did not know better. I was not built to consider even the others like me. We had no real minds to speak of, just hurt and anger.

I found my way to this planet through hurt and anger. I found a woman who carried her hurt and anger like it was precious and worshipped it. But her body was too weak. So, I pulled myself inside her daughter, who was so strong but also held hurt in her heart. Her mother had given that hurt to her. It broke every kind of love she tried to give in this world, and I caught on to it. I fed it. I whispered to it. I am not proud, but I pulled myself out of my existence and into this one through her tooth. She screamed me into this world against her wishes. And together we ripped a tear in the sacred fabric.

The GodThing's arms sharpened and stopped vibrating. They pointed directly above It to a spot in the night sky.

It's there. For hundreds of sun cycles, the Star People did not even see it. But when they could, they didn't know what they were looking at. They studied it and studied it. With the same devotion that some of you study me, worship me. They've now found a way into that tear and a way to travel to entirely new places. I feel it every time they pass through. The first time was two brilliant women, and when I felt them, I fell out of a tree. I started twisting animals because I could not understand this feeling. But now, more and more Star People are passing through. And I feel their hurt. A new kind of hurt. An indescribable one. And for a flash of a second, I know them. The Star People. They are killing each other over the right to pass through that tear. To pass through me. And they will destroy themselves until there's nothing left but shallow objects in space, rather than even thinking to return here.

I did not ask to be a god. Truly, I do not deserve it. I have done horrific things, and I know now that I must pay for them. I have to go back, to all the suffering, to that realm of pain, to reseal the fabric. To stop their endless fighting. Now that you're here, in the place you've called Equality, you can make a permanent home. You can live together in peace. So that when the Star People come back to Earth to live, you can show them how to.

I chose you, the elders and the clones, to say goodbye to, because you are the wisest. And my hope is that you will understand what comes after I go. I hope that I will remember you all, always. That through my hurt, my pain, and my suffering will be little sparks of each of you, reaching out. Tell the children goodbye for me.

The GodThing stretched Itself taller and taller. Was hard to make out in the night sky, but then It started to Shine. I never knew light could come out from a black that deep. The Shine started in the middle section of It. On humans and clones, we'd call it a stomach, but the GodThing doesn't need to eat. The light itself wasn't like anything I'd seen on Earth. It wasn't bright. The GodThing grew taller and taller, and Its Shine spread over Its body. I understood it once the GodThing was taller than the structure back in the woods. The non-bright Shine was the only light the GodThing could create. That's what passed for light where It was from. Made me feel sad.

We spent days walking and talking inside each other's heads. I let the GodThing into my dreams. It always had this unreal nature; I always knew It was otherworldly. But it made sense in my head for It to be here. So, now the place of pain and suffering where It came from didn't match up, like the GodThing would somehow stick out there.

The GodThing's Shine glowed harder but not brighter as the GodThing thinned down while still lifting taller and taller in the air. Its thousands of legs, once like the roots of a tree, shrunk down to branches, and then further, to thousands of twigs, vibrating like plucked strings.

I stepped closer, to get a better look, while everyone else stepped back. There was more GodThing in the sky than there was in front of me. Through the dark, I tried to follow the tiny vibrations of Its twig legs. I felt a tug whenever I focused down to just one, like all the food in my stomach would launch up at any second. I blinked until my stomach settled and tried again, not focusing on a single twig but trying to take in as much of this part of the GodThing as I could.

Finally, I noticed it. The Shine came from the vibrations. Every time a twig brushed against another twig, Its Shine would escape out. It was happening so many times a minute that I couldn't count them all. And then, at the thinnest and shiniest the GodThing could possibly be, it popped. There wasn't an explosion, but there was some force that leapt out from it. Racing like a giant echo. Since I was so close, it took the breath out of me and pushed me down on the sand. When I got up, the GodThing was gone. There was a young woman on the sand where the GodThing had stood and a new star in the sky above her.

Lok and Dash ran up on the sand to help me but stopped in their steps when they saw her. She had dark curly hair and was wearing the kind of clothes radys would have never seen on Earth before. They weren't like the clothes given to us on Mars, but they were close enough. She was huddled in ball, but the sounds of footsteps on the sand brought her out, and she began to blink and look around to all of us. More radys and the rest of us clones gathered around her. The radys' bent mouths hung open.

She began to speak, and we froze like stones because we couldn't understand her words. Me, Lok, and Dash were the closest to her. She crawled and then reached out for us to pull her up. Her body was sturdy, but she felt weak under her own feet. And she kept talking. Words none of us had heard before lingered on the beach breeze.

Dash and I helped her walk back to camp. Each of us wrapped an arm around her waist, steadying her as she walked.

I saw her before, Lok said, walking next to us. She was inside It the whole time.

At camp, the elder radys quickly sat children and parents down in small groups and began to tell them this new story. Jum didn't come with us to the beach, still locked down with the Forces. He looked like he hadn't moved at all. Until he saw the girl. His skin flushed like blood was suddenly pumping again, and his eyes narrowed. He stood up and began to raise a finger, pointing toward her.

A Star-Person!

No, Lok stepped in, blocking Jum from the girl. She came from It, not the stars.

That thing? Where is It?

It's gone. She's what's left.

I don't understand.

You don't have to.

Lok stood firm between Dash, me, and the girl, and Jum. I saw Jum's face twist, looking each of us in the eyes. He struggled to speak because the Forces wouldn't let him.

The rady children wanted to stare at the girl and touch her hair, but the parents said no, and everyone got ready for bed. The elder radys slept in a circle around her while Lok and Ged stood watch overnight.

Next day, while the radys went to work studying Equality and us clones planned for building, the girl kept trying to speak to us. Dash sat with her and began pointing to different things, like trees, flower, and dirt, to teach her our talk. By midday meal, she could say hello and her name: Lau. She sat with everyone, Dash following her, to say hello and her name, then wait to hear their names. Some rady kids blushed at the direct attention, but rady parents nodded with crooked smiles. 'Course she couldn't meet everyone during one midday meal, there's too many of us. When food was over, rady women took her hand and led her down with a small group, plucking leaves from vines growing over a tree.

Me and Ged spent the rest of the day talking out how to make the tools we'd need to build permanent tents. All answers seemed to point back to the structures just outside of here. Tomorrow we'd walk back there, inspect them, and see how to break one down.

That night during dinner, Lau again worked her way through the caravan. But she was stopped and sat in front of the big fire just in time for the dancing. Dash sat next to her and pointed words to help her through the story. In just a day, she was already picking up our talk real good. The children led the Earthfall dance, and Lau's eyes opened twice their size once she realized what the story was. She pointed to each of us clones and then pointed to the sky. We all shook our heads, except Jum.

Next dance was the rady men, telling the GodThing story. More people watched Lau watching instead of the dance itself. When the two men in black mud appeared, dancing the GodThing, Lau's face went stone. Dash pointed at them and then pointed to her.

You from it, Dash told her.

Didn't look like Forces took her; it was something else. Some kind of thought, landing inside her. It reminded me of when I woke up from my first Mars dream. She remembered something. After the GodThing dance, radys elders got up. They formed a half circle around the two mud men, directing them where to stand and what to do. They began to sing the story of last night. The place of pain and suffering. The tear in the great fabric. The Shine. They told the mud men to shake, harder and harder and then told them to sit down. Then the elder women crawled on the ground, singing, making their way to Lau. They stopped just close enough to touch her. Dash taught her how to say thank you earlier in the day, and she repeated it over and over. She blinked her eyes each time to emphasize it.

After the dancing, Lau continued introducing herself. I felt my food plunge into my stomach as Lau made her way to Jum. Being a Star-Person, Lau was taller than us clones but shorter than the radys. But her body was thick like ours. She sat down in front of Jum and crossed her legs. Jum was lost in the Forces, and his eyes were empty. Still, she tried looking into them.

She said hello and her name, and Jum didn't respond. She said it again, but this time lightly placed her hand on his knee. The contact jumped Jum back into himself. He twitched and then realized who was in front of him.

Hello, Lau, she said, pointing to herself.

I know I couldn't really see the Forces, they aren't here in our world, more like a feeling. Still, I saw them wrap around Jum like vines. They coiled and swelled up, and Jum began to move, and I jumped up to run to Lau, but I was too late. He slapped her hard across her face.

You, Jum screamed, standing up, shouldn't be here! You don't deserve here!

Stop, I screamed.

Lau lay on the ground, scared, while Jum stood over her. Lok reached him first and pushed him into the trunk of a tree. Dash gathered around Lau, checking her face.

You made us, made us like this! To build your world and then you threw us back here. Like we were nothing! Like we meant nothing! We built your homes, homes we never lived in. And I can't even remember them. I can't remember the Earthfall. I only know the stories. But it still hurts me! I feel it in my muscles and in the tips of my fingers.

Jum stopped yelling at Lau, but Lok still pressed him against the tree. Jum turned to me.

I can't do this! I can't build again. Not even for the radys, but especially not for her. Not for the Star People who will come back now. It hurts too much, Rom! How am I supposed to heal in Equality? With you all just building again. Knowing they're coming and building anyway! How can I? How can you?

The air out of Jum's voice faded, and he collapsed onto Lok. And in that moment, I saw, inside my own mind, the GodThing. It was quivering, holding the moon in Its thousands of fingers.

We have to learn how to change this. And then show them all how to.

I took Jum from Lok's arms, squeezed him tight, and then kissed him.

There's a place full of pain, I told Jum. And it's easy to choose it. Because it's powerful. Because it needs us. Pain and suffering need us to survive.

I felt tears running down my face and out of my nose. But I kept going.

It's okay to be hurt, Jum. We all hurt from it. But we don't choose it. We don't lay in it. I don't know Dash, Lok, or Ged's reasons, I just know mine. I want to be with people again! I remember living in groups, Jum. And I want it back! But sometimes we build things in our heads and in our hearts, and then we let them tear everything we love apart. Sometimes, we release our fears out into the world. Not just us, the radys, the Star People. We all can do it. Tell ourselves something deep down and then build on it.

I took a deep breath and remembered the GodThing and kept going.

The Star People may have made us. But we build ourselves. Every day, Jum. We build on what we choose inside ourselves until it's out in the world. That's how you heal your hurt, Jum. By building something new.

But I can't build again! I can't!

Then let us. Let us build for you.

That night, I slept with Jum in my arms. And I had dreams about the Star People. About their Earthfall back to us. It wasn't a celebration, but it wasn't pain either. It was just like this night. Talking. Releasing the Forces. The GodThing asked me how to find the moon of fear, and I think I found it.

Jum never lifted a finger to help us build Equality. And he never had to. No one asked him to help. But every day I would talk to him. Share little things about the GodThing or

Mars. Sometimes it was funny stories, sometimes we cried all night. But slowly he started to release. I could hear it in the way he breathed, see it flicker in the corner of his eye.

Some nights, after Jum would fall asleep, I would walk out to the beach. Sit down on the sand and look up to the stars in the sky and the black spaces between them. Lok followed me one night, sat with me with his arm softly over my shoulders.

I miss It.

I know.

This thing, this GodThing, was inside my mind for so long. Got used to It being there.

I know.

But what I keep telling myself, what I knew the whole time, is that It could have done anything to me. To us. And maybe I would have let It. But It didn't. It didn't force anything.

I know.

It just let me grow.

I think about It, Lok said. Out there, in the hurt and the suffering. But It's got a piece of us now. I think It remembers all our dances. I like to think there's a new kind of pain out there now, that's better, because of us.

In that time, we didn't just build permanent tents. We made gardens. We spread the river out to grow Equality. At night, Lau would tell us stories about her resistance. About the Star People before they left Earth, and all the bad ideas they took with them. Every night, we made new promises to each other. The rady children grew up and had their own children. And we told them about the sky, the stars, the

GodThing, about the hurt that we grow, and the fears we release. We tell them about the Star People who will come back to us one day.

We tell them the story about us. All of us. About the forces that drive us apart. And the ones that bring us back together again.

This is that story, and now, it's a story about you.

ACKNOWLEDGMENTS

So many people supported me through this book, from concept, to execution, to production and publishing. First and foremost, thank you, and massive appreciation to, Lisa Kastner, Cody Sisco, and the team at Running Wild Press and RIZE. Thank you also to my writers' group: Dudley Saunders, Tony Valenzuela, Dan Lopez, and Charles Jensen. Martine Lunis, Lauren Haugli, Luke Strong, and Nelly Nickerson, thank you for inspiring me. Thank you to Angus McGuire, Mariana Mendoza, Ruby Pinto, Ian Madrigal, Angela Peoples, and so many more at the Center for Story-based Strategy. Thank you to the amazing women and men who educated me: Sonya Huber, Patricia Price, Lori Amy, Porochista Khakpour, Hollis Seaman, Karen O'Brien, and Al Davis. To my story ancestors, Da Chen, Peter Christopher, and David Starnes, thank you for everything. Thank you to my mother, brother, and sisters. To Lesson Baker, Lani Brito, Astrid Edmondson, Santi Arevalo, Leek Reebus, and all my queer chosen family, thank you for holding me. Big thank you's to Jamila Brown, Jenni Swann, Agustin Calderon, Caitlin Parsley, Kyle Clausen, and Tory Locatell. Thank you to my beautiful community in Puerto Vallarta for encouraging me and steadying me: Kevin-Anthony, Kateri Brown, Jerianne Schmidgall, Luiz Lazaro, Curiel Raygoza, Brian McRonald, Alison Lo, Yair Luna, Omar Lopez, Effie Passero, and far too many more to name here. Thank you all.

ABOUT RIZE PRESS

RIZE publishes great stories and great writing across genres written by People of Color and other underrepresented groups. Our team consists of:

Cecilia Kennedy, Editor

Barbara Lockwood, Editor

AE Williams, Editor

Scott Schultz, Editor

Rod Gilley, Editor

Kelly Ottiano, Editor

Carolyn Banks, Editor

Evangeline Estropia, Product Manager

Pulp Art Studios, Cover Design

Standout Books, Interior Design

Polgarus Studios, Interior Design

Learn more about us and our stories at
www.runningwildpublishing.com

Loved this story and want more? Follow us at

www.runningwildpublishing.com/rize,
www.facebook.com/runningwildpress,

on Twitter @lisadkastner @RunWildBooks @RwpRIZE

RUNNING WILD

RIZE

www.ingramcontent.com/pod-product-compliance
Lightning Source LLC
LaVergne TN
LVHW011927070526
838202LV00054B/4529